MW01285835

By Francesca May

Wild and Wicked Things
This Vicious Hunger

THIS VICIOUS HUNGER

THIS VICIOUS HUNGER

FRANCESCA MAY

REDHOOK

Copyright © 2025 by Francesca Dorricott

Cover design by Lisa Marie Pompilio
Cover images by Shutterstock
Cover copyright © 2025 by Hachette Book Group, Inc.

Redhook
Hachette Book Group
1290 Avenue of the Americas
New York, NY 10104
hachettebookgroup.com

First Edition: August 2025
Simultaneously published in Great Britain by Orbit

Redhook is an imprint of Orbit, a division of Hachette Book Group. The Redhook name and logo are registered trademarks of Hachette Book Group, Inc.

The publisher is not responsible for websites (or their content) that are not owned by the publisher.

The Hachette Speakers Bureau provides a wide range of authors for speaking events. To find out more, go to hachettespeakersbureau.com or email HachetteSpeakers@hbgusa.com.

Redhook books may be purchased in bulk for business, educational, or promotional use. For information, please contact your local bookseller or the Hachette Book Group Special Markets Department at special.markets@hbgusa.com.

Library of Congress Cataloging-in-Publication Data
Names: May, Francesca, author.
Title: This vicious hunger / Francesca May.
Description: First edition. | New York, NY : Redhook, 2025.
Identifiers: LCCN 2024059814 | ISBN 9780316287531 (hardcover) | ISBN 9780316287982 (ebook)
Subjects: LCGFT: Fantasy fiction. | Novels.
Classification: LCC PR6104.O766 T48 2025 | DDC 823/.92—dc23/eng/20241213
LC record available at https://lccn.loc.gov/2024059814

ISBNs: 9780316287531 (hardcover), 9780316287982 (ebook)

Printed in the United States of America

LSC-C

Printing 1, 2025

For Athena.
If anybody ever deserved to live longer, it was you.

For Atlas.
My nurse, my faithful, my ever-sighing,
ever-loving sunshine-gremlin boy.

Blessed are all simple emotions, be they dark or bright! It is the lurid intermixture of the two that produces the illuminating blaze of the infernal regions.

—Nathaniel Hawthorne, "Rappaccini's Daughter"

THIS VICIOUS HUNGER

Prologue

I am no stranger to the intricate rituals of death.

From the age of five I assisted my father in the sepulchre, guiding mourners from the gilded coffin we called the "cradle" to the pyre room below, where tradition dictated that the sisters and wives and mothers and daughters must shear their incense-braided hair to the chin at minimum and toss the rest to the flames. Upstairs, my father stood by while husbands and fathers and sons and brothers watched to ensure the cradle was engulfed entirely by the fragrant smoke.

From the age of eight I was the one who held and rang the little brass bell, its mournful peal announcing the beginning of the Silence—the multiday vigil held by the women around the freshly cleansed coffin. I ensured that no word was uttered, no food or drink except for water passed their lips, and any insults upon the house of the departed were reported.

By thirteen, after the death of my mother, it was I, and not my father, who reported the infractions to the fathers and husbands: a sliver of bread for the girl whose twin had died of the influenza, placed between her cracked lips by her own aunt; the pregnant widow who fainted beside the cradle and could only be roused by the dabbing of the syrupy communal wedding wine between her lips; the crone who, having lost her husband and son, in a fit of grief made to return to the pyre room and throw herself into the pit rather than face her remaining life as a widow at the mercy of her son-in-law. I did not see the punishments, but I took them to my bed every night as if they were my own.

Death was indisputable. At times I both hated and loved these ritual beats, as familiar as my own skin. Just as there were those whose job it was to pioneer celebration—births and marriages and comings of age—my father always said it was our job as the chaperones of death to defend decorum, honour, and custom.

When my own father died two weeks into my marriage, I returned to the sepulchre and endured these old traditions easily. I had no desire to speak or eat anyway, wrapped as I was in my grief, and readily accepted the customary three-day vigil commanded by my husband. Three days of my life to honour my father and his decades of devotion to his craft seemed a fair price. I cut huge swathes of my braided hair for the fire, sweat pouring from every inch of me as I leaned close over the pit and sacrificed everything I could to the flames—determined that, although my father had no other family, his cradle would not go uncleansed.

Now it is my husband in the cradle upstairs, his body lying in silk-lined gold. It is not my father speaking the last rites, not his gentle hands that have arranged Aurelio's limbs and daubed his forehead with sweet perfume. I am surrounded in this unfamiliar sepulchre by Aurelio's family, not my own. They were never really mine. Aurelio's mother, his five aunts, his seven sisters, countless cousins, and their daughters all embrace their Silence, heads bowed, veils obscuring their unspoken prayers. I watch them bitterly.

Each of their husbands and fathers commanded the customary three days, and two fewer for the young and frail. Aurelio's mother volunteered for five and her husband did not argue. I did not volunteer for any—not that anybody would have listened. I have been Silent, in their eyes, since the moment my husband died.

No. For my sins, Aurelio commanded me one last time from beyond the gilded cradle. Not three or five, but thirteen days of mourning is his final wish. One to mark every week we were married.

I bear it, as he must have known I would, without complaint. But I am weak by the end, desperate for a wedge of lemon, a fistful of oily olives with their bitter pits, anything to smother the woodsy tang of frankincense from my too-short hair. I count each minute beyond death and wonder whether this is what it feels like to be free.

PART ONE:

KNOWLEDGE

Wonder—is not precisely Knowing

And not precisely Knowing not—

A beautiful but bleak condition

He has not lived who has not felt—

—EMILY DICKINSON, 1331

Chapter One

After Aurelio, only the university remains.

I have dreamt of it my whole life and I dream of it still. When I was a child my father described it like one of the Isliano palaces of old, a parade of white columns and sculpted stone women carrying water in vast urns. I imagined what it would be like to stroll through halls hung with masterpieces in gilded frames, to smell the smoky sweetness of clove cigarettes in the mouths of scholars.

My father described the university as though it was inevitable— as though I would one day see it. I did not realise until I was much older that he told such richly embellished stories because he never expected me to see it, and never expected he might see it again either, since he had never had a son. He took solace in the tales he told as I watched from my perch in the corner of the embalming room or looked on from the grassy slopes as he tended his garden of herbs; by the time I left home I could recount each story word for word, as I often had at bedtime to ward off the thoughts of what would come if my parents ever received an offer for my hand.

When I was a wife, the vision in my head became twisted

by desperation, the university an oasis of dark cubbies, vaulted arches, and the cool darkness of libraries recessed deep underground. I never stopped thinking of it as mine, my story, my fairy tale. I knew by this time that I would never have the honour of attending as I might have if I'd been a boy instead of a wretched girl, but I longed for nothing more. I should never have been a daughter of Death, learning my father's profession despite my mother's protests, condemned to a life as little more than Aurelio LeVand's wife. If my father had had his way—and if I had had mine—I would have been a son of science.

Instead, I was married and ordered to leave any childish dreams of education behind. I made a good match in Aurelio. His mother said he was charmed by my beauty, some softness in me that hadn't been lost during the years of constant mourning—or perhaps a softness that had emerged from it. My father said there had been some scandal, years ago, and while Aurelio was a very good match for me, with my rising age and my diminished dowry, I was also a welcome match for him, even despite my strange upbringing and his family's standing. He should have married a countess, but instead he got an undertaker's spinster daughter.

Although Aurelio's family settled for me, my husband himself was agreeable enough. He seemed relieved that I wasn't ugly and was eager to teach me the proper behaviour expected of a respectable lady. I'd never considered what might happen if I ended up with a society husband because I'd always hoped I would never be a society wife, but my father assured me on my wedding day that all fresh brides fear change, and my only duty was not to let Aurelio see it.

I assumed, naively, that Aurelio's teaching would open this new world up to me. After all, my father had nothing but my best interests at heart, so surely Aurelio must as well. I'd expected to make some sacrifices, of course—my father's rules for the rules of domesticity, the trade of mourning for other wifely duties—but I wasn't prepared, when it came to it, to release the hold my father's tales still had on me.

Women, Aurelio had informed me the week after our wedding, *do not read.* I'd been holding a paperback novel—hardly scandalous material—and he swept it from my hands without pause, dashing it straight into the open fireplace. *Now that you are grown you must set aside these childish fancies. Didn't your father know he was doing you no favours by filling your head with such silly stories?*

Aurelio never understood that these stories were the sun that warmed me through the winter days of my marriage; when all I had of my old life was the familiar scent of loamy dirt in the greenhouse and the steady growth of the unfurling leaves I'd cut from my father's prized pothos vines, these remembered fantasies of the university reminded me that Death had taken my father but he was not entirely absent.

I never told Aurelio that my father's stories about the university were perhaps the most normal parts of my childhood. The reading was foreign enough to him. Most women mourn perhaps five times in their whole lives: they celebrate their fathers and mothers, suffer the loss of their new babies, grown sons gone to war, or daughters taken in the birthing bed; if they are lucky, they might live long enough to mourn their husbands. I have mourned more in my life, spent more days in thoughtful, solemn Silence, than Aurelio has—*had*—spent days in the schoolroom. He might have assumed I had helped my parents on occasion, but I suspect if he realised how much of my life I'd spent wearing the veil of death, he would have decided to give me thirteen hundred days of mourning instead of thirteen.

And now Aurelio is gone and the ceremony, and my Silence, is done. There are no more secrets I must keep from him. The house we once shared echoes with his absence, with the memory of how much space he demanded, how much clatter and bulk there was to him, and I spend the days after my mourning ends rattling around it like I still wear the chains of my Silence.

The servants stay out of my way as I catalogue the house and all its contents through the lens of my widowhood. Uncertainty colours the airy rooms, my thoughts returning, as they did during my Silence, as they have done my whole life, to the familiar stories of the university.

I know it is callous to say, but as I wander the halls of our home I'm struck not by the loss of my husband, of the life we shared and the potential of our future, but by the sequestered dreams of the university. I hadn't realised how badly I had hoped, deep, deep down, that Aurelio might one day grow to be more like my father. How eventually he might have come around to my reading, my learning bits and pieces of science or history—and how one day, maybe, just maybe, he might have considered becoming a benefactor, letting me attend a few lectures as a guest... It was a stupid, senseless dream, not even something I paid much mind to while he was alive, but with him dead... It is even less of a dream than before, and the loss is a wave big enough to engulf me whole.

Now I am at the mercy of his family, nothing more than a tool to be bartered, another moving piece on the chessboard. I await my fate like the condemned awaits the axe. Is it too much to hope for a life of solitude, to be left alone to run my household and tend to my plants in the greenhouse? The alternative—the prospect of remarriage so soon after Aurelio's death—leaves an ashy taste in my mouth. Will I have to simply trade one set of chains for another?

I am in the greenhouse three days after my mourning ends when Madame LeVand finds me. She insists we all, her children and their spouses included, call her that—*Madame*. Perhaps she thinks it is sophisticated; perhaps it makes her feel strong. She always marches about this house as though it is hers, coming and going without warning, hosting dinner parties at our table without even so much as telling me in advance, directing our staff by first name in very nearly the same tone she uses on me. Aurelio always told me that it wouldn't be this way forever. *Once you have children*, he'd say, *it'll be different then*. Once *you* have children, as though it was my job—and mine alone—to create this new life.

With Aurelio dead it's exactly as it was before. Madame stomps into the greenhouse while I am in the middle of repotting my poison ivy—I believe its proper name is *Toxicodendron radicans*, though I'm not sure I'm remembering that correctly; I only ever saw it written in one of the books I left at my father's house before he died. This time I'm wearing gloves. The rash on my left arm is still there from my last attempt the day before Aurelio died; I'd thought it was a kind of creeper, a mistake I won't make again. Others might have had the servants throw it out, wretched little thing, but I'm surprisingly fond of it.

I half turn as my mother-in-law enters; I smelled her before I saw her, the clack of her heels accompanied as always by too much sickly rose perfume. Madame is tall and thin, not unlike Aurelio in the quiet strength in her shoulders, her stern jaw, straight nose, and piercing blue eyes, but she's lost weight with the death of her only son—just about the only visible evidence of her loss.

"What are you doing rooting around in the dirt?" Madame says sniffily.

Politeness dictates that I should have stood a little straighter to show interest when she entered, or at least pulled off my gloves; I still could do both of those things. Instead, some small spark of defiance holds me bent slightly over the potting bench with soil on my dress. I doubt my behaviour will change anything she has to say.

"Aurelio liked when I maintained the garden," I explain. "So I'm maintaining it."

That much was true enough. Or at least he hadn't *disliked* it. Growing, nurturing, those are women's work and they suggest a kind of maternal feeling I'm sure Aurelio was relieved to see. Of course, he never knew about the books I'd read about the *science* of plants, how sometimes I dreamt in kaleidoscopic images of what their leaves and stems might look like under a microscope. I never let him see how much I liked the germination stage, how I'd started to make my own herbarium sheets, and how badly I preferred this preservation and study to the endless flower arrangements I left to the housekeeper...More secrets.

Madame huffs. She glances around the greenhouse, which is already transformed from the pallid, empty space it had been when Aurelio and I first married. Now it is roaring with colour, the trellises overloaded with roses and honeysuckle, ivy and jasmine and clematis. The air is thick with the floral scent—and still Madame's perfume dominates. I try to hide my distaste.

"Well. You certainly have green fingers." She smiles as she says this, a wry smile the likes of which I've never seen on her face. It unsettles me. Finally I pull my gloves off, inching my sleeve down over the poison ivy rash and turning to face her fully.

"Did you need something…?" I ask. "Only I ought to go and talk to the cook if you're staying for dinner—"

"No need." Madame runs a hand under her greying chignon, smoothing it in the way I know she does when she is under pressure, the way I have seen her do during dinner parties when her grandchildren complain. *Manners*, I'm sure she is thinking. I shrug. "Let's not beat about the bush, Thora dear. With Aurelio…gone…" She swallows. "With him gone. Well. There's your future to consider, and I really don't think—"

"Ah." It's come sooner than I expected, the axe landing *thud*. I assumed I'd have a week at least before questions of my future began. "So soon?"

If Madame is offended she doesn't show it, blustering on as though I haven't even spoken.

"I still have three daughters looking for good matches—dowries needed, you understand, that are much larger than yours ever was. I simply do not want you here, cluttering up the house, nor do I think you'd wish to stay any longer than your mourning requires. The LeVand obligation was in sickness and in health, not into the great beyond."

I stay silent. Madame is not inclined to let me get many words out once she starts, and frankly I'm happy to let her talk.

If I was another sort of woman I might be panicked. All this talk of dowries and obligation—I should be wondering: What will happen to me? I have no father to return to. My mother is dead. I have no other family, no other marriage prospects. Aurelio was my only shot at this marital life. I suppose the fear is there, somewhere, in the questions I know I *should* ask, but most of the time it hides beneath the numbness, which I suppose looks a little like grief.

"I'm not trying to be unkind, girl," Madame continues. "I should never allow you to be thrown to the wolves. Which is why..." She pauses, her expression growing furtive. Then she pulls out an envelope from inside her spencer, bent where it has rested between the jacket and her gown. Its side is torn neatly with the edge of a letter opener. "I thought, perhaps, you might consider this."

She hands it to me. The paper is creamy, heavy, and I imagine that I can smell grass tangled in the weave of it, and the warm, dusty scent of books. Not only is it open; it is addressed to me.

I raise an eyebrow and glance at my husband's mother, but she doesn't flinch. She only nods at the envelope again, waiting for me to pull the letter from its sheath. I don't know if she is expecting me to kick up a fuss about her keeping the letter from me, if that's why she's come to speak to me herself, so it doesn't spread through the house and make her look bad—or if she wants to gauge my reaction for another reason.

Either way, I fight to keep my expression neutral as I pull the paper out and unfold it. I scan the letterhead, its curling scroll like the ironwork of an old gate, and my breath catches. The university. *St. Elianto.* I want to murmur the name like a prayer. My heart thumps wildly, pulse thundering in my ears.

Suddenly the numbness is gone. I read the letter, limbs buzzing nervously.

"What is this?" I demand, glancing at Madame and then back to the paper to make sure it's real. "This is postmarked weeks ago. Who is this Petaccia?"

"He's a botanist—a fellow at the university. I opened the letter by mistake," Madame says in a way that makes me think this is a lie. I wonder how many other communications I might have received if not for her. "And since the letter arrived so soon after your marriage I thought it best that I dealt with it. Your grief over losing your father was still much too raw to be responding to condolences." I say nothing, forcing my jaw to lock so I don't snap at the absurdity of this coming from the woman who forbade me from wearing mourning black after my father's funeral because it wasn't "befitting a new bride." "Apparently your father and this doctor of science were good friends years ago but lost touch."

"This says something about a scholarship." I force the words out. "What scholarship? Why does it matter?" The beginning of an emotion too big to process begins to unfurl in my belly. I clench my fists and my teeth and take comfort in the dull ache.

"That's what I wanted to talk to you about. There was an offer of some sort between this doctor and your father when he first married your mother. We received something similar for Aurelio's education—"

"Yes, I'm familiar with the general idea. If my father had a son, he would have had a free education," I say, bitter understanding washing through me. All this time, all those stories, they weren't just fanciful what-ifs from my father; he had an offer of a scholarship— only all he had was a daughter. A fresh mixture of guilt and shame curdles inside me. "Why is any of this relevant?"

"With Aurelio's passing I have taken the liberty of writing to this doctor on your behalf." Madame's expression shifts again, pride lighting her up like a candle. "I informed him of my son's death, your widowhood. He expressed his deep condolences, you see, and I thought he might be the sort of man who could be persuaded, given a little nudge..." She pauses, watching my face like I'm a mouse and she a hawk. I feel as though she has punched all the air from my lungs.

"You asked him to take me on?" I whisper. "As a student?"

"I did." Madame's smile grows, a little sly now. "I know it's not what you would have hoped, but really your prospects are extremely limited. And a life of study is far better for the LeVand name than that of the nunnery..." Madame says. There's a note of genuine condolence in her voice and I realise with a jolt that she has no idea. She has no idea what this means, how badly I want this, what I would do to get it. She does not realise that this is the gift I have prayed for my whole life. I forcefully straighten my face once more.

"Thank you, Madame," I say, infusing my voice with a hint of regret. Just a hint. It wouldn't be polite to argue anyway, but it's best she thinks I am speechless from courteous disappointment rather than sheer excitement. "I appreciate all you have done for me."

She takes in the riot of plants in the greenhouse again, eyeing the dirt on my gown with a flicker of disapproval. "Think nothing of it," she says. And I know what she is really saying is *Let's not speak of this again.* "It's what Aurelio would have wanted."

Chapter Two

Less than a week after my mourning ends, I leave my marital home and all its secrets behind. This morning when I dressed I shed my mourning clothes and headwrap and joyfully greeted the spring warmth where my shorn hair curled at my neck.

It takes three hours to reach St. Elianto from the city. On the journey I hum the marching song my mother always favoured and engage in polite conversation with the driver of my cart, delighting in the sound of my boxed luggage bouncing as we hit stones in the road.

"A female student," the driver murmurs to himself when we are long out of the city. "Well, I never."

"Yes," I say hesitantly. "I know it's unusual."

"Stranger things have happened, I'm sure. Though I've never heard it." The driver chuckles. "What are you going to study? Nursing or something?" I rankle a little at his suggestion. This Dr. Petaccia is a doctor of medicine, true, but just because I am a woman doesn't mean the care of others is what I'm best suited to.

"Botany, actually." I hide a smirk at his blank look. "It's the study of plants. A *science.* And maybe I'll take some classes in medicine too," I add, although the idea seems absurd. "I haven't decided yet."

"What's your husband have to say about that?"

I glance down at the ring I'm still wearing on my wedding finger—half because I know it will be easier to avoid attention as a widow than as a spinster, but also half because this is the last reminder I have of my father. I left all his plants behind this morning, and the small gold band was purchased with my dowry, money my father scrimped and saved for many years for my future. Madame could have asked for it back, but she seemed only too happy to get rid of it—along with all other evidence of my existence.

"My husband has nothing to say," I reply coolly. "He's dead."

The driver sinks into silence, eyeing me warily but asking no more questions. I turn my gaze back to the road ahead, delighting in the way the scenery changes as we draw away from the roll of open fields.

We first pass the small chapel used by the villagers, and then the market square and a tavern—silent at this hour. My father said that the village existed long before the university, but as we approach I am not sure how that can be possible. The village looks lived-in, the stone buildings old and heavy enough, but it exists entirely in the shadow of the St. Elianto campus.

The truth of the university is somewhere between my father's stories and my lonely dreams. It is a collage of white columns and twisted terra-cotta spires above pale flat roofs embedded in the hillside. It is dust rolling up around the wheels of the pony cart and flourishing fields behind us.

We leave the village and it isn't long before the only sound is once again the beat of the pony's hooves and my driver *haughing* and *hmphing* to himself. It is late morning and the sun is fierce, the air baked and green scented; as we approach the campus the air grows cooler, though, an oasis of dusty shade.

The driver guides the pony trap through the gates, scrolling text above giant columns, and along a lane lined with trees. Ahead I can make out what may be a clock tower, though all I can see are a turret and bells. I crane my neck back to read the words above the gate as we trundle beneath the arch, the hairs rising on my neck and arms as the temperature dips.

Doctrina est vita aeterna, the same words my father once muttered to me like an oath. Learning is life eternal.

I straighten my expression, wary of the excitement that flips in my belly. I may no longer be in mourning dress, but I'm not foolish enough to assume that the people here won't gossip about my arrival the way they would back home. I still wear the shorn hair of sorrow—though of course how are they to know I gave more of it to my father's cradle than to my husband's?—and I'm sure many of them would have opinions about my being allowed to study here in the first place, widow or not.

The driver stops the trap at the end of the lane. There is a grand central square ahead, a handful of robed scholars crossing with their heads bent together and bundles of books dangling from string. They look hardly old enough to be away from home. One shades the sun from his eyes with his hand, but I'm invisible, not yet one of them, and they don't pay me any mind.

"S'far as I go."

The driver's gruff voice startles me and I clamber down as gracefully as I can manage without taking his hand, my thick skirts swirling dust over my boots. Sweat drips down my spine. There's no way I can manage to carry all my luggage alone, or even one of the individual trunks, but most of it came from the house I shared with Aurelio, clothing and jewellery I never had a chance to wear during our marriage. I don't wish to be ungrateful, I'm lucky Aurelio had so many things made for me after all, but still I feel no attachment to any of it.

I leave the luggage on the edge of the stone steps and cross the square empty-handed.

The room I have been allocated isn't with the majority of the students here at St. Elianto. Generally the scholars and professors are men, educated in serious subjects—philosophy, medicine, astronomy, and mathematics—and the few women on staff are of the serving class, happily boarding in mixed accommodation.

Although I no longer possess the social rank I did before Aurelio's death, somebody, somewhere, obviously decided I was not a poor enough relation to share the fate of the staff. Mind you, I'm not rich enough (or poor enough) for my risk to the morals of the young male scholars to be ignored either; instead, the room that is to be my home for as long as the university will have me is a good walk—or, apparently, preferably a short trap ride—from the main halls, classrooms, and two libraries boasted by the central campus and its square.

It is a thin, tall building that looks something like an old miniature mill, with dozens of windows and small balconies. It hardly matters to me what it looks like, but I appreciate that it is quiet.

The day has been a blur of paperwork, of dim, smoky reception rooms and men who all look the same to me. My arrival is clearly a bit of an inconvenience to most of them, though I haven't encountered any downright hostility yet. For the most part they seem glad that I am somebody else's problem and have been content to point me onwards to get me out of the way.

I arrive at my rooms just as dusk is settling over the turrets and casting long shadows on the flat roofs below. In the distance the hills are hazy, purple and willow green. There is the softly distant sound of laughter, and I imagine the gentle rattle of clinking glasses and scratch of once-expensive cutlery on worn china in the dining hall, though this is pure fancy as I've yet to see the place. My own evening meal is waiting for me in my new room, or suite of rooms, which comprise a cramped sitting room with a desk pressed tight against the only window and a stove on the opposite wall, and an even smaller bedroom—washstand in the alcove that perhaps once housed a wardrobe, and another tiny window.

My luggage is already here. I try not to feel disappointed, but it looks about as out of place as I feel; the cream leather is flecked with dried mud and stands stark against the terra-cotta tiles. I press my back to the door, feeling the last of the day's warmth seeping away. The sigh that escapes my body might as well be the fleeing of my spirit.

This morning I was full of zest. Everything had seemed like a fresh start, even the maps and papers, the list of dos and don'ts, the warnings about summer storms and promises of isolating winters when the campus is closed to all except the year-round boarders. After the last hours in the baking heat of the administration office, no ocean breeze to take the edge off, not even a whiff of snow-scented air from the hills able to infiltrate the campus, the warnings of winter never seemed farther away and I am almost ready to turn tail and run.

The reality is I have nowhere to go. The feeling weighs me down like a sack of soil, crushing the air from my lungs. Fighting it seems impossible.

It is one thing to dream of this place, to replay the stories in my mind, but the truth of it is something entirely different. This room, isolated from the scholars and the staff alike, is a reminder: I am not welcome here. I may have been invited, but I am not favoured. I am not a scholar, not a student, nor a professor. I am not here because I have earned my place. I am a widow, here by sheer chance because my father once received an offer from a friend in the right place, and my mother-in-law couldn't wait to get rid of me.

Still, beneath the heavy exhaustion, my heart flutters. I feel sick with guilt, Aurelio's memory large in my chest, and yet I'm also giddy with excitement. Tomorrow I will meet Dr. Petaccia. A professor of botany—a tenured and respected academic whose work has no doubt been published throughout the country, maybe even the world.

By all the criteria I have been taught since I was old enough to think, my life is over. I have nothing but Aurelio's name and the clothes and jewels he once bought for me; I have no prospects, no social skills, nobody to broker another match, and nothing to offer in my favour even if I did. I am a charity case, standing here in rooms smaller than any woman my class should consider her own…

And yet, somehow, I am staring down the barrel of an education with one of the most well-regarded botanists in our fair world.

Chapter Three

Although my first meeting with Dr. Petaccia isn't until midmorning, I awaken at dawn, my limbs thrumming restlessly, the nightmare scent of smoke still in my nostrils from the dreams that twisted from one to another all night long. It's always smoke, the tickle of dust in my throat turning to ash as the walls crumble around me—my own golden cradle licked with the flames of death until I awaken gasping for breath.

My bedroom is dim and relatively cool, but I can tell from the warmth of the light that the day is already stifling. I stare at the ceiling for long minutes, where I fancy that the cracks in the paint and plaster look almost like the curling tendrils of a passion vine.

I have no idea what to expect from this doctor who holds my future in his hands. I never even knew he existed. For all my father's talk of the university, he never mentioned him in any of his stories—only lamented his damned inability to produce a son, which makes so much sense now that I know about the scholarship.

Perhaps I should feel betrayed. All these years there has been a way out for me, a future that didn't involve a lifetime of husbands or marriage or undertaking...I might not have felt so trapped if

I'd known—though, of course, I would never have been able to take this path without Aurelio's death, and it's not as if I could ever have predicted such a thing.

That thought sends a nervous shiver through me and I shake it off.

It's not that I would expect any different from Aurelio's mother, really. Her only interest was first finding her son a wife—even if said wife's background and rumours about her lack of suitors did raise a few eyebrows—and then keeping her spoiled son happy. How was she to know she held my future in her hands? Why should she care?

My father, though... I'm disappointed that he never fought for me. If the doctor was persuaded by Madame LeVand as she said, what's to say my father couldn't have achieved the same? This is the thought that needles me as I stare at my ceiling: perhaps my father was so caught up in his dismay at not having a son that he never stopped to wonder what his daughter might do.

Eventually I can lie still no longer. It isn't in my nature to dwell, but since Aurelio died it's all I have been able to do. I fling open the shutters and let fresh waves of sunlight into the room, shielding my eyes from the early golden rays. The view from this window when I arrived last night was disappointing, barely a view at all in the unfamiliar dusk. This morning I'm greeted by a much more welcome sight; beyond the isolation of my rooms, through that little square window, my desk is situated so that I may look upon a garden as I study.

The garden is lush and overgrown, surrounded by high walls topped with wrought iron and coiling plants, running in both directions as far as I can see. There is a tower at its verdant heart, the stone pale and shining, its base awash with colourful blooms and climbing vines. The area outside the garden closest to my window is sparse and scrubby against the retaining wall, the cobbles turning slowly to spiky grass and dusty dirt, in strong contrast to inside the walls, where I admire the riot of trailing leaves, flowers that look like bells and stars and sunbursts all tangled together. Despite my passion for all things green on this earth, I cannot identify most of the plants from this distance, and a sudden longing to catalogue them makes my heart thump with excitement.

I think of my father's small garden and wonder what he would make of this place—and if it was here when he was. I think not, or else he would have included it in his stories. He never exactly encouraged my love of plants, but nor did he ever guard his knowledge.

I dress with a wild smile on my lips. I have not unpacked more than the basics from my trunk, but the simple walking dress I've chosen is one I hope will make a good impression; it is modest, with a high neck and long sleeves, made from pale sage silk and printed with a gentle, repeating vine-like pattern. The wrap that goes with it is too warm for this weather, so I abandon it to the trunk. I can't do much with my hair except attempt to tame the rough-shorn curls with some water and a comb, though I forgo the headscarf in favour of letting my scalp drink in the sunlight.

I'd like to explore near the garden, but the pull of my stomach guides me instead towards the campus. Last night's supper was meagre and I have nothing left to satisfy my hunger. But then, it feels as though I have been starved for months—all the meals I ate during my life as Aurelio's wife could probably have fit onto the small desk in my new rooms—so the hunger isn't entirely new.

Ignoring the advice of the registrar, I decide to walk to the campus, enjoying the feel of the hot sun on my back and neck, the stiffness easing in my legs. Everything here is dust and terra cotta, so different from the damp green hills of my childhood. Aurelio grew up in the city, all cobbles and carriages, restaurants and boutiques and the opera; this was the life I'd come to accept would be mine for the rest of my time, and I'm not ashamed to say I did not like it and I'm almost relieved to not have to pretend any more. Although I'd still prefer my childhood hills, my heart soars at this freedom and space. I'll gladly take dust and terra cotta if I never have to see a city again.

I picture Aurelio's face as I think this, imagine the curl of his lip if I'd said anything like it in public, but the smile I might get in the privacy of our home would have been different; he liked to tease me, to call me his *bellezza*, his cutie—though only when I said something that would make his family regret their choice. I'm still not quite sure whether his amusement was at me, or at the turn of his life ending with me.

As I walk, I know that his mother is wrong; this life is not what my husband would have wanted for me after his death. He would have railed against it, fought tooth and nail to keep me trapped in morning rooms and parlours, drinking tea with neighbours I didn't care for—anywhere but here. Even the nunnery would have been far preferable. The thought fills me with bitter joy.

I stretch my legs longer, walk faster, until my heart pounds and my cheeks flush in the heat. By the time I reach the campus my forehead is dripping with sweat but I feel positively alive. Forget the city, and forget the sepulchre; this morning there is only me and the sun and the hot, lemon-scented air.

The feeling doesn't last. It's early enough that the dim, vaulted dining hall is still only half-full, countless scholars staring glassy-eyed into their coffee or stirring mushed eggs around their plates, but the server girl at the door can't decide if there's a table free for me to eat at.

"I'm a scholar," I say, smiling politely to show I'm not making fun. From the suspicion in her eyes it's clear she doesn't believe me. She can't be much younger than me, rosy-cheeked with her dark hair pulled back into a tight braid. "Really," I insist.

"Really?" She raises an eyebrow, taking in my dress, my hands—their new softness from my weeks of marriage no doubt a mark in my favour—my shorn hair, and my ring finger, which are no doubt both marks against me. Nobody likes to be reminded of the proximity of grief, least of all the young and beautiful. I fight the urge to twist my wedding band, a still-new nervous habit I can't quite bring myself to drop. Perhaps I should take it off.

"Really," I repeat. "Do you have the authority to seat me or do you need to ask your mother? I'm starving and I'd appreciate it if you'd let me eat while you sort it out."

The girl is not as surprised at the haughtiness in my tone as I am. It spurs her into action and she dips her head as if I've uttered the magic words—which, I suppose, I have. She leads me to a small table away from the men, unburdened from the fog of cigarette smoke by an open window, taking my order of coffee, cereal, and figs, plus rusk and hazelnut cream, without meeting my eyes. When she is gone I stare at the polished, slightly sticky wood of the table, my hands spread on top. They are shaking.

Thirteen weeks, it turns out, is more than long enough to become one of them. The wealthy. I spent my entire short marriage to Aurelio believing I could never be like him, could never adjust to a life with servants and six types of wine with dinner, gaudy gowns and endless supplies of hot bathwater. Four months ago I would have been just like that poor server girl, and I would never have spoken to her with such disdain. And now here I am.

I pick at my breakfast when it arrives, delivered by another server, whose gaze I avoid. Suddenly I'm not hungry at all. I crumble the hard rusk bread into dust on my plate, dipping a finger into the hazelnut cream before deciding to stick to coffee.

By the time I finish my sad meal the dining hall is filling up—though I note that my little corner by the window is still empty. Men of all ages trudge in, some in groups and some alone. Some eat heartily and others sip their coffee with an air of importance, all of them pointedly not looking at me. The scholars and professors eat together here; I don't know enough to know whether this is normal elsewhere or only here, but I can tell the professors by their robes. Some wear regular clothes, or plain black robes; others have their collars and cuffs adorned in a variety of colours: green, ochre, brown, mauve.

As I get ready to leave the hall, I cast my eyes about the room, wondering if any of these men is to be my new mentor. Of course it's no use, I have no idea what Dr. Petaccia looks like, nor would it be appropriate of me to approach him before our meeting. Still, I don't like waiting—and I definitely don't like feeling like an outcast. I wonder if I should have worn something less pretty; perhaps then they'd all take me more seriously. I almost laugh.

Outside the sun is unrelenting, the cobbles radiating heat through my thin-soled shoes. I raise a hand to my eyes, trying to work out which of the buildings crowding the dining hall is the library, or which path between them will lead to the square I landed at yesterday so I can *find* the blasted library. This place is so large I can't imagine I will ever find my way about. Panic rises in my chest. Maybe I'm not cut out for this environment if I can't even remember my way around, but I stamp on the feeling. *Don't be silly*, I tell myself. *This is your home now whether you feel like it or not. You'd better get used to being a little lost.*

I square my shoulders, deciding to head to the left, when I'm thrown backwards as a man on a bicycle hurtles across my path, his arm outstretched to push me away. His knuckles connect with the softness of my diaphragm. I stumble, my heels catching on the uneven cobbles, my stomach lurching and the breath knocked from my lungs. I let out an indignant cry but manage to keep myself upright.

The man on the bicycle doesn't stop. Another scholar on his way to breakfast guffaws. I shoot him an icy look that consumes much of my remaining energy. He takes in my now-dusty dress and my bare head and his expression morphs into something more like scorn. I imagine what he's thinking: *What's a silly, mournful woman like you doing in a serious place like this? You should be at home with children or a husband—or be content to arrange funeral flowers until your dear dead husband's deathday, when you can hurry up and get a new one.* I square my shoulders but keep my mouth shut.

"Apologies, lady," he says with a noncommittal shrug. "But perhaps you'd better look where you're going next time. Us scholars have got more important things to do than watch out for you. This is a college, not a salon."

I don't manage to find the library until half an hour before my meeting, so I have little time to explore. It's as cool and dim as I expected, with huge vaulted windows and row after row of wooden shelves housing so many treasured texts. What I never truly managed to picture in my dreams was the size; there must be ten or twelve floors above my head, each mezzanine guarded from the open atrium by a wooden railing between stone pillars.

The height alone makes me feel dizzy, never mind the thought of falling.

I wonder how many books there are in this place, how many worlds of fiction and endless treatises of power and race, religion and philosophy, science—all that science. I wonder, too, if there are any of *those* books in here. The kind Aurelio hated most. The kind I haven't even dared to think of since his death, the kind that changed it all. Inflammatory books. Passionate books. Books about—

I stop myself. I do not want Aurelio, or those books, to taint this place.

I turn instead to the familiar stability of my father. I imagine him in his youth, roving between these endless shelves, absorbing as much knowledge as he could by night, knowing that in the morning he would have to return to the chapel and his apprenticeship there. It isn't hard to see how his time here influenced his performance of the death rites—every undertaker has a style, a trademark of ritual, and my father's was at once solemn and erudite. Some undertakers prefer the cleanness of open air, grassy knolls, and cradles wrapped in moss; others prefer the darkness, warmth from a fire and the resultant dripping sweat symbolic of mourners' tears even for those who cannot—or will not—cry.

I instantly see the Grieve family's sepulchre echoed in these book-lined halls, the artificial, reverent silence here as holy as that of a family laying their loved ones in the cradle. Incense smoke curls blue from sconces on the walls just like at home, the stones underfoot polished by years of acolytes. It is airy, too, cool but not cold. Somehow even the smell, dusty pages and patchouli, is the same. A pang of grief surprises me, not just for my father but for the sepulchre he spent his life perfecting, likely demolished or sold off for a tidy profit by Aurelio's family as soon as my mourning days passed. I asked Aurelio once what would happen to it, but he refused to answer. The building was perhaps my only worthy dowry—and even that was never truly mine.

"Excuse me, miss, the archives are for members of the academy only."

I startle, turning to see a man with owlish horn-rimmed spectacles and salt-and-pepper sideburns so unruly they'd likely get him thrown out of polite society. The hunch in his back is distinctive of a man who has spent his life surrounded by books.

"Oh—that's okay, I'm a student."

"And I'm a maharaja," the man says without pause. "I've told your ilk before, I don't care if your husband or your brother's studying at that damned school in the village; that doesn't mean you can waltz in here and just help yourselves to our prized—"

"No," I cut him off quickly. "You misunderstand. I'm a student at the university. I arrived yesterday to read botany under Dr. Petaccia."

The man stops and stares at me. "You?"

"Yes." I try to curb the bite in my words, knowing that making an enemy here of all places would be a very bad start, but some of the poison sneaks in anyway. "I imagine it's hard to believe." I try for a small smile, but I'm not sure it's very convincing.

"Ah." A stalemate. Then, after a sneaky glance at the wedding ring on my finger, owl-glasses softens. "Yes. Well. Same rules for everybody. You need to sign in." He nods over to the imposing polished desk, replete with a rare electric lamp, ledger, mahogany book tray, and other minutiae. "You can't just wander around willy-nilly; we have a lot of textbooks that require checkout authorisation depending on who needs them. We have a lot of trouble in that department, people thinking they deserve access by proximity's sake alone, with no appreciation for the importance we place on endurance…"

I want to point out that I know how a library works, but the logical part of me knows it's not an unfair assumption for him to make. I might have grown hearing my father's tales, but it's clear Aurelio was right in this instance; my upbringing was unusual in more ways than one, and women rarely read.

"Yes, sir," I say. "Though I'm not here to study today. I have a meeting with the doctor. Can you please point me in the direction of the laboratories? I believe that's where I'm meeting him, and perhaps other members of the faculty."

The man looks at me with a puzzled expression for a moment. He once more glances from my wedding ring to the hems and sleeves of my dress, which are still as new as the day they arrived in silk ribbons and lined boxes in Aurelio's parlour. *She's young*, I suspect he's thinking. *She doesn't belong here.*

"Dr. Petaccia doesn't share a laboratory," he says, and the strange expression doesn't leave his face. "The doctor is very protective. But I believe there is a parlour in La Vita—the thin grey-brown building with all the vines up the side behind the square. Perhaps you should try in there."

Chapter Four

The librarian's instructions are, thankfully, right on the mark. LA VITA—so christened on the chalky baluster out front—is hard to miss, sandwiched as it is between two much newer white-and-terra-cotta stucco and brick buildings on either side with grander columns and grander titles. LA SCIENZA to the left and L'ASTRONOMIA to the right, both with arching windows and shining pale steps out front. L'Astronomia is crowned with a strange circular tower at its zenith that can only be for stargazing. La Vita hunches between them like a poor cousin, thinner and shorter, its stucco greying and crawling with vines.

The butterflies in my belly I've been attempting to still all morning are now wild horses. I chomp down on my lower lip and push into the old building; it is cold inside after the heat of the sun and a shiver snakes up my spine. What if the doctor doesn't like me? What if he changes his mind? The university, this life, is my last hope of making something of myself. Without it…I have nothing. I could try to set up my own sepulchre—I have enough experience in the business of grief—but I doubt anybody would bring me their dead. Mourning is a woman's job, but the burial rites belong to men.

I shove the thoughts deeper, so deep that I can barely hear them over the hum of my blood in my ears, the thump of my heart. There is nobody at the entrance to this building, and both doors that branch off in this dim hall are locked. Time is pushing on and if I don't hurry I will be late for my meeting.

Unlike Aurelio's family with their silly parlour games, seeing which sister could best seduce her current suitor by the long wait to see her dinner dress alone, my father always taught me that punctuality is the politeness of kings. So I hike my skirts and breathlessly make the climb.

Each floor of the building is near identical, the same two locked doors off each landing until I finally reach the top. This high up there is only a single door, also closed—but this time not locked. I turn the knob and knock loudly, the rap of my knuckles echoing.

This landing spills into one enormous room. It has two huge curtainless sash windows on all three sides, bright and hot and— closed. The air in the room is muggy and green and I catch a breath in shock as my lungs rebel at the heat. Sweat immediately prickles at the nape of my neck, along my hairline, and I'm glad for the loss of my thick curls.

The walls are overrun with greenery, plants crawling on every inch, some alive and growing and others pressed tightly between great slides of glass. There are trenches of soil in curious knee-high troughs, some newly sprouting, and two trees in tubs blossoming with out-of-season flowers—white cuplike petals and long, curling pistils. I don't recognise either.

Before me, creating an artificial divide in the room, is a large antique desk. It, like the rest of the room, is trailing with vines, some of which I could swear are moving. I let out a croak of greeting, startled.

"Yes?"

The woman—yes, woman—hunched behind the desk, the vines wrapped around her gloved knuckles, peers up at me with an expression of impatience on her narrow face, her dark eyes liquid.

"I...have a meeting," I stammer. "Sorry. With Dr. Petaccia. If you could—"

The woman's face shifts into a smile so bright that this, too, startles me. She looks younger then, perhaps mid-forties rather than fifties, her dark eyes sparkling with warmth. She stands, pushing the vines away impatiently, and approaches me; she is tall and thin, *willowy* might be the word, and dressed in a peculiar arrangement of layered skirt over tight trousers that gives her a range of movement I've never seen outside of Aurelio's sister's lady sports club. She sweeps some of the papers from the desk in front of her and into a small drawer, which she locks with a little key.

"You must be Thora," she gushes. "Come here, girl. Let me get a good look at you." She takes my face in her hands, so close now that I can smell her tart, almost bitter perfume. Her skin is clean and dry, no sign of the sweat that gathers on my top lip.

"I...Yes."

"It's a pleasure to meet you, Thora. I'm Dr. Petaccia—though you can call me Florencia if you'd prefer. I don't like to be too formal with friends, and of course I only work with friends."

"Friends?"

"Of course! Well, we soon shall be, I think." She shifts her hands to my shoulders and looks me up and down at arm's length. "You don't talk much. Not that it's necessarily a bad thing; I can't stand those gossipy society types—and I have to confess, the LeVand connection did make me think twice—but I thought, well, if you're your father's daughter..." She stops and gives a dry laugh, surprisingly deep. "I'm sorry, my dear. I'm getting carried away. Please sit. Would you like a drink? I have, oh..." She glances around. On her desk alone there are several cups and saucers, all coated in some filmy substance that might have been coffee with milk but now looks more like brackish marsh water. "Well, I can send for something. Or there's water?"

"No," I say hurriedly, taking a seat, "thank you."

"Good. That's good. Well." Petaccia's smile grows again, exposing her teeth, which are large and stained. "How are you liking St. Elianto so far? Although I'm very sorry to hear your circumstances, I won't say I wasn't pleased to hear from the LeVands. Your father was a good man and I was saddened to hear of his death."

I'm still trying to get my head around it all—that this eccentric person, a woman, seated before me with a vine once again winding around her gloved wrist, and I could swear it's moving without her training it, is the doctor who may change my life—so what comes out is a garbled mess.

"Thank you." I'm breathless and flushed and I feel like a child, desperately trying to impress. "I like the university so far. It's big, though," I hear myself say stupidly. "It's so big and...full of all these...men." The words come out coated in a layer of disdain—I was thinking of the scholar this morning, the one on the bicycle—and instantly I wish to take it back.

Dr. Petaccia's expression grows suddenly serious, her dark eyes flashing. My stomach drops. It's as if the air in the room has grown several degrees warmer and I feel my cheeks burn hot and red.

"I was going to wait to delve into the minutiae, but I suppose we'd better get this over with." The doctor leans back in her chair and steeples her fingers. "You understand, Thora, don't you, that

I'm taking something of a risk here with you. St. Elianto is a serious institution, an academy of learning. It is not that women are
not allowed to study here, but there is a certain expectation of
female frippery around learning."

"Oh yes. I know it. I very much appreciate the opportunity—"

"St. Elianto isn't a place for silly girls to meet the silly boys
they're going to marry."

I stop, a laugh building in me that would be wildly inappropriate to release. "I'm sorry?"

"You mention the men, and I know you can't be thinking that
this is the sort of place to come and while away your days until
you find another suitable match for yourself. Not because you
won't find one, Thora. I was led to believe that your father had
taught you to read and write well, is that true?"

Now the laughter comes out, coarse and ugly. I slap my hand
over my mouth.

"Is this funny to you?" Petaccia's eyes darken further, the effect
like a shock of cold water calming my hysteria. "Phytogeography—
botany—is a serious science. It isn't all fun and parlour games,
little walks in the public parks and flowers pressed for pretty
displays. I won't have myself aligned with any of that brainless
hedgerow theology they seem to play with in the polite circles.
You're here because I had faith that your father did not raise a silly
girl and I need somebody I can trust, somebody without precon-
ceptions about phytology."

"No," I blurt. "No, I'm sorry, you misunderstand—it's absolutely not funny. The funny thing is that you'd think I speak of
men in an...achievement-worthy way." I raise my chin and look
the doctor straight in the eyes, willing her to see how serious I am.
Men, and the way women are supposed to think of them, have

plagued me my whole life. But something tells me that unlike my father, Dr. Petaccia might understand. "I was married once, Doctor. I did not plan to be a widow at twenty-five—the Lord clearly had other plans for me—but I can assure you that I am not a silly girl, nor do I ever intend to be one."

Dr. Petaccia lets the silence gather for a moment before saying, "Good. Because I will tell you now, the men in a place like this have an agenda. They *always* have an agenda. Make sure it isn't you—d'you understand?" I nod briskly. "Good," she says again. "Now, your father, did he teach you much outside of mourning?"

I think of the stash of books my father kept in his study—the ones even my mother knew nothing about. We never spoke of them, he and I. To this day I'm not even sure if he knew I knew of them, let alone that I would often squirrel them away to read between mournings, but I suspect he did.

When he taught me to read, we used the Scriptures and later the death rites he'd written himself, but my father's collection of books strayed into more than just the rituals of grief; he always took his role as undertaker seriously and told me more than once that a man who stopped learning no longer had any right to facilitate the passage of life.

He kept titles on medicine and surgical science, on sewing—for those deaths where the rites required a tidy corpse—and on art and painting. He dabbled in poetry, in mathematics, in animal husbandry and, indeed, in phytology. I read every single one of his books, often by candlelight, hiding under the desk in his study, one ear pricked for my mother's slippered footsteps.

There were other titles I found, too, ones I do not think my father wanted me to see, which even now I try not to think of, a pamphlet hidden between pages of a phenomenally dry veterinary biography about how to determine manner of death—or the one about how to diagnose, or disguise, an accidental or non-accidental incident according to a family's wishes...

In public my father gave me titles on flower arranging, and religious pamphlets on the importance of fasting, the science of Silence. It is these, I am sure, Dr. Petaccia is referring to—the very border of respectability. The titles Aurelio's family would have just about considered appropriate for an undertaker's daughter— before I became a LeVand by marriage, at which point they became entirely *inappropriate*.

"I can read and write as well as my husband could," I say in answer. Petaccia nods, pleased. "I'm comfortable taking notes in both long- and shorthand and I write smoothly. I have a knowledge of plants from the *Funereal Flora*—"

"That will do nicely," the doctor cuts me off. "The rest I can teach you."

"I assure you, Doctor, I am committed to this life. I'm grateful for the opportunity to learn under a famed doctor such as yourself—"

Petaccia waves her hands. The vine is still coiling and I can't stop staring. It has little blister-like nubs all along its lengths, swelling to pustules the colour of sunspots in places, but its leaves are sharply green and it looks healthy enough. I wonder what kind it is, whether it is something the doctor has somehow created herself. I've read about botanists who do that, who aren't content to merely study and must *create*, but rather than frighten me this sudden thought sends a thrill right through my core.

"Stop schmoozing," Petaccia says languidly. "But please, do call me Florencia. My father was Doctor and I can't stand it."

"Yes. Sorry."

"Look, I apologise for jumping to conclusions about you. It is hard for me to open up my sacred space to somebody, even the child of a friend. But really, it's simple: work hard and you'll do fine here. It doesn't matter to me whether you were a wife or a daughter, whether you are a widow or a nun. I know this is not the life you were raised for, but it's comfortable, and I can offer you a future many women might never dream of for themselves. As I said to the LeVands, you'll want for nothing—St. Elianto provides both our rooming and living costs so long as we are working—and you won't have time to be lonely. The university doesn't have many ladies in its employ, it's true, but we are not none. Not any more." That wide-toothed smile is back and I find myself echoing it, my face stretching uncomfortably. "You will attend lectures as a scholar, learn with the little boys, and I won't hear any complaints even if they *are* little boys, only here to further their political or societal agendas. They may not be serious about botany, but you have a lot to catch up on and I expect you in the lectures with them."

"I will work hard," I swear, clasping my hands together tightly. It doesn't feel real, a dream of my father's creation. "I want to learn."

"Good. That is good." She leans back and I think our meeting must nearly be over. After a rocky start I'm proud that I have shown my mettle, and I begin to gather my skirts.

"Oh, and Thora? One more thing."

"Yes, Doctor? I mean, Florencia."

"Out there in the halls and the libraries you are a scholar, just like all the others. I don't care what you look or sound like, or what the boys think of it. You are one of them. That being said, we must have a conversation about your wardrobe, as it's really not safe for you to be stumbling about the lab in skirts."

"I understand—"

"No." She shakes her head. I swallow hard. Her narrow face is the gravest I have seen it, the hollows in her cheeks catching the light. She brushes the vine from around the wrist of her glove and reaches across the desk to me, grabbing for my hand in my lap. "Let me finish. Out there, you are just another scholar. But in here, in this room, you are my partner. Do you understand?"

"I...I'm not sure I do."

"I am taking a risk by bringing you here, and I expect complete dedication." She pauses, as if this will clarify. I open and close my mouth like a fish. "Your father was a good man, a clever man. He assured me, long ago, that you were the same. I had given up hope I might meet you, let alone have the chance to bring you into my life's work—but the Lord has his ways. Together I have faith we can push the boundaries of botanical science. I travel fairly often about the country, gathering specimens; I need somebody in the lab whom I can trust." Petaccia squeezes my hand tighter, so tight now the claws of her nails—very sharp even through her gloves— dig into my soft flesh. "So you see: out there, a scholar. My student. In here, my partner."

Slowly the realisation sinks in. She is not asking me to be a good student, to study hard—or not only that. Just as before she was not asking me only if my father taught me to read or write. I notice once more the pustule-like nodules on the vine on the desk and think again of my father's hidden pamphlets. Petaccia, I remember, is interested in both botany and medicine. There is more to the doctor than meets the eye.

"Yes," she says, seeing my face and posture change. "This is cutting-edge research, Thora, and I trust that you will take it more seriously than most."

Chapter Five

I leave the laboratory with Petaccia's words echoing in my skull like the ring of a gong. Friend. Partner. I don't know what I expected from my meeting, but it wasn't this. Petaccia is the kind of woman I was sure could never exist—the kind of woman who, if I'd known of her before, could have changed everything I have ever thought possible, everything I have ever known about myself.

Warring feelings of pride and anger distract me on the journey back to my rooms. I wonder if Petaccia ever felt she had to read books in secret, if a husband ever told her that learning, the delicious pursuit of knowledge, was not something that belonged to her. I wonder why my father, knowing this successful woman of science, still believed this life was not suitable for me.

If Aurelio could see me here, I know without a doubt that he would laugh—and it would be that same scornful laugh he gave the day he threw away the novel he caught me reading. I'm seized by the memory, pausing in the middle of the cobbled path; I feel the pressure of his fingers around my wrist as he tore the book away, his nails digging into my skin. The sun beats down on my shoulders, but it's the heat of the parlour fire I feel warming my skin.

Why are you crying? he'd demanded after the book was nothing but ash. *I'm trying to help you.*

How does this help me? I said, wiping the single tear from my cheek—anger, not sadness, writhing in my chest. *You want me to be stupid.*

You're already stupid if you think this sort of thing is appropriate. Aurelio's eyes were icy, but he wore that same smirk, the laughter always only moments away. *Don't you want to rise to your new station?*

The words echo in my mind as I push on, away from La Vita. *Your new station.* Aurelio thought I should be grateful that he'd deigned to marry beneath himself, that he'd lifted somebody like me up into the golden glory of society. The thought angers me even now, even with these gorgeous ancient buildings standing proud on my every side, even with Aurelio nothing but ash in the great beyond.

Faith in my father has always driven me onwards, but since Aurelio died there are new questions to haunt me. If my father was such a good man, why did he let me read all his books? Or, perhaps more importantly, why didn't he let me read them in the open? I feel caught in a limbo, half silly society wife and half scholar, both costumes that shroud the real me.

I suppose I expected to leave my meeting with the doctor with the confidence that I was on the right path. I did not realise until our conversation that thoughts of remarriage had never entirely left my mind, though they had never been my dream either; deep down maybe I had hoped to find another husband here, a man I could take with my meagre widow's dowry as a fallback. If Petaccia is truly my only hope, if I'm putting all my faith in academia, is that brave or stupid?

I walk without purpose, kicking up dust with my shoes. My thoughts stumble over Petaccia's comment about my wardrobe—I long to tear off the walking gown and stomp on it like a petulant child, but what would I replace it with? All I have are the clothes Aurelio gave me, all in shades of demure cream, rose, sage, more dresses and stays and chemises fit for a society lady, nothing like the doctor's strange hybrid choice of skirt and trousers. The thought of having to ask Petaccia for money to have something new tailored is intolerable.

But so, too, is the thought of returning to my rooms and trying to sort through my belongings to find something more suitable. I need the heat on my shoulders, need the sun to burn off this nervous energy that thrums under my skin.

Eventually I realise I've been heading back towards my rooms anyway—the only place I can find without asking for directions or a map. Once I reach the front of the building I stop. The sun is high now, the heat making the blood pump hot in my veins. And then I think of the garden.

I turn away from my building, following the line of trees out front until the cobbles fall away to grassy tracks. The grass is scrubby here, as it appears from my study window, and when I walk I can feel the crackle of it beneath my soles like thousands of fragile fish bones. The image comes unbidden and I stop for a moment, curious at my morbidity. Then I laugh.

There is such freedom in the loosening of my chest. I swing my limbs and walk eagerly along the path. It is shaded here, deliciously cool despite the heat of the day. The wall I've seen from my window rises beside me, maybe ten feet high and smooth to the touch, its top verdant between the iron spikes that run along its length. The stone is cool too; I run my palm along it as I follow the path. It is quiet—silent, in fact. I could probably pick out my room eventually given enough time to count the windows, but I suspect the rest of the building behind me is empty.

This is, I think wryly, the exact kind of hidden, secret place Aurelio would have warned me off if he was alive. *Propriety*, he'd say. *Think before you act, Thora. A woman alone in what is essentially an alley? What will people think?* What would people think, indeed? A bitter smile crawls across my face. The air tastes of freedom.

"There are no people here to think," I say aloud. This place is, for now at least, entirely mine. *Mine*. It is such a foreign concept that I bark another laugh. "Fuck propriety." The curse sends a thrill through me.

I walk until the edge of my building comes into sight, but still there is no sign of a way into the garden. Weeds grow along the base of the wall, but thinly, as though they daren't touch the stone and risk being compared to the riot of greenery at the top and on the other side. From here it's impossible to see any of the real beauty I can see from my room, just grey stone on one side, coiling vines at the zenith, and the softer, sandy bricks of my building on the other. From here I can't even locate the top of the tower at the garden's heart.

Just a little farther, I think, and then I'll head back and tackle the awful job of my clothes. I just want to see how far the wall goes, how big the garden is, since it's hard to tell from my window. Now the wall curves away, and instead of walking back around to the front of the dorm, I continue with my hand on the stone.

Here—eventually—I come to a large gate. It is arched stone and ornate ironwork, long crackled from vivid orange rust to faded brown and wide enough that I cannot reach from one side to the other. I wrap my hands around the lumpy bars and peer through the gaps; the garden is truly beautiful, even more overgrown than I realised. Tangles of green form the base, but everywhere I look there is a new colour, rose pink and lilac and the soft white of lilies, even some rare black blooms that look like a cross between a rose and foxglove, the centre of their flowers bell-shaped, so dark they seem to swallow the sunlight.

"Hello?" I call.

I press my face to the gate. There is no sign of a padlock, but it is either locked from within or rusted shut. It looks so peaceful inside, shaded in some places and full sun in others, sprawling in every direction as far as I can see. It would be the perfect place to study, away from the prying eyes of those horrid male scholars, and warmer than the library.

"Is the garden open?" I call. Quieter I add, "Even just for me?"

I wait in silence, fighting the inevitable swoop of disappointment when I receive no response. It was undeniably a long shot; it looks as if nobody has tended this space in years. There are hints of what might have once been paths, but they are overgrown, treacherous to the ankles. I picture with a good deal of childish glee lengthy thorns snagging the embroidery of my skirts, but I push the thought aside.

Despite the obvious abandonment, I can't shake the feeling that the garden isn't entirely empty. Probably rats, I think. Or mice. Or birds—though I can't hear any. It doesn't feel exactly like I'm talking to nothing, though perhaps I am simply sick of silence.

"Well," I say flippantly, patting the gate and startling myself with the volume of its rattle. "I'm sure I'll be back. So if you change your mind...kindly leave the gate unlocked, will you?"

Chapter Six

Strange dreams haunt me again—Aurelio's fingers around my wrists morph into vicious weed-like creatures, ugly pustules on their knuckles that remind me of Petaccia's pet vine. Flames lick at my back and a wall of thorns scratches my skin as I force myself away from the blaze and into the dark unknown. I toss and turn, my bed damp with sweat, my ears full of the rustling sounds of pages turning in a breeze.

I wake to find somebody has pushed a piece of paper underneath my bedroom door. The doctor must keep strange hours because it definitely wasn't there when I went to sleep, but I've no doubt that it's her handiwork; it is a clean, crisp sheet, folded on a knife edge, and spindly black ink crawls like skittering spiders into what resembles the most intense two-week schedule I could imagine. If it wasn't clear before that Petaccia wasn't joking about the seriousness of my studies, then it is now: every day from eight until three I am in back-to-back lectures with only a half hour for lunch. Not one of these lectures is with her.

The class names are wildly variable. I recognise some words from my father's books and pamphlets, but there are many more I've never seen before. A wave of panic overtakes me as my eyes scan the page, taking in lecture titles like "Medicinal Beginnings: From Athyner to Romeras" and others that have been asterisked, like "Folklore, a Historian's Introduction." There are recurring titles hosted by the English faculty—both poetry and drama—and in philosophy and medicine; two lectures pop up more than once this week with a professor whose name Petaccia has underlined: "The Philosophy of Death and Mourning from a Preacher" and "A Study in True Grit: The Survivors of the Landler's Ship Disaster, Fact or Clever Journalism?" There are a handful of simpler botanical science lectures, which I understand better, taxonomy classes or those with grandiose titles like "Plant Medicine, Alchemy or Science?" and "The Alarming Underpopulation of the Isliano Rose," which echo the titles, or central arguments, of the books I read undercover in my father's study.

From three until six daily I have private study, and, once a week, she has scrawled *tutorial* in thick black ink, starting in two weeks. My stomach flips, a mixture of excitement and dread, as I realise that I shall spend this time alone with her in her laboratory— maybe even with that strange, diseased-looking vine.

I sit back and rub my knuckles, gently prodding the dread in my belly like one might tongue the gum around a missing tooth. I realise there is a sharp disappointment beneath the dread. Only once a week? After all her talk of partnership?

A horrid thought makes me stop short. The sheaf of paper trembles in my grasp. Is this Petaccia's way of telling me that she doesn't think I can do this? That I'm not ready, or that I don't belong here? There is no way for me to attend so many scattered lectures and actually absorb any of the information, is there? Surely this isn't a normal schedule.

I glance out the window, where the rosy pink dawn is painting the top of the empty, overgrown garden in shades of mauve. A mosquito buzzes somewhere close by and its electric hum sets my teeth on edge. I push away from the desk and march to the stove, where I set a pot of water on to boil. I throw in a scoop from the pot of tea leaves I stole from the dining hall last night at dinner and inhale the slightly bitter aroma.

No, I tell myself. Petaccia doesn't seem the cowardly sort. If she was certain I wasn't suited to this life, then I'm sure she would have told me yesterday.

She wants me to prove myself.

I roll my shoulders and smooth the paper out across the desk again, studying Petaccia's scrawl with more care. The first class is this morning, a lecture on the enduring medicinal plants from Isliano's Dark Ages. If a two-week test of resolve is all that stands between me and this future I've dreamt of my whole life, then I won't let a thing as small as mental exhaustion stand in my way.

I dress just as carefully today, pawing through my trunks for the least cumbersome of my gowns. I settle on one made of a soft green silk; it flows like water as I slide it over my head and arms. Aurelio hadn't been as much of a fan of this one, though his eyes did soften the first time I wore it to lunch with his family. *You remind me of lily pads*, he'd said.

I chuckle to myself now. Lily pads. It's entirely the wrong shade of green. Coyotillo flowers maybe. I'd have given him that. Not that he'd ever have even heard of them. Natural wonders, especially natural wonders with a penchant for harm like the coyotillo berries, never were Aurelio's speciality.

With the stolen dining hall tea to fortify me, I skip breakfast in favour of exploration, determined to find the locations of all the lectures ahead of me today. Three are within a stone's throw of one

another, but the fourth will require some creativity if I'm to attend
on time. The campus is a hive of activity this morning; men of all
ages wearing all manner of robes move with purpose, zigzagging
between benches and lampposts decorated with colourful blooms;
I find it hard to keep up the pace, my legs tangling in my skirts, my
notebooks shifting my centre of gravity something rotten. Now I
understand Petaccia's comments on my wardrobe—forget the lab,
St. Elianto itself is dangerous if one wields only a skirt as armour.

The lecture halls are bigger than my father's sepulchre, though
lighter thanks to the many windows. Colourful beams shimmer
through stained-glass scenes in the natural sciences hall—fields
of glass grass below olive trees and twisting strikes of lightning
catch the sun as it moves overhead. In the halls the seats and desks
are slanted upwards, so it feels as though learning comes from the
sky itself; the speakers stand on raised podiums at the centre of
the room, like preachers on a giant anthill, and the feeling of the
learner—at least this learner—is one of smallness. I'm in rooms
crowded with people and I've never felt more alone.

Three lectures out of four before lunch I'm left with a seat at
the hall's bottom edge, craning my neck to see and my ears to
hear. I leave each one with a mess of spindly notes and a spreading pain in my neck, my bewilderment growing. Petaccia said she
wanted a partner. I assumed she wanted me to have a rounded
knowledge so I could help her with her own research—but all I
feel now is confused and stupid.

You want me to be stupid, I'd said to Aurelio. I replay his
response over and over: *You're already stupid*. I've never felt more
of a fool than I do today, surrounded by scholars who have been
preparing for this environment their whole lives. They have each
been fed a steady diet of learning from the cradle, where all I have

is my father's books. Shame prickles in the sweat beneath my arms as I fight to keep up.

I gather my notebooks after a lecture on medicinal beginnings, where I learned only that Professor Almerto does not speak loudly enough for a low-row seat, and stumble out of the hall. The corridor is swarming with lively scholars, cheerily elbowing one another, clapping backs, and ruffling hair. It is a far cry from the solemn silence in the philosophy hall.

At the edge of one of the groups is a man I think I recognise from more than one of my lectures—he is tall and thin, with broad shoulders and arms that narrow like the branches of trees to delicate, slender hands. His dark hair is oiled but unruly, curling across his forehead and over his spectacles, and the front of his sandy-coloured shirt is creased beneath his open scholar's robe.

"Almerto is a quack," one of the scholars says, loudly enough to elicit sniggers from his nearest fellows. "All this nonsense about mint and garlic, as though we don't all eat it every day. If any of this were true, Alec's dear, well-fed grandmother would still be alive." One of the men bristles but laughs gamely; the others show no such hesitation. "He's no proof but stories—and what good are those? What do you think, lady?" He turns to me, a smirk on his face, and I realise it's the man from yesterday who laughed when the cyclist pushed me. "Must all be for fun if they're inviting the village girls in to listen. I'm curious what perspective you bring." The bespectacled man catches my gaze, brief alarm flashing across his features. It's sweet that he's worried about me.

I match the other man's smirk. "I doubt that," I say. "But shall I confirm it with Dr. Petaccia in my tutorial later? I'm sure the doctor would be very grateful to know if a single colleague is ruining the department's reputation for you fellows."

It feels like a risk to mention Petaccia in front of these men—I don't know if half of them even know who she is, but from their reaction it's clear the risk has paid off and her reputation does in fact precede her. The mouthy one goes instantly quiet and his two closest companions shift uncomfortably.

"I thought so. Now, if you'd kindly move out of my way? I have only a half hour for lunch, and I don't intend to waste it talking to you."

I push out into the heat of the sun, blinded momentarily by its fierceness. My heart pounds but the blood rushing in my ears feels like triumph. Perhaps making enemies isn't something I should be doing this early in my career—here's hoping it's even a career—but it felt like the right thing to do. I need to channel Petaccia's energy; I'm not some sideshow to be laughed at.

I wander to the edge of the lecture hall and find a spot in the shade to rest my back against. My heart beats so fast I might be sick, but I breathe slow and steady, deep in my belly, until I'm calm again.

"That was something back there."

I spin, ready to scramble for a witty comeback, but it's only the floppy-haired scholar with glasses. I relax, feeling the roughness of the stone through my dress.

"They needed to be put in their place," I say fiercely.

"Clearly." The scholar's lips quirk in a small smile and pride rushes through me. I roll my shoulders back and ready a shrug, but he's already looking away, patting through his pockets and coming out with a cigarillo and a book of matches. He hesitates before lighting the match. "Do you mind...?"

I laugh. "No. I'm fine, my husband used to smoke. Besides, these breaks are short enough, you might as well enjoy them."

"Oh, you too?" He raises an eyebrow but I don't miss the way his eyes dart to my wedding ring and I wonder if he's not just talking about the length of the break. I can't see his left hand. "Some schools really do overfill the schedules. What department are you in? You mentioned Petaccia. I was very impressed."

"I wasn't lying." I bristle, holding my books tight to my chest. I can't tell if he's making fun of me. "I really do have a tutorial with the doctor, it's just in a couple of weeks."

"No, no, I didn't mean it like that." He takes a hurried drag on his cigarillo and then heaves a sigh. "Sorry. I'm not very good at any of this. Can we start over? Let me introduce myself." He wipes his hand on the cream slacks under his robes and then extends it to me with a smile. "I'm Leonardo Vanksy. Billionth-generation scholar at St. Ellie, though a huge disappointment to my father for deciding to become a phytologist."

"Ah," I say, understanding. Now that I think about it, he looks exactly like the kind of man who might make a career studying plants. "Are you one of Petaccia's as well?"

"No," Leonardo says regretfully. "I'm with Almerto. You should ignore what those imbeciles said about him; he's really very clever. His undergraduate lectures are dull because he's preaching to the unconverted, but he's done a lot of work to open up the field. There's a lot of snobbery that goes on. Petaccia is very, very highly regarded by most—not that I need to tell you that—but she never takes on students, especially not undergraduates." His eyes follow the bob of my throat as I shift uncomfortably.

"Am I the only one who didn't know the doctor was…" I struggle to find a word that doesn't feel as though I'm reducing her achievements to biology.

Leonardo has no such qualms. "A woman?" he asks, then laughs kindly. "No, I think it's just not widely discussed. The 'serious scholars' "—he intones this in an imitation baritone—"are probably embarrassed, and I'm sure it suits her just fine. She's done more for the university's status than anybody, woman or not."

"That's probably why she took me on." I'm not sure why I say it—it's not the first time I've thought it, but it feels like a betrayal of myself to even utter it aloud. There's just something very gentle about Leonardo. He doesn't seem like the other scholars I've met. Perhaps, I think wryly, because he's a botanist.

"Oh, I don't think so." Leonardo takes another long drag on his cigarillo but doesn't follow that up with anything.

The area we're standing in is shaded by tall cypress trees and the air is cool beneath them—but it isn't private. All of a sudden I'm intensely aware of how close we're standing. Leonardo is leaning casually against the building as he smokes, dangling his cigarillo lazily between puffs. There's nothing to it, but I can feel the eyes of other scholars on us as another lecture hall lets out and a swarm of them passes. My wedding ring only affords me a certain kind of invisibility, and not from this distance.

"I have to go," I say abruptly, pushing away from the wall. "I have another lecture."

Leonardo's eyes widen, but I'm not sure whether it's surprise or disappointment there. He doesn't follow me, though, and for that I'm grateful. My next lecture is in the building next to the library, and I'm not ready for more stares if he wants to walk with me.

He waits until I've reached the dusty path, a slight breeze stirring my cropped hair, before calling, "You didn't tell me your name. I can't call you Botany Lady, that sounds crass."

"It's Thora," I say, rewarding him with a small smile. "Thora Grieve. See you around, Phytology Man."

Chapter Seven

Despite the exhaustion, I soon fall into a rhythm of learning not too dissimilar from that of my mid-childhood, only here my father isn't around to corral me as he did back then, and the learning is in lecture halls instead of the dark beneath his desk or curled in the corner of the embalming room with my fingers and toes freezing solid even in the summer.

I think of my father often. Whenever I drink a strong cup of coffee dosed with fragrant cardamom, I'm haunted by the ghost of the same scent caught in his beard during the rites; during my lonely walks about campus, I can't shake the sensation that he's right beside me, studying the stone buildings. I often catch myself spinning my wedding ring, as if this might keep his spirit at bay. My grief is stronger here than it was even in the city, and I find it hard to shake.

It should be Aurelio I think of—and perhaps those who see me twirling my ring in lectures might think that it is, more fool them—but the more time that passes, the more those thirteen weeks of my married life seem like a bad dream, nothing more than an untenable enclosure.

Most days I wake before dawn, still clinging to the tendrils of nightmares I don't remember, to read over the notes from my lectures, readying myself for the upcoming tutorial with Petaccia in every way I can since I have no idea what it might involve. Then it's breakfast, classes—some more interactive than others—and a quiet dinner in my same spot by the window in the dining hall with barely a minute to think about anything else—although I have taken to counting the number of my classes where Leonardo Vanksy also occupies a desk in the outer row.

He catches my eye outside after class one day as I'm taking a breath of the warm summer air, making the most of a rare fifteen minutes before the next, and stands waiting in the shadow of the building until I wave him over.

"You can stop skulking and come say hello," I say, giving him a small flustered smile as he lights his cigarillo. I don't know exactly what possessed me to give him my maiden name last time we met, though I *do* know that the reason has less to do with Leonardo than it does with the way Aurelio's name never felt like mine. Still, I think of Petaccia's warning. Leonardo seems like a nice man, but is his friendliness genuine philanthropy? It pains me to admit, but I am likely the naive one here.

"Sorry." He laughs through a puff of smoke and comes to stand with me under the trees instead. "I thought maybe you were avoiding me, hiding over here amongst the foliage. I thought, 'If ever there was a woman trying to turn invisible, it's that one.'"

I return his laugh, but the comment lands hard. Invisibility used to come so easily to me—nobody pays attention to the funereal staff, especially not if the chief mourner is nothing but some gangly young girl—but that all changed when I was the new Mrs. LeVand. Our marriage photograph was even in the newspapers.

And here it doesn't matter if people think I'm married, divorced, or single—I'm still a woman and that's reason enough to pay attention.

"I can hardly avoid you; I see you several times a day," I say as lightly as I can muster.

"I'm sorry about that too," Leonardo jokes. "I wouldn't want to look at this ugly mug so often either."

"Don't be silly." Despite Petaccia's warning about the men here, something about the warmth in Leonardo's voice makes me like him. It's like talking to somebody I've known a lot longer than a week. "It's not you I'm hiding from. Besides, if I was planning to disappear, I'd do a heck of a lot better than *Cupressus sempervirens*."

"Ah now." Leonardo nods approvingly, taking a drag and blowing smoke away from us. "Somebody's been paying attention in taxonomy."

Coming from somebody else this might seem patronising, but from Leonardo it's a genuine compliment. I shrug. "Perhaps I have a knack for it."

"I think you probably do. It's not often Petaccia takes a new mentee."

"You said that before. Stop trying to butter me up," I say. Leonardo raises his hands in defence but his laughter tells me it's only part of the repartee. "Or are you simply jealous?" I add, playing along. It's nice to joke.

"Oh, very," Leonardo says earnestly, and there's more than a kernel of truth there. "I imagine my parents would be much less disappointed in their only son if he had such a well-regarded mentor."

"Perhaps we should petition to get her to take you on."

Leonardo chuckles. "Alas, I actually don't think my parents

would care to know Petaccia from Almerto, since neither is a law-
yer and neither would make a particularly good suitor for my sisters. I'm already a lost cause."

"You think you have it hard, try being the only daughter of an
undertaker," I say blithely. It's meant to be another part of the jape,
but Leonardo's face softens in a manner too close to pity for my
liking. I feel myself clam up immediately, the balmy heat against
my skin no longer pleasant. "I mean—we're very well respected,"
I stammer, desperately trying to claw it back. "But don't tell me
anybody's top choice for marriage is ever the girl they last saw at
their great-uncle's cradleside."

"I..." Leonardo pushes at his spectacles awkwardly.

For a second I debate simply walking away without another
word. Death is *not* a subject for polite conversation; I know that—
Aurelio beat it into me often enough—but what else do I have to
speak on? How will I ever make friends when this, mourning and
sadness and Silence—and less than four months as a wife—is all
I've ever known?

"It's all right," I say quickly. "You don't have to say anything; I
know that was strange. I'm sorry. I'm—"

"I was just going to say... You're right." Leonardo gives me a
tentative smirk, which widens when he sees my expression shift
from embarrassment to hesitant relief. "You *did* have it harder. Of
course, now you have a terribly big advantage. With you as such a
shining example of your kind, I think it might very well be more
difficult for me to get signed on under Petaccia than it would be to
get our fellow scholars to start marrying undertakers' daughters."

"You think?" I choke out.

"Oh, absolutely." Leonardo finishes his cigarillo and stubs it
out with the sole of his shoe. "So how about we call it a draw?"

Lectures aside, life at the university is lonelier than I expected. Most of the scholars keep their distance, and my evenings are quiet—I've yet to brave the library again and have taken to spending the hours between dinner and near dusk with more books for company. It occurs to me more than once that some would call this just another kind of Silence, an extension of my grief, but if that's so, then it is at least one of my own creation.

The truth is that I'm accustomed to being alone. My father was my closest companion after my mother died, and he spent so many hours working that it became second nature to either amuse myself or work alongside him—and even he was not my *friend*. An undertaker's life is one of fluidity; it's hard to develop any true kind of routine or connection when your days and nights are ruled by the constant unpredictable predictability of death and your home feels like it belongs to the departed more than the living. I never knew other children my own age, unless they were Silent or lying still in the cradle awaiting their flames, and my mother only ever gave birth to one living child, so I had no siblings.

It wasn't until my marriage to Aurelio that I knew what it meant to be so constantly near somebody—and with Aurelio's family, his mother, his sisters and their children and their husbands, it was often more than only one somebody. It was too much to bear. More than once during our short marriage I had to excuse myself from a family dinner early claiming a headache or indigestion. Aurelio was always disappointed, though he hid it well in public.

This is why I'm so surprised at myself when I accept the coffee Leonardo offers as we enter Professor Almerto's next Thursday morning lecture. He comes to the hall bearing two closed-top containers made of glass, the dark liquid topped with a creamy white foam, condensation beading on the sides.

I waver, thinking again of Petaccia's warning, and the way Leonardo gamely carried on our banter the last time we spoke, but I smile as he approaches my chosen desk and he returns the gesture. I don't know anything about Leonardo yet, not really, but I won't let Petaccia's fear that I'm shopping for a husband get in the way of a potential friendship just to reassure her of my aspirations—not unless she insists. Besides, having a friend in the same area of study is, I think, a wise decision.

Petaccia isn't the only reason for my uncertainty, though. The thing that makes me question myself is much smaller, and also much, much bigger. It's something I noticed when we first met and saw an echo of in his childish eagerness to continue our conversation even after I made him uncomfortable...

Why do the other scholars in all our lectures avoid him as they do? They don't engage with his questions as they do with other classmates, and even the professors seem to falter when he speaks. He isn't poor, that much is clear from the clean cut of his clothes under his robes, and he is well groomed and well spoken. Yet the seas part when he appears, as though the others fear catching something from standing too close.

"I hope it's not too forward of me," Leonardo says, handing the second glass of coffee to me and swinging into the empty seat next to mine. It's a move that is meant to look relaxed but comes off as jerky as he thumps down a little too hard. "It looks like today is going to be a hot one and it felt rude turning up without a spare." He takes a sip and sighs in relief. "There's nothing for days like these like Andanicci beans over ice."

I sip my coffee and give a surprised sigh of my own. It is good and strong, bitter and smooth at the same time, and icy cold. Better than I expected. The flavours dance on my tongue as I watch him.

"Thank you for thinking of me."

Leonardo smiles again and he reminds me of a child, only with skin that crinkles around his eyes. I notice his long fingers again, such slender hands; they are safe hands, not like Aurelio's were. He had the hands of a brute—it was the first thing I ever noticed about him, the way his knuckles rose like mountains and his nails were so square and shiny he might have been able to slit open skin with the straight edge of them.

"I stole the recipe." Leonardo leans over so he can whisper conspiratorially, and even his bragging voice is gentle. Could this be the reason the other men avoid him? Do they think he is soft? I tilt my head and study him closer, wondering if there's something in him that could be different, like me. "It's a secret."

"Oh really?" I raise an eyebrow. "Perhaps you'd better consider some form of retribution. It seems wholly unfair for you to be the sole keeper of such a secret. Have you considered writing a letter of thanks? Or posting a piece in the papers?"

Leonardo's expression shifts, his eyes narrowing—not in anger or annoyance, but something else. It isn't a delicate expression, though. There's a warning there. Then he takes another sip of coffee and releases another sigh, this one more theatrical than the last. A smile flits back over his lips, forced but not false, and I understand myself, and Leonardo, better already.

"Alas no," he says. "Sadly the secret is all mine now. Nobody else wants it."

The reason I'm hesitant around Leonardo has nothing to do with Petaccia, but it is the same reason the other scholars avoid him—though I'm not sure they know exactly why he makes them so uncomfortable. It isn't because he is soft, or strange; it's not because he is too gentle—though he is—nor is it because he's mean beneath that gentleness. The reason is also the reason I am holding home-brewed coffee in my hand, my attention half on this man and half on Almerto's lecture, warmth in my chest and pity there too. It is a reason I see myself in him, and I'm sure he sees himself in me.

Leonardo is grieving.

The lecture ends with the ring of a small gong that echoes around the amphitheatre-like hall, and Leonardo catches my eye as we get up to leave. I give him the smallest nod and we trudge together in silence to the same spot outside where we first spoke. My head is spinning.

I've never heard the theory that most medicinal plants have origins in cool oceanic regions and that's why we see few of them truly thriving in Isliano's mountain heat, but it makes sense. It scares me, too, that I've never noticed before how sparse common herbs like cattlethorn and amber grass have become; my father used to burn amber grass with mint for the cleanse after a grieving, but at some point he started to substitute that with double doses of mint, and although I often quizzed my father about his plants, I never thought to ask why.

"Are you seeing stars too?" Leonardo asks.

"Stars and moons and whole universes." I shake my head. I wonder if Petaccia knows all this and wants me to learn it, or if she wants me to report back like a little spy while she's busy with her own work. "I just can't understand why it's not talked about more widely. Surely there's the potential for huge problems if the supply chain dries up."

"It's what Almerto wants us to work on together," Leonardo confesses. "The academy in Romeras are trying to come up with plans for what happens if we have another influenza like the Fourth-Decade one; half of the counsellors think that the modern medicine will be enough—they're expecting breakthroughs in the next few years with some sort of synthetic vaccine or antidote— but others maintain we ought to have a backup and it doesn't make sense to funnel all our research away from tried-and-tested methods."

"So Almerto is trying to fearmonger the scholars into switching their studies?" I wrinkle my nose. "That seems like the stupidest way to get clever people to care."

Leonardo shrugs one shoulder and lights his customary cigarillo. The smoke from it is grey against the bright blue of the sky, its scent at once sharp and earthy. An image of Aurelio flits, unwelcome, across my brain: my husband smoking in the library, his feet up on his desk, a funeral summons in one hand as he told me, without punctuation or pause, that my father was dead. *He's dead. You can give him three days, if you* must, *but no more. I need you here.*

He'd not even tried to comfort me.

"It's not fearmongering if it's based in truth, is it?" Leonardo continues. I shake the memory with a physical shiver. "That's how he adopted me—he read a thesis I wrote on the decline in wildling flowers in my hometown back when I was a first-year."

"Fearmongering is exactly what it is when you're lecturing a student body that largely doesn't have a clue about botany." I wipe the sweat from my palms onto my skirts, wishing I hadn't finished

Leonardo's coffee so quickly. "It would be better if he encouraged the scholars to open their minds first, rather than grubbing them to support him when they don't even understand the severity of what he's talking about."

Leonardo sighs and pinches the bridge of his nose. "Yes," he agrees, "you're probably right. But you have to consider that half of these men have never considered botany as a serious science—and most of those have decided firmly against it once they realise it's a wo…"

I quirk my eyebrow and Leonardo hesitates. "What?" I prompt. "A women's issue? Just because they've all decided that medicine is only the real deal if somebody is bleeding doesn't mean there isn't a crossover that's spanned centuries."

"Look, you know as well as I do that most people don't consider what we do a serious science, regardless of its medical history. Just look at the way some of them flinch when Petaccia's name comes up."

"But you do," I point out. "So why even say it? You know it's not true. I've never been more convinced than in this last week that any scholar would take the subject seriously if they actually attempted to learn it. There is more to botany than horticulture and pretty flowers; it is the very essence of life, isn't it? There's evidence that plants were here long before we were, and I've no doubt they'll exist long after the human race is gone. As much as the scholars in their terra-cotta towers would wish to deny it, plant medicine and taxonomy benefit us all."

"I'm sorry," Leonardo apologises, and he looks genuinely stricken. "You're right."

"Relax, Leonardo. I'm only teasing. I mean, half teasing, anyway. And only because I know you can take it. I'd actually love to spend the next hour discussing all this, but I've got another class to get to now."

When Leonardo smiles it's crooked and his whole face shifts. There's that childlike quality again that it momentarily lost in sadness. If the other scholars could see him like this, I wonder if they would keep such a distance from him.

I push away from the wall in the shade of the trees and feel the immediate burn of the sun on my shoulders and the back of my bare neck. I should buy a hat—but I know I won't; I've enjoyed the freedom since I got here and I'm reluctant to go back to hats and shawls, although it would be proper. The other scholars already find me strange just by virtue of my being a woman; I might as well make the most of that.

"What would you say to dinner tonight?" Leonardo blurts. I stop, half turning. "There's a little place I know just off campus; it's not far and I can get a trap for you..." He trails off.

Petaccia's warning echoes unbidden like the ring of a bell. But I don't think Leonardo is trying to poach me, to rush me into a marriage or anything so silly. I think maybe he's just lonely—and I like his company. There's something refreshing about him compared to the other stuffy men in this place. Still, there's being kind and there's being naive, and I want to avoid the latter as much as possible. If marriage taught me anything, it's that men will say a lot of things to get what they want.

"No," I say after a thoughtful pause. "Thank you."

Leonardo's face falls instantly. There's something still quite childish about the expression—it isn't petulance, though, not like it would be in most men. It feels gentler. More like regret.

"I'm so sorry," he says quickly. "I didn't mean to offend you or be impolite—I just thought...That is...It's been a while since

I had a dinner companion. It would be nice to talk to you more…
about science."

The stammering is so different from our usual banter that I
hesitate, torn between laughter and sorrow. Have I made a mistake? I don't want to upset Leonardo, but Petaccia's words have
stuck with me. I'm not here for marriage. Is that what Leonardo is
hoping for? It didn't feel like he was proposing some sort of date
or trying to twist my arm. But who's to say his remorse is genuine?
Perhaps he's trying to make me feel guilty.

After all, that's what Aurelio would have done.

"I'm sorry," I say with finality. "I really do have to go."

Chapter Eight

That night there is a girl in the garden.

If this were any other night I would have believed it a mistake, but the moon is bright and whole tonight, the garden outside my window bathed in ethereal light so bright it might as well be day. Silver beams illuminate the strangled greenery, and at the heart of the overgrown tangle of vines where the tower grows from its grassy mound is the girl.

My breath catches in my throat. It's impossible to tell exactly from my window her age, but she's definitely young—maybe younger than me, although only by a little. Her hair is long and thick and dark, falling in unbound waves nearly to her hips. She floats between the vines and flowers in a gown as pale as the moonlight.

My first thought, as foolish as it might be, is that she is a ghost. An apparition conjured by my tiredness, maybe, or by too much squinting at my rows of cramped lecture notes. I have spent hours reading and memorising the names and properties of plants, their families and their cousins. In my weeks at St. Elianto, evenings and mornings studying at this desk, I have yet to see anybody in the garden. Twice I have attempted to gain access through the gate, and twice I've found it locked and rusted. Yet this woman moves through the plants as though she was born to them and they belong to her, her fingers trailing across the silky petals of blooms bigger than her fist, one the size of her head.

She stops seemingly at random, bending her head to inhale the fragrance from one of the black-blue flowers. A trick of the moonlight makes the dark colour dance across her cheeks like a swirl of ink in water.

When she raises her head, her eyes rise towards me. Although there is no way she can see me, and I have no reason to feel guilty for the dim lamp on my desk and my shutters thrown open to the balmy night, I hurry to extinguish the flame with a swoop of panic.

The girl's face remains upturned for a long moment as she basks in the light of the moon, revelling in it as most people relish warm spring sunlight on their skin. It isn't cold tonight and the crickets chirp beneath my window, but there's something about her behaviour that seems strange.

I press my palms against the hard wood of my desk, my heart hammering. Without the lamp to blind me, her features are sharper, her cheekbones highlighted in silver below large dark eyes. Her gown bears more form than most nightgowns but is cut scandalously low for a day dress, allowing her to swing her arms from side to side as she resumes her aimless wandering. My gaze is drawn to her collarbones as she loops nearer the garden wall, and my cheeks heat with shame.

The girl turns away from my window, finally, picking at the petal of another dark-bloomed plant. She has a basket, I realise, and she's filling it with flowers snipped just below the head using a shining, sharp tool. She glances upwards before culling each one, as if whispering a prayer—or asking for permission—her eyes firmly on the moon.

I press my hands to my flaming cheeks and inhale breath after shaky breath. I track the girl until she wanders into the shadow of the wall beyond, to my left, waiting until she is no longer visible before hurriedly packing away my pen and inks. I feel strangely shaken; I have come to think of the garden as my own private Eden, and this girl is an unwelcome intruder in the space.

Of course, this is ridiculous. The garden isn't mine. She obviously has more claim to it than I do—I picture the way she caressed the blooms, almost lovingly—but the heat in my cheeks is more than me simply bristling at the intrusion.

I'm jealous, I realise. But whether of the girl and her free-swinging arms and exposed collarbones, or of the plants beneath her gentle touch, I cannot decide.

Chapter Nine

I sleep little and wake long after the start of my first lecture, my mouth parched and throat rasping. My forehead is feverish to the touch and I wonder, briefly, if I'm coming down with something. I lie still for a moment, tensing my fingers and toes, but once I roll out of bed the feeling is gone as fast as it came. I fight the panic at missing the lecture; it's poetry, the second lecture I've had with this professor, and he speaks too quietly for my liking anyway.

I make tea and drink it while it is near scalding, relishing the burn. My dreams last night were muddled—but unsettling. I don't remember much except silver moonlight and vines as thick as my wrist rising through the floorboards to wrap me in my bed like shackles.

I can't stop thinking about the girl I saw in the garden. I sat by the window for a long time after she'd disappeared, and when I couldn't sleep, I'd donned my walking jacket and slipped out of my rooms and down to the garden. There is another path I've discovered if I turn left out of the building that takes me to the gate much quicker, and I chose that one without thinking.

When I got to the gate the garden was silent—eerily so, in fact. It must have been the wee hours, but I was wide awake and could hear nothing, not the chatter of distant students, not the call of a bird or even the gentle hum of a fly. I stood by the gate for minutes, perhaps longer, the time passing as liquid through my fingers. Up close I noticed how well tended the blooms were, the scent of the ones closest reminding me faintly of something at once familiar and somehow entirely foreign.

In the end I didn't dare to break the silence; I crept back to my rooms as softly as I'd come and slipped into bed still wearing my stockings. After that I remember only the dreams, the vines, and a premonition of some strange icy heat surging through my veins. And then morning.

Perhaps I dreamt the whole thing. I touch my hand to my forehead again—it's warm but no longer strikingly hot—and then clamp my palms over my face and heave a sigh. I don't have time for this. Today alone I have three more lectures and the tutorial with Petaccia, and I've still no idea what the latter will involve.

I dress in my least flouncy dress for the occasion, white button sleeves and plain grey kirtle. It's as close to mourning black as I will willingly get, and even then I stare at my reflection with reservations. It makes the brown-gold of my hair seem duller, the hazel of my eyes muddier—but perhaps that is what Petaccia wants. A serious scholar, not a silly girl. Part of me is happy to slough away Aurelio's bride and play the role of his widow; part of me wonders what might be left underneath them both if I scratch the surface hard enough.

Leonardo is conspicuously absent from my last lecture, even though it's a botany lecture on plant procreation. I've read all the science before, stamens and stigma and nectar, so I'm grateful for the opportunity to relax my writing hand and listen only for new information. There is a blister the size of a raisin forming on the first knuckle of my middle finger, and I pick at it absently. It reminds me of the strange pustules on Petaccia's vine and of my dreams last night. I wonder if any of the plants in the garden have a similar illness—or whatever it is—and if that's why the gates are locked. But then what about the girl?

I snap back to attention when the scrape of chairs across the uneven wooden floor signals the end of the lecture. My notebook is bare before me with the exception of a few jotted words— and many, many drawings. I hadn't even been aware of my pen moving; the ink is blotchy and irregular, brown here and black there, concentrated in several spots where my mind has obviously wandered. They're vines, I think. Rambling, crawling plants. If I squint, I can make out flowers amidst the scribbles.

Hurriedly I sweep the notebook closed, tucking it tight to my chest. My palms are slick with sweat, my spine and armpits too. I glance around, but fortunately nobody seems to have noticed my inattention. Even the professor is long gone.

I lean back in my chair and let my head rest against the wall behind me, my eyes drifting to the domed glass roof over the central podium. A sharp pang of grief takes me off guard at the reminder of my sepulchre. I miss its predictable, quiet darkness more than I thought I ever would. When it was mine it felt like a prison, the only walls I would ever see, but now that it's gone I realise how little I know of the world. I miss my father too, the comfortable discomfort of all his rules—and, worse, I miss Aurelio, the stability of my planned future, as much as it was a future I hated. Here I feel all at sea.

I don't move until the next round of scholars begins to trickle into the room, and even then I wait until the last possible moment before slinking away. My legs ache something rotten. What's wrong with me? It must be tiredness, lack of sleep after so many days studying. I ought to be more careful.

I stumble out into the daylight and almost run straight into Leonardo. He catches me about the shoulders with surprising strength and I blurt a curse—followed by a swift apology.

"Thora!" he exclaims. He steps back, clearly remembering my coldness yesterday—we haven't spoken since then—and shoves both hands into the pockets of his robes, as if to say *Don't worry, I won't touch you again. I don't want to offend you.* I shift awkwardly, regretful at this new distance. "Are...you all right?"

"Sorry," I repeat. I resist the urge to dab my forehead with the back of my hand. I feel dazed and quite warm. I can't shake the feeling that my dreams, so vivid and serpentine, are partially to blame.

"Thora...?"

"What?"

"I asked if you're all right." Leonardo's brows furrow. "You came barrelling out in such a hurry, I thought something had happened."

"Oh." I let out a rattled laugh. "No, I'm sorry for rushing. I don't know what's wrong with me today but I was in a world of my own. I'm fine—though I didn't sleep well. I have my tutorial this afternoon."

"Ah." Leonardo maintains his distance, but when I step out of the direct sunlight and into the thick shadows under the trees, he follows. I wonder if he's got a lecture in La Scienza, if that's why he's here, or if he just makes a habit of frequenting all my usual haunts. A few days ago, yesterday even, this might have made me wary, but after my dreams—and after seeing that girl in the garden last night, so alone, so *lonely*—I realise with a jolt that there might be worse things than encouraging Leonardo's acquaintanceship. "It's your first one?"

"I'm terrified," I say. Only as I say it do I realise how true it is. Dr. Petaccia scares me more than I'd like to admit. I actually think I'd be less afraid if she was a man.

"Don't be," he says warmly. "You'll be fine. She's not going to expect you to know everything already. That's why she's teaching you."

"No, I know, it's just…" I shrug. "There's a lot riding on it. I've wanted this my whole life. You probably don't know what that's like—sorry, I don't mean it like that. It's just…I never thought I'd get to be here. What if I'm not clever enough?"

Leonardo is silent for a moment, genuinely thoughtful—and seemingly not offended by my lack of tact. Then he says, "I'm sure Dr. Petaccia knows how you feel. Nobody makes…Well, excuse the presumption, but nobody makes the kind of commitments you, and she, have made without knowing the cost. I know being a—a lady in the sciences isn't easy. Regardless of what brought you here, and when, you're here now."

My heart swells. "You don't have to be nice to me. I was rude just now, and I was rude yesterday too. I regret both times. I'm… I guess you could say it's been a while since I had anybody new to talk to."

"Oh," Leonardo says breezily, his smirk cutting through any tension between us. "Don't worry, Botany Lady. I won't take it personally."

"You probably shouldn't. It's a little-known fact that undertakers' daughters don't get out much." I know I'm slicing off the three months of my marriage as if they're the tip of a candle wick but I don't care.

Leonardo's smirk softens. "Like botanists," he agrees.

"Worse. My only companions growing up were the dead."

"I grew up with five sisters. Nobody ever paid me any mind, so my friends were pretty much all plants. At least yours *used* to talk."

I can't help the chuckle that burbles in my chest as I picture a pint-sized Leonardo surrounded by potted plants wearing hats and spectacles and little pencil moustaches.

"So... At risk of getting my head bitten off again—have you changed your mind about dinner?" Leonardo raises an eyebrow. "Or coffee. If we're going to have classes together it might be useful for studying. Almerto always says I don't participate enough. We could do tonight if you wanted, chat about your tutorial. Like I said before: there's a place I know off campus—"

"Not off campus," I say firmly. "And not tonight." He winces, but we both know why I have to be so stern. I'm already the odd one out at St. Elianto. I don't want to give anybody, not least Dr. Petaccia, reason to think I don't belong here. "But... the dining hall tomorrow evening would be nice."

"Really...?" Leonardo beams.

"*If* they'll let me sit with you. I usually get shoved at the table by—"

"By the window?" He chuckles, his eyes bright with a gratitude of his own, though I don't think I'm the one being kind here. "Yes, I'm familiar with that one. I suppose it's just where they put the botanists."

By the time I set out for my tutorial in La Vita I'm rushing, but I make it with five minutes to spare. The building is just as dim and cool as on my last visit, and all the doors are locked as before—I try them only out of curiosity. I pause for a second outside the upstairs laboratory to catch my breath and push a hand through my slightly sweaty cropped curls; it's just as warm in here today too.

Inside I'm met with a scene that is almost eerily similar to our first meeting—Petaccia at the desk with a pen in her gloved hand and papers scattered before her, and that diseased-looking vine crawling beneath her empty hand as she...what, pets it?

I close the door behind me.

"You're late." Petaccia glances up from her work, a frown furrowing her otherwise creaseless skin.

"I—"

"Well, no mind. You're here, which is something. Now, come and make yourself useful, will you? This little beast has been making my life hell."

"I'm...sorry?"

"The *vinea*, the liana. I call her *Paruulum arida*, though in truth she's more of a bastard trumpet creeper. Come and hold her for me while I finish up these notes, and then we'll get started."

"Oh," I say, and drop my notebooks onto an empty wooden stool. Petaccia shifts the vine from her fingers and I could swear it wriggles in response.

I put on a spare pair of the doctor's gloves and take the length of vine from her. It's a lot longer than I thought, growing from a pot below her desk where the sun filters through the window. It's swelteringly warm in here again, but the vine is cool to the touch—and farther down its length there are curious clusters of sickly yellow flowers, several of them wilting although the soil at their base is perfectly moist.

The vine wriggles again, and this time I'm sure it's not a trick of the light, or false movement, or some phantom breeze. I feel the pressure of the green matter against my covered skin and fight not to recoil as it trembles slightly, shifting to sit across my knuckles as I hold it awkwardly.

Up close I realise that what I'd thought were pustules, oozing wounds, are in fact scaly buds covered in a layer of sticky, protective gum; the buds themselves are not unusual, many plants have them, but the colour... The colour isn't right, dark reddish pink in places and pus yellow in others.

"How are you finding your studies?" Petaccia asks, either oblivious to my discomfort or content to ignore it. "Are you settling in?"

"I'm enjoying them." I don't really know what to say, what answer she is expecting of me here. The reality is I've hardly had time to think, even though I spend every day thinking so hard my brain feels like ooze. "I would prefer more time dedicated to the science, although—"

"Yes, I know. It's regrettable that you're having to split your focus, but there's much you need to know, and I need as well rounded a partner as I can get. My father always said that life breathes science, and the older I get, the more I'm inclined to agree with him."

Petaccia scribbles something with a flourish—all I can make out is *P. studies incomplete... movement gaining traction though not without... pause,* which means nothing to me—and then looks up at me expectantly.

"Oh, of course," I stammer. "Whatever I can do to help. I

didn't mean to criticise. I'm finding the other lectures very valuable. I suppose I always knew there was a lot to learn, I just didn't realise that the arts and the sciences were so...interconnected? I think that's the right word. Your father sounds very wise...Was he a botanist too?"

"Yes. And my mother, though her focus was more taxonomy than anything else." Petaccia scratches the tip of her nose, leaving an inky smudge that looks a little like dirt. "She was the author of a wonderfully detailed botanical dictionary, though not many people have heard of her. My father was renowned."

"Did they raise you to be interested in science, then?" I ask. Not for the first time since I found out about the scholarship I'm struck by an unfamiliar bitterness towards my own father. I thought I'd made my peace with the parts of me he nurtured and the parts he bade me keep hidden, but how much of what I thought I knew was a lie? I could have been like her, like this doctor with a career behind her as well as ahead, if he hadn't been such a coward.

"Yes, my sister and I were both educated from a young age. A little like yourself, no?"

"Oh, uh—"

"I knew your father when he was a student here. That was before the chapel laws and the bruising fever, I think."

My father did mention this in his tales of the institution, usually as almost a footnote. In his last year of study at the mortuary school, there was an outbreak of a fever that mottled its victims in bruises the size of apples. There were so many deaths they had to open a new chapel and sepulchre in the village, which soon became the primary site for all rites. The campus was quarantined until an antidote was discovered, and the schools remained separated afterwards.

"I remember my father telling me about the antidote," I say.

"How it was like a kind of miracle, coming right at the point everybody thought the university would have to close. That's probably the first time I thought about the science of *life* instead of just—well, death. I...I read a lot of my father's notes growing up, his books too. I always wondered who thought to try something as simple as purple saltflower..."

Petaccia inclines her head, watching as the vine coils in my hands again. Her expression gives me pause, half amusement and half more like... *pride*?

"It was you?" I mouth, jaw agape. My father always said that the bruising-fever cure changed the place of herbal medicine in the sciences, pulling doctors back to its research for decades despite advancements elsewhere—the same shift Almerto is fighting for again now. "But you must have been so young?"

"My father and I worked together on the tonic." Petaccia shrugs. "Plants like saltflower have been used topically to reduce immune response for hundreds of years, but the antidote was a little more complicated."

"Did you get the credit?" I blurt. "Or did he?"

I realise the moment the words are out of my mouth that this is a huge mistake. I was thinking not of my own father but of Aurelio, knowing he would not allow me to claim such a prize for myself even if I was responsible. Speaking freely with Leonardo might be acceptable because he, too, is a kind of outsider. But Petaccia? She is a university fellow, and she holds my future in her palms. I slap my free hand over my mouth stupidly.

Petaccia's eyes are cold, but they glitter with a surprising amount of humour.

"We shared the credit," she says. "I was young. At the time I thought that was fair."

"I'm sorry—"

"You needn't worry so much about upsetting me, Thora. We have a lot of work to do and I don't have time to mollycoddle. If you've got questions to ask, speak up. If you think we should do something differently, tell me that too. I didn't get here by pandering to the whims of others but, well"—she pauses and smiles and there's something unsettling about it; I think it's the largeness, and the dark colour, of her teeth—"perhaps it's time to try another tactic."

Petaccia pushes away the papers, sweeping them into her top drawer, and gently takes the vine from my hands. I peel the gloves off and wipe my palms on my skirts immediately, hoping she doesn't notice.

"Forgive me," I say then, "but you still haven't really told me exactly what it is we're trying to do. They say you never take mentees or apprentices and yet you've made an exception for me—and I'm doing my best but a handful of classes won't make me well rounded overnight. So why me? Why now? My father always lamented the fact I would never attend the university and yet here I am."

Petaccia lets the vine down onto the desk gently—I get the distinct impression neither of them is happy about this development—and gestures for me to follow her to one of the windows on the far wall.

The heat here is something fierce. Sweat beads on my forehead and I feel it gathering across my collarbones and at the base of my spine. Once again I regret my outfit choice, envious of Petaccia's short sleeves and unhindered legs. The air is wet and green and cloying, like soup in my lungs. I wonder why she never opens the sash—just a little breeze would make this room so much more bearable—but there must be a reason for it. Still, perhaps the reason is that the doctor doesn't feel the heat, since her skin looks entirely dry to the touch.

"You're like me," Petaccia says. "I think."

I wait as she studies me, her gaze trailing with scientific precision from my cropped hair right down to my barely used shoes—another of Aurelio's marriage gifts.

"I married late," she goes on slowly. "Out of...well, some would say it was necessity, though I know that's a dirty word. My husband was quite a bit older than me. He and my father had collaborated on a number of projects as young scholars, and his first wife died young. A curse that struck twice—I was widowed within just a few years. Or..."

Petaccia's gaze becomes unfocused. I wait, but she doesn't continue.

"Or?" I prompt eventually.

"I assume so anyway. Niccolò was halfway around the world collecting specimens—oh, such excitement, but then he always was very daring. I always preferred to remain in my labs, it's where my skills are best used—and he simply...Well. He never came home."

"I..." I stumble for the right words. Condolences for my own loss always feel so unwelcome that I haven't the words to comfort anybody else. I never pictured Petaccia as a widow, though I suppose given her stature it makes sense that she was once married to another academic. I settle for "I'm sorry."

"So you see," Petaccia says, shaking herself. She redirects her gaze to me and gestures to the window ahead. "I think that you and I will be able to work together very nicely. We understand each other, I think. We've both seen loss firsthand, and know how the mind appreciates a project. I'm hoping this could be the kind of project you will sink your teeth into."

Across a bench in front of the window there are multiple low boxes of soil, seedlings of various sizes sprouting in shades of emerald and hunter and sage, white and a silvery sort of transparency that reminds me of moonlight. Underneath the bench there are more of the large troughs with much more established plants, and on the wall to the left of the window, where the bench stretches across, there are diagrams of various plants' biology, and a crosscut image of a plant that looks similar to Petaccia's precious vine only with great trumpet-shaped flowers and spotted leaves that curl inwards on themselves.

There is a microscope—I've never seen one in person before and it's bigger than I thought it would be—and slivers of plant matter between sheets of glass. There are also small buckets filled with what looks like sand and reddish clods of dirt, plus a bucket of what looks like plain water. Beside them is an open book, the paper filled with the doctor's spidery scribbles. Petaccia stands by the rows of seedlings, direct sunlight on her face, and looks at me expectantly as the cogs in my brain begin to whir.

"This is what you're working on?"

"Yes."

"I assume it all has something to do with Almerto's work in the same area? His opinions about the loss of important plant families due to lack of environmental care are sincerely striking."

"Almerto is a quack," Petaccia says. I bristle at the phrase Leonardo disagrees with so vehemently, but I try to keep it to myself. "But yes, you're right. It's similar stuff. His focus is purely on medicinal plants—which are important, you understand. I know that better than most. But what I'm doing is more important."

I wait for Petaccia to clarify, but she's already lost in an inspection of the seedlings closest to her. Their leaves are curled and a little wilted. They're not coping well with the heat. I move closer, attempting to get a better look. I've read pamphlets on proper plant growth, it's what I started with really, and it's pretty plain to me that the issue here is the heat and too much sunlight. I don't know where these plants are from, or even what families they're part of since it can be hard to tell at this stage, but they look like Elver clover, which grows in the mountainous regions to the north where it's much cooler this time of year.

I say nothing. Eventually Petaccia looks at me. "Drought," she says, as if that explains everything.

"Drought?"

"You said yourself, Almerto concerns himself with environmental care. He's not wrong to worry. It's true that a large portion of Isliano's medicinal herbs have traditionally been imported from oceanic regions like Indonolsea and Farlospel since our coasts are so rocky, but it's a system that's been working well for centuries, so what's the problem?"

"Drought...?" I suggest.

"Drought," Petaccia agrees. Her dark eyes are shining now, taking on an excited sheen. "The summers are getting hotter, record temperatures here every June and July wiping out entire crops of spring and summer jewels. We're lucky that we don't need them, as we usually import, but isn't it better to get ahead, and stay ahead, of the game?"

"So you're investigating how different plants grow in our climate so we can grow them with less water?"

"No, my dear." Petaccia grins, and it's that same unsettlingly broad, stained grin. It sends a zinging feeling from my belly right to my limbs. Suddenly I'm not so hot any more. "Better, in fact. I'm working on a genus that can survive without any water of its own *at all.*"

My eyes widen as I finally understand. It sounds crazy. It sounds absolutely *insane*, actually. I turn back to the clover and peer closer, at the burnt bits on its baby leaves, and at the soil. I hadn't noticed before, but it is completely devoid of any moisture. Not a single drop. The only liquid these plants are getting from Petaccia comes from the syrupy warmth and moisture in the air. They should be dead already—but they're not.

"You're trying to train them to draw moisture from the air."

"Bingo."

Petaccia's smile is worth my exhaustion. With a thread of guilt in me I note how easily I'd allowed myself to forget why I'm here. This is everything I've ever dreamt of, and it's my future. *Mine.* I grin back. Petaccia closes the notebook on the desk with a thump and hands it to me. We walk back over to the door together.

"Read that over the next few days," she says, "and then I'll give you the next one. Ask me about *anything* you don't understand, clear? Even if you can't read it for my handwriting. But read it fast. I've wasted enough time on this as it is, and I won't have Almerto deciding he's going to write up something similar. I'm sick of men always getting the credit, aren't you?"

She doesn't give me the chance to answer.

"I'm also going to have you doing more research for me; I'm better with the practical things, and you've got fresh eyes, so each week I'll give you a reading list. The lectures are important, but this, *this* is the real work, Thora."

"I understand, ma'am."

"I told you. *Florencia.* I'm nobody's mother and I hate being made to sound like it. Oh, and I believe we discussed your ward-robe. It looks like you're no closer to a solution, so I've taken the liberty of getting in touch with my tailor. I assume you'd like something like these"—she gestures at her outfit—"though I sup-pose just plain trousers wouldn't hurt either—"

"I'd rather have trousers," I blurt without thinking. Petaccia is stunned to silence and I swallow the brick in my throat. "That is...if I may."

Petaccia raises an eyebrow and then shrugs. "You may. Just don't make a fuss about it. Any of your fellows have a problem, send them to me."

"I...Yes, ma'am—sorry. Florencia."

I stand awkwardly in the doorway clutching the book, and within seconds it's as if Petaccia has forgotten that I'm even there. I watch curiously as she wanders back over to her precious vine on her desk, her gloved fingertips dancing over it the way the girl touched those flowers in the garden, so much earnest love in her face, but something else too. Something fierce and a little frighten-ing. Almost like a hunger.

Chapter Ten

I wasn't sure you'd show up."

Leonardo is waiting for me at my usual table in the corner of the dining hall. I ignore the server's expression as she watches me approach him—she'd tried to tell me she couldn't seat me at all tonight—and slide into the free seat closest to the window. The evening air is stuffy and smells like fresh, crusty bread. I realise I haven't eaten all day, and can't actually remember the last time I *did* eat.

"I need to eat, Leonardo. Of course I was going to show up."

"You could have fooled me. I've hardly seen you since yesterday. I was beginning to think you were avoiding me again."

"Oh, don't be cold," I say with a smile. "You were the one missing from our lecture again today." Leonardo looks hurt, his eyes crinkling behind his glasses as he winces. *Was* he missing? I thought he was, like yesterday, but maybe I simply didn't see him. Maybe I ignored him without realising. "I'm sorry. I've had a lot on my mind, that's all."

Leonardo helps himself to a glass of fruity red wine and attempts to pour some for me, but I place my hand over my glass and pick up the water instead. Tonight's meal is some kind of stew, red meat and vegetables cooked in the same university house wine. My mouth waters at the sight of other scholars receiving their bowls and bread. Leonardo watches me with interest.

"Have you eaten at all?"

"Bits here and there."

"Thora."

I sigh. "What?"

"I don't mean to sound like your mother, but you've got to take care of yourself here. The schedule is punishing—you're exhausting yourself already. I can tell."

"I'm fine. I didn't sleep well again, and I've had a lot to think about today."

"Because of your tutorial? How did it go?"

"She's remarkable." That's all I'm willing to say about it. Leonardo might be studying the same field, and he might give me insight into Almerto's studies, but doesn't that make him some kind of...rival? Petaccia's comment about sharing credit has been knocking about in my brain since yesterday.

Leonardo pushes his glasses back up his nose as he attempts to take a sip of wine, and I almost laugh; he's not exactly a threat, though, is he?

"You still need to eat—"

"Leonardo," I intone seriously. He blinks, shaken, and then that slow childish smile creeps across his lips.

"Sorry. Sorry. Can we start over?"

I shrug. "Again? You're the one who invited me to dinner. You make the rules."

"Then we start over." He puffs out his chest. "I'm sorry I was an ass. We seem to take it in turns, don't we? But I'm just trying to look out for you—and no, no, I know you can do that yourself. It was something my wife…" He trails off. Short of clapping his hand over his mouth, I'm not sure there's a way he could have made it more obvious he didn't intend to talk about her, but rather than whatever emotion he was expecting I'm merely pleased he finally mentioned it—though it does raise more questions.

"You're married, then? I did wonder." Here in the dim light of the dining hall I notice what I've missed so far during our outdoor conversations: the pale band of skin on his wedding finger—not a ring, but where a band once sat.

"I was." Leonardo takes a hasty gulp of his wine as the server finally brings our meal. My stomach rumbles at the sight of the stew, fresh bread and butter, a platter of cured meats and cheeses on the side, plus a fresh bottle of wine. I flex my fingers and take a second before diving in, rich onions and beef and wine melting on my tongue.

"What happened?" I ask, at least remembering to swallow first.

Leonardo breaks off a piece of bread and rolls the soft inner part between his fingers thoughtfully before answering. It looks like he's torn over what to say. *So it's not death, then*, I think. *Nothing so simple.* It's customary for widowed parties to keep their wedding rings, not least because it's a sign of morality.

This isn't a man who has been able to lay his grief to rest. No undertaker or sepulchre here. No, the grief is still very much there, raising its greedy little head in the tears that well in the corners of his eyes and that untanned band of skin.

My father used to tell me tales of his early years reading the death rites, and I'm reminded now of one of the stories he related, in which a young man was widowed only days into his marriage after a long, angry battle with his new bride-to-be's father, who delayed their marriage for nearly five years. The man was so distraught over his lover's death that he chose to starve in his family's private sepulchre rather than process the loss through his sister-in-law's Silence and his own celebratory wish upon the cradle.

Leonardo strikes me as the kind of man who would struggle to let the women around him do his mourning for him, though I'd never say this aloud. He is gentler than most men I've met before in my life. He takes off his spectacles and wipes the lenses on the sleeve of his shirt beneath his robe.

"If you want to tell me," I add, speaking quickly. "You don't have to. I know you don't really know me—"

"She left." Leonardo stirs his already-cool stew but doesn't eat much. I wait. "She...I don't really know what happened. She was the one who pushed me to become a scholar. I met her just after I finished my undergraduate degree. I was torn between going to work with my father—it's a good living but neither of my parents really wanted that—and continuing here. Almerto approached me about continuing my studies and Clara was so very supportive. She even came to live with me."

"At St. Elianto?"

"Yes. You probably don't know this, but they have rooms to the west that are larger, better suited to family living. It's where most of the professors live with their wives."

"I've never seen another woman anywhere except in the dining hall." *And the garden.* Though this feels different, so I don't say it.

"They don't mingle." Leonardo shakes his head, finally tucking into more than a tiny bite of stew. "It's absolutely not the done thing. But they have a little community, sort of a campus within the campus, with a greengrocer's and on-site restaurant. Most of the women don't work—"

"But those who do are servers here, right?"

I glance guiltily back towards the server who refused to seat me—not the same girl as on my first day, but they all look kind of similar after a while—and a hollow forms in my belly. I'd assumed most of these women were from the village. I cringe inwardly. It shouldn't matter where they're from, they're still women, and that's one vital lesson I didn't expect to receive over dinner.

"Right. Some of them like the independence, and the professors like to keep it in the family, as it were. I don't know about you, but I can't think of a worse job, dealing with hungry scholars all the time."

"Not least the ones like me who make horses' asses of themselves by being rude."

Leonardo's face softens from amusement to kindness. "Don't beat yourself up," he says softly. "It's a big change for you. Most of the men in this hall have been bred and born and raised to know that they'll spend several years of their lives in a place like this— and many of the scholars' wives are also scholars' daughters or sisters. Education runs in the family, and they're *still* wary about you joining our ranks. So you're not the only one with prejudices."

I shift uncomfortably. Leonardo might be right, but that doesn't change the way I've been acting. You'd think after my first day here I'd have learned. I can blame Aurelio for a lot of things, but not all of them.

"So your wife liked living here?"

"Oh, she loved St. Ellie." Leonardo smiles, but there's no heat in it. "She'd be out every day walking the grounds. She loved to walk! Lord, she'd never stop. Dinner was always late or burnt, but she always had a collection of fresh flowers for the vase and lemons from the trees. A year after she joined me here, things started to change. She got distant. I started to think she was having second thoughts about staying here. My mentorship with Professor Almerto was only newly underway, and I don't know if she maybe decided that a few years was all she could take and that an indefinite tenure was too much?

"I thought about teaching," he adds. "At first. It was my main motivator really. Maybe here, or maybe back in Scandessa, where Clara and I are from. And then I got into things with Almerto and I was enjoying taking all these different classes. It's so different from when I was a young thing, always choosing my lectures based on what they could *give* me. Now I choose based on interest alone. I dabble in arts and science and photography and psychology...What?"

"What do you mean?" I ask.

"Your face changed."

"No, sorry. I was just thinking. Petaccia has me taking all these classes and I wasn't sure what the point was. I'm a scientist. I've read books on everything else, but science is my truest love. So why waste all that time? She said that life breathes science, which I understand logically, but not emotionally—but then you talk about it as if its *freedom* and you're right."

"Oh." Leonardo tilts his head. "Yeah, learning for the sake of learning is my favourite kind. I guess Clara didn't agree with me, though."

"So...she just left? Without saying anything?"

"It wasn't so straightforward. I was really busy with some paperwork and prep for Almerto's spring classes, and Clara was distant but *fine*. Vaguely I started noticing her coming home later, long after dinner, but I thought maybe she'd just made friends with some of the other wives. She was out so late, though, and she always smelled so strange...I didn't really pay enough attention. I was distracted. And then she was gone."

I let the silence sit for a minute while we both eat. It feels wrong to talk about Leonardo's wife, or speculate on her motives, when I know him so little.

"I didn't realise you'd done your three years here before working with Almerto," I say eventually. "You always struck me as kind of..."

"What?"

"Kind of hapless." I laugh, and fortunately so does he.

"I suppose I deserve that one. But, yes, I've been here for, what, five years now? With a little break in between."

"You must know the campus well, then. I'm still finding my way. I've heard there are two libraries? I've only been able to find the one. And that little box of free books in the square, but that's not what people are talking about, is it?"

"No, there is another one—right by the gates. It's sort of hidden. Kind of useless unless you've got an in with one of the librarians, because the sorting system is absolutely bonkers. It's worth a visit, though, if you know what you're looking for and can find a way to ask without offending any of them."

"I'll give that a go, maybe once I've settled in a bit more, then, if my relationship with the serving staff is anything to go by. I'm learning a lot since I got here. My husband was a society man and he tried his best to teach me, but I guess I'm still a little rough around the edges."

"Your husband isn't here," Leonardo says, his eyes going to my wedding ring, "or you'd be in the base with the rest of us. Well, not me, not now, but you know..."

"No," I say abruptly. "He died." I watch his face as Leonardo carefully wipes his lips with a napkin.

"I'm sorry."

"I'm not." It comes out before I can stop it, but I soften it with a wry smile. I wipe my palms on my skirts beneath the table and fight the tremble in my chest. "That is—we were married only a few weeks. I miss him, but not the way you must miss your wife. Aurelio was... Well, he didn't appreciate learning, especially in ladies. So while I *am* actually sorry he's gone—I'm not a total monster—his death has brought me here. And I like it here. New company, and learning."

"Cheers to that, then," Leonardo says, his voice full of false bravado. I can tell he wants to ask more questions, but politeness wins. He picks up his wine and clinks the glass against my water.

He finishes his meal with a flourish then, wiping the bowl with his bread. The ghost of his wife is gone from the table now, and I'm glad. Grieving is my bread and butter, but Leonardo is such a soft, gentle person, I don't like the shadow it casts over him. I wonder if I have the same shadow—if it's the shadow that all women wear until their hair grows back and they forget the dryness of Silence in their throats.

I look down at my hands, the same hands that held fast and unwavering for thirteen days; they're still slick and shaking after talking about Aurelio. The glint of my wedding band reminds me, tonight, of him more than it does my father. I should take it off; I'd willingly slough off every memory of my husband, burn them all, if I didn't think being visibly *unmarried* would gain me more attention here than I already receive.

No, I don't think my shadow is the same as those of other widows after all.

"Speaking of the campus"—I change the subject, pushing my bowl away—"do you know anything about the walled garden to the east? I found it when I was out stretching my legs." *And I visited it again last night when I couldn't sleep,* but I don't tell him that part. I'm already kicking myself for not asking Petaccia about it during our tutorial—but Leonardo is my next best option until next week. "I figure it must be part of the university, but I can't find any information on it."

"To the east?" Leonardo clears his throat. His eyebrows furrow slightly, a ghost flitting across his face. "Hmm, no. I'm not sure. I can do some research for you, though, if you'd like?"

When I meet his gaze, his brows are smooth again, his expression elastic—almost as if I imagined it.

Chapter Eleven

I wake to the sound of paper being pushed under my suite door. It takes a moment to orientate myself; my dreams were full of the roar of burning, though I'm not sure now if it was my own— flames licking at the sides of a cradle designed by my father—or somebody else's.

I slept with both sets of shutters open last night, hoping to stir the slightest breeze into the stuffy rooms, but the sun's barely pinking the sky and the air is already soupy. I shake the dreams from my limbs along with the sleep as I shuffle to the door and pull the crumpled piece of paper from under it. It's another note in Petaccia's scrawl, familiar to me now that I've spent much of the last few weeks pawing through several of her messy notebooks.

Ignore lectures today, it reads. *Come to La Vita. I'll wait for you. Bring notes.*

I puzzle over the letter for a moment, trying to work out what could have got her so riled up. Our tutorials are the highlight of my week and I'm often giddy in the hours that lead up to them, but they are normally like clockwork, more like mini lectures than the partnership she promised, and we're not due to meet again until Friday.

Last week we spent the afternoon discussing pigmentation and photosynthesis. There's a page in her notebook dedicated to how plants with darker leaves are able to produce the energy needed to thrive; some, she writes, are actually brown or red and have other pigments in addition to chlorophyll in their leaves that may mask the green to the human eye. The following page features a sketch of a plant with black flowers and dark, near-black leaves. In the margin she scrawled *Black eg. Nigrescens: protects itself by shielding chloroplasts against stress.*

"She's a genius," I'd said to Leonardo afterwards. "I spent an hour just staring at that sketch. You know, I don't think I've ever seen a plant with properly black leaves, but I don't doubt they exist."

"She wrote a paper last year, potentially from those notes," Leonardo replied. "I'm amazed she lets you see the primary material. All I get from Almerto is proofing his papers as he's writing them."

"Right?" I gushed. "She wrote another one around the same time about toxicity in plants as a defence mechanism; what's interesting there is the idea that there's a tolerance level for animal exposure and how contact with intoxicating plant life can give extreme reactions at first, but with repeat exposure the level of tolerance builds—until it reaches a crescendo, at which point the body stops metabolising the toxins and the symptoms escalate. So plants that aren't entirely poison, in theory, could be metabolised and tolerated, to a point."

Leonardo was quiet at this, his face thoughtful.

"Honestly," I said. "She's making groundbreaking hypotheses as often as you or I make coffee. Do you think she ever gets tired?"

"Not like you or I do," Leonardo replied with exaggerated remorse. "That's why we're the ones always making coffee."

Discovery is invigorating, that much is true, so Petaccia must be up to something this morning if she's posting notes under my door at dawn. I crumple the paper into the waste basket and get to dressing.

When I let myself into La Vita I barely have time to blink my way into the dimness before Petaccia is there, looming in front of me like a ghost. I jump and then let out a surprised laugh.

"You got my note. Good."

"Have you been waiting long? I skipped breakf—"

"Don't worry about any of that."

I'm exhausted, limbs humming with tiredness after my restless night, but I nod anyway. There will be coffee today, and a lot of it. Petaccia drinks it near black most of the time, so thick it might as well be tar.

"I thought something was the matter," I say.

"The matter?" Petaccia raises an eyebrow. "No. We're going to do something different today. I know I said we'd have a look at the difference between anatomy and morphology in phytological study but, well." She claps her hands together excitedly. "Come— you'll see."

She walks away, not towards the staircase and our usual room at the top but instead to one of the locked doors on this ground floor. She pulls a key from her pocket and unlocks it with one quick, smooth movement. The latch clicks.

"Now, hurry," she says. "Quickly."

She ushers me into the room ahead of her, turning and closing the door swiftly behind us so that the latch clicks again, loudly. I jump. Petaccia thumps both hands down on my shoulders, guiding me to the left while she cuts ahead and gestures grandly.

The room is mostly bare, concrete and stone, with more large floor-to-ceiling glass windows dyed green so that the world swims in shades of emerald and chartreuse. The light along with the sodden heat that makes my clothes instantly stick to my skin make my stomach swim uneasily. A thermometer tracks the temperature, and there's a gauge that looks to measure humidity too. In the centre of the room is a huge wooden box closed with nails as thick as my pinky finger.

"What is it?"

"A very exciting new specimen," Petaccia says. "Sometimes providence smiles on us scientists when we least expect it. I wanted you to be here when I unpacked it. Let me just check the humidity—" She crosses to the gauge, tapping it with her fingernail before turning back to me with a wolfish grin. "Ready."

"But…what is it?" I ask again. I approach the box with caution. It's nigh on four feet in height, just about thin enough to fit through the door. Petaccia wastes no time pulling a metal bar from the only workbench in the room and attacking the side with the nails.

"So far we've dealt with mostly theory," Petaccia says through gritted teeth as she works to prise the box open. "But you'll know from the laboratory that I do most of my own work with live specimens. Dried plants are useful enough for some learning and research, but they're pallid corpses compared to the real thing. I'm wary of over-collecting samples to the point of destroying precious plant life, but sometimes the Lord smiles and I'm able to get my hands on something truly special."

With a crack that reverberates through the room the final nail releases the wood and Petaccia can peel back the side of the box, and then the top, and then the other sides until we are left staring at what I can only describe as one of the most hideous plants I have ever seen.

It's near four feet tall, more a squat kind of tree than flowering shrub, but its dark purplish leaves and thick black branches hide small white fruits that look almost like a hundred tiny eyeballs.

"It'll need to stay in here for a while. I've had it shipped from the rainforest in Odyll. Once it's had some time to adjust to our clime, I'll move it to one of my glasshouse nurseries. Today we need to get it settled, take some vital statistics to aid growth. I think it will do you good to use your gardening skills a little differently with me, so you can get a feel for how to handle unfamiliar vegetation. The principle can be applied to dried plant life as well, of course."

I step closer despite myself, inhaling the strangely bitter scent— it reminds me of the garden near my rooms. I smell it sometimes, distantly, as I lie in my bed. Sleep evades me more often than I'd like and it's this same bitter smell I catch often, just at the edge of my consciousness as I drift off.

"*Not* too close," Petaccia says, stepping between me and the tree. "I believe the sap is a little caustic."

"Is that what I can smell?"

Petaccia looks at me curiously.

"The bitterness," I prompt. "Can you smell it too? I assume that's what I'm picking up. It's like lemons, only—not fruity." It's more than that, but I find it impossible to describe: woodsy, a little citrusy, like the rind of a lemon after the lemon has dissipated. Perhaps a little more like the pit of an olive mixed with something more animal, more tangy, like the iron in blood.

"You have a good nose." Petaccia's gaze is narrowed but I can't make out if she's dubious or impressed. "I've only ever heard one other person describe it that way. My father always claimed that certain plants have a stronger scent than others—not the flowers, you understand, but the stems and the leaves. Not simply the earthy green scent that we all catch but something beneath it as well. He always said it was stronger in plants with stingers, nettles, and thistles and the like. There's no scientific basis for it, of course, and since scent is so variable it's impossible to test."

I frown when Petaccia turns her back.

"So, he thought every plant smelled different on its basic level and some had underlying smells too...But—if I smelled two plants with a similar scent, say, that same sort of bitterness, would that be unusual...?" I'm thinking of the garden, and the girl. I'm sure it isn't the plants I can smell when I'm in my rooms—more likely the ghost of them, a scent memory—but through the gate they smell strong and bitter. Is it exactly the same as this tree, or am I imagining the similarity?

"I suppose *unusual* is one way of looking at it. Why?" Petaccia is staring at me again and there's a glitter in her eyes I don't like. It feels accusatory. I wonder if I've crossed some invisible line, betrayed the hidden boundaries of this new "freedom." "Where have you smelled it before?"

A strange thought surprises me: What if the doctor tells me the garden is private, and I'm not allowed inside? If I ask, and I'm told not to enter, I'd be at risk of breaking the rules when I do eventually find a way in—and I desperately want to find a way in. Perhaps it would be better just to plead ignorance...

"Oh, I've never smelled anything exactly the same as this," I say hurriedly, sweetening my lie with a smile. "I just wondered if it would be possible. If plant families have similar appearances, why not scents? When I was a little girl my father taught me that no two flowers ever smell the same and that always amazed me. It doesn't feel as though it should be possible, especially when some types of flowers *look* similar—"

"No," Petaccia says, appeased. Her shoulders relax—and only then do I feel my own drop from near my ears. "Appearance and scent are not the same. But we can talk about that another day. Now, come—put on these protective armbands and gloves and help me lift this from the base. I need to check the soil."

When I arrive at the dining hall later, Leonardo is being seated at my normal window table, his curls wild where he's run his hand through them. He waves me over with a grin.

"Good timing," he says. "I would have asked if you wanted to join me, but I didn't see you around today." His eyes travel to my arms. The cuffs on my sleeves are grubby, stained slightly green. I was too hungry to get changed before heading here.

"I was with Petaccia." I sit and hide my hands under the table. "She called for me—all day. So I didn't go to my lectures."

Leonardo leans in with interest while the server pours our water. "Oh? Anything exciting?"

I hesitate. I'm sure Leonardo is only curious, but it feels wrong to share Petaccia's excitement with him—not when she keeps it under lock and key the way she does. "It was a delivery," I say honestly. "A fairly big one. She wanted an extra pair of hands."

If Leonardo is disappointed in my answer, he doesn't show it, just tucks into the warm bread and good, salty butter on the table. It isn't long before I follow suit, letting him lead the conversation. My head aches, not badly, but the pulsing sensation is distracting.

We've finished our meal and the servers are clearing our plates when I get a whiff of that odd, bitter scent again—likely from my sleeve as I dabbed the napkin to my mouth. I realise I've not asked Leonardo about the garden again like I planned to. Petaccia's strange response gives me pause, but I know Leonardo better than I do her and I don't mind pushing a little harder.

"Leo, I was wondering…" I spin my wedding ring beneath the table and then catch myself, laying my hands on its surface instead. Leonardo shifts uncomfortably. "I'm sorry—can I call you Leo? Or did Cla—"

"No, no," he says quickly, almost as if he can't bear me saying her name. "She called me Ardo, actually. The same as my parents."

"So…"

"You can call me Leo," he says. "That sounds nice."

I give him a small smile and he waits patiently. "*Leo*. I wondered if you'd had time to learn anything about the garden I asked about…? Only I tried to find out more myself today and I'm not getting anywhere."

Leonardo sits back, and this time there's obvious disappointment in his gaze.

"You said you'd help me," I add, "but if it's too much trouble—"

"You won't find anything about it because it doesn't belong to the university." Leonardo's eyes are dark and earnest in the dim canteen light, his lips quirking in a twitch I can't read. I curl my toes in frustration but otherwise keep my face straight; I can't pinpoint how I know, but in this moment I *know* Leo was lying to me before. He knew which garden I meant from the outset, even though I've never seen any of the scholars go near it.

I lean my elbows on the table. "No?" I ask lightly.

"No." He shakes his head, dark curls bobbing so that he has to brush them back off his forehead. "That land doesn't belong to anybody."

"How can that be? Somebody's got to own it. It's right there." I wave my hand in the direction of my rooms, feigning carelessness. "There's a tower in the middle and everything. Somebody had to build it." I don't mention the flowers, how they might look overgrown from a distance but through the gates they look healthier than any I've yet seen at St. Elianto. And I *definitely* don't mention the girl. The more time that passes, the more I'm starting to suspect she was a figment of my imagination.

"It's abandoned," he says with a shrug. "But I'm pretty sure it's locked up tight because it's unsafe. Nobody locks up a *garden* unless they're worried about people hurting themselves. Promise me you won't try to get inside."

"Oh, Leonardo," I say. "Come on."

"No, Thora, please. Promise me. That tower looks like it might collapse at any minute. There's got to be a reason nobody goes there."

"But there are some lovely-looking specimens in there," I try. "Aren't you curious? Maybe there are some plants we could use for our—"

"No, Thora," he repeats, and this time his eyes darken further. Whatever the flash of emotion is on his face now, it unsettles me. While before I'd been playful, pressing him half out of curiosity and half out of a desire to see how much he cared, this new, commanding Leo reminds me too much of Aurelio to be a fun challenge.

I hold up my hands placatingly. "Will you promise to help me find out more about the garden, at least?"

"I'm sure there's nothing more to find—"

"Please, Leo?"

"Fine," he says. "But you've got to promise you won't go there again."

"Okay, I promise," I say. "I won't go near the tower."

I'm quick to change the subject once more as we gather our things to leave the dining hall, and if he notices the careful way I phrased my promise, he says nothing.

Chapter Twelve

It is over a month before I see the girl in the garden again.

I check the window habitually as I study at night, or as I walk past the garden's gates—which I do more evenings than not—but it has been still and dark, and Leo's warning has never felt more asinine. Tonight is no different. The library would be quiet at this time if I chose to read there instead—I'd even likely get a carrel to study in, which is necessary as a woman studying after dark—but I've come to associate nights with the garden—and the girl. Deep down, I knew there was a chance I'd see her again, and I didn't want to risk missing her.

It turns out I was right.

This second time, a night just as warm as the first, I spot her right as I finish making tea. The moon is a sickle, a silver seedling amidst a velvet blue. The air smells of jasmine and lemons and the fresh honeyed scent of the echinacea in my tea. This time I refuse to just sit and watch idly, but I am as entranced as before and it takes a moment before I can breathe.

She drifts amongst the blooms again, trailing her hands, thanking some unseen deity for each specimen she snips and adds to her basket—just like before. When she bends close to take each cut, it looks like she is whispering to the flowers and my hair prickles on my arms and neck. My pulse crashes in my ears like ocean waves. I feel hungry and thirsty and dizzy all at once, desire wicking away all sense.

I watch long enough to be sure she is definitely there—not some wistful trick of my tired brain—then ram my feet into my shoes so hard my toes protest, before dousing the candle and hurrying to the door. I close it quietly even though there's nobody around, just in case it spooks her. It's a ridiculous notion, but what about my behaviour, or hers, is normal?

As I stumble down the stairs and out into the cool balm of the night, I can't help but think of Leonardo's warnings about the garden. I haven't had time to give it much thought, between classes and another tutorial with Dr. Petaccia—the mystery eyeball plant still locked away in its own private room—and reading and more classes. I sleep with Latin plant names swirling in my brain, their given names heavy on my tongue. Until this exact second I'd managed to convince myself that Leonardo truly was concerned only for my safety—but a feeling unfurls in my belly as I hurry towards my goal. I've been stupid to assume it's that simple.

After all, if Leonardo knew about the garden, how likely is it that he *didn't* know about the girl? I've been here only a couple of months and I've seen her twice now. Neither time was I particularly looking for her—though obviously it's not as if I *don't* look either. Part of me wants to think that she is all mine, she appears here, and only I see her—both times have been in the middle of the night with only the moon to witness. But the other part of me thinks of the way Leo looked when I mentioned the garden, that flash of his eyes that reminded me of Aurelio, and a seed of doubt starts to grow.

I push onwards, ignoring the thoughts, distracted now by the fresh rush of blood as my limbs pump. What if she's gone before I get there? I'm practically running, feet pounding the scrubby path with zero dignity, dressed only in my thinnest evening dress and satin slippers, when I skid to a halt outside the gate.

From here I can see even less than I could from my rooms. I've lost my bird's-eye advantage, the joy of gazing down unseen. I peer through, heart still pounding, into the darkness. The garden is cast in silver shadows. There's no sign of the girl or her basket of flowers, but the walls are high.

I curse myself inwardly. I was too slow. I allowed myself to get flustered and missed my chance. What if she doesn't come into the garden again? I might never learn any more about its contents and why it remains locked while she is allowed inside.

Maybe she heard me leave my rooms and decided to flee; it's not far from here to my window, close enough that the scatter of my pencils or the slam of a notebook closed too hard might alert her if she was close to the wall.

No, I tell myself firmly. *Don't be foolish. She's not on your schedule. And what's so important about her anyway? It doesn't matter if she's here or not if all you want is the chance to get a closer look at those flowers. Admit it, it's not just about the garden, is it?*

But that's a thought I refuse to acknowledge and I bury it immediately. My father would be ashamed. I *should* be ashamed.

"Hello?" I call. "I'm sorry to bother you, but I saw you and wanted to ask about the garden. I'd come back another time, during the day of course, but I've never seen you here then, so I had to grab the chance..."

Nothing.

"Hello? Please, I'm not trying to be a nuisance. I'm a scholar. I study botany—and I'd love to talk to you about some of the specimens you have. Apparently you're not affiliated with the institution, and I understand that perhaps I'm being very rude, but I'd really love to talk."

Still nothing. It's useless. When I left my rooms the girl was close to the wall, her basket in hand and her attention turned towards the tower. From here I can hardly even *see* the tower, only the edge of the sloping mound where it sits. There's no sign of her, or her pale dress, or her bundle of flowers. I don't know how far the walls even stretch, only that at some point they diverge from the campus. This gate probably isn't even used.

I begin to turn away, but a rustling stops me in my tracks. My heart stumbles. And then, near enough to make me jump but just out of sight, comes a husky voice.

"You shouldn't stand so close."

"Excuse me?" Despite the warning I step closer, my hands going to the rusted gate. The cold metal sends a zinging sensation right up my arms, and it's...delicious. I tighten my grip.

"I said you shouldn't stand so close to the wall. Some of these plants are dangerous. That's why there's a gate."

"Where are you?" I ask. Then: "I've studied plants for half my life. Maybe I don't recognise some of them, but surely they're mildly toxic at best. This one closest to my feet looks a little like some kind of mistletoe—is that right? I'm not going to get contact burns from anything I can reach."

"Are you absolutely sure about that?"

At that the girl steps into the light, her high cheekbones and full lips limned with silver. Up close I am even less sure of her age; her skin is dewy and perfectly smooth, her eyebrows thick and dark over full-lashed eyes that are darker still. Like liquid pools staring back. My throat thickens at the curve of her plump lips.

"I...Well. Isn't that a safety issue, then?" I demand, bristling. "Anybody could walk by and touch them. You can't just assume some rusty old gate is going to keep people out. There are hundreds of scholars here and any one of them could walk by and get hurt. It's a hazard."

The girl laughs and it's a throaty sound that ripples through me. She is empty-handed now and raises her arms in a kind of surrender. "Relax," she says. "You're right about the ones closest to the gate at least. They won't hurt you much."

"So why the warning? That's hardly a polite way to talk to somebody you don't know. Another scholar might report you for incitation—"

"A polite way to talk..." The girl barks another laugh and my heart responds by hammering a staccato beat. "From the person who's just interrupted me going about my private business by screeching through a locked gate like a drowning cat?"

I start to bristle again, but the girl is smirking and the expression on her face is so...so damn captivating that I can't help but back down. She's right, after all. I'm the rude one in this situation. For all Aurelio's family tried to make a society woman of me, I suppose they could never truly eradicate the effects of an isolated childhood. My affiliation with Leo has shown me that.

"You're right," I say. "I didn't mean to shout. I just...I saw you from my window and I wanted to talk to you—about your garden. It is yours, isn't it?"

"Oh, that was you," she says, ignoring my question. The way her eyes shine makes my knees weak. She licks her lips before continuing. "I've seen the light and I did wonder. They so rarely use those rooms any more. It's why—since you ask—I never have to worry about the scholars touching my plants. They don't bother me here."

"I'm the only one living in the building." I shrug, trying to hide the tremor in my hands. She's haughty and beautiful and—I stop myself. "As far as I know they've stopped using these rooms entirely. I'd have to walk all the way back to campus for a cup of tea if I hadn't stolen leaves from the dining hall."

"What did you do to deserve that?" The girl's smirk doesn't change, but her eyes narrow as if she's trying to solve a complex puzzle. Her chest rises and falls with surprising rapidity, reminding me of a small bird, fragile and hollow boned.

The question is so absurd, and the answer so big, that all I can manage is a laugh of my own.

"I didn't do anything."

"Ah," says the girl. "I understand. You're one of us—the outsiders, I mean." She pauses for a second and her eyes are on me with such fixation that I feel the urge to check to make sure my dress is buttoned properly. But it is, and despite the flutter of my pulse and the dampness of my palms, she retrains her gaze and the moment passes. A small gust of wind sends the flowers around her feet dancing, and my nose is assaulted by their floral perfume—so strong it makes me feel woozy. It's bitter and warm and aromatic and sits on my tongue like anise, the same scent I've grown used to but so, *so* much stronger—as if the girl has disturbed the flowers with her presence. "Are you really a scholar?" she asks.

"Yes. I mean—I'm pretty green but it's what I'm here for."

"Green." The girl's dark eyes sparkle with amusement. "I like it." She's thoughtful for a second and I half think she might walk away, but then she adds, "Pretty green if you don't know what these plants are, though. I thought you said you're studying botany."

"I am." This time I don't fight the urge to bristle; it simply happens. "And I'm good at it too. I can identify hundreds of plants by sight, I know their given and common names and their families and..." I trail off when I see that the girl's smirk has grown to a grin. "You're just baiting me, aren't you. There's no way I could know what most of these plants are. They're not in any book I've read."

She gives a little curtsy and her laugh reminds me, impossibly, of running water. "I'm sorry. You just looked so serious and it was fun to tease."

"I get enough of that from the rest of them. I don't need it from a woman as well."

"No, you're right," she says, but her smile doesn't disappear. Her whole expression mellows, though, less cheeky, and somehow it makes her more like a statue. "These plants are unusual. They're from around the world; some are even endangered. Collecting them is a...It's a hobby. A passion." She looks me up and down once more and then she shifts, her posture changing. It's only a minute change but I notice it the way you might notice an insect landing on your skin—an almost phantom sensation. And I realise that she's decided something. "It's getting late and I should go. I have a lot to do elsewhere. But before I go...My name is Olea," she says. "What's yours?"

"Thora."

"Well then, Thora. Now we're no longer strangers, does that make us friends?"

Her tone reminds me of the way Petaccia said *I only work with friends* and a chill skates up my spine. What, exactly, makes somebody a friend? And...what makes them something more?

"I suppose it might," I say cautiously, "if we were to meet again."

Olea's smile is like none I have ever seen. The curve of her lips reminds me of a plump fruit, the flesh so dark it looks bruised. I want to touch it, to test the skin like I might press my fingertip to check the ripeness of a peach.

I want very badly to meet her again. To be her—*friend*.

"Come again tomorrow night," she says. "I tend these plants by moonlight. They prefer it that way."

"And you'll let me inside?" I prompt. I wipe my clammy hands on my gown, ignoring the flutter in my belly. "I'd love to see what else you're growing in here."

"Midnight, please," Olea says again.

And then she's in the shadow of the wall and I can no longer see her. I wait for several minutes at the gate, palms still sweaty, heart still pounding, but she doesn't return.

By the time I head back to my rooms, the garden is still and silent beneath my window.

Chapter Thirteen

The next night I dress carefully before heading to the gate, choosing one of the new pairs of trousers that Petaccia has had made for me and a shirt that reminds me of a man's, except looser than most. It's so warm outside that it feels like midafternoon, the air syrupy against my skin. We've had no rain for five or six days now, and the grass path is parched and crispy beneath my window.

I could hardly concentrate through my lectures today, and although Leo caught my eye, I managed to make sure I was long gone from the hall before it was time for his customary break-time cigarillo. I felt guilty about it, but not guilty enough that I stopped. My head is too muddled for him. I worry that if he asks me, I might tell him about Olea—and I want to keep her for myself, at least for now.

My father dominates my thoughts more than he has for weeks, and I know it is because of her. Because of the way speaking to her made my pulse flutter and my stomach flop; this is not a way I should feel, not about her, not about anybody but my husband when I was a new bride—only I didn't feel it then.

Her name has been on my lips all day, every time I open my mouth, threatening to pour out like sweet, treacherous honey. Olea, *Olea*. It sounds like the plant oleander. Is this a coincidence? Like sweet poison. I spend my break pawing through one of my taxonomies. *Nerium oleander.* Rose laurel, dog bane, sweet sea rose. It's evergreen, subtropical, hardy, and fragrant. Like many plants, it has a myth for its name, though this is one I don't know by heart and I've yet found only references to it.

Olea.

Part of me is frightened by the feeling this girl has stirred within me. It's as though I shouldn't think of her, shouldn't talk of her. As if she really *is* a ghost. I even consider not leaving my rooms tonight because the feeling has unnerved me so. I could sit and watch from my window and see if she waits for me—I'm half convinced her offering to meet me again is all part of some hoax— but in the end I can't do that. If there's any kind of caper at play, I'm old enough to deal with it.

I spend so long debating whether to go to the garden that by the time I leave my rooms it is already midnight and I have to run along the path to reach the gate. I arrive panting and completely out of breath. But I needn't have worried—for there is Olea, just out of reach on the other side of the gate, her usual basket in her hand and her long hair swinging about her slender hips.

"You came," she breathes, and the sound of her voice is like the first sensation of sinking into a warm bath in midwinter. I shiver. "I'm glad. I thought maybe you wouldn't. I know it's all a little bit strange, this midnight gardening."

"It's nice to have some nocturnal company," I say truthfully. "I always seem out of time with the rest of the university. Nights are my favourite."

I lean my shoulder against the wall while I catch my breath and watch Olea place another flower in her basket. She does it with such care; I want to touch the velvet petals, to feel what she feels as she lays it down.

"I didn't ask you yesterday, but when you say you're tending your plants—what are you doing? These flowers look happy enough, so I assume you're not deadheading them."

"I'm cataloguing them." Olea tilts the basket so I can see what's inside. It's hard to make it out exactly in the dim moonlight, but it appears as though the flowers she has picked are held between sheets of some kind of waxed paper beneath a smooth grey rock.

"Are you an artist?" I ask. "Will you draw them once they're pressed?"

Olea's expression shifts from openness to something more wary. "No," she says coolly. "Why does everybody always assume all I'm doing is painting them? If I were to write my catalogue into a book, which I *might* one day, I certainly wouldn't only be responsible for the drawings."

"Oh, I didn't mean it like that—"

"And anyway, there's nothing wrong with drawing or painting them. It's just not the only thing I want to do." She lifts her chin with defiance. Her skin, in the moonlight, is pale as cream. Her lips are dark, thinned by her annoyance. My scalp prickles with embarrassment.

"I didn't mean anything," I say again. "Honestly. I ask because—well, if you're a scholar, I wondered why I haven't seen you in any of my classes. The professor who has taken me on never said anything about another woman studying botany, and you're clearly a student."

"I'm not a scholar."

Olea speaks so softly that I can hardly hear her. I step closer to the gate, wrapping my hands around the bars so I can lean more comfortably. She doesn't move any closer—still a careful few feet away. She grips the basket with both hands so hard they look as if they've been stained by shadows, her fingernails darkening away from the tips. Her feet, I realise with a small thrill, are completely bare beneath her gown. She reminds me of a dryad.

"You're not? But you know so much. Were you *ever* a scholar?"

"I'm not a scholar because I don't want to be one," Olea says pointedly. "Just because there is a university here doesn't mean I have to be a part of it. I can still be educated without having to attend lectures and silly little seminars—no offence. I like the peace and quiet here."

I raise an eyebrow, hurt but trying not to show it.

"But you've obviously spent so many hours learning what you know to be able to build a catalogue. Isn't that the same thing as being a student?"

"Well, exactly, and I don't have to prove myself to anybody. Books have taught me most of what I know, and they don't care if I'm a woman or a man or clever or stupid."

I'm truly not sure what to make of this girl. And what's more, I'm not sure that I believe her. It's a noble thing to want knowledge for the sake of knowledge—but is it realistic? There's something in Olea's face that tells me there's more she's not saying.

"No, that's true," I say, "but if you learn in isolation you don't get the credit for it either. Isn't that something you want?" I think of Petaccia's comment about sharing the credit with her father for the cure she developed because it seemed right at the time, and it rankles. "If I put that much work into something, I'd expect to be credited for it. Why wouldn't you publish it? Aren't you afraid

somebody will steal your work? Why must women always be condemned to the footnotes?"

Olea pauses at this. She's watching me carefully again, her
dark eyes sharp as a tiger's, fixated on my every breath. She wants
something—but what? My belly swoops and I push my face closer
to the bars of the gate, wishing I could peel back the moonlit shadows so I could see her better.

Who *is* she?

"I like you." Olea lays her basket on the ground and puts her
hands on her hips, her nightgown—I'm sure now it *is* a nightgown—
flowing around her legs in the faint breeze that whips up. I train
my eyes on her face, instead of the visible shape of her thighs
through the gown. "You're funny and you speak your mind. Some
of my friends beyond the gate haven't been so...strong."

"Friends beyond the gate?"

"I don't get to know many people from the university," Olea
says with a shrug. "The scholars tend to avoid me. They're all afraid
of the garden."

"Well, you did say it's dangerous—were you joking?"

"Oh no, not at all."

"So it *is* dangerous?" I swallow.

"Yes." Olea laughs and it's that same throaty chuckle from last
night. It ripples through me. "That is, it's dangerous for you—and
for them. Not for me. These plants know me."

A sound comes then. It's the rustle of leaves in a breeze, only
there is no breeze. The plants nearest to Olea's hands sway. If I
didn't know better I'd say their flowers might be intentionally
angling towards her body. As if they hear her. As if they *do* know
her.

I yank my hands back through the bars of the gate, a strange sensation bubbling in my belly. Something isn't right here. It's like Dr. Petaccia's vine that seems to move of its own accord. I know plants grow using sunlight and a sophisticated biological system, I know they're *living*, but they're not usually so...sentient? How could a plant know one person from another? It's not a cat.

"You...raised them?" I can't keep the suspicion from my voice, though it is tinged with awe.

"Most of them. And those I didn't raise are still sort of...my wards? I've tended them and helped them to grow. It's symbiotic. Does that make sense?"

I can't quite understand what she means, but I don't say that. Instead I watch closely as Olea gathers huge handfuls of her thick hair and braids it over her shoulder before reaching down to one of the plants growing near her bare feet. It's a thin type of grass, looks a little like wheat only shorter, with little black bushy fronds. Olea's lips part, and it looks like she's murmuring something, though the sound doesn't travel even this short distance. Then she picks one of the pieces and pops the stem in her mouth.

"Wait, isn't that...?"

"Sweetgrass," Olea admits. "I'm partial to the, well, the sweetness of it."

My mother used to put sweetgrass in the vodka she brewed—she'd grown up with traditional farming parents and it was pretty common—but she always warned me not to play around with the stalks, as their sweetness was not without risk. *It thins the blood*, my mother would always say, *and then the mind.*

Olea's eyes are wide and dark, and her shoulders droop a little as she chews on the stalk. When she smiles it's without her teeth and it gives her face a haziness it didn't have before. I want to ask her more about the plants, or about what she meant when she said she had friends "beyond the gate," but my head is clouded—as if I'm the one chewing on sweetgrass.

"Your hair is very short," Olea says suddenly.

I run one hand through the rough-shorn curls. It's growing a little, coiling around my ears and at the nape of my neck. Sometimes I forget what it was like to have hair down below my shoulders, but on nights like this when the breeze plays against my skin I'm more grateful than unhappy.

"My father died." I curl my toes inside my slippers. I don't want to talk about my father here, with her. He wouldn't have understood. "And then my husband."

"Oh." Olea pauses, chews the stalk some more, and then lets it drift gently down to the earth. "That's sad. But what does that have to do with your hair?"

I stare, dumbfounded. Olea's face is that of a child who has asked the most innocently stupid question, her dark eyes round and her lips slightly parted as she waits for an answer. Only the effect is less childlike than it is eerie, a grown woman playing pretend. *Surely*, I think, *surely you can't be this removed from the world?*

"Have you … have you never grieved?"

Olea wrinkles her nose, as if she's really thinking hard about this. "Mm, no, I don't think so. Well, maybe once? I don't really remember." Then she tilts her head to the side, playing with the end of her plait absently. "Is this something you do when you grieve? You cut your hair?"

"It's not just me. It's something everybody does when they grieve. It's a sign of honour and of love, from the ancient world when Memephestia shed her earthly form and sheared her threaded golden locks so that the burial fire might send Andynedes's ashes skyward, back to the gods. Women re-create the sacrifice into the funereal fire."

"But you said everybody. Do the menfolk too?"

"I...Do you really not know?"

Olea shrugs. "No. The walls are thick and I'm pretty happy here in my little paradise. Like I said, I don't meet many people and that's—well, generally that's okay with me. The hair cutting make a lot more sense now you've explained it. It seems obvious now I know that's something people do. Although I would quite like to hear that story—the one of Memephestia and the burial fire."

I think of my father, what he would say if I could have told him I would one day meet a girl with absolutely zero concept of grief or the art of mourning. Olea is a blank slate; she has no idea about sepulchres and cradles, about women's Silence while their men celebrate life over death in the world above. She knows nothing of incense and dried procession flowers, of punishments for breaking the fast or the significance of the shearing of hair. For a long minute I'm entirely speechless.

Olea, meanwhile, has started to drift away. She's back to collecting her flowers—a big, fat black rose-like plant with a stem studded with hundreds of tiny round white berries in her hands—and seems to have forgotten all about me again.

"Olea," I call.

She turns, her neck arched gracefully, flowers in both hands and the basket hanging from the crook of her arm. "Yes?"

"You said you liked me—before. Because I speak my mind?"

"Yes." Olea smiles. "And you're funny."

"Well. I..." I wipe my palms against the rough linen of my trousers. It feels wrong, what I'm about to do. Olea isn't like anybody I've ever met, though, and her knowledge of the garden alone...I think of what I could do with that knowledge, so much of it untapped and trapped in a naive recluse who barely leaves her garden. "I guess you're funny, and I like you too." It isn't a lie, I tell myself. It just isn't true *yet*.

Olea's smile widens. "Oh good," she says warmly. I ignore my guilt—and more, the swell of my heart that says there's more than just the garden to like. "You're the best friend beyond the gate I've had yet. I can't wait to get to know you better."

"And maybe you'll let me come inside and have a look around?" I prompt gently, as if she's a horse I might spook at any moment. "I'd love to help you with your catalogue."

"Tomorrow night," Olea urges. Her dress slips off the tip of one shoulder and my heart lurches. "Come again tomorrow, won't you?"

Chapter Fourteen

I visit the garden the next night, and the one after that. I don't tell Leo about my discovery of Olea. Nor do I mention the garden again, content to listen to his chatter and daydream about the evening to come.

At first I stay beside the gate for an hour, maybe two. Three on the fourth night. Then I stay until Olea decides it is time for me to leave, when I return to my rooms and lie unsleeping in my bed until nearing dawn. When I do sleep I am chased by winding dreams, of air thick with rain and the taste of fresh soil on my lips, and I wake up with my stomach clenching, ravenous. Whatever these dreams are, they are better than the ones of burning.

Often Olea narrates to me as she picks her flowers; she teaches me how to spot *Hyoscyamus niger*—or black henbane, which I know from stories of old as the original devil's eye, with its yellow-green leaves, purple veins, and scent so disagreeable that even Olea doesn't enjoy it—and she explains how she wants to have blooms at all sizes and points in their growing cycle that she can press and dry for her catalogue. Her passion is not just botany, but the plants that others have, often rightfully so, decided are dangerous.

"How did you know that's what you wanted to do?" I ask one night, as Olea runs her finger along the moon-shadowed red of an opium poppy's petals thoughtfully. I imagine the touch of her finger across my jaw, and I clench my teeth. "Dangerous plants aren't exactly easy to come by."

"I didn't know," Olea replied simply. "It just...happened."

"What do you mean 'it just happened'?"

Olea licks her lips and they glisten in the moonlight. When she swallows her throat bobs. The gate feels thick and heavy and ancient between us. "It's...a long story."

"We have time," I say gently. Olea hovers just out of reach of the gate. Her feet are bare as usual, but her nightgown is shorter than most, not far past her knees. Her skin is so pale in the moonlight it's almost translucent, and not for the first time I wonder why she dresses so plainly. It doesn't seem the kind of clothing somebody might choose for the work she does, which opens up the question: If she doesn't choose it, who does? "I'd like to hear the story. And— I mean...I can help, if it's not something you want to do."

"Help?" Olea wrinkles her nose. "It's my life's work, of course I want to do it. I was born for science whether I liked it or not. But if I'm doing something, I want to do it well, and the catalogue is my pride. That doesn't mean I'm always happy with the cards I've been dealt, though."

My lips twist in wry humour. It's ironic that the very cards Olea was dealt would have been my dream, while I'm sure this strange, thoughtful girl would have loved being a daughter of Death instead.

"What about your parents?" I ask.

"What about them?"

"You've never mentioned them. Do they make you do this?"

I lean harder against the gate and inhale deeply. Olea watches my inhale with that same tiger-like expression, always on guard. What is she frightened of?

"Did your parents make you come here?" Olea asks instead. "I didn't know that was common."

"My father would have wanted nothing more than for me to study here, but no. I came here because my husband died and they had nowhere else to put me. They didn't want me clogging up the family home. You know, since I wasn't family."

"So they sent you away, like you're some kind of inconvenience." Olea steps closer to the gate, one hand drifting towards the bars—and then stops so abruptly she skids in the dirt.

"Yes, but it's worked out well for me," I say. I'm aware, instantly, of the way my body curves towards the gate; the thickness of my tongue in my mouth; the way I want very badly to lean through and grasp Olea's hand. I want to touch her. Her presence is a spell, the tightness of my lungs, the tremble of my hands—it is all her.

"It has?" Olea breathes. I could swear I see the flutter of her pulse, just like mine.

"Yes. I met you."

Our eyes meet. Hers are so dark I can't see her pupils. They are dark gardens so deep I could lose myself in them, a bitter perfumed maze with no way out. And then Olea backs away, hurrying to pick up her basket, and the air swirls and all I can smell is green—and the moment is lost.

Another night I ask Olea, "How is it you can touch the plants when they'd be toxic to the likes of me? That one alone would give me palpitations something rotten, break me out in a cold sweat."

The thought has been bothering me for a few days. Once again, I woke up drenched in cool sweat, dreams of twisting vines haunting me as badly as my dreams of fire ever did. Mornings always find me parched, hungover from our garden hours, and I'm starting to get suspicious that the plants might be partly to blame. Of course, that's a ridiculous thought—but that doesn't stop it from coming.

"I told you," Olea says. "They grew to like me. You'd be surprised how you'll feel when they like you too. I promise I won't put you in any danger."

"How will you protect me?" I press my face to the bars of the gate, inhaling the garden's scent. Olea, as always, is just out of reach—though if I stretch my arm I might be able to snag the edge of her hem.

"The gate protects you."

"But how will *you* protect me?" I urge. I push my hands through the bars and make to brush my finger against one of the plants—some kind of stinging nettle. I'm not really sure what's come over me, only that I do want to touch it. To see what she would do.

Olea's dark eyes meet mine. Her cheeks grow flushed. What would she do if it wasn't the plant beneath my fingers?

"Don't," she breathes. Her feet don't move but her body leans, ever so gently, closer. If she moved her hand, just an inch, she could brush mine. I imagine the meeting of our skin, a jolt like lightning. Olea's lips are parted, her breath coming fast, and I wonder if she's thinking the same thing. "Not yet. The garden doesn't know you yet."

"What will it do to me if I touch it?"

"It'll hurt."

I glance down at the plant, which almost seems to stretch itself towards my fingers. Olea lets out a gasp that ripples through me, right into my core. For a moment I'm adrift, lost in the sensation of the balmy night air, the sharp, green garden, the moon on my skin—and Olea, so close I could touch her.

And why shouldn't I?

I meet her gaze again, can see the pink in her cheeks like a flame of recognition. Her throat bobs. She leans a little closer—tantalising. Her perfume overwhelms me. I breathe deep, press a little harder against the bars of the gate. It creaks, like the clang of a gong.

It shocks me as much as it does Olea. I curl my fingers away from the plant and yank my arm back through the gate as she jerks backwards, gathering the skirt of her nightgown in tense, pale fingers. She's trembling.

"I wasn't going to touch," I say shakily.

I don't know if I mean the plant or Olea; I'm not sure she knows either. She lifts her hand to her chest and breathes slowly.

"I'm sorry," I say softly. Olea's lips part as she starts to speak and then stops. She glances at the nettle-like plant, which still twists towards the gate, almost as if it's looking for me, and she smiles.

"I will protect you."

"Will you let me come through?" I ask. Perhaps a silly question, but I am burning to know the answer.

Olea's hand is still at her chest when she laughs, that same rippling liquid laugh tearing through me, and says, "Maybe."

Questions and answers are never so confused as when I'm with Olea, but I'm often so tired and foggy-minded from my days of lectures that I don't truly consider her responses strange until I'm back in my rooms dozing before dawn. I do not mention the garden, or Olea, to Petaccia, and I don't mention Olea to Leo either, though I come close more than once. I want to know if he's ever seen her, spoken to her—if he knows who she is, or how she came to her little paradise. But I also want to keep her all to myself, and this is the instinct that wins.

When my dreams aren't filled with the coil of vines or the lick of flames, I find they feature Olea more and more. These dreams are just as dark and unsettling, but I prefer every inch of them. I dream of her knuckles whitening as she grips my thighs, my lips against the pulse in her neck, her mouth twisted in expressions of ecstasy—or agony. More than once I wake panting, heat building between my legs, blood on the sheets from the shallow cuts my own nails have left imprinted on my skin. It isn't long before the nights seem more real to me than my days, dream and waking irreparably intertwined.

Some nights we abandon the gate and I follow Olea along the wall of the garden, although we can't see each other, and call back and forth through the stone. The sound of her voice is like an echo, a ghost—a reminder that she is always out of reach.

"Will you ever come join me out here?" I ask her more than once. The answer is always different, though a variation on the same theme: *I have too much work to do; I don't like it outside; I can't.* Or won't? It cannot be that simple, though. I've seen the way her gaze falls to the low buttons on my shirt, the way she licks her lips whenever she says my name. I can see the race of her pulse, the agonising hesitation whenever she drifts just too close to the iron bars that separate us.

"I'll cut the lock," I joke after weeks of these nights. "If that's what it will take for you to let me in. I'll pretend you're some maiden in need of a knightly rescue."

Olea smiles coyly and snips a stunning peony-like bloom from one of the flowering shrubs against the wall, its petals the colour of river water. I can smell it from here, fruity and dusky, its scent like grapes growing right out of river silt. She carries it tentatively to the gate, hovering nearby until I draw back, when she gently threads it through the bars.

"A token, then," she says, her voice smooth as glass. "For I will need to know it is you, when you come in silver armour to rescue me from my tower. And then we will ride into the sunset on mounts of pure white and leave this hidden place behind." She pauses, the colour high on her cheeks, before adding, "Please don't actually *touch* the flower."

It is a joke, of course, to imagine Olea somehow *trapped* in this private paradise, she its sole protector. I get the sense that wherever else she goes during the day, Olea doesn't have much contact with anybody, but I'm not sure if this is by accident or her own design.

Still, the thrill of the flower token is, despite my best attempts to convince myself, not a joke, and when I leave the gate for my bed, I wrap the bloom in my skirt, careful not to let it touch my skin. In my rooms I set it to dry near the window on my desk and I'm scrupulous not to jostle it as I work, watching with interest how the petals take days upon days to dry. And sometimes, when I lie in my bed after hours by the garden, I swear I can still smell its riverbed perfume and imagine it paired with the salt of Olea's skin on my tongue.

If Petaccia notices the dreaminess in my eyes when we meet for our tutorials, she doesn't comment; she's far too interested in tracking humidity levels and the effects on her current seedlings in the lab. Some grow weedy and thin, stretching their stems dangerously to draw as much moisture as possible from the air or claw for nutrients from the sun; most simply waste to nothing, blackened stubs in bone-dry soil.

Two months after our first tutorial I suggest to Petaccia that we try black-leaved plants next. She raises an eyebrow and waits for my explanation, though I hardly thought before I spoke so I don't really know what to say next. The words slipped out as if delivered by a spirit.

"You wrote yourself about the possibility of darker pigment being utilised to create a reduction in environmental stressors," I say. I think of how Olea's blooms, most some type of dangerous to the touch, have their fair share of black leaves and stems. "I'm paraphrasing a bit, but isn't it possible that the darker pigment could help to retain the heat—"

"And therefore aid in water absorption in a wetter clime," the doctor finishes, her lips pursing.

I have no idea if my suggestion is sensible, but Petaccia rests her chin on her knuckles and spends much of the next hour deep in thought. And a week later there is a new batch of seeds growing in the lab.

I tell myself that my time with Olea is just as much study as it is flirtation. She relays her catalogue, both scientific and Latin names, and I read snippets to her from whatever book Petaccia has me studying. I've never brought the doctor's notebook down here—it is, in fact, returned safely to its table in the laboratory—but I try to turn the conversation towards rainfall and drought whenever I can, hoping that Olea, or her garden—my secret weapons—will somehow provide the missing piece to Petaccia's puzzle. I imagine the acclaim, Petaccia's pride. Perhaps then I'll feel worthy of her mentorship.

Most nights I ask if Olea will allow me into the garden. Every night she either avoids answering or declines politely with a smile that is half coy and half genuinely distrustful. In the beginning I take it personally, leaving like a whipped dog with my tail between my legs. Within a month I realise it isn't something to be ashamed of, and I start viewing it as a challenge.

It goes on this way until the next new moon, when Olea says she will not be cataloguing for a few days over the weekend due to the darkness. Last month I wasn't visiting the garden every night, and I didn't really notice if she was missing during these nights of the moon's darkness—but now the thought of three nights without a visit fills me with abrupt, overwhelming panic.

"What do you mean you won't be here?" I blurt. She's left it until late in the night to tell me. The panic begins to bubble under my skin, as if the threat of it might expand until it explodes. I grab the bars of the gate with both hands. "Why not?"

"The plants don't like it." Olea's face is shadowed; her cheekbones are sharp as knives. "Don't worry, I'll be back the following night, or perhaps Sunday. You should get some rest, Thora, you must be exhausted with me keeping you up yapping every night."

Her face is so earnest, each night a little less silvered by the moon and shadowed instead by its growing darkness. It isn't me who's tired, I realise. She's the weary one. *Won't you miss me?* I want to beg. There is a brief gleam in her eyes as though she can see right into my thoughts.

I gaze upon the hollows in her cheeks and at the curve of her dark lips, at the way her collarbones look deep enough that they might catch garden dust in them, and I long to draw the neck of her nightdress together with a piece of twine to cover them—that, or tear it off and drink the darkness from them.

I don't argue, though the feeling deep within me is an ache I can't describe. I feel adrift, not willingly lost in my dreams any more but controlled by them.

In the end it doesn't matter. For some reason it is easy to do as Olea asks of me.

Chapter Fifteen

Leonardo and I have dinner most nights this week, as has become our custom, including the night of the new moon. I've been irritable all day, stumbling my way through the day's lectures without taking much usable information in, and by the time I get to dinner I'm downright ill-tempered. I've been queasy since yesterday, constantly covered in a sheen of sweat although it's cooler than it has been since I arrived at the university; my head pounds a sick, steady beat.

Leo is already at our usual table when I arrive for dinner, and he's taken the liberty of ordering us a fresh pitcher of ice-cold lemonade. He pours as I sit, and I gulp down the glass in one go, tartness tightening my throat, before I say anything at all.

"Well, hello to you too," Leo says.

I glare at him, irrational annoyance curling my lip. "Don't you have anything better to do than criticise me, Leo?"

Leonardo's lips thin and he draws his hands back towards himself on the table, where he presses them against his napkin. The normal clatter of the diners is so loud it feels as if my head might explode, and I rub at my forehead angrily.

"Are you unwell?"

I sigh and lean back in my chair. "Who knows," I say. I certainly feel unwell. Everything is too bright, too loud. I miss the quiet, dreamlike darkness of the garden. "Could be. It's been a long week. I feel rotten."

Leonardo waits for my apology, and when he gets none he signals to the server that we'd like to order. An icy silence falls over the table, but I'm too tired to much care. I have a document to write up for Petaccia's next tutorial—one I've been putting off for several days, but now thanks to my reduced garden hours I should be able to get it finished tonight. I'm just so damned tired. My whole body feels on the edge of collapse, mild aches and pains in every joint.

"Thora," Leo says. "Hello?"

"Sorry, what?"

"I asked if you'd been to see the physician. Perhaps they can give you something."

"Oh, don't be silly," I say, this time trying to warm my words with a smile. "I'll be all right. I'm just tired, that's all. And actually *starving*." I feel like I've been hungry for days. Have I? I hadn't noticed before. I felt fine until yesterday.

When the server returns to the table, it is with a platter of fresh salad, green leaves and tomatoes, soft, milky cheese, and herby vinaigrette. Thick slices of chicken gleam tenderly. I pick at the olives first and swallow two of them nearly whole in my hurry to eat. Did I skip lunch again? I actually can't remember. It's laughable how quickly I have forgotten the rules of propriety and society: four square meals a day, tea and juice and coffee, polite chatter over a meal.

"*Thora*," Leonardo says.

"What?"

"Are you sure you're all right?" he asks. Concern has etched itself into the lines around his eyes and across his forehead. His glasses are slipping down his nose and he doesn't even bother to push them back up. "You seem very distracted."

"I'm just tired," I insist.

Leonardo is silent again, but this time I pay attention to the silence, my stomach no longer screaming loud enough to drown it out. He's hardly touched his food and he plays with the tines of his fork before opening and closing his mouth several times fruitlessly.

"Say it, Leo," I say tiredly. "Whatever it is."

"It's nothing," he says. "Well. Not nothing. Only…" He sighs, blowing warm lemon-scented air across the small table. He's so different from Olea; he takes up so much more space, even though he doesn't mean to, and he smells different. Although I've never been that close to her, she always has a fragrance. I notice it when she walks by the gate, or when we're moving down the wall together, an earthy and yet somehow bitter floral scent. Like burnt coffee on a bed of wild roses.

"So, what is it?" I prompt. "Nothing, or something?"

"I'm worried about you. Is that so impossible to believe?"

"Nobody ever worries about me," I scoff. "I'm fine."

"Not even your father?" Leo knows what he's doing, mentioning him. I can see in his face that he thinks he's doing the right thing. Trying to get through to me. He meets my gaze steadily. My head thuds and my food squirms undigested in my belly. I don't want to rise to the bait but I can't help it.

"My father didn't worry as long as I was following his rules. His rites, his Silence," I say bitterly. The betrayal sits like ash on my tongue, dusty and drying. I'm not sure, as I say it, whether I have always felt this way, or if being here—seeing the life I could have had for longer if only he had asked—has made me change my mind.

Leo listens intently but doesn't speak while I chew on the words that follow, although I can see he wants to. The frustration of the day threatens to overflow and I have to clench my fists. "Not that it matters, but he had a view of me, and it didn't quite line up with the reality—but only because his view of *himself* was distorted. We were too alike, and too unlike everybody else." I rub at my knuckles, remembering the lash of the whip the first time I dared suggest I might avoid marriage and take over the sepulchre. The idea that I was just like him scared my father more than anything else ever had. "He wanted me to be normal," I say, "but he refused to relinquish me, kept me hanging on with a string of hope that he never would, which is what I thought I wanted. It's why my marriage wasn't finalised until he knew he was sick."

"You didn't know he was unwell?"

"No. He hid it from me until the end." I bite back the angry tears that well, nipping at my lip until I draw the sobering blood. "So, no, Leo. My father didn't worry."

Leonardo is silent again, though he watches me intently. I see flickers of sympathy and empathy in his eyes.

"Well, I *do* worry," he says eventually. "Thora, I'm your friend. I'm going to be honest: I'm seeing something and—I'm praying I'm wrong. But it's happening again."

I blanch. "Excuse me?"

"I told myself I would look out for you. There's—something's happening with you and it's just like before. You're not yourself. Distracted, irritable." He ticks the list on his fingers.

The pieces slot together and I have to fight not to laugh.

"You're talking about—about what happened with *Clara*," I say. "You think I'm—like her. That I'm going to run off or go mad or something. Is that what all this is about?"

The look on Leo's face says it all.

"You're getting distant, just like she did. Moody. I know I wasn't the best husband, but Clara was my best friend. I knew she was unhappy, and because I was too...I didn't help her. I'm sorry, I have to say it: Have you been..." He trails off.

"Have I been what?" I demand. My head pounds with my rapid pulse. I'm going to be sick.

"Have you been going to the garden?"

I lay down my fork. When I meet Leo's gaze I don't like what I see. My stomach clenches, a sheet of cold water down my back. How does he know? He couldn't possibly—and yet, he does. What if he finds a way to stop me from visiting the garden? He could tell Petaccia, or *somebody*. Maybe nobody official knows about Olea and the garden. Maybe they *should* know. And, oh god, maybe Leo knows about Olea.

A flash of jealousy roars to the surface, drowning my other thoughts. I'm not sure why, but the thought of Leo knowing about Olea—and keeping her a secret from me—makes me feel sick. He can't know about her, can he? If he did, why would he hide it?

"You said you'd help me find out more about it," I release through gritted teeth. "I thought that meant you didn't know anything."

"Okay, so I lied. But you promised not to go there!" Leonardo throws his hands up, nearly sending his fork flying. He glances around, panicked, and then leans forward and lowers his voice. "I didn't want you to go there, Thora. I warned you. I told you it's dangerous."

"And what's so dangerous about it?" I play dumb despite the sick feeling, tilting my head, pretending to myself and to Leo that I'm not about to get up and walk out. "All this silliness about the tower being unstable. It's hogwash. I told *you* I wouldn't go *inside* and I haven't. So what's the problem? What's got you so twisted up?"

"It's not just about the garden or the plants or the tower or any of that."

"Then what *is* it about?" I demand, breathless despite my attempts to hide it. Olea, and the garden, are *mine*. "Why are you being so pigheaded about this?"

"It's because of *her*."

All around us is the clatter of knives and forks, men talking and drinking and laughing together. But the silence between Leo and me at the table is sharp enough to cut glass. For a second I consider lying; Leo has no proof that I know anything about Olea, and I'm not sure I want to have this conversation. Yet—I need to have it. Because Leo knew about her, and I need to know how, and why he lied.

"What do you know of her?" My words come out so cold and slow they might as well be ice. "And why didn't you say anything about her before?"

Leonardo wilts under my gaze. He steeples his fingers against his lips and lets out another long sigh that does nothing to abate the unfamiliar jealousy inside me.

"I didn't say anything because it isn't my place to spread gossip. And I especially don't want to say anything negative about... a woman. To you."

"Right. But you've changed your mind," I say bitterly. "Why?"

"There are rumours about her. She gives me a very bad feeling,

Thora. I've felt this way for a long time. Since before you came here. I...Look, I have my suspicions. It's not my place to spread—"

"Gossip," I cut him off. "Yes, you said. But that's exactly what you're doing."

"You know she's your Dr. Petaccia's ward? I bet she didn't tell you that, did she?" Leonardo's cheeks are pink—though I'm not sure if it's anger or embarrassment. Both emotions war within me, too, bile rising in my throat, the sharp stab of betrayal in my chest. "She likes to float about and warn people about entering the garden, trying to make them think she's going to—going to curse them or something."

"She's what?" The words are like pollen in my brain; I can't understand them. "She's her ward?"

A wave of confusion engulfs me. Why has Petaccia never mentioned her? And somehow worse: Why has Olea never mentioned the doctor? Not for the first time I feel as if I'm on the outside, a waif staring through the window of a bakery, starved. Am I so naive that everybody thinks they must keep things from me?

"I don't know the details, but people say she has some sort of illness. The kind you have from birth. Her parents abandoned her and she was left on the steps of the St. Ellie chapel years ago, and Dr. Petaccia—being the only woman on staff—took her in." Leo takes his spectacles off and lays them on the table, his mouth twisting urgently.

The next wave of my thoughts is much muddier, a mixture of regret, and still that spiky jealousy, but also—*excitement*. This could be an opportunity. If Petaccia were to support my budding friendship with Olea—lonely, strange Olea—what favour might await me? My mind is abuzz.

"You have to understand, I'm not saying this to upset you

or monopolise you. I just…This girl is strange, Thora, and she doesn't have a job or a family so far as I know. She can afford to spend her time however she wants, flouncing about not sleeping or whatever it is you're both doing. But you—you have work to do here, and you're distracted."

I'm distracted. Am I? I disagree.

I'm angry. At Leo and at Olea both. But this could be a beginning; it could open more doors than it might close. Alongside Petaccia's award-winning works, my name might only be a footnote, a mere acknowledgement within—but with a friendship with Olea, if she is truly the doctor's ward…I might have something else to bargain with to show my worth.

"I just thought it was important that I said something before you got yourself into a mess with the doctor," Leo adds, much more quietly. So quiet I can hardly hear him over the hum of my thoughts. "I've heard she'll come down like a tonne of bricks on anybody who dares mess with the girl. Thora…I don't know if you understand what's riding on this—but you're in a more vulnerable position than I think you know."

"Thank you, Leo," I say, giving him my best winning smile. I'm not sure it's entirely convincing, but I also think the poor man would thank me for scraps if it meant keeping our gentle friendship alive. "It must have been hard to bring this up, and I wish you hadn't lied to me before, but I'm glad you've told me. You're a true friend."

Chapter Sixteen

I don't visit the garden for nearly a week after the new moon. The first two days the delay is intentional, anger and frustration warring with possibility as I turn Leonardo's words over and over in my mind. How could Petaccia keep Olea—and the garden—from me? I thought we were supposed to be partners. And Olea... why didn't she mention Petaccia when I told her I was studying botany? This lie feels bigger, almost too big to address head-on.

I mourn the valuable time I've wasted assuming I might learn some secret knowledge from Olea that I could use to impress the doctor—but the more I think about it, the more I know I'm repeating this phrase, *valuable time*, like my father repeated his mantra to me about how I was a *normal marriageable girl*. No funny business here, no daughter who looks at men like loose pebbles in her shoe but studies women as if they are uncharted territory on a map. No, sir.

Perhaps my interest in the garden started as a way to impress Petaccia, but I'd be a fool to pretend the plants alone are what draws me to that damned gate every night. It is the plants I dream of most, curled thick around my wrists and neck, squeezing tight, suffocating me—but it is still my dreams of Olea I fight waking from more.

I feel like nothing more than a child, naive, trickable. Leo, Petaccia, Olea—all of them have kept information from me. Do they not think I can handle the truth? Am I so stupid? Or do they each wish to manipulate me? My thoughts spin, and I am wounded by Olea's omission most of all, because with each hour that goes by I miss her more and more.

By the third night the reason I don't visit the garden is different. It isn't because of my mixed-up thoughts; what started at first as a semi-voluntary escape from the garden's midnight clutches now feels like a punishment. As if the garden's presence is leaching itself from my very bones.

I wake that morning with cramps in my belly so severe I question the date, but my courses aren't due for another two weeks and this ache feels somehow...deeper. It's a clawing sensation, as if somebody is scratching at my insides with a rusty knife. And on top of that I'm so hungry I can hardly think.

I lie in bed and try to recall when I last felt such pain. I've heard of stomach flus that can make you sick, and Petaccia herself talked about some sickness that causes hydrophobia in its victims, which also extends to a fear of food due to the painful spasms it causes, but I've not heard of anything that can make you feel this hungry. Maybe my body is fighting something off, an infection— that's the most logical suggestion, but other than tiredness I've felt fine until now.

I skip three days of classes, lying in bed until the arc of the sun convinces me it's time for dinner, when I make sure I'm ahead of Leo and gorge myself on platefuls of fresh bread and olives and syrupy balsamic vinegar before he even shows up. The first two nights of my illness I'm too exhausted to leave my rooms, curled beneath my worn sheets, praying that the morning will find me hale and well once more.

The dreams are rotten, too. The heat of the flames licking from inside my body, a fever that builds until I'm ready to explode; I dream of Olea's skin on mine, but the heat is too much and her skin sloughs away like the dead leaves of Petaccia's failing plants. Olea is Leo. Leo—he looks like Aurelio. And then it is Aurelio who is burning, screaming, skin crumbling to ash as the whole world burns.

When I wake the heat is sticky, the air building with the kind of static that signals we're due for a big storm—only it never comes. Every time I move, my skin sticks to something, my hair, my dress, my pillowcase, and I wonder how much of it is fever and how much is simply the weather.

When I begin to feel better, my first thought is the garden. And not just the garden, but Olea. It doesn't matter what Leo says, whatever the truth may be about the plants in her care, and whatever the illness or disfigurement that keeps her in that garden is, I want to know now for the sake of knowing. It is like a scab I have picked once too often, finding watery blood underneath, only now I must keep picking for the scar.

Thursday, when I'm finally well enough to go to the garden, I have a plan.

Olea is there, waiting.

There is a track in the earth across the front of the gate as though she has done nothing these three days but pace it. There is no basket in sight, none of her usual snipped blooms or wax paper. The hem of her dress looks dirty, as if she's worn the same one for several days, and her fingertips are stained with soil or ink, the nails unkempt. She jumps off the stone bench hidden between the fronds as I approach, wiping her cheeks hastily. They're streaked with translucent tears, her dark eyes still brimming with them.

The sight of her is a cooling balm. Instantly I feel any remaining anger drain away, my whole body relaxing as the familiar scent of the garden envelops me. It has, if possible, grown thicker and lusher since I saw it last; I notice fresh white blooms atop the goddess's arrow plant near the bench, and two new, thick tubular fruits the colour of emeralds from the one called widow's row.

Olea, too, is radiant with the thickening silver moonlight. I drink in her creamy skin, her dark gaze, the sway of her hair against her gown. My stomach swoops, and it is like staring at the ceiling in an unfamiliar chapel, the cradle burning at your feet.

"Thora!" she cries excitedly. "Oh, I thought you'd forgotten all about me. I was turning it over and over trying to see if I'd said something to upset you. If I have, I'm truly sorry. I only sent you away for a break because I was worried about you. I'm just a stupid girl—"

"Be still," I say. So many more words swell on my tongue. I want to tell her how much I've missed her, how the world out there feels like grey and brown dust but the garden is all colour. I hold it back, not afraid now, just waiting. The ghost of my father's disapproval does not belong in this place. "You've done nothing to me. I just haven't been well, that's all."

"You haven't?" There is a gleam of something in her eyes, not exactly pleasure, but close. Now that I know she is Petaccia's ward, there is something in this expression that reminds me of the doctor; it's subtle, a faint look of almost calculated curiosity.

I shake my head. "I wouldn't have stayed away otherwise."

Olea folds her hands nervously in front of herself, her eyes jumping from my face to my chest and back up again hurriedly.

If she can feel the difference in me she doesn't say, but I sense the acknowledgement between us the way I can feel the change in the air, storm clouds gathering in the distance. She missed me the way I missed her. She is *like me*—she has to be.

I produce the basket I have brought with me tonight, scavenged from the greengrocer's in the village. It's the first time I've been off campus since my arrival and I did not relish the experience, but it was worth it for the contents.

I beckon Olea to come a little closer, and she does so—skittish, like an untamed horse, eyes wide and wild. I tilt the basket up so she can see inside. Layered beneath a festive chequered cloth in white and blue and several embroidered napkins are a bottle of rare chocolate liqueur and two freshly baked Romesco-style Romeras pastries, their golden tops encrusted with flecks of sea salt.

Olea cocks her head curiously.

"Poplinock. Have you ever had one? They're delicious. My mother used to make them on the holy days, and when I got older my father and I would sometimes get them from the bakery after we worked. Would you like one?"

She licks her bottom lip, her dark tongue darting like that of a serpent. In all the time we've known each other, I have never seen Olea eat, but she has never mentioned any intolerances. I lift the basket up towards the gate, but it is too awkward for Olea to reach inside. I gesture—*May I?*—and gather one of the pastries in a napkin before holding it through the bars.

Olea stares at it. She doesn't come any closer, but I can see the tension in her limbs.

"Go on," I say. "I've not poisoned it."

"It's not that." She gnaws on her lip. "I'm ... I'm not really very hungry."

"Oh, well, you don't have to have one," I say hastily. I've begun to wrap it back up when she blurts, "Wait!" and I stop.

"Sorry...I want—I'd like to try it. Please."

I lower the corners of the napkin again and wait as Olea approaches the gate gingerly. Step by step, her fingers curling up towards the bars. I hiss a breath. This—no, *this*—is the closest we've ever been. Her proximity is like a drug. The hairs on my arms stand to attention, gooseflesh sending a delicious shiver down my spine. I swallow the racing of my heart, the accompanying throb of excitement deep inside me. It is as if the garden walls are coursing with electricity.

Briefly I wonder if she thinks I will try to grab her—though why she would opens up another much larger question about her other friends beyond the gate. Did they, too, feel her nearness like the pluck of a string?

Slowly, carefully, Olea reaches out. She uses the very tips of her fingers to lift the pastry from the napkin, leaving the cloth to flutter to the ground. When she steps away—just a little—my stomach drops with dismay.

We eat together in companionable silence, the last few days stretching between us. I devour my poplinock as if I've never eaten before, while Olea picks at hers and lets each sliver of honeyed pastry melt on her tongue. I drink my fill of the chocolate liqueur before passing it through the bars where Olea can pick it up from the earth—though she makes no immediate move to do so.

"I was thinking..." I say eventually, when the pastries are gone. The night has cooled significantly, though the air is still thick, and we are both sitting on the dirt—one on each side of the gate. Olea picks idly at strands of grass that grow between her plants, clearly not giving them the same reverence as her babies.

"That must be hard," Olea says with a weak smile. I smile back.

"No, really," I go on. "Wouldn't it be—wouldn't it be nice if we could meet somewhere else? The garden is beautiful and I love the peace and quiet of these nights together, but... But why can't we do other things too? I know we haven't talked much about it, and I assume—well, I assume you don't feel especially comfortable leaving the walls. But I'd look after you. Could we perhaps have dinner together? It could still be at night, if you want. And it doesn't have to be in the dining hall if you're not comfortable coming to campus. I could order something to my rooms, or we could visit one of the restaurants in the village...?" I trail off, unable to read Olea's expression. It is at once open and vulnerable and entirely unfazed.

"Oh, thank you for the invitation, but no. I told you, I don't leave the garden."

She climbs to her feet and brushes the grassy tendrils from her dress. I clamber up quickly as well.

"You don't, or you *won't*?" I ask.

Olea licks her lips before answering. Is it just me, or does the flesh around them look more bruised tonight? I lean in some more but I lose my balance, clanging against the gate, my knees and elbows barking as I catch myself.

Olea raises her eyebrows in surprise, though I can't tell if it's at my clumsiness or my question.

"Neither. I can't."

"Are you saying you're a prisoner in the garden?" I ask. Anger builds in me, humming in my fingertips and the restless energy in my legs. For a split second I want to track Petaccia down and slam her against a wall—

"No, no," Olea soothes quickly. She rubs one arm awkwardly and fumbles for the words to explain. "But I can't leave the plants. My work here is too important."

"You're talking about your catalogue?" I scowl, adrenaline still coursing through me. "That's hardly reason to turn down dinner. You have to eat, don't you?"

"It's not the catalogue," Olea says. "Or not so simple as *just* that." She looks at me carefully, as if deciding how much to tell me.

"Olea, please," I encourage her softly. "I thought you were my friend. I'm just trying to understand. I heard—well, it doesn't matter what I heard, but I want to know you. If you're unable to leave, I just want to know why. You appreciate how unusual this is, don't you? I haven't asked specifics before now because I don't want to press, but—I'm offering my help, if you need it."

When Olea speaks, the words gush out like a torrent; so much excitement is in her voice that I have to strain to make out the individual words. But it's not just excitement; it's passion stronger than any I think I've ever heard.

"It's so much more than the catalogue," she blurts. "The garden is a living thing, living and breathing and growing and thriving. These plants are nothing like anything you've ever seen. I tend the ones closest to the wall at night because of the emissions. The potential in these plants—oh, Thora, if you only knew."

"But I'll never know because you refuse to tell me more than riddles and rhymes," I snap, my anger brimming again, this time directed at Olea—or at least at the gate that continues to separate us. "I thought you wanted to be my friend, but friends don't keep so many secrets from each other. You didn't even tell me Dr. Petaccia is your guardian when you must know by now that she's the only reason I'm here in the first place. Everybody thinks I'm just some dogsbody, an experiment at best. Well, I'm *neither*, okay? I'm smart. I taught myself most everything I know, just like you, and nobody ever handed it to me. My father wanted a son, and I wanted to prove to him that he didn't need one. But honestly, he was right. What good is being a woman in a man's world when even other women don't take you seriously?"

I've had enough now. I push away from the gate with steely resolve. Perhaps Leo was right and I should have been more focused on what I could achieve on my own instead of what I could help others achieve. I should focus on my work with the doctor, on making a name for myself so I don't need to rely on her mentorship. Olea is a distraction, nothing more.

"Thora, wait—"

"No, Olea," I say firmly. "You've had me at your beck and call for weeks and I'm not playing by those rules any more. Don't you think I have important things to do too? I've missed lectures and nearly failed two written assignments because of you—and all of that pales in comparison to the exhaustion. Have you got any idea how little sleep I've had to spend time getting to know you? And all for me to sit on the other side of this wall and wonder if there's a reason you won't let me inside or if it's simply that you don't trust me enough to get close."

"You don't understand," Olea says feebly. "It's not...it's not that simple." I begin to leave. "Please!" she cries, her voice cracking. "Don't go, don't leave me. I can't bear it."

"Explain it to me, then," I say slowly. "Make me understand."

"I couldn't let you into the garden, not at first. The plants... Like I told you, it's important that they can't hurt you. I couldn't let that happen."

"Olea, you're talking in riddles again and I'm sick of it."

Olea steps closer to the gate. And another step. One more. Her bare toes wriggle in the dirt. This is the closest we've been since she took the poplinock from me so gingerly.

"What I'm doing here in this garden is vital," she whispers. "Dr. Petaccia is a genius—you don't need me to tell you that. But what if I told you that her public work, the things she has you helping her with in the lab, is a mere speck in comparison to what I'm helping her with in here...?"

"I'd say you're full of shit," I answer coldly. "Because, frankly, what proof do I have? I'm willing to bet you won't tell me exactly what—"

"I can't," Olea begs. "You must see why I can't tell you. If even a whisper of it gets out...It's too big and far, far too precious." She rubs a hand along the line of her jaw, her eyes going soft and misty. "Before you came I'd have given everything for this—for your friendship. I was so—I was so lonely, Thora. Florencia is gone often, for conferences and more research, and I'm always left behind. And the plants...even they couldn't get me through. I started to wonder how long I could do it, how many more times I might sit in that tower and cry myself to sleep.

"And then I met you. And suddenly it didn't feel so hopeless. The nights didn't feel like a punishment any more. The plants noticed, you know. They want you the way I want you. Your friendship is the most important thing to me in the world.

"And that's why you must understand that I'm not keeping secrets from you to hurt you, or because I don't trust you. It's the world I don't trust. Here, in my garden, I have control over it all. Inside these walls the secrets are safe. If I could tell you, then I would, Thora, I truly would. I don't want to keep secrets from you."

I jam my hands into my pockets like a petulant child, half to hide the way my fingers shake. I want nothing more than to believe her, to believe that she feels the same for me as I do for her. And the truth is I can't stay angry at her. And I would never, ever want to risk her passion.

"If you can't tell me, then I don't know how we can go on..." I begin. Olea worries her bottom lip between her teeth and, completely unbidden, I picture biting it. "I want the same trust and friendship you do, but there will always be secrets between us as long as this gate divides us, won't there? It isn't fair and it isn't right, but it's true."

This time Olea doesn't flinch—and this is the only proof I need to know I have her. Guilt swirls like an oil slick inside me, but I console myself that I'm not manipulating her any more than she wants to be manipulated. She wants this just as much as I do, only she's too frightened to admit it. I won't be cowed any more.

"You still want to come in here?" she asks quietly. "Even though you know it's dangerous? I can't guarantee you won't be hurt. You asked me to promise that I'd keep you safe... What if I can't do that?"

"Olea." I reach out and wrap both of my hands around the bars of the gate. The air is rich with the promise of summer rain, but most of all I can smell her—that bitter, floral perfume. It's in my nose, under my tongue. I want to bathe in the scent. "You said it yourself: in the garden you have control. I won't fight that. You don't have to tell me anything about the work you're doing—you can deny it to the doctor if it's her you're worried about. I won't tell her I've been inside, and I won't touch anything. We can just talk as we've done before. I want to learn about your passions. I want to learn about *you*. And this way you won't have to be alone.

"So I'll ask again. Will you let me in?"

This time I know that Olea's silence does not automatically mean no. She looks down at her hands, flexing her fingers. They look as if she has dipped them in ink, murky tendrils dancing from her nails right to her knuckles, as though she's plunged her fingers in black wax. When she finally meets my gaze there is a resolve in her eyes that I have never seen before.

"Florencia is at a conference next week," she says. "Monday—come at midnight."

Chapter Seventeen

L eo is already in the dining hall when I arrive on Monday night. Our first dinner after my illness was awkward, full of staccato pauses as our frosty conversation thawed, but within an hour we were talking like old friends. It's amazing how quick he is to forgive my moods, and I'm amazed at my own ability to forgive his secrecy about Olea. Still, I planned to avoid him tonight to save him a night of my anxious clock-watching.

I ate a large dinner intentionally early, two plates of string pasta with rich, creamy sauce and a doorstop wedge of white bread and butter on the side; by the time I left the hall I was hardly able to walk, but the fullness was worth it knowing I'd need the energy to be alert when seeing the garden for the first time. Alas, by seven o'clock I'm absolutely famished again. It feels like there's a vortex in my gut, just waiting to suck up everything I put in my mouth. I can only assume it's keeping such strange hours, how when you don't sleep enough your body flits between extremes of hunger and thirst simply trying to regulate itself. And when I sneak in, hoping for another meal—just a snack—there is Leo, already at our usual table.

Leo looks happy to see me and I pretend I'm happy to see him. No, that's not fair, I *am* happy to see him. We didn't have our originally scheduled lecture with Professor Almerto today—I found out he's attending the same conference as Petaccia—so I've not seen him since last night, which seems like an awfully long time given how long I've been awake today. I'm just not in the mood for any conversation where I have to be present. My brain is far too fixated on later, on the garden and Olea.

We fall into our usual routine, ordering our meals and chatting about our day's lectures and reading in the short time it takes for the food to arrive. Normally now is the time Leo changes the subject, to something less *messy* than science, but tonight he doesn't do that. Instead he watches me as I wolf down yet another portion of the ridiculously creamy pasta, buttering yet another thick slice of bread.

There is a war happening behind his eyes. I can see it, but I can't stop it. He rubs at the day-old stubble on his chin, clears his throat, and refolds his napkin into what looks a little like a swan. I chew my food carefully and swallow, waiting for him to speak.

"I saw you in here earlier," he says finally. "Through the window."

Ah, I think. I knew I should have avoided him.

"You were eating then, too, weren't you?"

"Honestly, Leo, you're not much better than those mother hens in the family rooms you told me about. Is it really any of your business how, or when, I eat?"

"I'm just looking out for you. I know you weren't well last week and I..." He leans in. "I wanted you to know that I can be very discreet."

"Discreet?" I raise an eyebrow. "And why, exactly, would you need to be discreet? Just because I'm hungrier than usual? I've been working hard over the weekend and today felt endless."

"Well... I'm no prude." He hems. "You know. And maybe I'm wrong because I thought... Well. Anyway. I've noticed things. You have that strange sort of... bitter smell. And your moods. I can help if you... In case you're..."

"In case I'm *what*, Leonardo?" I spit. "Wearing too much perfume? Getting fat? Apostles forgive me, but if you think it's your duty to tell me that I'm gaining too much weight, then I'm more than happy to tell you what I think of you." Of all the ridiculous, rude, absolutely banal things he could choose to have a problem with, this is the one he's decided to tackle me over? For the first time in weeks I find myself missing Aurelio's sarcasm; at least I knew where I stood with all that. That's the trouble with Leonardo—he's too kind-hearted, and damn nosy, for his own good. Petaccia was right about men and their agendas, but I didn't expect this kind of *mothering*.

"No!" Leo exclaims, his eyes going wide. "Goodness *no*, that's not what I mean at all." He wipes his forehead with his napkin and it comes away wet.

"Well, what, then?" I demand, anger flaring in me like a lit wick. "I was *hungry*. So I decided to eat. What's your problem?"

People are looking at us now, but I won't back down. I don't care what the LeVands would have said about this kind of drama at the dinner table; at least they never called me fat to my face. And anyway, if anything I've lost weight since starting at St. Elianto. Whether it's all the walking or the lack of sleep, I don't know.

Leo rests his palms on the table and lets out a breath as he tries to calm me—and himself—down.

"Lord," he groans. "I'm sorry. I was trying to say... if you were in the—in the…" He rolls his shoulders back as if he's trying to pull courage out of the ground. A quick glance to make sure nobody is still listening to us. "*In the family way,*" he says, barely above a whisper.

I stop dead, my fork halfway to my mouth. The laugh that breaks from me is raucous, absolutely inappropriate for the size of the dining hall, and now people are staring again, but I can't help it.

"Oh, Leo, no," I heave. "Absolutely not on this earth, no. You have no idea how far up the wrong tree you're barking."

Colour comes back into Leo's cheeks in a flush so pink he looks unwell. He sips at his ice water and makes a few shapes with his mouth before another apology comes out.

"What would make you think that?" I ask.

"Well, I…I don't know. You didn't talk about your husband much anyway, but you *never* speak of him now. You've been so— unlike your normal self. You hardly say anything over dinner, and you're eating more and you snap at me when I try to make sure you're all right. And…"

"And what?" I prompt, amusement draped over my annoyance. He's such a busybody. A haunted look shivers over his face, his lips thinning. It's as if he thinks I'm lying—and he's *afraid.*

"I remember when Clara…She and I were trying for a baby— when she—did I tell you that? I feel like that's why it all started. She was so frustrated by it all. We were doing this thing together to try to grow our lives, our family, but it wasn't working. And that's when she started getting distant and angry, sick all the time on and off, just locked in her thoughts in this whole other world sometimes when I'd try to talk to her. And you…it's so similar. It frightens me."

"Oh, Leo." I reach across the table and grab his hand despite myself. "I'm not Clara. You've got to stop with this. It's—" I want to say *strange*, but I hold it back. Leo's already been hurt enough by Clara leaving him like she did. "It's not appropriate."

"It's just..." He sighs. His expression flickers from troubled to a softer display; it might be remorse, or perhaps...guilt?

"You really loved her, didn't you?" I say. "You're grieving her, and you're grieving the life you had together—or the possibility of it, you know, with a baby."

"I never really wanted that." Leo doesn't look at me as he says this. As if he's embarrassed. "I only wanted what Clara wanted. I wanted her to be happy."

I pause at the echoing pang in my chest as another realisation slams into me with such force it leaves me breathless. Is it possible Leo wanted Clara to be happy like I wanted Aurelio to be happy? Because it was easier and simpler and less painful that way? If he was happy, then I didn't have to address the rest of it, the way I *wasn't* happy, and could never be in his arms. I lower my voice. "It's normal to want your spouse to be happy, Leo. But...you don't talk about her like other husbands talk about their wives. And—forgive me if I'm wrong, but I don't think I am, because it's the same way I've always felt—I don't think you *loved* her like other men love their wives either." I lean in, lowering my voice further. "That's why you feel guilty about what happened to her. Isn't it? Like you believe if you'd been a better husband, if you'd given her what she wanted, she wouldn't have left...? And I'm not just talking about a baby."

Leo is stunned for a moment. There, in his conflicted expression, is the real divide between Leo and his wife; his stare, devoid of any hint of anger, or disgust even, that I might dare to suggest he didn't desire his wife, is instead filled with *panic*. He doesn't even acknowledge the confession of my own feelings.

Leo is the same as me, like calling to like, and maybe he doesn't truly know it but I can see it. Leo loved Clara—but was he *in love* with her?

"Clara was my best friend," Leo says shakily. Sharply. "And this isn't about me." He glances around awkwardly, refusing to meet my gaze. I give his hand another squeeze, daring him to look at me and see that I know how it feels, that I understand more than he knows. But he keeps his eyes trained on the window instead before adding, "I'm not making this up, Thora. You can tell me I'm blinded by Clara all you want—but... you smell different."

I freeze. "What do you mean I smell different?"

"It's getting stronger. I thought, with Clara—maybe it was a baby. I've read that it happens—"

"Leo, what do you mean that I smell different?" I yank my hand back from his.

"You smell exactly like Clara did before she left. She used to visit the garden when she couldn't sleep. She came back—*perfumed.*" Leo finally meets my gaze, and it scares me. This mention of Clara's perfume... I can't explain it, except that it feels like she's here right now, between us. A ghost.

I can't do this. I can't be here. Not with him—or her. I can't talk about the garden, or picture Clara in it. Hysteria builds inside me, a mixture of horror and alarm that rings like a bell.

"I told you, you shouldn't compare me to your wife, Leo," I say, forcing ice into my tone to hide the panic. He's lying about the smell—he has to be. Otherwise why is he only mentioning it *now*? He's trying to distract me. Or worse, he thinks deflecting his own feelings with flirtation is the way forward. "If you're noticing the way I smell, sir, frankly, that is nobody's problem but your own."

"I'm only saying there's something—"

"I know what you're saying," I cut him off. "You're obviously trying to make me feel sorry for you. You need a new wife to hide behind, and you think this is how you get one? There's no other explanation for this ridiculousness. Maybe you should admit what you're doing to yourself and talk to me like an adult. Maybe then I'd feel differently about a conversation about my goddamn *perfume.*"

I shove my plate away and get to my feet, my appetite suddenly gone. Instead I feel a wave of dizziness, the kind of nausea that comes with having your feet on unsteady ground and a long drop below. I swallow hard, bile burning the back of my throat. If all I am to Leo is a marriage prospect so he can hide how he truly feels, or some way to forget about Clara—and if he thinks scaring me is the way to woo me—then he has another think coming.

"Thora," Leo argues. "Come on. You know I'm not trying to—"

"No, Leo. I think it's high time I remind you that we are *friends.* You are not my husband, nor is it in any way appropriate for you to act like you are. We have dinner together here because I'm willing to push the boundaries more than most, but if you can't behave yourself, then maybe we shouldn't."

"Thora," he says again. I hold my hand up and he stops.

"I'm going to leave now," I say as calmly as I can muster, still fighting against the dizziness that threatens to capsize me. I hold on to the edge of the table with one hand and hope Leo doesn't notice. "I trust that by tomorrow night you'll be back to minding your own damn business."

Midnight crawls around like the slow, inevitable march of a snail. I watch the clock in my study with such ferocity that I grow faint and dizzy again, resorting to locking my fingers in place with my nails in the polished wood of my desk. I know I should be more concerned about falling out with Leo, but the thought is distant, the toll of a bell two villages over, something for me to think of later—probably in those dim dawn hours when I cannot sleep.

When I grow so faint I worry I might fall off my chair, I drag myself to the stove and make tea peppered with the fresh, shrubby strawflower, otherwise named "immortelle" or "everlasting" flowers—*Helichrysum*—which grow in the boxes beneath my window, wild and untamed but still good, and which Almerto's lectures assure me are treatments for both sickness and mild digestive discomfort. If I'm no better tomorrow I might make the trek back to the village for something stronger. Perhaps it is just excitement. Or fear.

I stare at the flower from Olea's garden with fascination; its leaves and petals are still dewy and fresh as the day she picked it. Its scent has faded, though, and I miss its riverbed tang. It might only be in my mind, but before the scent faded I almost imagined that the flower's mere presence on my desk was like a bracer of sorts, keeping me afloat.

I'm at the gate early despite the dizziness. The fresh air helps. We've still had no rain, but as I walk I hear the distant rumble of thunder and a slash of lightning splits the sky. It isn't long before the first specks of rain begin to fall—and I hardly care, because there already at the gate is Olea.

She has combed her shining dark hair for the occasion, pulling it into a tight braid. Her dress, too, is clean and more structured than her usual fare, a bodice drawing her in at the waist and ruffles at the sleeves. She beckons me close with a silent wave of her hand.

The gate does not creak when she opens it. It is as silent as she is. The scent of the garden envelops me, so strong I have to pause to take a breath—damp and verdant and bitter. I ignore Leo's comments, push them to the farthest corners in the maze of my mind. Is it the garden he can smell—on my skin, in my hair, on my clothes—or is it Olea? And if he can smell it, can others?

But now isn't the time for such questions. The garden awaits, thrumming with greenery, beckoning me the way a dream lulls you deeper and deeper into sleep, the real world slipping away with every heartbeat, every breath.

I slip through the gate.

And suddenly everything is different. The walls and the gate, I soon realise, have done the space a disservice. The view from my rooms is little better. From up there everything looks tangled and overgrown, the spikes atop the wall blocking the best views, and from the gate I'd become convinced that Olea had perhaps fifteen or twenty different plants growing in this immediate area. Quickly it becomes clear how wrong I was.

To the left the garden beds ramble along the wall as far as the eye can see, and behind the tower I can see from my window there are trees and trees and trees. Some are tall and straight; others grow in great crooked waves, leaves and branches and hanging fruits in all directions. The plants directly in front of me—which I feel I've grown to know a little—are well tended, groomed so they grow along narrow, winding dirt paths. Most are tagged with little wooden signs where somebody—Olea—has scored their names.

"Olea..." I breathe. "It's magnificent."

"You haven't seen it yet," she says, but her smile is broad.

She still stands her careful few feet away, but I can barely bring myself to notice much less care. This is what I've dreamt of since I saw the garden from my study on that first day here. It matters less that these are plants I have never seen before, and more that they are now right here—right at my fingertips.

"Can I touch them?" I ask.

Olea shakes her head fast. "I wouldn't. Not yet. Follow me and I'll show you more."

"There's more?"

Olea chuckles. "This is...perhaps a tenth of what there is to see."

"Olea!" I exclaim. "Why didn't you tell me it was so big?"

"You never asked." She shrugs. "And besides, these plants are my...not my favourites; I don't have favourites. But they're the most fascinating to me. They hold the most potential. It's why I tend to them so often and why they hold a dear place in my catalogue."

I begin to move forward, but Olea lets out a little bleat of dismay. I freeze. My hand hovers beside one of the small trees I don't know the name of yet. Its narrow, dark green leaves look similar to those of common oleander, and its sprays of starry white flowers smell sweet as jasmine. Hidden beneath its flowers, however, I spot small, round, fleshy-looking fruits, and something in me—something primal—stills. Understanding the likely reason for Olea's panic, I lift my hand away and then step back slowly.

"*Cerbera odollam*," she hisses. "Those fruits are dangerous. Even the juices...Please, please be careful. Don't touch *anything* until we're beyond these trees where I can keep an eye on you. I need time to—assess. They won't mean to hurt you, but they might."

Logically I know I should be afraid. By the sounds of it, most of these plants could make me marvellously unwell with just a single touch, and the rest might even kill me, but this garden at night, gentle rainfall pattering amongst the blooms releasing bursts of bittersweet aroma, is the most peaceful place in the world. Besides, I'm not planning to put anything in my mouth.

It is near silent here. And I feel fine—better than fine, in fact. The everlasting flowers must have helped because I'm no longer dizzy or nauseous. I feel the best I've felt in days. In *weeks*, maybe. Even my tiredness seems to have abated. I run a hand through my hair, casting off raindrops and listening to the smattering sound they make amongst the petals and leaves.

I don't struggle to follow Olea as she guides me along the twisting path. It must be the open air, the rain making leaves and stems and hidden roots glitter in the moonlight, but I can see just fine. I step between rows of plants—their size growing the farther we walk—with ease, and soon we are within the trees. Rain falls in fat droplets now and the air hums with the scent of wet soil and crushed leaves. Everything is hazy, even Olea, who I'd swear is surrounded by a silver halo of light, her gown reflecting moonlight like a mirror.

These trees provide the tower with some privacy, though as we reach the other side it becomes clear that the privacy isn't needed. The garden spreads farther, fewer "specimens" now with their hand-carved tags and more wild abundance of hedges and saplings, flowering plants and weeds and twisting vines. And there are signs of old human life too; whatever this place was before it was Olea's garden, the people left behind the crumbling remains of fountains and statues, a winding maze of low stone walls and benches amongst the poppies and lilies, all growing good and strong and vibrant even in the moonlight.

There are trees and cacti and vines here I've only read about in books, and more I've never seen even in illustration. I spot what might be a mousetrap tree—something like *Uncarina grandidieri*—with its three-inch-long yellow flowers and fruit laden with vicious spines, and a weedy-looking thing, four feet tall with white flower clusters that I'm convinced at first sight is white snakeroot. Everywhere I look there is something else that can maim or poison or kill.

I listen. There is no birdsong at this time of night, but I can't hear the rub of crickets either. There is only my heavy breathing and the faint trickle of water. It is nothing like the Silences I am used to; this is peace, not pain.

Olea gestures to the right, and through two curving tree boughs I see the banks of a narrow river, still rich with water despite the recent lack of rain. It must come from the mountains. I want to rush to it, to put my hands in the freezing trickle and drink until I am made whole again.

I stop myself, hesitating, but Olea nods and the motion is so joyous and encouraging that I begin to run. Olea follows and our laughter is bright and buoyant. I drop to my knees at the river's edge and thrust my hands into the water; it is just as cold and refreshing as I thought it would be. The rain falls around us, warm compared to this, and I lower my arms into the river up to the elbows.

Slowly the excitement fades. I sit back on my heels and look at Olea, who is smiling at me from her spot between the boughs of the trees. It is dimmer here, in the shadow of the trees, and her skin is ghostly pale. She is an angel in chiaroscuro.

"Welcome to my silent little world," she says.

Chapter Eighteen

In the day and in the night it is the garden I think of before anything else. Its scent follows me from breakfast to class and dinner and bath and bed, that same strangely bitter perfume I have grown to associate with her. Between sleep and waking it isn't the garden I dream of, but Olea. Olea, Olea, Olea. Her raven hair and eyes like dark pools, her smooth white skin and collarbones and shoulders and the hint of her breasts, her fingers, her lips. Her lips beneath mine.

I wake often, panting, my mouth dry and heart pounding and a slickness between my legs. I am haunted by her the way I was haunted, once upon a time, by my secret books—not the ones I stole from my father, but the ones I hid from Aurelio, and which I cannot allow myself to ever consider again. I will not think about them, I will not...

But when I do not think of them, I think of her.

The laboratory is hot and stinking. Soil and mulch and manure mix in the thick air. We had more rain in that single night than we've had for six weeks straight, though just two days later there is no evidence at all and the sun is as fierce at the windows as before.

With Petaccia and several other professors off campus this week, there is an aura of festivity. Scholars who would normally be entrenched in lectures and seminars or squirrelled away writing essays take their books out into the square and sit eating havijillia, the little vanilla sugar pastries Isliano is renowned for. I meet Leonardo for both breakfast and dinner for three days—no lasting bitterness from our argument save the now-familiar awkwardness of Leonardo's apology; we have not spoken of any of it again, of Clara or babies, of strange perfumes or shared delinquencies, and I think we are both glad to push it all aside and start fresh. Again.

This morning we strolled the cobbled pathways between the science buildings. Leonardo chain-smoked his fragrant cigarillos and I did my best not to trip on the uneven stones, my dizziness worse than ever. It seems now to attack me strongest during the day; I wake uneasy and unsteady, and by the time the moon rises I'm about falling over and faint with the same strange hunger—but my nights in the garden, sitting and talking and inhaling the green scents with Olea by my side, help. I should probably try more herbal medicines like the everlasting flowers, but I'm wary of drinking or eating too much, for I know both can cause further problems.

The stench in the laboratory does not help with my nausea today, yet it also doesn't abate my appetite—a double curse. My stomach gnaws at itself angrily and I drink cup after cup of cold tea in the hope of keeping it quiet until lunch. Petaccia has left me strict instructions for while she is away; I start by taking cuttings of the stronger seedlings in the window troughs and making the slides she has requested, and then I water those of her plants that aren't part of her current experimentations.

Then there are notes to write and new seeds to plant, some to be mixed with the brown dirt the doctor will apparently be bringing back from her travels. I do it all wearing Petaccia's custom-made gloves, which have artificially narrowed fingertips so I can select what I need with ease, and rubber tips to help me grip. I avoid thinking about the difference between Petaccia's scientific approach, her tools and her laboratory, and Olea's wild garden. I avoid thinking about Olea at all when I am in Petaccia's space.

Instead I busy myself between tasks by poring over the doctor's first notebook. I've returned to its pages more than once, flicking back and forth, hoping desperately to find something for me. Some hook that drags me in, wakes up the scientist inside me. I'm hungry for discovery, to prove to Petaccia that I can be worthy of her mentorship. Some of the notebook's pages are exactly what I would imagine from a professor of her tenure—tidy thoughts, well rounded if a little ambitious; other pages are like the ramblings of a madwoman, barely legible in places, what-ifs that question the very basics of nature and the world around us. I return during my laboratory hours to thoughts such as *What if it is possible for humans to have a complete life cycle as plants do? Is it possible for man to become perennial?* And *If it is true that fungi grows through mycorrhizal networks, could the same symbiotic relationship be possible for other life forms?*

I've heard murmurs amongst the other scholars, usually when they think I'm not listening, whispers about Petaccia and her "unorthodox" methods. I thumb the pages and scoff. Don't they see that she is a genius? Yes, her work is unorthodox, but it's more than that—it's *unprecedented*. They're just jealous because she's a woman.

But even when I'm focused on my work, it's hard to avoid

thinking about Leo's warnings about Olea, and about her connection to the doctor—which I've yet to get any real answers about. And the idea that Petaccia might smell the garden on me as Leo did is disturbing to say the least, though our conversation about the bitter scent of her odd little eyeball tree gives me hope that it's not something she might notice. Still, I don't have to think about that yet, so I push it away and busy myself with more planting and more reading, and with imagining that this laboratory could one day be mine as well as hers.

The worst part of having the laboratory to myself—aside from my own endlessly whirring brain—is the note that the doctor has scrawled at the very bottom of her list, in capital letters so I have no choice but to pay attention. DON'T FORGET MY PARUULUM ARIDA.

For the last two days I have avoided touching the vine as much as possible, except for moving the pot towards the window as I know Petaccia does every morning so it can bask in the sunlight before the light through the window gets too hot. I have always loved plants, always, but I can't help the way this one makes me feel. There is a vulgarity about it that rubs the very hairs on my skin the wrong way, almost as though it shouldn't exist.

Petaccia hasn't yet explained the purpose of the vine to me, nor how it came to be, but I have a sneaking suspicion she has cross-pollinated and bred it herself, which begs the question: Given how sickly-looking it is, why does she have such a fondness for it? She's usually so ruthless with her failures. I've been wary to even approach it, but Petaccia's note is staring at me and I know what she means by it. She doesn't mean I should water it and move it from place to place; she means for me to hold it, to give it some contact time with my body.

I wait until the fiddly slide making and seed planting are done, and then wait until I've been to the dining hall for my lunch. I wait until the afternoon starts to cool into evening before realising it is no use and I can't keep putting it off. That the sound I can hear in the laboratory is the gentle *swishswish* of Petaccia's pet as it tosses against the desk or the window or its pot like the flick of an angered cat's tail.

I'm struck by the instant knowledge that if I do not hold and pet this bloody plant, Petaccia will know. And I know, deep in my heart, that no excuse I give will be good enough—and she will not be happy.

I could interrogate why making the doctor angry scares me so, but in the end it doesn't matter. Petaccia is strange and wonderful and all things in between, but at the end of the day she is still the single reason I am here at all. Not long ago that only meant learning and knowledge and the potential for a future, for all the acclaim and esteem that goes with such a position under her tutelage, but now it means the garden—and Olea—too.

I settle down at Petaccia's desk to write up my notes. The vine, Petaccia told me, prefers contact with skin—though how it can tell the difference between leather and flesh is beyond me. I've avoided it until now, but I can't go the whole week shirking this part of my duties. I peel off my gloves with a sigh and lift the vine, wilting yellow trumpet-shaped flowers and all, up beside me and do nothing to encourage the way it coils itself around my wrist, my fingers, right up to my elbow—and still it coils. Like before, it is cool to the touch, unexpectedly dense and soft, a little like thin velvet. I whisper my notes aloud as I write with my right hand, stopping occasionally to brush its leaves, which are also softer than I expected despite their sunburnt appearance.

An hour later we are both still sitting there.

"You know, this isn't so bad," I say. "I'm sorry I waited until now." It feels foolish to talk to a plant like a person, but I suppose people do it with dogs and cats and horses—and I'm certain Olea talks to the many plants she grows in the garden. So perhaps it isn't foolish. Perhaps that's how they grow so well. "And I'm sorry if I was mean before, even in my head. I didn't mean to offend you and I certainly don't want that held against me."

It occurs to me that I could talk to the plant about things I might not be able to tell anybody else. Speak thoughts that no human should hear. A wobbliness begins in my belly and I laugh it off, the sound echoing in the silence of the lab.

"Does the doctor keep it so warm in here for you?" I ask, lifting the *Paruulum arida* up slightly, crooking my arm so I can look into the eye of the trumpet flowers. They look smaller than they did earlier, though surely that's a trick of the mind. "Or is it for those other fellows? You mustn't mind it. Even I don't mind it so badly today."

It is true that the heat doesn't seem to bother me as much today. Only now am I starting to feel the buildup of sweat on my skin, whereas in days past I would have felt it hours ago and been relieved for a break. In the dining hall at lunch I found myself almost *cold*. The dizziness, however, is back with a vengeance. I wonder if maybe I'm developing an allergy to milk or eggs—I had both at lunch—but the nausea doesn't feel anything like true digestive discomfort. It feels as though I am so hungry I have never eaten before in my life. The sunlight burns my eyes, and my *skin*, and my whole body feels weak. A deficiency, then. *It must be*, I think. *What else?*

The vine wriggles less than I'm used to, and although an hour ago I might have been glad, now I notice it with mild concern. It's true, too, that the flowers *do* look smaller than they did earlier, and more wilted. I glance down at the soil, but it is still only the correct level of moist. I check to make sure I'm not crimping or compressing any part of the vine, that none of its leaves are caught against the desk by my chair, but everything looks fine.

Everything, that is, except the *Paruulum* as a whole. I'm sure now that something is wrong. I peer closer at the body of the vine, at the buds I once thought were pustules. They are paler in colour than I recall them being. Paler than earlier today, or only paler than yesterday or the last time I paid attention? I can't be sure. I move my hand into the beam of sunlight and watch in horror as the edges of the leaves at that side begin to curl and darken, the faintest hissing sound erupting from them.

I yank the vine back into the shadows. The curl of its body around my wrist grows slack. When did I last see it move? A sick feeling begins deep inside me, a tightness in my chest, panic growing so big and so fast that I drop the plant entirely. The leaves and flowers scatter on the desk, their precious nubs coming away from the body of the vine; the yellow flowers crinkle and turn to fine dust, a scatter of gold atop the unpolished wood. All that is left of them is ash.

I mutter a string of choice expletives, but I don't move. I watch as the rest of the vine continues to curl, to shrink, to thin and twist in on itself until it slithers, lifeless, off the desk and back into its pot. There it remains sitting atop the soil, stained dark like ink in places and so translucent in others it might as well be made of air. Its leaves and flowers are gone—just like that. It is nothing.

I stare, my mouth agape, my notes scattered across the desk and the floor. The air smells rotten, like matter turned to mulch, like soggy leaves and forgotten compost. The stench assaults my nostrils, lines my throat. I gag once. Then, beneath the badness, all that decay, there is another smell—faintly bitter and floral, like old perfume.

Petaccia's vine is dead, and somehow, though it must be impossible, I could swear it is entirely my fault.

Chapter Nineteen

I run straight from the laboratory to the garden. My hands are sticky with the vine's ashes, my fingertips stained grey. I scrub them against my trousers but only succeed in smearing the ash across my palms, mixing it with my sweat.

Relief floods me as I reach the garden. It is only when I see the way the sun catches on the dull iron, the way the shadows dance against the wall, that I realise: it is day and I have no idea where Olea spends her days, or if she's anywhere close enough to hear me.

"Olea!" I scream. I don't care if anybody *else* can hear me. Let them chalk it up to some kind of female hysteria, or the shriek of long-extinct wolves. I smash my hands against the bars of the gate, feeling the clatter of the metal in my rattling teeth, in my bones. "Olea!"

She is a vision in white, a scarf pulled up over her dark head, the tasselled edging flying behind her as she darts down her well-worn paths. Her hands are filthy, her feet black to the ankles, but with ink or mud I can't tell.

This is the first time I have ever seen her in daylight, but I can't even enjoy it. I'm going to be sick and my nose won't stop running; tears streak my cheeks.

"Olea, let me in, please, please," I sob.

She throws open the gate and stands on the other side panting. I am breathless, too, but I've long stopped noting the feeling as unusual.

"What?" she demands, urgency making her voice high and sharp. "What is it? What happened?"

I fall into the safety of the garden as if its walls are a mother holding out her arms. I inhale deeply, drawing in its familiarly bitter scent. It smells less strongly than it does in the night, and many of the flowers closest to the walls are closed against the glare of the sun. Olea holds her hand up to her eyes, which are narrowed— perhaps sleepily?

"Did I wake you up?" I say, sniffling. I reach up to wipe my nose and then remember the ash on my hands and use my sleeve instead.

"No," Olea says, but her voice is thick with suspicion. "It's just...bright. I have to be very careful in the sun. It—hurts."

We walk together into the shade of the trees just beyond the tower. It is cooler here and I can think much better in the dimness. Olea drapes herself over the low bough of a tree with succulent-looking peach-like fruits and I sink onto the remains of a stone pillar or bench, now just a round, uneven block of pale stone that digs into the soft flesh at the back of my legs through my trousers.

"What happened?" Olea asks again, this time with more gentleness. "I've never seen you so distraught. Do you need to...to *grieve?*" She says the word as though it is secret, leaning closer. Her hair falls over her shoulders, the shawl over it slipping down to rest in the crook of each elbow.

"I…" It occurs to me that this is exactly what I need. I need the cool Silence of my father's sepulchre on the day before a funeral, the sooty incense to wipe away the memories of the vine's death, to shear myself and absolve myself of my guilt—

"Thora?" Olea prompts. "You can tell me. Even if it's a secret."

"It isn't a secret." I wipe my hands once more on the legs of my trousers, feeling the material bunch beneath my fingers and almost missing the freedom of my skirts, to wipe away my sins and hide them amongst their folds. "You know about my work with Dr. Petaccia…?"

Olea stills. Almost as if she's waiting for me to reprimand her again. We have not talked about why she didn't tell me of her relationship with the doctor, but I'm not raising it now because I'm angry. I have more important things to worry about.

"You know her science," I clarify. "The work she's doing in the lab with the drought and dry-living plants?"

Olea relaxes a little and nods. I pick at my nails awkwardly, still feeling the dusty ash beneath them, wanting nothing more than to boil my skin and get rid of the sensation forever.

"She left something in my care. A plant. She wanted me to take care of it—it's… it was very tactile and liked to be held."

Olea's expression shifts as she realises what I'm getting at. "What happened to it?"

"I don't know. One minute I was holding it—only exactly like I've done before—and the next it was like…" What was it like? "It was like it turned to ash before my very eyes."

"You burned it?" Olea's dark eyes widen.

"No! I didn't *do* anything to it at all. It was fine and then all of a sudden it went completely still and began to sort of melt inwards and go all brown and white. And the leaves and buds just fell off and turned to dust. Have you—please tell me you've seen something like that happen before?"

Olea's face has changed, but I can't read it; I'm not sure whether she's horrified or intrigued, and I suspect she isn't sure either. Curiosity wins. She sucks her teeth thoughtfully, and she looks nearly like Petaccia, her brow furrowing as she considers everything.

"All right," she says slowly. "First off: don't panic. I'm sure there are a lot of things—okay, not a lot of things, but *some* things that could cause a reaction like that."

"Like what?" I throw up my hands uselessly. "Cosmic intervention?"

"Amongst other things." Olea's amused smile is almost worth the pain. It lights up her whole face, her dark lips standing stark. It is only now that I notice them, how purple-red and plump they are. I have always assumed they only looked that way in the moonlight, a trick of the shadows, but she is even more beautiful by this hazy light of early evening.

"Other…things?"

"Like acid, I suppose," Olea continues. If she notices me staring at her lips she doesn't say anything, but she must be able to see me—I can't stop myself. "Vinegar maybe? Did you have anything on your hands?"

I think back. I'd eaten lunch not long before, but I doubt the rye bread and soft cheese could have caused such a reaction. I shake my head.

"What about sweat?" Olea tries then. "Perhaps your sweat was salty and when you touched the plant it transferred."

"Salty enough that the *Paruulum* virtually caught fire?" I scoff, trying to punctuate my words with a laugh. It comes out as more of a grimace and Olea's expression flickers in response.

"How about…something from the garden, then?"

"Like what?" I repeat my earlier question. If it was obvious, surely I'd have thought of it by now.

"You've not taken anything out of the garden, have you? Any blooms or pollen?"

I recoil at the suggestion. "No! I wouldn't do that. You said—"

"All right, all right," Olea soothes. "I was only asking."

"Wait." My stomach lurches. "Do you remember…the flower you gave me as a token?"

Olea stills. "You took that with you?"

"I thought—since you gave it to me…I thought that would be okay. I wanted…" I trail off. Would Olea understand if I told her why I took it? "Do you think that could have done this?"

"Did you touch it?" Olea asks. Her expression is a mixture of worry and again that same open curiosity. Her gaze flicks from my face to my hands, then her face melts to a softness I can't pinpoint.

"No, never," I swear. "I carried it with my clothes and it's been on my desk ever since. I haven't even been back to my rooms since this morning."

"It's—it's okay. It was only an Ophelia. They're a little troublesome, can cause some nasty stings, but they're only risky with prolonged contact." Olea's shoulders bunch and then relax as she smiles. "I'm surprised you took it, though."

"How could I not? It was a gift—from you." I tremble as I say it. It's the closest I've come yet to telling Olea how I feel, and even this is dangerous. What if she doesn't feel the same way? Worse: What if she tells Petaccia, and she thinks I'm some sort of pervert?

"I…" Olea's smile falters and then widens—and it's like the moon between clouds, bright and cool and good. "I'm glad it made you happy."

I rub my hands over my face, cheeks burning, exhaustion threading through me. "What am I going to do?"

"I would say try not to worry about it. There's a lot you haven't told me, and I assume, given—Florencia—there's a lot you likely don't know. Maybe it had a life cycle, or maybe it was all part of her thesis."

"Wouldn't she have told me, though?"

"Maybe." Olea shrugs. "Maybe not. She's...difficult, sometimes. Anyway, there's no use bolting the door after the horse has left the stable. Isn't that what they say? You might as well wait for her to return before you panic."

"I'm already panicking."

"I know you are. I know." She smiles. "But all I'm saying is try not to. And maybe..." She trails off. I wait for her to speak, but it's a long minute. I breathe in the greenery around us, feel the blood singing in my ears slowly reduce to a gentle flow. "Maybe this is a good thing," she says finally.

"Good?" I can't help the crack in my voice. "How can this be good? You sound like Petaccia. She's always on about how science is about learning from mistakes and failures. Does anybody ever stop to consider if we shouldn't be making these mistakes in the first place?"

Olea doesn't answer. Instead she begins to pace. The shadows from the tree branches flicker across her face, one way and then another, and I stare. Everything seems farther away here. As the moments trickle past, the laboratory seems so hazy and distant I could almost forget about it. Olea is right: Here in the garden, what does it matter if I fail? What does it matter about anything at all? Anything except her—

"Come with me," Olea says suddenly.

"What?" I blink. Olea has pulled the shawl up over her head once more, its fringe framing her face. Her dark lips curl, her cheeks rounded and tinged with faint pink.

"I want to show you something." She pauses breathlessly, and when I don't immediately get to my feet she flaps her hands at me. "Come *on*," she insists. "I promise it will help you see that this isn't the end of the world."

Olea guides us until we reach the heart of the garden. The sun is just beginning to set, the trees and plants surrounding us gleaming in the gentle pink-gold. The grass around us is lush and green, peppered with dwarf nettles, rhubarb, and tiny black mushrooms I suspect must be *Coprinus atramentarius*—inky cap—amongst brambles with thorns as long as my thumbnail.

Just beyond us are the crumbling remains of a fountain, its white stone shining as the sun hits it; the statue atop is of a young woman riding a horse, bare of all clothes and her modesty preserved only by the long hair that winds around her body. The horse, however, is missing its head.

"That"—Olea points at one of the trees to the fountain's right—"is a type of manchineel. Traditionally *Hippomane mancinella*, though I'm not sure she truly shares the name, as she was brought over from the Old Continent. Some people call it 'little fruit,' or sometimes 'beach apple tree.' You see how it leans towards you? It likes you."

The tree Olea refers to is young but no longer a sapling. Its bark is the colour of dusty sage, cracked silver farther away from the roots. Between the thick, equally dusty-looking leaves grow apples the size of Olea's tiny fists.

"Wait, I've seen this in one of my books. Isn't the fruit meant to be—"

Olea reaches for one, and before I can stop her she's pulled it from the bough with a triumphant smile. I step back hastily. I've read about the manchineel. Its fruit is otherwise known as poison guava; even its bark, its leaves, its sap, are caustic and can burn skin and cause blindness. Olea, completely unperturbed, raises the apple to her mouth and takes a bite.

"Olea," I warn.

The juice that runs down her chin is pale, milky white, and she sighs at its sweetness. Her eyelids flutter closed, long, dark lashes almost brushing her cheeks. She looks different in the sun, so pale she could almost be translucent.

"*Olea*. Whatever you're trying to prove, this isn't the way to do it—please. I don't want you to hurt yourself just to make me feel better about—anything. I know you're good at what you do. I trust you, but you're scaring me. Please. *Please*."

Olea opens her eyes and looks at me. Her pupils are so large they seem to swallow the irises; she is sweet-drunk and her smile is lazy and slow.

"Is that what you think I'm trying to do?" Her voice is soft like honey. "Thora, I'm not trying to scare you. I'm not trying to prove anything, except to myself. I just wanted to show you..."

"Show me what? That you don't value your own life?"

"No, of course not."

"Then what?"

"That the tree isn't—she isn't just a *tree*. She won't hurt me. And look how she leans, how the fruit on her branches looks almost too heavy for her to bear. I think she *wants* you to take it. She doesn't want to hurt you either."

The setting sun is hot on my shoulders and I can feel the burn of it through my short hair, across my forehead, my nose, and my cheeks. I long for shade or shadows. How is it so insufferably warm at this time of day? I wipe the sweat from my forehead and squint. Olea lowers the fruit to her side and lets out a soft sigh.

It does something to me, this sigh. I feel the quiver deep inside myself. A release. Olea steps closer. Her bare feet *are* stained, I realise. Her fingers too. It doesn't look like dirt or ink, though, more like their natural tint—if that natural tint was midnight with a touch of dark forest green. She takes another step closer. And then one more. The fruit still dangles casually from her right hand. Too casually. Her eyes are on mine and they are anything *but* casual. They are so dark they're almost black, but they're *not* black. They are actually hazel.

I begin to tremble.

"Does it frighten you to be close to me?" Olea asks. She is so close now I can see the pulse at her throat, rapid like the fluttering wings of a bird. My own pulse echoes. Gone are all thoughts of Petaccia and the vine, of Leo—even of the garden. There is only Olea.

"No." My mouth is dry, my lips stiff as I try to lick them. The heat is too much, the sun and its damned pink rays. "You are the one who's normally afraid." I recall the way she flinched away from the pastries I brought, the careful way she holds herself so there's never any chance of us touching. Not so now. Now she leans towards me, her body bowing like the arms of the manchineel.

"I used to be afraid," she says. "I don't think I am now."

She lifts the fruit and holds it out to me. I continue to stare at her. Her chin still drips with the juice, some of the pulp there too; it makes her lips especially dark and her teeth especially white and I can hardly breathe.

"You said I shouldn't do that," I croak.

"That was before. You've been exposed now, long enough that it's safe. I'm sure. I told you I would try to protect you—and now I'm telling you—taste it."

Olea closes the last of the distance between us. She is so close I can sense the warmth of her body; the tassels of her shawl brush my shoulder and I feel them like shivers through the loose weave of my shirt. She holds the fruit to my mouth and I raise my own hands without thinking. As she presses the surprisingly soft flesh to my lips, my hands close around her fingers and the apple. Olea startles at my touch, making to pull away, but I tighten my grip, sinking my teeth in and hissing as my mouth floods with flavour.

It is bitter and then it is sweet—sweeter than anything I have ever tasted. That first bite is like an awakening, the rush of adrenaline when nearing the edge of a high bridge. The giddiness too. I inhale and swallow and then take another bite. I know my eyes must be glazed because I can see the same in Olea's face, a contentment that is somehow both hollow and gilded. I close my eyes and let out a hum of surprise.

"You see?" Olea breathes. "Some have called the manchineel cruel, a devil tree, a death tree. She is only protecting herself and her fruit. This tree should dislike you, but she doesn't, because now she trusts you. Do not assume that because things have always been so they will always *be* so, or they were always meant to be. Apologise to Florencia. She knows, like the manchineel, that you are pure at heart and you meant no wrong. Do you *see*?"

I realise I am still holding Olea's hand. My fingertips tingle like the aftermath of a sting, heat beneath my skin, so pleasant it is painful. It is the heat of a flame in the second before the sharp, white-hot agony begins.

"Yes."

She lowers the apple but does not allow me to let go of her. My heart skips. I sigh.

"Do you feel better?" she murmurs.

"Yes."

Our foreheads come together, the shawl shielding both of us from the sinking sun. I let out a breath and Olea smiles. The smile grows. Neither of us pulls away. My heart continues its rapid beat and Olea swallows so hard that her throat bobs. She drops the fruit and it rolls away; we stand, uncaring. Still, there is the heat. I cannot move away—the thought of it fills me with panic. Now that I know the feeling of her skin as it touches mine, I *need* it. Even if it will hurt—and something primal inside me tells me it will. I am like the starving man who eats until his stomach bursts and only tastes the sweet nectar of release.

In the end it is me who moves first. It was always, truthfully, going to be me, wasn't it? I know what I must do and I must do it now, right this second, or I shall go mad.

"May I?" I whisper.

Olea gives the faintest nod, and this is all I need to ignite the fire that has been burning in my belly and between my legs since that first night I saw her in the garden. I crush my lips against hers and the taste is so sweet it is bitter; it is honey and freezing fire, her skin cool against my own burning.

This is not like an Aurelio kiss, chaste and matte and perfunctory. This is everything a kiss should be, everything, *everything*. I am so lightheaded I can barely think, my blood crystallising to sugar in my veins. My vision swims and it is Olea I see in multiples like the glittering sand repetitions inside a child's kaleidoscope.

Olea, Olea, Olea.

Chapter Twenty

Kissing Olea is like being plunged into a freezing bath on a hot day. My whole body tingles with it, from the soles of my feet to the tips of my fingers. From my deepest, darkest, most secret depths right out to the places the world can see. It is better than any dream. Better than *any* of the hazy, dawn-peach-stained moments of weakness I've had between sleep and waking since I was first old enough to bleed, when I would wish that things could be this way—and then wish fervently that they never would be. Because if this is the depth of feeling I have been missing...how can I believe in any god or apostle?

I see the same fear echoed in Olea's face, but the same smooth relief and open longing too. With her in my arms I don't care about what my father would have thought, or how the world might see us. I don't care about any of it.

We kiss until our lips are swollen, until our lungs scream at us to take air. We kiss until the moon rises and begins to fall once more in the sky, no sound but the faraway trickle of the garden's private stream. Every touch is a jolt of pleasure-pain, white-hot and agonisingly moreish. It is like being drunk, being swept into an ocean of feelings so deep I might drown. It is bewitching.

When our mouths grow sore of this new adventure, Olea makes us a bed amongst the brambles that grow around the fountain, soft grass cushioning us and Olea's shawl as a pillow. We lean back against the stone fountain and count stars and name constellations. Olea knows a story for each one, every tale more outlandish than the last.

"Once upon a time," goes one such tale, "there was a bird. When she was very young and weak she fell from her nest, whereupon she was captured by a mage, who had a fascination with such small-boned beings. The mage kept the bird in a cage the size of a palace, with gold bars and plenty of enrichment—but the bird grew lonely. One day she happened upon a fox spying on her through the bars.

"'What a pretty little bird you are!' exclaimed the fox. The bird was flattered, for she had never had a friend, and she thought the fox beautiful too. 'Won't you let me inside your cage?'

"'Oh no,' replied the bird. 'My cage is to keep me safe, and the mage always warned me of cats.'

"'But I'm not a cat,' said the fox. 'I'm a fox! And foxes want to be safe too. Please let me in; there's more than enough room for both of us.'

"She told the fox to come back again the next day and she would have an answer. Now, the bird considered the fox's proposition hard, for she was a lonely thing, a tiny little bird in a cage the size of a palace. And she thought to herself: Well, what could go wrong? Perhaps the fox will eat me, which would be unfortunate, but the mage might protect me. And loneliness is as painful as being eaten, just in a different sort of way. So she decided that the fox could come into her cage palace, and together they worked to bend the bars—which weren't real gold after all."

"What happened to the bird?" I ask, turning my face to Olea's.
"It's a horrible ending."

"Tell me."

"The bird said to the fox, 'You can come into my cage, but please don't try to eat me.' And the fox agreed. The bird was excited for their friendship, but she didn't consider the mage's feelings. The next day the mage came to visit the little bird and discovered the fox sleeping in a pile of autumn leaves.

"'How dare you bring a filthy fox into this palace I have built for you!' screamed the mage. 'You have defiled the safety of this place, and I shall banish you from it forever.'

"The bird begged and pleaded for forgiveness, and the fox apologised to the mage.

"'Please don't hurt her, Your Kindness,' said the fox. 'I was only looking for a nice place to sleep and a friend to share my days.'

"'You are a liar,' replied the mage. 'A filthy liar and a cheat! For I know you were planning to eat my little bird and take this palace for yourself.'

"The fox denied such a thing, and the little bird cried. The mage would hear no more, and bade them both leave the safety of the cage forever."

"And then what happened?" I ask. Olea blinks and looks at me again.

"The fox and the bird left the palace together. They huddled together at night under the boughs of a tree, and the bird began to wonder if the mage had been lying. But on the second night outside the cage, well, the fox tried to eat the little bird after all. Only—it turned out the little bird had claws, and it scratched the fox's eyes out. That's why the stars look like that." She points to the dip between two points that might be ears, and to tiny specks that might be the place where eyes once were.

"Oh lord," I say. "You're right—that ending is horrible."

The next tale Olea tells has none of the sadness of the last, a story about a hen who became trapped in the body of a human and developed the ability to talk to certain types of animals.

"You're making them up!" I laugh as she finishes yet another story. "There's no such thing as a dog the size of a bear."

"Not any more," Olea says morosely, and I laugh harder. She is different here, bolder in these lively moments than she ever was near the walls of the garden. It's as if some part of her has come alive, happiness carved from chunks of ice. But she is still a know-it-all.

"What about the wolves?" I say. "We haven't had wolves in Isliano since the Dark Ages."

"And you think these tales weren't told during the Dark Ages?" Olea turns her face towards mine and arches an eyebrow. "Thora, stories about the stars have been told since man first told tales around fires, long before our Descalous separated from the Old Continent.

"But they don't *mean* anything."

"They don't have to mean anything." Olea props herself up on her elbow. Now that our lips aren't locked, she is careful to maintain a small distance between our bodies, though my heart is screaming for anything but that. My skin tingles where she has touched it, like the white-hot itching of a hundred nettle stings. "They're stories. Stories exist for a lot of reasons."

"Yes, parables and fables and—"

"Sometimes a story is just a story," Olea says, but something in her face says otherwise.

"Do you really believe that?"

"You like to interrogate everything, don't you." It isn't a question, but she doesn't say it with disappointment, merely interest.

"Don't you?" I ask. "I learned young that you can't stop learning about the world just because somebody tells you that you should. Out there"—I wave my hand—"women hardly read. They hardly write. It's only by virtue of my father and the death rites that I know to read any written stories at all. And even then, if you just accept everything you're told..."

"Accepting a story for what it is doesn't mean you have to stop questioning the world," Olea says quietly. "It just means that there is a time and a place. Some stories teach you to be brave, some teach you to be strong, and some make you laugh. Does laughter come cheaper than bravery or strength? Do you need all of these stories at once?"

I fold my arms behind my head and gaze upwards. The sky is smooth as dark water, speckled with thousands upon thousands of tiny flecks of light. Olea's insistence makes me think of the gossip Leo so desperately said he didn't want to spread about her—and her supposed "illness"—the likes of which he told me anyway, and I wonder if she has been haunted by this before. Perhaps she and Petaccia are the same, both trapped by expectations of gender, of rumours and stories told by people who don't know better.

"So it's like with the trees and plants in this garden," I say, giving myself the time to think. "You're saying that there are tales about them—like the manchineel being the death tree—but we don't always have to believe them?"

"It's not about believing really," Olea says thoughtfully. "More that we shouldn't take everything at face value. I'm certain there is truth in the stories about most of the plants in this garden."

"So, the tree is poison?" I ask, reaching to prod at my lips.

They still feel swollen, though I think that's likely more from the kissing than the fruit. But was the kissing *because* of the fruit? This thought doesn't sit well with me, and I drag myself a little more upright against the fountain.

"Yes," Olea says. Then, "No. It's... Can't it be both?"

"You know that's not how this works."

"But it sort of is," Olea argues. "It's poison. Its natural defence is one that could easily hurt you, or me, or anybody else. It hasn't hurt us, though."

"Did you *know* it wouldn't hurt me?" I ask.

"Well, no—"

"And you didn't think to tell me I was taking a risk?"

"The tree chose not to hurt you," Olea argues. "It accepted you. It's providence."

"You think I didn't get hurt because the tree *chose* for that to be so?" I shake my head to clear the fog in my brain, but it feels like I'm wading through treacle. She sounds just like Petaccia with all her talk about fate of discovery. "Meaning, what, you gave me that fruit to eat based on a hypothesis alone? Surely that's exactly the kind of arrogance that gets people killed by plants like these."

"It's not arrogance! I'm telling you the tree *trusts* us. It's like..." Olea clenches the fingers of her left hand together and spreads them apart as she gropes for an explanation. "Okay, so that tree—do you see the one in the far ditch?" She points and I follow her finger to the edge of the tree line. There grows a small moonlighter, maybe six or seven feet tall with palm-sized leaves and hanging clusters of pinkish berries that might be similar to raspberries—though it's hard to tell from this distance.

"The slightly fuzzy one? I noticed it the other night. The whole thing is like the skin of a peach."

"Some people call it a stinging tree," Olea says. "*Dendrocnide moroides* officially, imported from the rainforests in the south. Those fine hairs are—I'm not sure what they call it, but each one contains a virulent neurotoxin so strong, if you even brush up against it you'll be in agony within minutes. And if by some virtue you manage to deal with the pain the first time, heat can reactivate the pain later if you can't remove the hairs."

"Okay...?" I say hesitantly.

"So the thing is, other people have called it the suicide tree. The pain can last for months after you get stung, and to make matters worse, the tree sheds like crazy. You can get the hairs in your eyes or your nose or your mouth. The hairs are so fine they're almost impossible to pull out."

"Olea, you're not selling this tree to me," I say. "What's your point?" She quirks her lip in a half smile but holds up her hand.

"My point, Thora, is that you walked right past that tree earlier today on your way into the garden. You were so distraught over Florencia's vine that you didn't even notice how close you got. And I was frightened for you at first, because I know the stories of the tree, and I've seen what this garden can do to people. I told you I couldn't always promise to keep you safe—and I thought, *It's happening, she's already in danger.* Yet here you are. Completely unscathed."

"Did I?" A coolness snakes down my spine, but I keep my composure. "I didn't think I got that close."

"You didn't touch it—but you might have. If you had known the story of the stinging tree I'm sure you would have been more careful, and that's fine and good, but if, like me, you'd known the story and decided to place your trust in the tree itself...?"

"That could be pure luck!" I exclaim.

Olea shifts to better face me. "It might be. But what is luck if not the winds of change blowing in the right direction? Providen—"

"Don't you dare say providence again," I cut her off. "You'd put my safety in the hands of *luck*?"

"No," Olea says quickly. "You did. I warned you not to touch any of the plants. But I watched you walk right past that tree and pass by unharmed and I knew then that we *trusted* you. Do you see?"

I could get angry at this, but it doesn't seem worth the pain. Is it arrogance if she's right? I'm here, and I'm safe, and I'm with her. My whole body still feels warm and cool at once, tingling with Olea's kisses, and the heavy bitter-rose scent of the garden surrounds me like a soft blanket, so I just inhale deeply and shrug.

"You did warn me."

Then the thought comes. The one I've been playing with since I first remembered Leonardo's warning about Olea being danger-ous. And his complaint about the bitter smell that follows me now, that followed his wife too...

"Olea," I say, an urgent note creeping into my voice despite the haze in my brain. "I have a friend who knows about you, and about the garden. His name is Leonardo Vanksy. Have you ever spoken to him?"

If Olea notices my urgency, she doesn't show it, her face thoughtful as she says, "Vanksy...? No, I don't think so."

"What about his wife, Clara? Did she ever visit you?"

"Mmm, no, I don't know her either. I really don't know many people at all. Just you and Florencia. Why?"

"He was the one who told me that you are Dr. Petaccia's ward. He warned me to stay away from the garden—and from you. Is this why I should be wary of the stories I hear outside these walls?"

Olea's expression grows serious, but she doesn't move away from me as I almost expect her to. Instead she catches my gaze very, very carefully and holds me in place with a look so earnest I want to kiss her again. I want to do more than just kiss her.

"Do you even want to do this, to be stuck here?" I push gently. "The garden, the tower—"

Olea shakes her head. "What a question."

"Leo is my good friend. I'm sure he would have no reason to lie about any of this, but he's really very...uncomfortable around the subject of the garden. Around the idea of *you*. Why is he so suspicious? Are you *sure* you don't know of Clara?" I press. "You can tell me if something happened. If that's why he's spreading rumours about you. How else would he know about you? I worry that with the garden and your work here with the doctor, you've got so much you need to protect and—"

"Thora," Olea says. She lifts one dark-stained fingertip and holds it to my lips. The scent of her overwhelms me, nearly capsizing me entirely. I could fall into her arms and stay there forever. "You're worried about me and that's sweet."

"I'm not just worried about you," I blurt. "Like I said, Leo is my friend and I can't bear the thought that he might have some reason to hold a grudge. He's looked out for me a lot since I got here."

Olea holds her hands together, twisting the small gold ring that she wears on her pinky finger—plain gold, like a wedding band, and slightly too big. If I didn't know better I'd think she was nervous. "Okay, I will be honest with you." Olea sighs, a light breeze ruffling her hair and wafting her bitter-coffee-and-roses perfume my way. "I did know Clara, once upon a time. She was one of my friends beyond the gate. It was, oh, a long time ago now. She stopped coming. It's true I never met her husband. I didn't even know his name until you said it, but the name Clara is unusual, isn't it?"

"Why did you lie?"

"I don't like to think about her." Olea shrugs, twisting the ring again, around and around, hurt plain as anything. "She left me. She said we were friends. I wanted to...to get to know her. I wanted to invite her into the garden. And when I said she could come in, she—she stole things from me. Plants. From *my* garden. Do you understand why I am so wary? Why it took me and my plants so long to trust you?"

Relief flows through me like the sun's gentle warmth on a winter's day, though there's something about the edges of the conversation that bothers me. *Did you love Clara?* I want to ask. *Did you kiss her the way you have kissed me just now? Did you let her touch you?* A bitterness whips through me that has nothing to do with the garden and its green perfume and everything to do with my own green jealousy.

"I'm sorry she did that to you," I say earnestly. "And I'm sorry I believed Leo's stories. I'm sure it isn't malicious, but I shouldn't have let myself be taken in."

"Don't be sorry." Olea's tone is simple, her face open and honest and full of hope. "You're here, aren't you? The garden trusts you. You're not like the others."

And then she kisses me again and the hunger within me is all-consuming. I need to taste her, to devour her, to blot out the rest of the world. I suck her lips, graze them with my teeth. Her hands find my shoulders, my chin, guide my own hands to her chest and the plump softness of her breasts.

In this garden, tonight, I have been made anew.

Chapter Twenty-One

Olea rouses me just as the sun is beginning to creep over the horizon, painting the garden in shades of dusty green and gold. The grass is damp around us and there's a delicious chill in my bones, welcome after the days and days of endless heat.

I yawn and stretch. The skin on my lips blisters and cracks, an iron tang leaching into my mouth. Olea is crouching a little distance away, her nightgown pulled down over her knees and a smattering of crushed leaves in her lap.

"You'd better get back," she says, brushing her hands clean. There is a shyness in her that wasn't there last night. She peers up at me over thick lashes. She looks soft and relaxed and gentle. "You'll miss breakfast."

"I'm not hungry," I say. And I actually mean it. I can't remember the last time I woke without that gnawing hunger in my belly, the desire to gorge and gorge until my whole body feels leaden with food.

"You still might be yet. You missed dinner too."

Olea's crouch deepens and she reminds me of one of those wild children the newspapers love to sensationalise; her curls are dew-damp and loose, her feet bare and dirty. I resist the urge to check my fingernails for the same dark stain as hers. In the end, what does it matter if mine are black too?

"You're avoiding things," Olea goes on. "I can tell."

My chest hollows. "Am I?" I think she means last night. The kissing. My lips tingle at the thought. I don't want to avoid anything—

"I know it's uncomfortable, but I'm certain it will be better for Florencia to hear it from you, rather than arriving back to the lab and finding it—gone."

Gone. Dead, in fact. The guilt swoops through me. Yes. I should be thinking about the doctor's vine, her ruined experiment, and my failure of responsibility. Instead all I can think of is the doctor's ward, the heavenly way she tastes and how badly I want to kiss her again. I clear my throat and clamber awkwardly to my feet.

"You're right," I say briskly. "But..." I pause, a sudden thought coming to me. "Olea. Do you think I should tell the doctor I've been in here, in the garden?"

Olea blinks, her face otherwise entirely still. "Why should you do that?"

"I...I don't know. You asked about—if I took something out of the garden. What if something, some pollen or thorn or dust, like from that awful tree, what if it got on my skin or my clothes and I took it to the laboratory by mistake?"

"You didn't, though."

"How do you know? You asked the question. I'm just saying..." I lick my lips. "Why is it such a secret that I come in here to see you? I'm sure the doctor would approve of our—of, of..." I don't know what this is—or what we are.

Olea clenches her fists against her knees. "No," she says darkly. "No. I'm not allowed visitors."

"Why? I'm not just a random visitor," I argue.

"As far as Florencia is concerned, you are. She rarely visits the garden herself. It's—it's its own biome, a complete ecosystem. Her experiments don't factor you into them. She wouldn't want you in here. You could ruin everything just by being here, don't you understand?"

"I..."

"Oh, Thora." Olea reaches out to me and grasps my hand, squeezing it tight. My fingers tingle painfully. "I'm sorry. I didn't mean that. You know I didn't. It's just—Florencia and I have worked so hard to create this place, to culture and nurture it, and she's so very protective of it. And me. You *don't* understand, but this isn't like her other work."

"I don't understand because you won't tell me."

"No." Olea's expression shifts to sadness. "I know. I wish I could, but—not yet."

"What if she can smell it on me, though?" I ask. "I know the garden has a scent."

Olea thinks a moment. "If she does, just tell her you've visited the wall—like before. It isn't a lie—or at least it doesn't have to be if you tell it carefully." She wrinkles her nose. "But...I don't think she will notice, or if she does she might assume it's from her own clothes maybe. I don't want you to lie for me, Thora. I'm just saying maybe don't mention it to Florencia if she doesn't bring it up first, not over something like the vine. When we bring you into the experiment, we want it to be on positive terms, don't we?"

I still have no idea what the experiment is. This garden is a wonder of toxins and poisons, a veritable treasure trove of death, but still I cannot see why there is the need for such secrecy. They are, at the end of the day, just plants.

But at the same time, I want it. I *want* to be included; I want desperately to be a part of whatever this experiment might be. So until Petaccia invites me in, I'll keep Olea's secrets.

"You look tired," Olea says. "I'm sorry. I've kept you awake again and you've got such a long day ahead. You should—why don't you stay away from here tonight. Get some sleep."

My chest tightens, regret and a new kind of grief pricking tears at my eyes, but Olea adds quickly, "Come back tomorrow night instead. The garden trusts you now. Please don't stay away."

She stands, the fragrant crush of leaves in her lap tumbling to the grass, leaving a patina of the garden on her dress. Her voice is urgent. "You *will* come back tomorrow, won't you?"

My appetite doesn't return for breakfast. I'm too anxious for Petaccia's return; I sit in the laboratory, watching the slow tick of the hands on my wristwatch and listening to the building settle around me. Without the vine, the room feels empty. I know this is ridiculous, and almost certainly a result of the ebb and flow of my guilt, but still I jump at every small noise, catching the scent of the garden in my hair though I've dabbed it liberally with rosewater.

I get up and check my reflection in the small mirror over the sink. My skin is grey tinged from poor sleep rather than its normal golden tone, my hazel eyes shockingly dark. The smattering of freckles across my nose reminds me, sickeningly, of the ash of the *Paruulum*. There's a small speck of blood at the corner of my lip, and I wipe at it impatiently. Despite all this eating I've done recently, I think I've lost weight—I can see it in the sharper jut of my cheekbones and around my neck. Olea is right. I need to sleep tonight, to get some proper rest.

I wash my face with cold water, scrubbing at my lips and at my hairline, where normally sweat would be beading already. Today the heat in the lab doesn't feel so bad, as if my night in the garden and the cold that leached into my bones are insulating me against it. Hopefully Petaccia won't notice that the cuffs of my creased shirt are stained with grass, and that the seat of my trousers is dusty with the garden's dirt. I don't want to lie to her, but I will if I have to.

Another noise from below startles me. There are a lot of noises, I realise. From the gentle whistle of each gust of wind outside to some unknown ticking and clicking somewhere beneath me in the building, La Vita is not silent like Olea's garden. Its thick green scent and muggy heat feel artificial, too, like a paste spread too thick. I can't quite put my finger on it but the laboratory feels almost like a facade, like the real work is missing from this picture, and then the guilt becomes real once more. Petaccia's *Paruulum arida* is dead...what if she no longer needs me as her partner?

I think myself into such a spiral of doubt and panic that by the time the doctor arrives at just after eight o'clock I am sweating profusely and the room stinks of it on top of its usual heavy scent. It is mildew and dank soil combined with dust and heat and gently seared leaves. I've tried to hide it the best I can by brewing a fresh pot of coffee, but I can still smell it.

I leap out of Petaccia's chair at the desk and clasp my hands in front of myself like a schoolchild. Petaccia seems a little surprised to see me, but she recovers quickly.

"Thora, my dear. How have you enjoyed having the lab to yourself?"

"Hi, ah, it's been—well. Did you have a good trip?"

Petaccia drops several bags by the door and closes it behind her. First she strides to the window and checks the temperature on the gauge there, then each of the little black seedlings, none of which look much different, each wilted and sad but still growing. Then she turns back to the desk and my stomach lurches. I'm going to be sick. I'm—

"What happened?" she demands. Her eyes flash and she steps closer. "It's gone?"

"Yes, but—"

"Did something happen? Did you change anything?"

"No!" This comes out as a yelp and I swallow hard, trying to unstick the words I've practised from my throat. "No, I didn't... it didn't..."

Petaccia closes the final steps between us. She's studying me hard, her gaze darting from my face to my clasped hands. *Guilty*, I think. *I look completely guilty.* I need to do something, say something. I can't keep standing here like a naughty child.

"Thora," Petaccia says sternly.

"Yes, ma'am?"

"Sit down. I'm going to make us both tea—no, coffee's on the go so we'll have that—and you are going to tell me everything."

"I..."

"Everything, Thora. This is serious. Do you understand?"

I fight the tremble in my limbs, clinging to Olea's advice and reassurance from last night. This can't be the end. I won't let it. But my knees are weak and they betray me; I sink into the chair and rest my head in my hands.

When Petaccia brings our drinks over, I snatch mine before she can place it on the desk, my mind imprinted with the image of the vine as it withered, blackened, and turned to ash, nothing left but dust motes in the sunlight. The coffee is thick and black and sludgy. Petaccia sips at hers, taking the seat across from me—the very one I sat in for our first meeting.

"Well?" she says coarsely. "Tell me."

I sip gingerly from my own mug, nearly gagging as the bitter liquid clings to my tongue and burns my throat. It is like chicory, harsh and raw. Now that I'm seated, my hands are still, my limbs unshaking, my panic over. Olea was right: I can do this.

"It wasn't my fault. I did everything you asked. I watered only the plants you said, did all the prep and wrote up the notes. I wore gloves for all of the small work and made sure to change pairs so there was no cross-contamination—"

"I didn't ask for excuses," Petaccia cuts me off. "Just tell me what happened." Her features are so sharp they could cut glass. I can't read her expression.

I take a deep breath. "I didn't do anything unusual, is what I'm saying. Everything was fine. And I took the gloves off to handle the *Paruulum*, just as you said it prefers. I held it for perhaps...an hour? If that? I was writing up some more notes. I don't know if any ink got on the vine, or if I got anything corrosive on my shirtsleeve, but one minute everything was normal and the next..."

The memory of it is surprisingly painful. I might not have cared for the damn thing, but I'd started to see it sort of like a pet. And the fact that it wasn't *my* pet almost makes it worse.

"And the next?" Petaccia prompts. She's crossed one leg over the other and rests her chin on one hand while the other clutches the top of her mug. Her eyes are dark and thoughtful, and maybe a little damp. The sick feeling twists in my belly again and I'm glad I didn't eat breakfast.

"It just sort of . . . died? I appreciate that's not very scientific."

"Make it scientific," Petaccia returns coolly. I don't argue.

"It stopped moving first. Then it started to blacken, the leaves first and then the vine itself. The whole stem went part translucent and part black, like it was cooking over a high heat. And then it crumbled to ash."

Petaccia says nothing for a second. She sips her coffee. She leans forward to inspect the desk where I've been gesturing, and into the pot with the withered, blackened remains of the stem. And then she surprises me completely.

"Interesting," she says.

"Interesting? That's all you've got to say?"

"Well, words aren't going to make it un-happen." Petaccia shrugs but her face is shrewd. "You say you were holding it at the time?"

"Wrapped around my wrist like normal."

"And you didn't tug or squeeze or trap it in any way?"

"No, I even checked."

"Good," she says. "That's good."

"Is it?"

"Good that you checked, I mean," Petaccia says quickly. She gazes somewhere behind me, running a finger along her jaw while she thinks. She looks tired. This surprises me—in all the weeks I've known her I've never noticed her looking any different. She is always harried and slightly unkempt, but I've never seen such dark circles under her eyes.

"I'm sorry," I say quickly. "I know it doesn't mean anything for me to say it and words are cheap, but I truly am. I honestly don't know what happened. I was so shocked I've not even cleaned up; there's ash everywhere."

Petaccia's smile is unreadable and it doesn't reach her eyes, but there is some warmth there, and as always that flicker of curiosity. It's almost as if she's seeing me for the first time. I want to cry but I blink furiously until the threat of tears is dulled.

"These things happen." Petaccia gets to her feet, slopping coffee over the side of her cup. "Part of all of this"—she waves her hands at the laboratory—"is accepting that failure does and will happen, and that success isn't linear. There is always an element of fate, or luck, or heavenly intervention—or whatever else you want to call it—at play. Now, wipe your eyes, the lab is no place for tears, and get out."

"Ma'am—"

"For goodness' sake, Thora, I've told you to stop calling me that. I am *nobody's* mother," she snaps.

"I'm sorry, but please don't throw me out. There must be some way I can make it up to you."

"Make it up to me?" The doctor's sudden laugh is harsh and foreign and it makes me jump. "Girl, I want you out of the lab so I can catch up."

"You're not angry?" I swallow my pleas, my cheeks flushing. Olea was right. I should have listened and now I've made a fool out of myself.

"I'm not. As long as you have told me everything." She pauses. "You have, haven't you? Told me everything?"

"I..." I think of Olea's pleas, her insistence that I keep my visits to her garden a secret. Guilt threatens to capsize me, and for a second—just one second—I consider opening my mouth, but then I think of Olea's lips on mine, the press of our bodies, the heat deep within my core, and I know I can't tell the doctor. I nod instead. "Everything I can think of."

"Good. Now, get out and leave me in peace for a while, will you?"

I wince. "All right."

I make to take my barely drunk coffee to the sink, but Petaccia waves me off with a hand. "Leave it," she says. "And the ash. Enjoy the rest of your day off because tomorrow we begin again. I've got a *lot* of thinking to do, and I'm going to need your help."

I leave La Vita with my head spinning and my stomach gnawing itself in knots. I can't help feeling that despite Petaccia's positive outlook on things, I've somehow managed to fuck this up so irreparably that she'll have to give up on me.

I'm ravenous, and sick, and dizzy with pining for the coolness of the garden. This heat is stifling, it is *unbearable*, but I can't think of anything worse than returning to my rooms, where I can *see* the garden but I can't touch it—can't taste its sweet bitter greenness on my tongue. The sunlight burns my face as I cut across the campus; it's quieter today, most of the scholars returned to their usual studies in the dim lecture halls and classrooms, hidden away from the baking heat. Petaccia has left no lectures for me, and I don't feel much like pawing my way through any of the histories I've been reading. My mind is simply too full of bees.

Still, I'm surprised at where my feet carry me. The library is just as daunting and exciting as it was when I first entered. I've had most of my books delivered to my rooms or the laboratory— it's easier than trying to find a private study area according to St. Elianto's rules—and I haven't had the time for any other reading since I started. Today, though, the library's cool halls and hidden nooks call to me.

I slip into the building silently, wasting no time crossing the atrium and climbing up to the mezzanine. My appearance still garners more attention than I'd like around the campus, but at this time of day there aren't many scholars to pay me any mind, and those who do quickly go back to their reading. I stride in my trousers, grateful to Petaccia for her insistence on them, and head up another spiral staircase.

I'm not looking for anything in particular, not any section or author or theory. I don't want to read about politics or philosophy or science, I can't think of anything worse right now than filling my head with more *things*, but I'm burning with exhausted energy. I continue to walk because if I stop I will simply collapse.

I consider titles on death and mourning. My father always said there was more to learn—I wonder if there have been any advancements since he died, in the ritual preparation of bodies or the casting of new cradles, a process that has had bloody wars fought in its name for centuries. But it isn't death I want to read about. Not bodies or thoughts. I want—the realisation hits me like a carriage—I want to read about love.

I've gravitated towards fiction, most of the library's offering here of the elegiac and temporary variety. Novels by poets, pretty in prose and heavy in ideas, or great tomes by old professors in their waffling prime. I have never really been one for fiction, except—

I stop. The book—right ahead—with the black spine, completely innocuous in both appearance and title, is one I would recognise anywhere. The image of it is seared into my mind; my whole body flushes at the sight of it, cheeks hot, palms sweating. I recognise it because it is a book I have seen before. Not in my father's private stash—he would have been disgusted if he knew such things existed—and not in any public collection I have seen since. But it is one I had once, hidden, in my marital home.

More than most of the titles I secreted away, concealed from Aurelio's prying eyes, this one was special. And not only because of what made it worthy of a secret, the scenes that burned behind my eyelids in the darkest hours of night, throbbing deep in my belly, but the story.

I creep closer. It can't be—can it? It is small, about the height of my palm, and sits nestled between two much larger companions. It is a slender thing, no more than a hundred pages, and I might have missed it if I hadn't seen it before. What is a book like this doing here? Dimly I wonder if the author is a scholar or professor at the university. It's the only thing that would make sense. Such inflammatory material...out in the open?

My chest rises and falls rapidly, my heart a bird fluttering inside a too-small cage. Part of me wants to scream, to run, to demand that the librarian remove it at once, or better, to run away and never come back again. This isn't the part of me that wins.

It's as if an unseen hand guides me, my arm that of a puppet and somebody upstairs pulling the strings. I swipe the book off the shelf and shove it deep into my trouser pocket, where it nestles against my skin through the thin material, warming with the heat from my body.

I glance quickly up and down the stacks, but there is nobody up here. Then I head back out the way I came, trying to affect the same innocence. It isn't possible—I can't pretend. I'm convinced that any second somebody will stop me, will demand to see what I've concealed in my pocket.

Nobody stops me. And I can't stop myself. I'm back at my rooms, hot and sweaty and trembling with fear and hunger and deep, impossible delight before I even realise what, exactly, I have done. I pull the book from my pocket carefully; it looks nearly new, not thumbed and creased like its shelf mates, and I stare at it in awe.

The first thing I think is that Aurelio is going to kill me when he finds out what I have done—and then I remember. Aurelio is dead. There is nobody here in these two rooms of mine to care what I read or what I think. Or whom I think about.

I hurriedly start the task of closing the shutters, giving the hot, sun-filled garden one longing glance, before carrying the book through to the bedroom. I glance down at my hands, then remove my wedding ring. I strip down to my underwear and crawl between the sheets, limbs singing, skin already prickling with anticipation.

There are no thoughts of fear now. No worry about whether this is wrong of me to want or need. I remember the same antici-pation in my study in Aurelio's house, the way I would hide behind my husband's desk with my knees propped up against the wood and my hand circling hesitantly beneath my skirts. Back then I was afraid—petrified—of being caught and crucified. I wanted noth-ing more than to wipe the memory of his touch from my body, to reclaim the burning feelings that were mine alone.

Now I read with delight, page after curious page of the chapter I have always loved best. It is an ancient story within a story, the leg-end of the nymphs Hekaline and Orithyia, who were cursed by the great Lord of Death to exist eternally opposed—one condemned to the night, the other to the day. In this version of the tale, Orithyia discovers the ambiguity of the greyness in dusk and dawn, and the lovers meet under a secluded rocky overhang where they satisfy their desires beneath the golden-edged shadows of the sunrise.

It is a story of beauty and daring and resolve. It is trust, and the risk of betrayal, for each of the nymphs must wholly believe in the other or risk death. When I first discovered it I felt like Hekaline, and I would have given anything to trust in the greyness; now it is Orithyia who speaks to me, the one who holds the cards—and the responsibility if it all comes tumbling down.

Of course, like the rest of this novel, this chapter spares no details of their passion.

As I read I think of last night, of the crush of Olea's lips on mine, of the delicious softness of her skin, her breasts. I want to gorge myself on her. I want to hold her body with every inch of my own, palms and nails and lips and teeth; I want to crawl inside her skin. My body grows loose and comfortable—and as my fingers reach the soft, warm flesh between my thighs, all I think of is Olea.

Chapter Twenty-Two

When I wake my bedroom is dim, threaded with golden pink strands of fading sunlight, the air still pleasure scented. My skin is slick with cool sweat, almost feverish, and my hair is soaking. I dreamt, I think, of the garden—but I don't recall why.

My stomach pinches painfully. My limbs feel weak, as if I have run and run for days without rest or food. I'm thirsty, too, my tongue parched and sticking to the roof of my mouth. I lick my lips, tasting the faint crusting of blood from last night, and I think, again, of Olea. Oh, the sharp pain behind the pleasure in our kiss.

Normally I would be getting ready to head to the garden with her now. I've hardly made it past sunset the last few days. I don't like the disruption of our routine, though I can't deny the sleep—and what came before it—was necessary. I'm still tired, muzzy-headed, but at least it isn't the same bone-wrenching exhaustion as when I finally collapsed against the pillows, my right hand and arm aching fiercely.

I flex the muscles now lazily and consider my food options. The dining hall will be closed before I get there, and I have little to eat here except some stale bread and cheese I put in my pockets a few days ago for a snack. Everything else I've systemically polished off. The thought of food makes me want to cry; I'm not used to being governed by it like this. Why am I so famished?

I lie in the evening dimness for a while trying to gather the energy to move, and it is only the call of a fresh breeze that drags me from my bed to the study, where I throw open the shutters and let in the everlasting-flower-scented air. I stuff the bread and sweaty cheese into my mouth in one go and make tea with some of the flowers mixed with peppermint and a small amount of vanilla, all crushed together with the tea leaves to create a fragrant stew. Hunger pangs grip my belly, one after another, as I sink down at my desk and rest my chin on my hand.

For just one minute I allow myself to fantasise. Not about Olea this time but about the feasts my mother cooked, once upon a time, whenever my father would return from performing the death rites. It was a celebration of his work, of his patience, of his ability to keep us clothed and fed—but most importantly a celebration of his rites. The gentle but unrelenting way he shepherded the dead and pushed the mourners through their grief. My mother was a wonderful cook; the table would be laden with jellied meats, candied bacon, and tart apple stew, fresh bread folded in the *moeror* loaves, and seasonal vegetables or salads dressed in expensive, thick vinegars and honey. My mouth waters at the thought, my bones hollow for the need of it.

Then I force myself to stop. There is no use thinking of the past. Tomorrow my work with Petaccia begins anew. It would have been wiser for me to spend my afternoon studying so that I am prepared for whatever the doctor may ask of me, but it is too late for that now. The demise of her precious vine still niggles at me; there is something about what happened that I can't ignore, but my thoughts are jumbled, as if everything is coming through brackish water. When did it become so hard to think? I don't recall it being this way when I first arrived here. I felt fresh then, ready to tackle the world. It feels now more like I am swimming with my eyes open, fingers clawing for purchase on nothing but silky water.

I sip my tea and try to make it last, hoping that the mix of leaves and flowers will settle my stomach and soothe the dizziness in my eyes and my tired brain. I must have overtired myself earlier. What was I thinking? I attempt to shake my head, to clear my mind, but I only succeed in rattling myself badly enough that I think I might vomit.

There is something wrong with me. The thought comes so suddenly that it takes me by surprise. I stop mid-sip, the cup of tea partway between my face and the desk. My hands begin to tremble something awful, a rotten sensation unfurling from my core right out to my fingertips. *There is something wrong, and I don't know what it is.*

I think back. When did I last feel normal? When was I last completely well? I've lost all track of my days and weeks, but I think it must be weeks now since I woke from a sleep without the painful, gnawing pit of hunger in my belly. Weeks, too, since I could walk without some mild dizziness. Leo has been complaining of my distractedness for longer than that—though of course I've mostly ignored him. I've been too busy to worry. Should I worry? My father was taken by some meandering, withering illness that started a few months before my marriage to Aurelio. He complained of no dizziness or hunger but often said that his chest ached, though he—and I—brushed it off as nothing.

I lean forward and then backwards again. My chest feels fine. The inside of my mouth has the tangy iron taste of blood, but I'm almost certain that's from the bruises on my lips—and I'd take Olea's hungry grazing again despite the pain.

Olea. It is early yet for her gardening hours, and I know she'd hate the idea of me watching for her, but I lean out the window anyway, just in case I can spot her. The hours stretch before me without the promise of the garden. I want to see her. I want to talk to her and hold her. And the plants, too, I realise. I miss them. It feels as if I've been severed from them, although they're so close I can almost smell them.

I wonder if this is what Leo was worried about when he warned me of the garden. Did he suspect I would become addicted to it? Does he know for sure that his Clara was there, at the gate, visiting with my Olea? Does he think that's why his wife abandoned him? He drove her away with his desperation for her happiness, drove her right into Olea's arms...

I haven't seen him in two days—or is it three? And I've barely thought of him either. I wonder if this is how his Clara was, captured, enraptured by Olea's private Eden, haunted by the garden's scent and dreams of Olea's lips. I wonder, with a laugh, if Leo is wrong, and if Clara isn't still here on the campus, hiding somewhere, biding her time, waiting for Olea or to steal from her again.

The memory of Clara is bitter and my thoughts are jumbled and nonsensical. I don't like that Olea lied to me about her. More than that, though, I don't like that Clara claimed to be Olea's friend before betraying her.

Olea is fragile, too gentle to be at the mercy of people like Leo's wife. A thief no less. I wonder if Leo has any idea what Clara was up to, if that explains the fervour of his mistrust more than just fear. Perhaps he is frightened of Olea because Clara told him her plans to rob her; perhaps they were in on it together.

No, that's a ridiculous notion. Leo is too kind to support even his wife in such an act. Perhaps she told him and he disagreed, though? That would be reason enough for Clara to abandon him. If I was caught trying to steal something so precious—for there's no denying that half of the specimens in Olea's garden would be worth a small fortune in some academic circles—I'd want to disappear too.

I blink. The sun has nearly set and the light is that hazy in-between, blue and purple with shadows that stretch uncannily, but I could swear there's somebody in the garden. It isn't Olea; the figure moves too fast and furtively, dressed in black or brown so they virtually blend in with the tangle of thorny plants that grow near the garden wall.

My stomach lurches. Olea has left the gate open. She must have. Or I did when I left this morning. How else could somebody gain access to her secret place? Freezing panic drips down my spine. I want to shout, to wave my hands, or to run down and shoo the intruder away. Yet something holds me in place. I remain, fixated, as I watch the figure hurry towards the boggart's posy—or *Mercurialis perennis*—a patch of weeds that grow close to the wall with toothed leaves shaped like spears. The weeds grow thick in places, but not there.

It's impossible for me to tell whether the figure is male or female, only that they are tall and fast; they wear a hood over their head, some sort of travel cloak, and long dark sleeves that stretch down over their hands, maybe gloves too. I angle closer to my window, careful to keep to one side. I'm not sure what I am planning to do aside from watch, but if there is a thief targeting the garden, I'm determined to be able to tell Olea exactly what they came for.

But the figure doesn't grab and run. If they're familiar with the risk these plants pose, then they're confident in the safety provided by their conservative clothes. Once they've reached the shadow of the wall, the figure pauses, glancing around. I catch a flash of pale skin, but then the hood is in the way again and they're kneeling down amongst the weeds.

I narrow my eyes, waiting for the snap of stems. My mind flits between fear of arson and fear of some kind of poison that might kill the plants, but the figure bends lower over the earth and they seem to be *digging*? They brush the plants away with little tenderness, scooping aside handfuls of what I assume is dirt.

There is a flash of metal as the stranger removes something from inside their robe, whatever it is large enough to catch the last rays of the setting sun, and then the stranger rolls their shoulders, climbs to their feet, and begins to dig in earnest.

I don't know what to make of this. I'm still torn, hovering with indecision, when the intruder in the garden stops and drops something in the hole they have made. I can't see what it was, only that it was small—no larger than a silver coin. They cover the hole quickly with the shovel and then with their hands, laying the shovel down and bending low over the weeds once more.

A sneaking, trembling feeling starts deep inside me. Not quite a suspicion, but closer by the second. I hold my breath, waiting, waiting, until the figure in the garden reaches up to brush their forehead. The deed done—whatever the deed may have been—they have grown careless, and the hood slips back. Dark curling hair slides across their forehead. An inky-clad hand reaches up to pull the hood back.

Not gloved, I realise, but stained.

Olea.

It feels like deceit. The sun has nearly set, but I know I'm not mistaken. I would recognise her hair, the frame of her beautiful narrow face, anywhere. She was a stranger in shades of pink and gold, but now, in the early moonlight on this clear, cloudless evening, she is Olea again.

Olea, digging in the garden. More: Olea digging in the garden by the light of the setting sun, so out of character for her when the sun seems to cause her such displeasure, on an evening when she has explicitly asked for me to stay away.

My heart thuds and the stale bread and cheese threaten to make another appearance. I'm hot and dizzy, gripping at the frame of the window for support. She doesn't glance up here again, nor does she resume her usual garden duties. She looks lost, bewildered, but also strangely satisfied—her body language, the gentle slope of her shoulders and casual dangling arms, that of relief.

Am I chasing rabbits? Is this a foolish scene to try to pick apart and understand? I've learned before that more harm than good can come of such questions when answers are too far away. I could go insane trying to understand this girl. Maybe I should return to my bed and gaze instead at the ceiling and its cracks, imagine the crawl of *Mandragora officinarum* roots. It will do me as much good as standing here.

Yet I can't tear myself away from the window. Olea stands, frozen. I half imagine I can see the rapid rise and fall and rise and fall of her chest. She looks as if she could be laughing, or crying, and a violent little niggle at the back of my mind whispers: *What if she is laughing at you?*

What was she digging for? What was she burying? I grasp at straws, my sluggish mind churning and turning over possibility after possibility. She wasn't planting seeds, nor would such behaviour align with the checking of her soil or the gentle snipping of blooms for her catalogue. But why would she keep secrets from me?

I wilfully ignore the secrets that have always been between us, her silence around Petaccia's mentorship and her request that I keep my admittance to the garden a secret. And Clara, too.

Clara.

Is it a coincidence that Olea has asked me to stay away tonight—so soon after I raised my questions about Leonardo's wife and the garden? Olea was cagey in her response. She *lied* to me. I recall, too, the way she grew nervous when I asked, the fiddling of her fingers, the gold ring spinning and spinning. And even then I had wanted her to touch me.

The ring—it is about the size of the object she buried. Why would she bury it? Is there more to her friendship with Clara than she admitted, some closeness she is too ashamed to reveal? I squirm in place, embarrassed by the heat that still coils between my thighs, unsated and out of control. Did she bury the ring for me, as a gesture of moving on, or did she bury it because of what I asked? Because of my friendship with Leo? I pull at my hair, scratching my scalp mercilessly, as though I might pull the answers from my skull with the right amount of force.

I am so deep in my thoughts that I almost miss what happens next. It is nothing, a nothing thing, an event that happens a hundred times a day—and yet, in this garden it does not. Only I'm not sure I've ever noticed before.

Olea lowers the hood of her cloak fully. She has resumed her usual casual air, though perhaps only I can tell how forced it is. She has hidden the shovel amongst the weeds and begins snipping small green flowers, her nose turned away from the boggarts' rotten scent and buried in her shoulder as she snips bloom after bloom. I'm almost certain that she doesn't need these flowers for her catalogue, but she works with a fervour that borders on religious.

Whether it is because of her distraction or simply that she doesn't expect it I don't know, but when the little sparrow swoops into the garden Olea doesn't see it. I don't either, not until it's too late, but even as I watch what unfolds I marvel at the tiny bird, realising with curiosity and faint, unfurling horror, that I have never seen a bird in the garden before. No, not a bird, not a bee, not a fly—not during the day, and definitely not at night. I'm sure they must exist, for the garden ecosystem to function, but I have never seen one. Why?

This bird flies straight for the boggart's posy and its unleashed rotting-flesh scent—or swoops directly for Olea, perhaps, a nonsensical attack. I don't hear anything from my vantage, but I see Olea flinch and pull back from the bird as it dives. She covers her exposed face with her hands as she throws herself out of its way, knees skidding in the dirt. The bird continues its flight.

A frantic flap of her hand. The bird connects with the exposed inky flesh of her palm.

The bird drops like a stone.

My breath catches. At first I think that the bird is only stunned, that it will shake itself in a second and fly away. That is before I see the way Olea stares at her hands, both outstretched before her. The rising moon casts silver across her features and I recognise the expression: resignation, tinged with the faintest disgust.

The horror unfurling inside me is no longer slow and dawning. The feeling slams into me, leaving me sick and shaking, realisation not far behind. All this time…all this time I have believed Olea when she said the garden trusted me. I have believed her when she said that the plants were toxic to everybody but her—and now me.

I was wrong. The bird isn't stunned. It doesn't get up and fly off. Olea walks to where it fell, calmly, calmer than I have seen her all evening, and gathers the poor, tiny thing in her hands. I can see the way she cradles it, curiosity merged with her resignation. She lifts first its wings one by one, and then its head. The bird wriggles once, one last fighting flare of its heart, and then goes still. Something liquid, dark in the moonlight, drips down Olea's arm. She lifts the bird to her ear and listens, then whispers something to its lifeless form.

Piece by piece, the puzzle slots together. When Olea said that the plants were not toxic to her because they trusted her, that was only a story she told to draw me in, to lull me with the harmless side of her and her miraculous Eden. The notes in Petaccia's book were more to the point. *Tolerance*, I think. *It's all about exposure.*

I can see it now, plain as the inky stain on Olea's fingers, plain as my body's rejection of—followed by complete intoxication with—her. Her and the garden both. When we're apart I crave them, and if we're apart long enough I am sick and shaky as an addict without opium; when we are together my body is filled with overwhelming sensation.

Yes, the bird might have been sick, dying already, but…the coincidence is telling. Death by a single touch. Look at what her kisses have done to me, even after months of low-level exposure to both her and the plants.

When Olea said that the garden was dangerous, I should have

listened. I should have listened to my body, the feverishness and sleepless nights, the sweet-bitter scent of the garden, so similar to Petaccia's wretched eyeball tree; I should have heard Leo's warnings and taken Olea's caginess about Petaccia's experiments to heart.

Bile burns my throat as I slowly, carefully, close the shutters and back away from the window. I back away until I reach my bedroom once more, fingers at my lips, teeth grinding as understanding finally hits me in wave after wave after wave. I picture without trying the burning shock of Olea's kisses, the heartsick *need* to be near her. No, it is not only the plants that grow close to the wall that can maim or poison in one toxic touch, nor those on the other side of the trees; it is not just the garden that can kill.

It is Olea too.

Chapter Twenty-Three

I know about Olea."

I stand in Petaccia's lab the next morning, feet apart in a fighting stance. As usual, even on a Saturday, the doctor is starting her day behind her desk, writing notes from some overnight spark of genius. She is dressed in black and it highlights the pallor of her skin. She looks tired, her hair frizzing around her head—but I don't care. I need answers.

She glances up when I speak, pausing her writing, but doesn't say anything, just peering at me expectantly. A rush of fury over-takes me.

"I know about the garden too," I say. "How long were you planning to keep me in the dark? I thought we were supposed to be partners."

Petaccia purses her lips. "What," she says coolly, "exactly is it that you think you know?"

"Olea told me everything." It's a bluff, and one that I know within seconds hasn't paid off.

"Well, if you know everything, why are you here?" Petaccia steeples her gloved fingers. It is strange, I realise, talking to her in this room without her vine coiling around her wrist. A pang of guilt almost stops me in my tracks, but I refuse to back down.

"Okay, not everything," I admit. "But I know about the poison plants. I know Olea tends them at night. I know she's your *ward*, for god's sake. Why didn't you tell me about any of this? All this time you've had me fannying around playing children's science with those—" I gesture at the seedlings in the window, bigger than they were but still stunted by the full sun.

"The drought is a serious problem, Thora," Petaccia snaps. "I wouldn't exactly call it children's science."

"No? Then why is it that you share it with me but not Olea's garden? What on earth are you doing in there that is so, so…" I can't say it. I can't even think it. The memory of the bird touching Olea's skin and falling down dead comes unbidden and I feel sick, a mixture of revulsion and vicious hunger deep inside me. *Unnatural.* "I've been in the garden. I've seen it all. I know that there's more than what it seems."

Finally, I think, I have Petaccia's full attention. She closes her notebook—different, I realise now, from the ones we have always written in together. Different, too, from the one she gave me to read her notes. She slides this into the top drawer of her desk. Her eyes are narrow, but thoughtful rather than angry.

"If you have spoken to Olea, then you must know I spend very little time in her garden. And what time I do spend there is focused on helping her to create a—a catalogue of sorts. Olea is a very talented gardener and she has been working on her little…project, I suppose you could call it, since she was young. All I have done is encourage her affinity."

"For poison plants," I say. As if that is the most normal thing in the world.

"Yes, poison plants, amongst other things." Petaccia shrugs. "It's also an area I myself find fascinating. And why not? All of nature's miraculously self-defensive plants being encouraged to grow in one place—it's quite the marvel, isn't it? And as I said to you when we first met, it has always been my goal to encourage other women in science. Olea's science is just a little more…unorthodox. Scholarship does not suit her, she is too…" Petaccia searches for the word. "Frail."

"That doesn't explain why you didn't tell me about it," I grind out. "Do you not think that I deserve to know? I live right above the garden."

"Well, I can hardly be blamed for that." Petaccia's face is a mask. *I don't know*, I think. *Can you?*

The anger rises in me again. This whole conversation is going nowhere. I want to know how much Petaccia knows about Olea's *affinity*, as she calls it, and whether she has seen the results like I have, or whether she, too, has been kept in the dark, if all her notes about exposure and tolerance are just that—notes. Half-baked ideas at best. The doctor must see the anger in my face because she shifts in her seat and rolls her shoulders.

"Look," she says. "It's true I haven't been entirely honest with you about the real nature of my research at St. Elianto. My work in the lab *is* important, and it's better I do it than that hack Almerto. Can you blame me for keeping a little back for myself? You've seen what the others are like, how they crave fame and fortune without wanting to work for it. What real proof have I that you are any different from those praise-grabbing male students out there? And, yes, maybe you've gained some trust. But let's get one thing straight: I haven't any obligation to share my other research with you. I told you that you would have to prove yourself, and my ward's work in the garden is not mine to share."

"But—" I protest. Petaccia stands so quickly that the creak of her chair startles me and I step back, instinct reminding me of every time Aurelio ever did the same. I let out a frustrated breath.

"Let me finish." She clasps her hands behind her back and strides around the desk until we are truly face-to-face. Up close the dark circles under her eyes are more apparent than ever, and I wonder if she, too, is struggling to sleep at night. "We stand upon a most important precipice. And, yes, perhaps it is time for me to open up to you."

"Tell me," I say urgently. "Please. I'm so tired of always being one step behind. Let me prove to you that you've made the right choice."

It isn't what I intended to say, nor is it what I expected when I marched into the lab ready to walk away from it all if Petaccia dared lie to me again. As always, the lure of true knowledge, of being part of the inner circle, turns me into that same child who begged to learn to read, who stole books under the cover of night, who risked her whole life and future for just *one more page.*

Petaccia shakes her head. The ground rushes beneath me like a river, lightheadedness threatening to engulf me. I lean against the doorframe, breath coming in short bursts. The doctor doesn't move, only watches me curiously. I pull myself together.

"Tell me," I spear through gritted teeth, "or I will make sure that everybody knows just how dangerous your little garden experiment really is."

Do I mean it? I don't know. In that second, maybe I do. I draw myself up to my full height and give the hardest stare I can muster.

Petaccia smirks. "*There* she is." It is almost a croon. "Good girl." Her smile grows at my confusion, like that of a wolf, slow and sinister as a snarl. She rubs her hands together and then claps them. This time I don't jump. "You're finally starting to think like an achiever. Devour all the knowledge and fuck the rest. I think... rather than tell you—perhaps it will be better to show you. Come with me."

"La Vita has always been a hub of cutting-edge research," Petaccia lectures as she leads me out of the lab. I follow her into the dusty stairwell, grateful for the cool dimness and a chance to slow my racing heart. "My parents met at the university and worked here all their lives. I was practically raised here. Of course, it was very different back then. They had half the funding and twice the inexperienced staff. Work was stolen, names changed on academic papers. It was a mess."

The doctor turns to smile at me over her shoulder and it's that same wolfish grin, a flash of stained teeth in her ghostly oval face. *She's mad*, I think abruptly. *It's not genius, but lunacy.* But it's a fleeting concern. I'm more focused on making sure I don't trip. Until I know more, I plan to reserve my judgement.

"Anyway, there's a lot of their theories at play in my own work. My father, especially, was fascinated by the life-death cycle, in both animals and plants. He became convinced that the end of life was merely another stage, like birth or adolescence. Not just in words but...how do I put this—in essence?"

"My father believed something similar," I say despite myself. "That's why he used to say that grieving and care of the body were so important."

"Ah yes, but you see this is where your father and I always differed. Don't misunderstand me, he was one of the most respectful undertakers I've ever met—and I've met a handful over the years.

But when I talk about life stages I don't talk about birth, adolescence, adulthood, death. I talk about birth, life, and afterlife."

"Of the soul...?" I venture. We've reached the middle landing of La Vita, whose locked doors I have tried many a time to no avail. I've assumed they were the same as the room on the ground floor, where we unpacked the imported tree, though I've never stopped checking, just in case. Petaccia holds out her hand to halt me.

"Not an afterlife of the soul," she says. "Of the body."

She pulls a ring of keys from one of the pockets of her top skirts and inserts a tiny brass one into the lock of the door to our right. It swings open to reveal a deceptively large, dim room. There is a single window draped in muslin; a long metal table runs the length of the room, ditched in the middle like the base of a valley, with grates in the floor at several intervals and taps for running water.

On the back wall runs a battery of metal cages, perhaps ten feet tall stretching from floor to ceiling—covered at top and bottom by some kind of spongy material. Some cages are larger than others and many are empty. Those that are not house shredded hay bedding and rats, mice, the odd small bird, and in one even a rabbit.

I glance back at Dr. Petaccia uncertainly. This was not what I expected, though I'm still not sure what that was. The animals are all fairly quiet and unusually subdued; some twitch frantically when we enter and others stare with glassy eyes. My stomach churns at the sight of them all.

It is cool like a natural sepulchre in here, or one of the memorialist churches—or, I suppose, one of the mourning tombs of old. And there is death in the face of every creature in here. It is a far cry from the laboratory above, which is hot and living, green and yellow in every direction; in this room there is only the dull ache of grief.

"What do you need with them all?" *It's inhumane. It's unforgivable.* I can't say so aloud, but Petaccia's expression says I don't need to.

"Come, now. Where's that spirit I saw only minutes ago? You don't mean to tell me you've lost your nerve already."

"No, I just...I wasn't expecting—"

"Science has never been clean, Thora. It has never been won the easy way. As my father always used to say, 'You've got to crack a few eggs to make an omelette.' Do you think we learned how to survive by accident? We humans have made our fame by stealing and bartering, by carving our knowledge out by the flesh. How do you think we learned to operate to save lives? How do you think doctors and midwives have learned their crafts for centuries?"

"Yes, but you're a *botanist*—"

"Thora." Petaccia turns from the survey of her kingdom, and I'm impressed by the disappointment her frown conveys.

"You haven't told me what any of it's for," I say weakly. "Maybe then I'd understand. What does any of this have to do with the garden or Olea's plants? All I see is suffering. I would expect this in—in one of the bigger laboratories maybe, anatomical science. These animals...look at them. Doesn't it look like they wish for death?"

"Ah." Petaccia guides me farther into the room and closes the door. Instantly I'm more aware of the stillness in here. I can't hear anything from outside, no noise from scholars in the distant square, no creaks or clanks of pipes. It is the kind of stillness that usually only comes after death, after the mourning and the cradle and the burning; the flutter of my heart might as well be the only living thing in here.

Petaccia says nothing as she watches me. It's only a few seconds but it feels as though she's waiting for something, some proof that she can trust me. I try to raise my chin again, to square myself up against the horror. *It is science,* I think. *This laboratory is a frontier of discovery.* She must be satisfied, for her next move is across the room; to the left of the cages there are long, thin wooden shelves that look older than anything else in here, each one crammed to the gills with bottles and jars, filled colourful pipettes sitting in saline and cubes of what might be salt or sugar injected with similar colours. There looks to be a certain order, or progression, amongst the vials, but I can't make any sense of it.

"What are they?" I ask.

"Every single one of these is a failure, or a representation of a near miss, which is essentially the same thing, I suppose."

I'm tired of waiting for Petaccia to explain herself. I have an inkling, the tiniest blossom of an idea, but the thought horrifies me so much that I push it down. *Impossible.*

Each of the bottles, jars, and tinctures is a different size and colour. Some are similar but none are the same. Each has been labelled. *Antidote #1, Antidote #238, Antidote #654...* My blood runs cold with the suspicion that each of these "antidotes" is probably worth at least one animal life.

Many of the liquids are green in colour, though the higher numbers are also frequently red, rust-orange, and such dark colours as to be almost black. Then I spot one whose colour is a milky white, and within the mixture there is a single spiny brackish-red castor seedpod. I recognise it from Olea's catalogue. She'd said that three or four of the large, speckled seeds inside the seedpod contain enough poison to kill a person.

I turn back to the doctor. She is checking the notes strapped to one of the rat cages with a resigned shake of her head. "What is the end goal?" I ask.

"What do you think? Talk me through it."

It's clear that Petaccia considers this a genuine question. It's a test, but one she believes I will pass. She waits patiently while I sort through my thoughts, wading through the horror that curls deep in me, so deep it is pain, but also so deep I am able to sift through it like sand. I hold up one hand and count on my fingers, hoping the gesture will calm the hum of my nerves and the sickness in my belly.

"Okay. Well. You're likely using toxins distilled from Olea's plants to attempt some kind of medical healing. I see the *Ricinus communis* in that one, and given that you *are* both a botanist and a trained medical doctor, I think it's a fair assumption that you'd want to combine the two. I know that toxins have been used before now for experimental trials—isn't it foxglove that's been discussed for an irregular heartbeat? And of course poppies— *Papaver somniferum*—yield opium, which is often used as a pain medication."

"Good," Petaccia encourages. "Go on."

I shift awkwardly, glancing around the room. There is little other indication to me of the doctor's end goal. These animals are obviously very, very sick, but what with?

"May I examine them...?" I gesture at the animals.

Petaccia lifts one shoulder in a half shrug. *Go ahead.* I am not familiar with most animals in the flesh. I have read countless books borrowed from my father detailing the aspects of animal husbandry, and my mother's childhood on the farm gave her a few choice stories that she often told me, like the time the family dog had puppies—but I have never had an animal of my own, never owned a working horse or dog, or any kind of pet. I wander to the cages.

Up close things are no clearer. The rats and mice are not skittish like I would expect; they sit with laboured breaths or burrow deep in their bedding. My heart thuds and my hands are clammy with cold sweat. I reach up to the bars of the cage housing the bird and it does nothing. The rabbit is the same.

"They all look critically ill." Petaccia waits expectantly for me to continue. "But I can't see a common cause. Is it... something in the body or the blood?"

"There is no common cause," Petaccia says. "And the cause itself is not important."

A shiver snakes down my spine as the pieces slowly fall into place. But I can't be right—I simply can't. "Right." I count off on my fingers again. "So it's a medical trial in which plant toxins play a role, and it looks as though you're trying to combine them with something viscous—something that can travel around the body when... injected or ingested? But the cause of comorbidity isn't vital, so..."

My thoughts twist to Olea. She killed that bird in the garden, stone-dead from a single touch. I'm almost certain of that now. The two of them are harnessing the power of these plants at the risk of death, which means the potential payoff must be huge. And what do each of these animals have in common? Not the illness— but the end.

"End of life," I blurt in horror. "You're studying the process of death after illness."

"Not just studying, Thora. I am trying to find a universal cure for all ailments." She turns to look at the row upon row of antidotes, her expression hard to read. She chews on her lower lip.

"And it's not fucking working. You're right—it must be ingested. Intravenous delivery doesn't work as the site of injection is prone to necrosis. Water isn't a strong enough carrier. Saline is better but the salt ruins the balance. I've tried blends of countless vitamins and minerals, different toxins too—but everything in my gut and my research says that the toxin itself is almost irrelevant once you find the correct thing to bind it with. It could be a...a *vaccine*. The best success I've had is with crushed animal offcuts, blended offal, as the body doesn't reject it so fast, but you can't blend it fine enough for injection unless you water it down too much. And the mice and rats won't drink it; they choke if they're forced. There's something in the offal, something...I'm so close."

The doctor turns to me now and her eyes are wide and wild. The shiver down my spine is now a full-body tremble. I feel sick and—and excited too. I think I understand. I think I can see it.

"Has there been any progress?" I ask shakily. "Have any of your cures worked?"

"If there is any kind of positive transformation, it fails almost immediately. I think it's breaking down inside the body, so it—it needs to act *faster*. A failure is still a damn failure. I narrowed down the toxins but, in the end, had to open it back up again to ensure my tests were broad enough. Do you understand? I am on the cusp of something so great here, so great it will upend life and medicine as we know it. A cure for all—do you see the potential, Thora?"

And suddenly I do. It hits me like a hurricane. *A cure for all.* No more babies or mothers lost in childbirth, no more soldiers lost to gangrene, no more pneumonia or fevers or cholera or dysentery. No more mourning and grieving, undertakers and sepulchres and cradles.

"A cure for..." I whisper.

"A cure for natural death."

Chapter Twenty-Four

I leave La Vita a ghost. I must stride with such purpose, such an air of determination, that the other scholars in the square avoid me, a few even shivering when I cross their paths. My stomach gnaws with its familiar, aching hunger, but I ignore it. I feel faint. Sick. Heavy and light at the same time.

"Is the toxicity catching?" I asked the doctor before leaving the lower lab. I think of it, already, as *the Tombs* because that is what the cages remind me of. Petaccia gave me a look filled with curiosity. I added, "Is that why the vine died?"

I was thinking of Olea, of the bird, and the way my own skin seems hot and crackling to the touch sometimes, but it was her own hands Petaccia looked at. I didn't wonder until now if that meant she has spent more time in the garden than she is willing to admit.

"I had never considered that any of the plants' toxicity could be transferred outside the garden by a carrier such as yourself," she said simply. "But perhaps now I will think on it."

As I walk back to my rooms, I stare at my hands. The nail beds are faintly blue-black, as if I've bruised each one. There is a sore inside my mouth, at the corner of my lips, and I worry at it, opening the wound so that my tongue floods with the iron tang of blood. My skin feels scorching in the sunlight, a low-grade fever burning at my very core. I wonder, just for a second, if I might be dying.

The thought is so maudlin, so extreme, that it shocks me to stillness. I reach my rooms, driven there by the desperate need to escape the heat, the blinding brightness filling my vision. Sweat curls my upper lip, my mouth claggy with blood, my trousers rub the skin between my legs raw, and my shirt sticks to every exposed part of skin.

I tumble into my rooms, throwing the shutters closed against the daylight—and the garden. The thought of it makes me sick. Sicker than I have ever been. It is not nausea, rather a squirming oily tide that crashes like the roll of an ocean and then falls into hollowness with each hammering breath. I strip the clothes from my body, ripping and tearing until there is nothing left but anaemic skin, bruises upon bruises on my arms and legs and stomach. I don't know where any of them came from.

I glance down, seeing the faint imprint of Olea's fingers carved in blue-green on my left breast. *I know where those are from.*

The sight of them is too much. The memory of her hurts like an ache—I toss myself onto the bed and lie, arms outstretched, until the heat leaches from my bones and the sickness stops its crashing inside me. How much of what I feel for Olea is real? How much of it is the natural, unnatural magic of the garden? I am drawn to her like bees to pollen, but how much of the enchantment is mine and how much is hers? Am I only an addict, rooting for my next fix?

More hours pass. I roll on my side and read more from the book I stole from the library. Whereas before I chose my favourite chapter, now I read from the beginning, as I once did in secret in my husband's house, determined to purge myself of all thoughts of Petaccia and Olea and their unnatural, incredible science. I must become myself again—I must start anew.

I don't know how long it takes. Hours. Days. At first Olea is all I see, in the curl of the book's text, in the shadows of the darkened room. Her lips, her eyes—and then her panic as the bird fell, dead. The sun and moon become the tick of my clock as I lie in sweating silence, waves of fever rolling over me, a withdrawal I never expected I'd have to endure. I finish the book, the first time skipping the scenes inside I know will make me ache for Olea— the second time reading them, touching myself, crying for her anyway. More than once I consider dragging myself to the garden, to her. But I don't.

A new week begins and I do not consider the lectures I must be missing. They seem so paltry in comparison to this. Nor does Petaccia chase me for my presence. I am a ghost—she, lost in new potential discovery, and I merely a distant memory. That suits me well.

The fourth afternoon, I think, I'm roused by the flutter of a note underneath my door. I lie in bed, staring at the ceiling cracks, feeling the gently receding heat of the day creeping around the edges of my shuttered window. My mouth is dry and a little cracked but no longer caked in blood; my eyes don't hurt when I move them, and neither do my limbs.

I stumble unevenly to the stove to make tea, a pit of hunger in my belly but no more than would be normal after days without food and with little water. I drink a pint of the stuff, tepid and metallic, and shiver with relief as my hunger abates.

It is only then that I remember the note under the door. I open it warily, half expecting a letter terminating my scholarship with the doctor—a ridiculous thought, given what I now know about her research, but one that I realise still terrifies me—but it is from Leonardo.

> *Thora. Forgive my intrusion, I knocked but received no answer. I am worried about you. Ignore me elsewise if you like, but please, please just let me know that you are all right. You know where to find me. As you said, you still need to eat.*
>
> *Yours,*
>
> *Leo*

I turn the note over, searching for…what? I don't know. The warmth I feel at seeing his handwriting surprises me, and I realise with a jolt that I miss him. I miss the familiarity of his face. A pang of guilt swiftly follows. He has been kind to me since we met. I would be a fool to let his kindness go unappreciated. But now…I think of the ring Olea buried in the garden—for I'm sure now that's what it was—and the thought plays in spinning golden circles in my mind.

If the ring was Clara's, or given to Olea by Clara at least, that signals more than a short friendship gone awry. And if Clara treated Olea so badly, stealing the plants that belonged safely in the garden…Why did Olea keep the ring, and why bury it only after I asked what happened between them?

And, perhaps more importantly, how much did Clara know—about Petaccia's research, about the garden, about Olea…? And how much does Leo know still? His warning tugs at me, a suggestion that if he does not know the truth, then he at least suspects it.

I can't sit and ponder any more; I feel as if I am going mad. I dress in one of Aurelio's gowns, soft peach silk, which I hope will hide the new pallor of my skin. I've lost so much weight that it hangs off me, but I'm right about the colour. My hair has grown past my ears in places and the peach makes it look burnished, like gold. I almost cackle at my reflection, wondering what Aurelio would make of me now.

I arrive at the dining hall just as the server is seating Leo at our usual window table. He sees me instantly and the relief melts across his face like butter, a reaction he doesn't even try to hide.

Part of me is wary. This is where our friendship risks the kind of familiarity I can't afford, and relief could so easily turn to more. I've not forgotten my revelation about the truth of his romantic feelings towards his wife, but I'd be a fool to assume he doesn't still long for the kind of stability that another marriage could provide. I must tread carefully. Still, whatever his intentions, he is always kind, and I have so few friends. I'm pleased to see him.

"What," he says thickly, waiting for me to be seated before pouring us both a glass of the dark red wine already on the table. "No trousers?"

"Not today." I don't have the energy to muster a witty comeback. We order our food and I sip at the wine, but it is bitter and ashy. I almost miss the way things tasted when I was visiting the garden. It was as if food was hollow and I was ravenous, but when I ate—oh, even stale bread was glorious. I know the way I feel tonight is closer to *normal*, so why does it pale so in comparison to the hunger?

"Are you..." Leo leans in when the server has gone, his dark eyes earnest behind his glasses. He's had a haircut since the last time I saw him. How long ago was that? A week? Without the lectures to mark my days I've lost all sense of time.

"I'm fine," I say. It comes out with a caustic edge I don't intend, but I try to soften it. "Honestly. I'm sorry."

Leonardo's gaze indicates he's not so sure. He takes in the new cut of my cheekbones, the jut of my collarbones under the soft silk of my dress.

"I haven't been well," I explain hesitantly. I want, desperately, to tell him everything—about Olea, her kisses and her poisons, about Clara's ring, about the doctor's groundbreaking, impossible work—but...

Leo is my friend. He is kind and caring. I open my mouth and then stop myself. He might be my friend, but he is still a rival scientist and—a man. A vision of Aurelio comes instantly to me, his face, the book, the library. *Fuck*. I can't tell Leo about Olea, can't ask him what he knows without opening up about everything. I will not be vulnerable to a man like that again.

"I think I caught something last week. And then with running the lab, I guess I was exhausted. I'm feeling a lot better now. I just needed to sleep."

"You slept for nearly a week?" Leonardo raises an eyebrow. "I was worried when you missed your classes. Did you need help? Why didn't you send a note? Did you at least see a doctor?" He peppers questions at me as though he can't help himself.

"I saw Florencia—Petaccia." I shrug. "She's a doctor."

"Sure, of academic medicine. She's not a physician." Leo's lips thin.

I've never noticed before, but I see it now clear as day. Leonardo does not like to talk about Dr. Petaccia. He applauds her achievements, but he doesn't respect her. He's just like the others, grousing about her as if she got where she did by accident, not design. Last week I would have been angry, but now...part of me—only a very small part, a tiny speck of doubt at the back of my mind—wonders if the scholars are at least a little bit right. Petaccia is a genius, she *is*, but I know there's a fine line between genius and madness, and her secret research treads it with one foot on either side.

"It's fine," I say, impatience just beneath the surface. I didn't come here to be grilled like some common criminal. Why *did* I come? "I feel much better."

"Are you sure? It's just…you seem different."

Am I different? What I felt in the garden, what I have felt since…Have these feelings changed me? Or have they made me more of who I already was, who I've always been, the very wife Aurelio sought to twist into submission?

"Do I? You said that before."

And then it hits me. I miss Olea, I miss her with such fire it licks at my bones, but I miss the garden too. Not as a person misses their friends, or their loved ones even, during a short separation— no, this is more like the grief after death. I miss them like I would miss breathing, with an ache so sharp it maims. Despite the illness, despite everything I have learned about Olea, I long to be amongst the quiet greenery—to study alongside her. I don't want to be in this crowded dining hall; I don't want to be here justifying myself to Leo.

Olea is toxic to the touch. I wasn't sure, before, how I felt about that—but now I am. It isn't her fault. It can't be. I remember the way she avoided my question when I asked if the catalogue and the tower, her time in the garden, were her choice. *What a question*, she'd said. Well, that wasn't an answer.

Whether the doctor knows or not what sickness has developed in her ward doesn't really matter. *Olea* must know about her condition, understand it a little; that is why she wouldn't let me into the garden at first, why she let our friendship unfold slowly, and at a distance, just as she bade me keep away from the plants until I'd acclimatised to them. It's all about tolerance.

She is lonely. And sad. And resigned. What kind of a life is it? Beholden to science whether she likes it or not? But—I think with a jolt—Petaccia's antidote research could save her. I wonder if this is part of the doctor's plan. Whatever toxins flow in Olea's blood, whatever sickness locks her in her poison paradise, a cure for all— it could fix everything. For her—and for me.

Only then will I know how much of myself, and my feelings for Olea, are real—and how much is the seduction of the garden itself.

I look Leonardo directly in his eyes and fix a gentle but firm smile on my lips. He doesn't know it, and I'm sure he would hate it if he did, but he has helped me to decide.

"I promise, I'm fine," I say. "Now, let's eat before the food gets cold. Tell me about your week, I'm sorry I missed it."

I am going back to the garden. To Olea. I am going to find that cure.

Chapter Twenty-Five

Thora."

There is so much longing in this one word, it seizes my guts and makes my blood pump hot and thick. I am breathless from my walk to the garden, grateful for the moonlight. I'm still not recovered from my fever, my lungs aching and my limbs weak.

"Olea," I say.

She ushers me into the garden, but there is hesitation in her movements, a jerkiness I've not seen before. I try to reach for her, to draw her to my chest; I want the crush of our lips, the heat of her skin on mine. And I know Olea wants the same; I can see it in the tension in her limbs, the tautness of her jaw.

I inhale, the sweet bitter greenness filling my lungs. It smells like home, but then—not quite. There's an acrid tang that follows, settling on my tongue. I've been away too long. I—

Something in my body screams in warning, that old haziness clouding my mind and my vision. I stagger, leaning against the wall for support.

"Are you okay? Thora—Thora, look at me. *Look at me.*"

I see Olea's face through the flutter of my eyelids. She doesn't touch me, but with her as my guide I stumble through the plants and along the dirt paths until we reach the tower. I have never been this close before. It is taller than I thought. I sink down at its base and rest my back against the sun-warmed stone, still baked from the day's heat. My chest heaves and I have to take long, deep breaths to calm my slamming heart.

"You should leave," Olea says, panic lacing her words. "The garden—something's happening. I can't let you—"

"Just. Give me a few minutes," I squeeze out.

Olea sinks into a crouch, knuckles white with tension. Her beautiful face is distorted with worry, but as my breathing finally begins to slow and my dizziness abates, her brow smooths and her dark lips soften. I wipe my lips, the sweat from my brow.

"Better?" she asks softly.

"Yes."

"Good. You…you haven't been to see me for so long. I thought…"

"Olea." I let out a sigh. "Petaccia told me about the antidote you're working on. I've seen her labs. I know everything."

"Oh." Olea hugs her knees to her chest. "So that's why you've been gone. You understand more about me, then." It isn't a question, but I nod anyway. I wipe a hand over my face again and it comes away damp with fresh sweat. I feel as if I have run the length of my father's sepulchre after a mourning, my mouth dry and ashy. "When you didn't come back after…I thought maybe you wouldn't come ever again. I was worried it was because…" Her eyes are locked on my lips and I feel that now-familiar pulse of desire within me. I want nothing more than to touch her, to kiss her. I don't move. "Then I started to think maybe you'd realised— it isn't safe. I warned you. I wanted so badly for you to ignore that warning, and I should have been more forceful."

"I needed time away from the garden." I don't want her to feel guilty but she must understand that none of this is simple.

"You needed to be away from me." Olea rocks back on her heels. "I understand."

"No," I say sharply. Though isn't it true? "Not that. I wasn't well and I didn't really think about how staying away would look after what happened between us. I'm sorry—"

"You were unwell? What happened?" Olea's eyes are huge and dark in the moonlight.

"I'm okay now." I run a hand through my hair and try to explain the thoughts that have been brewing in me. "Being in the garden, being here with you, it made me feel…strange. At first it was very unsettling. Then the garden became a safer place. I used to feel very dizzy and lightheaded and that all stopped—except for when I wasn't here. When I left the garden this time, and was away for longer, I got sick and it's as if my body had to purge… I had a fever. So I had to stay away even longer. I feel a lot better now. But coming back is a lot for my body to process, I think."

Olea's expression is one of abject horror, but I can't tell if it's at the idea that she hurt me or if it's something else. Does she realise that it isn't just the garden and its plants responsible for what happened to me?

"Did you *know* that I would become immune to the worst effects of the garden after a while?" I ask. *And to you, your body, and your touch?* "Is that why you kept me coming back to the wall for so long before you let me in? And why you didn't want me to stay away again after—why you said to come back the next day?"

"No!" Olea blurts immediately. I wonder if she realises that she's lying. Perhaps she believes I will think better of her if all this is an accident. It might not have been consciously calculated, but there's no way I believe Petaccia's ward would take such a risk without care. "It was never my intention for this to happen the way it has. I just…I noticed that you seemed different the longer we spoke, the more you came to the wall. And…I'm so selfish. I wanted so badly for it to be the case that things would get better if you came more, and stayed longer. I wanted you to be my friend and for the garden to welcome you."

"Does Petaccia know?" I press. "About you, I mean. About how the poison flows through you?"

She looks as if I've struck her. Did she think I wouldn't notice? She won't touch me now—because she can't. The air hums between us and yet we can't cross the divide. Despite everything, I want her hands on my skin, in my hair; I want her lips at my neck. But neither of us has any idea how much of my tolerance I've lost by not being here. She is silent for a second, as if she's deciding how much to tell me. I wait patiently but my heartbeat increases with every second.

"Well…" She gnaws on her bottom lip.

"Olea," I insist. "Tell me the truth. No more lies. I don't care if you're trying to save my feelings, there's no sense keeping things from me now—you understand that, don't you? I can't help if you keep me in the dark. Petaccia trusts me, so why can't you?"

"It isn't that simple," Olea moans. She rubs her knuckles against her scalp. "I'm an experiment, aren't I? I look after the plants. I always have. She trusts me like she trusts nobody else, and she has since I was just a baby."

"A baby?" I want to shake her. "Olea, did you ever have *any* choice in this?"

Olea's face is a mask. "Florencia always says she knew that I'd been sent to her so I could help her solve this puzzle, the research she's been working on her whole life," she recites, as if this is the story she has told herself—and been told—forever. "From the moment I arrived at her door, these plants accepted me. They don't sting me when they should; I'm fine when I'm around them. I've never been in any danger from them. Of course Florencia noticed quickly—I was a gift with half the solution to her questions. How can I be alive when everything says I shouldn't be? I'm a monster."

"Oh, Olea." I reach out, nearly grazing her sleeve with my finger, but she yanks her arm out of reach. "You're not a monster."

"No, she's right. I shouldn't exist but I do, so maybe I am the missing link. The way the plants…they treat me like one of their own. And because I can touch and care for them, I can harvest what Florencia needs without anybody else getting hurt. What a boon." Olea smiles but the movement is jerky. "I've been getting sick more as I get older, but that's nothing compared to the possibility of what we could achieve for mankind because of me. And anyway, it's too late now. We can't just stop. And it's not as if there's anybody out there to miss me if I do succumb to the poison."

A hollow forms deep in my chest. I picture Olea, small, fragile Olea, in this beautiful cage. And then I think of the story she told me, of the little bird and the mage and the fox. It is Olea's story—at least in part. If Petaccia is the mage who keeps her in this gilded cage, does that make Clara the fox who lied?

"You can't succumb to it," I whisper. "I would miss you."

Olea melts, finally sinking so she sits firmly on the ground. She crosses her legs, inhaling deeply. Her lips are so dark. My skin crackles with her proximity, but I hide my lips with the collar of my shirt, afraid. I can't deal with that hunger again. I will go insane.

"I wanted to kiss you tonight," she says. "I missed you so very dreadfully. You know, I was alone so often for so, so many years, and it never hurt the way it does knowing I can't touch you—and you're right here with me. Oh, Thora. What are we going to do? I can't live like this any more. Every night it's the same emptiness. Leaves and flowers and moonlight. I'd had enough long before I met you, but you—you've made it wonderful. Without you..." Her dark eyes glitter with unshed tears. "I can't do it."

"We work harder," I say forcefully. "All Petaccia's experiments—they can't be for nothing. It has to work. And my intolerance won't last forever. If I come back into the garden my body will acclimatise again." I'm not sure if this is what I want, if the wretched hunger I experience anytime I'm away from these walls is worth the price for access to what's inside them, but if the alternative is never touching Olea again, I know it's a price I will pay. Even just to be near her is worth the pain.

"Florencia has been working on this research my whole life," Olea argues sadly. "If she was going to make a breakthrough, surely she would have already."

"She said she's come close, though. And now she has me to help. A garden go-between." I give her a reassuring smile.

"Close isn't the same as *there*," Olea says, and she sounds just like Petaccia. "I have provided her with strain after strain, different genera and families. I thought the answer was in the plants, not the carrier."

"Petaccia is convinced it's the carrier."

"I know. But." Olea sighs, blowing her hair off her face. She looks so old when she does it, ancient and wizened and sad. "Either way it's not working and I'm so, so tired."

"Florencia will find a solution," I insist. "She will find a cure, for the world—and for you."

"Maybe." Olea wilts and my heart breaks. "But Florencia doesn't have to live with it like I do. And I honestly don't know how much longer I can."

Every second without touching Olea is agony.

At first the pain is physical. It is like the lash of a thousand whips, my skin so sensitive to sunlight that it opens with the gentlest touch. I'm dizzy and sick in unpredictable waves, always worse during the daylight hours, though it returns with a vengeance if I stay too long in the garden at night. It is a balancing act, razor-sharp pain on either side of the wire.

And then, slowly, as the toxins begin to metabolise in my body and the physical symptoms subside, it is in my heart that I feel the pangs of longing. I am not acclimatising fast enough. I *need* her, and I need her now.

The garden calls to me, sweet whispers on the evening breeze; I spend my days in Petaccia's labs, my lectures long forgotten, stacks of notes and microscope slides, blisters on my fingertips from burning solutions blended to form differing strengths of animal-organ colloid. Petaccia does most of her work in the Tombs in the night hours, when I am poring over the pages and cuttings of Olea's catalogue in the garden by candlelight. The doctor has two current strains on the go, her current focus the reduced, gooey sap from a *Pueraria lobata* kudzu and the fibrous remains of a piglet heart reduced to pulp.

I try to make sure I manage three or four dinners a week with Leonardo, just to keep him happy, but that lasts only about as long as my first antidote attempt. With my first experiment—quickening breath of the rat, heart racing, pupils dilating, followed by immediate cardiac arrest—the dinners and breakfasts slow to a trickle.

Leo doesn't mention the garden or Olea, though I can see the question in his stare. The way he looks at me sometimes, just a little too long—as if he's silently comparing me to Clara again, as if he's monitoring my health, my moods, my hunger. I don't know what I'd say if he asked; if he smelled the garden on me once, he must know I'm visiting again, and he must also see that my interest in my lectures has waned since I'm spending so much time in Petaccia's lab. I'm not sure I could bring myself to lie to him about it.

So I can't talk to him about my research, and I can't talk to him about the garden. There's only so long I can listen to him ramble about Almerto and the drought, or the lectures he's attended on mythology, poetry, philosophy, before I'll snap. How is any of that important when I'm dealing with life and death itself? How long will Leo let me keep pretending that everything is the same as it was before he stops wanting my company?

When I visit Olea's garden, I take fresh care. I wear long sleeves and cover the nape of my neck with a thin headscarf. Gloves, socks, any spare scrap of clothing to cover as much of my skin as I can...It all helps to control the rise of my appetite and the painful rush in my ears. I begin to weigh myself daily, to document my cravings—even the ones that flush my cheeks and coil with tension in my innermost parts.

Although my dinners with Leo often make me question myself, most of the time I am filled with fresh purpose. I wake early, working amongst the animal cages, often falling asleep with my head propped in my hands against the metal workbench. My clothes are stained with blood. I haven't yet discovered why Petaccia has had more success with the offal, whether the type of toxin truly matters. There is a whole world to uncover.

At first I am squeamish with the animals. I don't like to inject them, and Petaccia is right: feeding them medicine is worse. Still, there is no other solution bar experimentation on myself, and that will hardly do. I grow a backbone, start small, administering Petaccia's antidote tests so she can spend more time in the other lab on this floor, a darkroom where she keeps deep-sea and night-crawling specimens. She tells me, for instance, of the blind aquatic salamander—*Proteus anguinus*—which spends its whole life in the darkness of caves in the southeast, living for nine or ten decades. She has already depleted the number she brought back to St. Elianto.

I start calling this other laboratory the Cave. The darkness, so complete Petaccia must navigate the equipment by touch alone, unsettles me more than I'm willing to admit. But even in the Tombs I don't touch the animals more than I have to; I hardly look at them even. It makes it easier to pretend that what I'm doing has no consequence beyond my own success.

Of course, it isn't long before that changes. After the third bloody, gurgling death with Petaccia's Antidote #689, I start to monitor the surviving subjects closely, finding that the birds die easier than the rodents. The rabbits are the worst of all. I push the sickness down in my belly and create a chart, body mass to antidote, time since consumption versus severity of end-of-life indicators.

Then I move to concoctions and experimentations of my own.

I wear gloves, just in case there are still traces of the garden in my skin, but it doesn't help with the guilt. I take deep breaths and think of Olea—and, I won't lie, of the golden acclaim that will be laid at our feet when we succeed. First I try a rat. Then a goldfinch. I finely dice offal and mix it with a paste of crushed leaves and ibogaine from one of Olea's *Tabernanthe iboga*, try cubes of fresh cow meat injected with a saline colloid. I switch tactics, microdosing a red-eyed mouse with pure powdered strychnine. This works better, three weeks of slow sickening, a brief reprieve from the symptoms, then death.

It is thrilling. A doorway of discovery opened. I think of my father, of his constant desire for change, for betterment. Better equipment, better delivery, better results. Like him, I am an angel of death.

Unfortunately, all my experiments end the same way.

Failure. Failure. *Failure.*

When I arrive in the garden tonight Olea is crying. She wears her usual nightgown, and I my armour of cloth. We walk six feet apart in the silence of the balmy night until we reach the fountain—*our* fountain. Olea doesn't speak until we are settled; she sinks down in the exact place where we kissed, and I perch on the stone fountain, my hands and feet and face well away from any of the plants below.

"Talk to me," I urge.

She glances up and her face is a pale oval. There is no moon tonight and the garden is stranger and more beautiful than I have ever seen it. She's never let me in during total darkness before and I can see why. Some of these plants *glow*, a faint blue-green bioluminescence that is barely visible at any other time. She was right that I would have once been afraid. Things are different now; I see it for its truth. The garden is a fairy world, unnatural and terrifying and yet the most natural thing in the world.

Olea does not glow, but the faint plant light catches on her skin, playing in the shadows under her eyes, the dark fullness of her lips. She is ethereal. The tears on her cheeks only exaggerate the effect. If I could, I would smother her with kisses, roll her into my arms and hold her there. I know I can't, not without the same commitment to poisoning myself as before, and oh god, it is agony.

"Florencia had another failure today, with the lizard."

"The salamander?" I haven't seen Petaccia since yesterday morning, when she'd been sunny and cautiously optimistic in her lab notes. My heart sinks into the pit of my stomach. *Another failure.* How long before we accept that the hypothesis is flawed? The thought pinches my throat closed.

"She was so incredibly hopeful this time. She swears there's something in the darkness. It's like..." She gestures at the garden helplessly. "It's like we have all the pieces and just can't put them together. How many times can we twist the same variables and get something close-but-not-quite? At what point do we have to accept that it doesn't work?"

My same thoughts from Olea's lips sound unholy. "It *will* work," I insist. *It has to.* "If the toxins were only ever going to kill, why do the survival times vary so much?"

"Temperament. Health. Physical characteristics. Breeding. Thora, the possibilities are endless. Every time you pick a new subject, how can you guarantee you're not changing something irreversibly by moving from one subject to the next? Nothing is universal."

I turn this over in my mind. Desperation is the rocks in my pockets, dragging me into a murky lake of despair.

"We can't stop now," I say. "Imagine—"

"Don't you understand?" Olea snaps. "I'm so fucking sick

of *imagining*. I can't keep doing this." She jumps to her feet so suddenly I'm thrown off-balance, grazing the back of my leg on the crooked stone of the fountain. Pain shrieks up my leg, even through my trousers.

Olea's lip curls as the blooming metallic scent of my blood tinges the air. We both smell it. I clasp my gloved hands over the scratch, surprisingly deep, and I hold it there until the pain abates and my trousers stick to the skin. I'm standing now, too, frightened to rest against the wall again. Olea is close enough that I could reach out and touch her. God, I want so badly to touch her. It is like the first taste of wine, the opening of a window in spring, full of promise. I grind my teeth.

"We're trying our best."

"It isn't fucking good enough!" Olea slams her hand against the fountain rim, opening a bloody gash of her own between her knuckles. She stares down at the glistening crease in the black skin of her hand before hesitantly licking it. "Don't you understand," she says again, this time quieter, pleading, "how much of my life I have wasted on this? If I'm nothing but a burden, a time pressure, an *affliction* to be cured...what does that say?"

"Olea, please," I beg. "Just a few more weeks. A month. We're close to something, a breakthrough, I—"

"Don't lie to me." She's panting. How have I not noticed how thin she's grown? The circles under her eyes are no trick of the dark; the green-blackness that covers her hands like a pair of gloves has spread beneath the end of her white sleeves. "Don't coddle me, Thora. This is no joke. I'm not just an experiment. I'm a living, breathing, real-life goddamn woman. I'm tired of waiting."

"What are you saying?"

"I'm saying that I will not continue to do this. I will not stay cooped up here, watching the sun from my tower and giving my everything to these plants when I will never see a return. Once upon a time I believed that Florencia could save me, that her science could ignite the world—and I would be free. It's never going to happen. Instead I'll die here, nothing more than a glorified gardener, not even able to touch the woman I..." She stops.

"The woman you what?" I prompt. It isn't gentleness that flows in the static air between us. "Don't act like this is our fault. Making me feel guilty isn't going to get a cure any faster."

Olea's gaze narrows and she licks at the cut on her hand again. The liquid that drips between her fingers looks too thick, more like sap than blood, and it glazes her teeth when she bares them.

"I'm not trying to make you feel guilty."

"Yes, you are. Can't you see? It's what you do—"

"That's not fair!" Olea exclaims. "You're acting like I'm the one making you do this. I'm not. I'm..." Her expression shifts as she realises what she's saying. "I'm..."

"I know you feel trapped," I say gently. "And you're lashing out at me because I feel like the safe choice."

"You're my only choice."

I freeze. Olea's eyes grow wide. I open my mouth to reply, anger already burning bile in my throat.

"That's not what I meant," she blurts.

"What did you mean, then?" I say coldly. "You're right. How could our feelings be mutual when I'm your only friend? Besides, you hardly know me," I say.

"That's the point!" she cries. "I want nothing more than to know you the way you want to know me. Don't doubt me when I say that, Thora. You're...you're the brightest part of every night. But don't you see? I want to know you, but if this carries on I never will. I am trapped here. I will die here. So why not move things along a little and save us both some hurt?"

"Olea," I growl. Panic threatens to engulf me, but it is anger in my voice. "You don't know what you're saying."

"I know exactly what I'm saying. Without a cure, I'm going to do the one thing I possibly can to take some control, Thora. I'm going to end it. And in the nicest possible way, you won't stop me. It's better for you too."

Horror curdles in my stomach as the full realisation of how deadly serious she is settles in. She has spoken before of this option, but I never thought she would need it—now that she has me. I push the hurt from my face as quickly as I can. This isn't about me.

"Just a little more time. The garden needs you—"

"Don't," she says. "The garden doesn't need me any more. The catalogue is a disguise for my real use—as a human guinea pig to test Florencia's potentially winning antidotes. They don't hurt me like they do the rats." She scowls. "We all know that's why I'm still here, why I can never leave the garden. It's got nothing to do with safety. She's protecting her investment."

"Do you really think she wouldn't let you leave?"

"She has *never* let me leave."

Rage shakes within me. I know Petaccia cares about her research above most things, she's made that clear, but above even her ward? The girl she is supposed to look out for? How can this place be *safe* when Olea is so eternally lonely? Does she even understand how unwell Olea is becoming?

"She used to visit me often when I was a child, you know," Olea says sadly. "But then she stopped. And now she's rarely even *here*, travelling the world, doing her work and leaving me behind again and again. Everybody leaves. One day, you will leave me too."

"I'm not Florencia," I argue fiercely. "I know people have treated you badly before, but I know the truth and I'm still here, aren't I?"

Olea goes quiet. She stares at her hands, examining her fingernails. Then she looks at me, and there is so much hopeful love in her eyes that it breaks me. Maybe I started out as an escape for this girl, but that look...You can't convince me she doesn't feel the way I do.

"I hate that I can't see your whole face behind that scarf." Olea closes her eyes and sighs. "I feel so cut off from...everything."

"Then we change that."

"What?" she demands, her wounded hand dropping away from her mouth and leaving tiny specks of blood—a blooming blue-green glow in the leafy fronds.

"Do you trust me?"

Chapter Twenty-Six

The next night after a hasty dinner with Leo I meet Olea at the garden gate. She is dressed in the dark cloak I saw her in the night she buried Clara's ring, a memory that still unsettles me. I brush it aside, along with the wobble of nerves, and gesture for her to follow me. We move silently until we are barely a foot apart, neither of us up to talking. The moon is the barest sliver of white in an otherwise completely dark, cloudless sky. I brought a candle, but in hindsight it's not important. Olea has lived her life in the shadows; she doesn't need candlelight to follow me now.

"Are you sure you want to do this with me?" Olea's voice is low and uneven. I think she's been crying again.

"Yes," I say.

No. The truth is, this is perhaps the stupidest thing I have ever done. My mind has been whirring with it, round and round like a child's pinwheel. Removing Olea from the garden seemed like the only solution when I broached the idea last night. Olea's sickness—that final stage of tolerance where the body stops metabolising for good—must be progressing slower than mine, and being away has helped me to reach some sort of equilibrium. I still don't feel wholly well, but I don't know how much of that is the fact that I can't make myself stay away. And if Olea hasn't been outside this place in years, how do we know that distance won't help?

The other voice in my head, less insistent but just as insidious, is more concerned with Dr. Petaccia. Olea is her ward, her project. From Olea's perspective, her *property*. How exactly is she going to react when we take that away? I feel as if I've made a split-second decision and only now realise the risk I'm taking.

Yet, here I am.

The university has been my dream my whole life—but that was before I met Olea. Whether it is the magic of romance or something less natural, I can't lose her.

"Come on," I insist. "Quickly."

Olea pauses at the threshold to the garden, standing beneath the arched gateway like a shadow. On her face flickers the same indecision that lies within me. Our eyes lock. A rush of warmth fills my chest. My thoughts shift to the book I stole from the library. I have never admitted it to myself, but a romance like theirs—all-consuming, a love between women that is both soft and fierce—is the only other thing I have ever wanted. Aurelio would never have understood. I never thought it was possible. And here it is.

In this second I know we're making the right choice. Fuck the science.

Olea's fear melts, and she tumbles the rest of the way through, her legs unsteady like a newborn foal's. We wait. I look down at the plants beneath Olea's bare feet. Nothing happens. Nothing shrivels and dies; there is no crash of thunder or dramatic bird diving into her path.

A laugh burbles in my chest. Olea joins me. We walk briskly

and then push into a run, Olea's cloak flowing behind her like a dark flag. We reach my assigned rooms breathless and giddy.

"I love being here with you," she says.

We've done it. Whatever happens now, Olea is free.

We sit in my study, separated by the distance of my desk. I've drawn the shutters closed against the rising sun and the lure of the garden and placed steaming mugs of tea before both of us. In a small vase, Olea has placed an already-wilting leaf from her precious stinging tree. "A little garden comfort," she says with a smile. I make a mental note not to touch it but can't bring myself to deny her this.

The air is filled with nervous energy. The skin of Olea's hands looks different in candlelight, the green patina running through the darkness more evident as she spreads her fingers against the grain of the desk. She's already thumbed through my most recent notes, corrected several of my taxonomies, and lectured me on the genus of a thorny bramble I've sketched from memory as a potential future option for the colloid.

I'm uncomfortable in my heavy clothing. Normally I would have stripped it off by now, rolled my sleeves up, and set to my reading or note taking—or my bed, fingers curled and grasping for release. Tonight I've settled inside in all my garden protection bar the mask across my face, though I feel I'm naked without it.

It's worth it. We've spoken more than we ever have before, as if the garden's privacy was that of another world. There we spoke in riddles, flirty and suggestive. Here it is all laid bare, our lives opening up like one of her night-blooming flowers. She's told me tales of how Petaccia used to leave her for three or four days at a time from the age she could successfully wield a knife to cut her own fruit and cheese, how at first she hated it but grew to hate her guardian's intrusions more. I tell her of the sepulchre, the Silence of grief.

"I don't understand it," Olea says. "All this ritual, these rules. Isn't it just a prison of another making?"

"Death is a common human experience," I explain. "People find things less scary if they know how to act, what to feel and when. The death rites help people to process what they feel."

"Do they?" Olea worries at her lips. "I mean, really, do they? Because all I have ever known is sad people beyond the gate. Sad and lonely and alone. Grief follows them like a cloud, and nothing gets the stain out, not things like cutting their hair or burning their herbs. It's what brings them to my garden, isn't it? They're not okay. And I know grief isn't just something you feel when somebody dies, but it's such a universal experience that you would think we would be able to coach each other through it—"

"No, but ritual *does* make people feel like they are a part of something," I argue. I think of all the days my father would come home from the sepulchre stinking of smoke and wine and green incense and how it always felt so...so holy. "Like a community."

"And what about after the ritual is over?" Olea asks. "When the undertaker has gone home and the women return to their families after the days of Silence and the men stomp about in their leather work boots with all that bravado. You tell me either group of them forgets the person they loved? That they don't wish something different had happened?"

"Yes, but—"

"No," Olea says. She is fervent now, waving her hands. "It isn't that simple. You can't put grief into a box and tie it with a ceremonial bow, the same way you can't stop feeling happiness or anger with a blink. It might not be on the surface any more, but it's still there. Isn't it better to admit that and let people feel for as long as they need to? When I die I want anybody who mourns me to feel what they feel for as long as they need to feel it."

"You're right," I say eventually. "But I don't think you have to take away the ritual either. If it brings people comfort, then surely that's a good thing. When my father died I wanted to mourn him in the way I knew both he and I would appreciate."

"What about your husband?" Olea asks. She tilts her head curiously.

"What about him?" I don't want to talk about him. Not here—not with her. It feels wrong, knowing how he would have dismissed this conversation, my choices, my voice. Knowing, too, how disgusted he would have been to see me now, sitting in my rented rooms with a woman I have kissed.

"Did you want to mourn him in the way he made you? You said he wanted you to hold your Silence for thirteen days. Why would anybody do that to somebody they loved?"

I avert my gaze, turning it to the mug of tea cradled in my hands. "It didn't matter what I wanted. *He* wanted—"

"Exactly."

Olea is right. My whole life I've been trained to believe that grief is holy, that serving mourners is an honour. But my father, the holiest man I've ever known, was so disgusted by the idea that his daughter did not want to marry that he found her a husband as his dying wish. If I thought the sepulchre was a tomb, then my marriage was a prison—still of my father's creation. Aurelio's thirteen-day mourning Silence is only a reminder that my husband's detention of me was, deep down, approved by the man I trusted most.

"Either way." I brush it off. "It happened, it's in the past."

"That's my point," Olea says. "Aurelio made you mourn him in the way *he* wanted after he was otherwise dead and gone. So you could argue that ritual is all about guilt, rather than grief."

"Guilt?" I push back from the desk and carry my mug to the sink. It's still half-full, but I refuse to let Olea see my face. "What's guilt got to do with anything? Do you think I *should* feel guilty about the death of my husband? We'd hardly been married five minutes—"

I see the flicker of flames behind my eyelids. Blink.

"I'm not accusing you of anything, Thora." Olea's voice is soft.

She is on her feet now too. I hear the scrape of her chair and the light pad of her bare footsteps as she crosses the room to my side. I hold my breath, not turning. I don't want to talk about this. Aurelio is gone. I should not have to feel guilty for something that wasn't my fault, even if it brought me here. To her.

"I'm not saying you should feel guilty," she murmurs. "I'm saying that he wanted you to. And by following his instructions for how you should grieve—"

"I don't want to talk about it," I cut her off, my back still towards her. "I'm sorry. I know you want to—"

There is a loud crash behind me. I spin, nearly throwing myself off-balance. Olea is on the floor, supine, hair flowing around her head like spilled ink. I rush to her without thinking, instantly grateful I kept on my gloves and then cursing myself for the way they get in the damn way. I hesitate only a second before grabbing her chin, checking her temple for bruising where it's pressed against the floor. Her eyelids flutter and she groans.

"Are you okay?" I say in a rush. "Olea, can you hear me?"

Her skin glistens with a sheen of sweat. I can see the rapid pulse firing in her throat. Her lips have paled to the shade of a healing bruise, the dark circles under her eyes now grey-toned where the rest of her skin is pallid as off milk. I try to shake her shoulder, but she is limp and unresponsive as a doll.

My throat thickens and I feel tears prickle uselessly behind my eyelids. It is too warm in here. Can I open the window? Will the sunlight hurt her? Can I get her to drink? I have to do something. I pull her head into my lap, trying to raise it as gently as possible. I wipe the sweat off her brow and attempt to blow cool air across her face.

"I didn't think this would happen so soon. I hoped it wouldn't happen at all, but you'll be okay," I soothe. "It's your body trying to purge the toxins. Just hold on. It will pass."

It will pass.

It *will* pass.

It doesn't pass.

I manage to get her into my narrow bed, though my lungs burn and I can feel my old dizziness returning the longer I battle with her limbs and the dead weight of her. She comes to briefly, long enough to moan for "Water, please, *water*" but not enough for me to fetch it so she can drink.

I gather a damp cloth, sponging at her skin when the heat of the fever rages and covering her with sheets and blankets when it abates. She is conscious enough to feel pain but these moments are fleeting, her eyes glassy and her skin dull as paper. I remove her nightgown, barely registering the state of her body, bruises blossoming everywhere, some turning yellow already; I can see her ribs.

The second evening I pull back the sheets to bathe her and yelp. The blackness at her hands has spread to her elbows, and at her feet it has seeped up her skin nearly to the knees. It is like a slowly creeping necrosis—and it smells like it in places too. The cut between her knuckles has opened up again and weeps continuously, reopening every time she reaches for a glass or flails in whatever nightmare wracks her body.

"Just a little longer." I can't keep the urgency from my voice. "Just until your fever breaks. Come on, Olea, you can do this."

But the fever doesn't break. It comes in wave after vicious wave; the sweat pouring out of her smells entirely of the garden, that same bitter green perfume. She shivers between punishing waves of heat, her lips cracked and dry and bleeding, the blood nearly black. It stains the bedding, the wooden floor; there are even splatters of it on the walls where she has lashed out with an arm.

At first I do not leave her side, but unlike Olea I need to eat. On the second day I venture out. I avoid Leo in the dining hall, making sure to send a note to his rooms explaining that Petaccia has me working late on a project and that he shouldn't worry, and then I load up on stacks of bread and cheese, hiding napkin bundles in the pockets of my trousers and carrying the rest. I run back to my rooms with my heart pounding in my ears, near convinced that Olea will not still be breathing when I return. She is—thank god, she is—but she appears to fresh eyes like a living corpse, pallid and damp and shrunken.

By the fourth day it is clear that the sickness is not running a natural course. Whereas when I was unwell, that deep, painful sickness and the accompanying dizziness rose and fell, in Olea it is so persistent that when she is awake she can sometimes hardly speak. At first I try to encourage her, desperately urging her on—and then I know that no amount of encouragement will drag her through this.

"Olea," I say, waking her gently with a fresh cup of warm

herbal tea. "It's not working. None of this is working. I think it's time we..."

She rouses, bruised eyelids flickering. She opens her eyes and they are black slits. I can see hardly any whites, no iris, just pupil from lid to lid. For a second I am drunk with panic. She is not herself. I don't know what lurks in the darkness of her smile, but I know it's nothing good.

"*Thoradarling*," she enthuses. It all comes out as one word.

"We've got to try something else," I insist. "Olea, you're—"

"No, no," Olea groans, sounding more like herself. "Don't."

"Olea, you're—" I try again.

"I said *don't*." She grabs for my arm, quick as a snake strike. I drop the mug of tea, warm liquid splashing down my legs, dripping, the porcelain smashed against the wood. She's using her wounded hand. Blood mingles with the tea, drip-dripping. Her fingers curl around my forearm, stronger than I expected, her nails digging through the material of my shirt.

"Okay," I bleat. "I'm sorry."

"Don't say we are done," she hisses. She thrashes, surging forward and then back against the bed so hard that the frame rocks against the wall. She won't let go of my arm. I try to pull away but her grip only tightens. "I can do this. I can do it."

"You don't have to do anything!" I cry. "Come on, please. Let's just agree that this isn't working. We'll go back to the antidotes, we'll—"

"I have to, I do." Olea's voice is a cry of pain, nails on a chalkboard, her throat cording as a wave of agony ripples through her. She clutches at her stomach with her other hand, clawing, scratching at the skin until it is streaked with ragged lines. "Florencia was right. I shouldn't have left."

"No," I say. "We had to try it. She was wrong to leave you there for so long—Olea, please let go. You're hurting me."

"She took me in, she cared for me." Olea's face is slick with oily sweat. "Anybody else would have thrown me in the river. The loneliness, oh, it's a fair price, isn't it? Look, look what I can do."

She squeezes my arm harder, pushing at the sleeve until my bare skin is exposed. I cry out at the pain; it is like needles, like the sting of a nettle a hundred times, all in the same place. I try to pull away again, but Olea grips tighter. I stare at her. The panic ebbs and flows but beneath it is my realisation that she doesn't know what she's doing. This isn't her.

I pull my free arm back and slap her firmly across the face. She shouts, more in shock than pain, I think, instantly dropping my arm. The skin pulses where she held it moments ago, and I have to prop myself against the bed frame so I don't collapse, or throw up directly over her.

"I'm so sorry," she sobs. "This is all my fault."

"It isn't. Don't be silly."

"I knew this would happen." She breaks into full-body cries, her face still contorted in pain. Once I'm steady on my feet, I back away to the chair I dragged in from the study and wilt into it. My arm is tingling, the pain now a numbness that appears to be spreading.

"You knew leaving the garden wouldn't help you to get better," I say quietly. Then I realise something. "You've done it before, haven't you?"

"Once," Olea admits through her tears, wincing as she shifts onto her side. "I'm...that was a long time ago. I thought things would be different this time. I've spent all these hours with you and you weren't that sick. I thought that maybe things had changed."

"You should have told me what happened last time."

"This is punishment." Olea sniffs, then tenses as another cramp tears through her. She curls into a ball and holds herself tight, dark hair sticking to her forehead, the sheets damp with her sweat.

"You don't deserve this."

"Oh, but I do." Olea's eyes are normal again now, their usual brown-green, infinitely sad. "I'm not like you, Thora. I should never have been born. I killed my mother, you know. Probably my father too. It's how I ended up with Florencia. She always told me I should stay in the garden, that I shouldn't have friends, because of what I did when I was young. And she's—she's right." She breaks into another bout of sobbing.

Slowly I begin to understand. When Olea said that she was born this way, she didn't mean she was born with an affinity for the plants. She meant she was born with poison in her veins. And it has killed before.

Part of me wants to reach for her, to stroke her back in comfort. Another part of me flinches away at the pain she has caused. Instead I do neither, sitting stock-still on my chair and waiting.

"It's not just your parents, is it?" I prompt when she has calmed herself.

"No."

"You've hurt others."

She blinks salty tears, rubbing at her eyes with one inky green hand. "My friends beyond the gate," she whispers. "I never wanted to hurt them. You understand that, don't you? I never wanted any of this. I just wanted...I was so fucking *lonely*."

"Clara." The realisation hits me, and I'm stunned at the depth of the horror I feel. "She's dead. You *killed* her. That's why you won't talk about her. All this time I thought you were guilty because—because you loved her. Because she tricked you. But the guilt goes deeper than that, doesn't it."

Olea doesn't look away. She doesn't even try to hide it. Her bottom lip quivers and fresh tears roll free; this time she doesn't wipe them away. Leo was right to warn me about her, I realise. Does he suspect the truth about Clara? About Olea?

"I didn't mean to," she whispers. "But yes. I let her in too soon. The garden...I told you. It doesn't take kindly to strangers. You need to earn its *tru-ust*." She curls tighter in pain. "I deserve to be punished. I deserve to be lonely. God, this pain...It must be what they felt when *the-ey*..." Her eyes roll back and then she squeezes them shut.

I stay where I am. I hardly move at all.

"I deserve this," Olea cries weakly. "And when I die that will be the retribution for what I have done, to my friends, to my parents. Florencia was right. I should never have wanted more. I should have stayed in the garden forever."

Chapter Twenty-Seven

Once upon a time there was a little girl who lived in a tower in the middle of a poison garden. Every day she waited for the good doctor who had rescued her from her cruel and unusual fate to visit—and every day the sun rose without her. It had not always been this way. When the girl was a baby, she knew the doctor had mothered her as well as she could, feeding her cow's milk from a spoon and teaching her to damp her lips with tart apple paste. Always at arm's length, with gloves or a shawl, but the doctor did her best.

The child who was once a baby nobody could love grew to become a girl who did not even love herself. She doesn't remember the comfort of the sun, a warmth without prickly rashes all over her tender skin or boils and blisters erupting in the places her clothes didn't reach, though the doctor says she did once feel its heat on her face and rejoice. She doesn't remember what it felt like not to be hungry, the worm—she likes to think of it as a worm, not her own feral self—in her belly never satisfied. These days she eats out of necessity, not because it fills her but because if she doesn't she will eventually go mad.

The girl in the garden doesn't have friends; she has flowers and trees and poisonous blooms. She can't remember a life before the garden and its savage beauty, and most days she doesn't want to. The plants are hers; they are her friends, her confidants. Unlike the doctor, they never leave her. From the first light of the moon the girl tends her garden, chosen—no, *blessed*—by its trust, and giving faith in return. It delivers fruits to her on the days the doctor does not come, the soil damp with the water she has carried in calloused hands making the plants grow big and strong.

The garden is her slice of paradise, an Eden untouched by the rest of the world, and she likes it that way. Until, that is, the day the first stranger comes. The first of three friends beyond the gate, each of them a fox in disguise. The first, Pietro, is a student of law. His father was a botanist, and the garden, its locked gate a deterrent to most, is of great interest. Of course, the girl inside becomes his next-best interest when he finds the gates locked. He lavishes her with gifts, sweet treats from the bakery, bulbs and seeds of the non-poison variety, which she sows, and which subsequently fail to grow.

Pietro tells her stories of his travels around the country, and wider—to the mountains of the northeast and the world across the ocean; he laughs when she doesn't know what horses or dogs are but is sombre when she tells him of the rabbits that sometimes stray into the garden; she often cooks them. She leaves out the part where they die, twisted and foaming at the mouth or with eyes glassy and black as coal, but Pietro senses there is more to these tales.

He is a beautiful man, big and broad with rippling muscles he likes to display under overly tight white shirts. His legs are great boulders, stacked in khaki and navy slacks. The girl, barely seventeen, has never met a man before and she assumes that this is what all men are like: big and loud, charming and coy. When she looks at him she feels nothing but curiosity—but her books have taught her only that curiosity is like a window that will always remain open until it is firmly closed up tight.

The doctor warns her that people will take advantage of her beauty, that they will want to take the garden—and her gifts, or her curse—for themselves. The girl doesn't understand why anybody would want to steal what she would willingly give away, but fear keeps her in the doctor's pocket. She does not like to hurt, or maim, or kill, but it is all she knows.

Pietro asks her every day about the garden and its locked gate. At first she tells wild tales hoping to scare him away, and later she tells an approximation of the truth, which is wilder than any story she could concoct, and only seems to make him want her more. In his eyes she is tragic, untouched, and vulnerable, her curse a romantic challenge to overcome. *Is this what it feels like?* she wonders. *To be desired?* She, who has never had friends, who has never known anything but these greying walls and her books inside the tower, likes the way it makes her feel.

When Pietro asks her if he can enter her garden, the girl always says no, but his promises get grander with the passing days. He will break her free of her tower prison and carry her to Romeras himself so she can be seen by the finest physicians in the land; he will burn the garden for her, if only she would take his hand. In the end he wears her down, day after day, gift after gift, question after question. Perhaps, she reasons, the doctor has no real reason to be cautious, and her curse extends only to the rabbits and bees and occasional small bird. She has never harmed her plants, after all.

Pietro is in the garden barely an hour before he becomes worth less to her than even a single one of his gifts. In the meadow beyond the trees he shows his true nature, not a strong, brave hero, a fighter of curses, but a brute. *Just a kiss*, he sneers. *A repayment for all of my gifts.* He chases the girl into the safety of her angel's trumpet and its giant white bell-shaped flowers, bruises already forming on her arms from the strength of his hands. It takes less than a minute for him to collapse, and it turns out it isn't just the rabbits, the bees, or the occasional small bird; whether the garden or her curse, something has saved her.

She buries him beneath the oleander.

It is two years before she meets her next friend, a quiet scholar by the name of Michele. He has no family history of botany or science. He is a poet, gentle and dreamy. He finds her garden in the hour before dawn after crying over the death of his late grandmother—late, because she died five years before Michele was born.

The girl does not like Michele. He is too soft and too gentle. Everything makes him sad. At first she tolerates his company because it is better than the silent moonlight, the endless lonely nights tending to her flowers. She teaches him the poetry of the ancients, which she knows a little by heart, and in return he reads sections of his latest works to her aloud as they wander along the walls.

Soon the girl grows tired of the poet. Unfortunately, the poet does not grow tired of her. He is weak and frail with the scents of the garden, and he, like Pietro, begs to come inside. This time she does not tell tales, either wild or truthful, but it's clear that Michele wouldn't listen if she did. He likes to tell his own stories, the act of committing them to speech the same in his mind as the creation of truth. He believes, in turn, that the garden will balance his humours; its poison leaves will cure his melancholia; if it were to kill him, he would become a martyr after death and his poems would be published far and wide.

The girl does not intend to let Michele inside. In fact, she stops going to the gate altogether, worried for his sanity—and his life. Michele, however, does not take this rejection well. One day, while the girl is sleeping, he scales the garden wall, finding a precious gap in the broken spikes atop it and dropping to his knees beneath a canopy of trees. By the time she finds his body beneath the arching flowers of the golden rain laburnum, his skin dusted with fine yellow powder, it is too late.

She buries him with his book of poems, all twee or bawdy or downright embarrassing; they are his alone in death. She is not sad, or at least only for herself. He never belonged here anyway.

The girl doesn't tell the doctor about the poet—she does not tell her much of anything these days—but she suspects that somehow she knows about his death. The girl does not argue when, two weeks later, the gap in the wall's spikes disappears overnight, fresh grey metal glinting like a warning.

The third time the girl makes a friend, everything is different—and, somehow, nothing is. This time it is not a weedy man at the gate, or a brute, but another girl like her. She comes to the gate in the early hours of night, smoking cigarillos and pacing a rut in the grass out front. She talks aloud to herself, mostly nonsense, but the girl likes the sweet cadence of her voice.

For many nights, our garden girl does nothing but watch. This other woman is everything she dreams of being: chic in narrow, ankle-length skirts and shirts that ruffle at the sleeves and collars, and she wears her hair in a bob, cut severely at the chin. The nights go by and this new stranger visits the garden most evenings after dusk, talking and smoking and staring at the sky, as if this is her own private chapel. It isn't long before the girl cannot resist making herself known, not least because she worries if she doesn't, then more strangers will eventually come.

The other woman's name is Clara. She is married to one of the scholars, but she speaks of him little. When she was alone, she was always wound as tightly as a spring, but when the two of them talk she is soft and gentle, asking questions but not minding if the girl doesn't, or cannot, answer. She knows a little of flowers and loves to learn. She tells stories of her childhood, in a town not so far away, where the homes all have front gardens overflowing with colourful blooms and children run in the grassy meadows after school. She misses the town and hates the university—that much is clear.

At first, the girl doesn't notice the feeling. It grows beneath her breastbone like a seed, and without realising she feeds it a steady diet of sunlight and water. As the seed sprouts its tiny leaves, she begins to see what is happening, though she doesn't understand it. Clara doesn't ask to come inside the garden, not like the others, but she is always there at the gate when the night falls, and soon the girl is counting the hours until she arrives. This time it is *she* who invites the stranger inside, revelling in the warmth of Clara's sun, taking every offered moment, every gift, and basking in them all.

It hurts, a knife right to the belly, that she cannot trust her body, her skin; she is cautious not to touch Clara in case she might share the fate of the rabbits and birds, and of Pietro buried under the oleander. She hides behind trees, whispering to her plants. *Just make her like me*, she begs. *Please. If you trust her as you do me, make her as baneful as I am.*

If Clara notices the girl's reluctance to touch, the way she appears like a ghost and is untouchable in the same way, always out of reach, she doesn't say. She thrives on the giddy, stolen romance, the casual brushes with danger a drug, and the girl... she laps it up like cream.

Until, one day, the fairy tale ends. Clara—stupid, greedy, *hungry* Clara—wants more than her husband, the university, and the girl can give. This ghostly romance—is it even that?—is not enough; she wants riches and freedom too. One or two carefully chosen specimens could set her up for a lifetime, but she makes plans to take *five* of the precious seedlings the girl has cross-cultivated. The girl notices the change, the withdrawal a kick to her already fragile heart. She is suspicious but not sure why.

Clara is not as careful as she thinks she is. She might keep her plans from the girl, withdrawing from the garden's poison influence, but the garden can read her intentions like a book. The girl doesn't want to believe it, the way the plants seem to turn on her beautiful friend. At first she thinks Clara's new sickness is natural, born of disease or overworking. She coughs and splutters her way through her cigarillos, many nights arriving with the stench of vomit on her breath. The girl tries to tell herself that these things, romances and the like, take time, that perhaps the garden is only a little jealous, but it *will* see: Clara is good for her, and that will be good for it.

The longer the sickness progresses, the harder it is to deny: Clara is plotting, and the garden is withdrawing its trust. The girl's feelings sputter and die like a candle flame drowned in wax. Did Clara never care for her at all?

The next night, when Clara visits the garden, the girl is ready to administer an experiment. Although she is a daughter, and an orphan, of science, this is the first thesis of her own suggestion.

She will settle for truth but prays for honesty. If the girl feels any guilt at the prospect of this test, she buries it deep, deeper than the empty hole beneath her breastbone where the seed of hope once grew. It is simple: if Clara's intentions are pure, then she will endure no ill effects from their touch, and the girl can proceed with their romance with caution. If not... Well. It wouldn't be an experiment if she could guarantee the outcome.

In the end, the garden is right. Clara lies, denying her plans without a blink of guilt. But the girl, and the garden, have prepared for this, and neither will let Clara leave without repayment in kind for her dishonesty. All it takes is a single kiss on the mouth. And oh, the kiss is *everything* the girl hoped such a thing might be. And then Clara's throat closes as the guilty confession pours from her poisoned lips.

The garden, and the doctor, were right all along. And now the girl is alone once more.

PART TWO:

POWER

I took my Power in my Hand—

And went against the World—

'Twas not so much as David—had—

But I—was twice as bold—

—EMILY DICKINSON, 540

Chapter Twenty-Eight

I watch Olea sleep. It is not a peaceful sleep, not smooth skin and gently fluttering eyelashes like in the old ballads. No, Olea's is the sleep of the damned. She tosses and turns, waking in agony and then crashing back into the land of nightmares once more. When she wakes properly next, I'm not even sure she will remember our last conversation—but it is not one I will ever be able to forget.

Olea killed Leonardo's wife.

She might not have meant to, but she did. I do not know what to do with this information. Should I go to him right now? Should I tell him what I know? Is it what he already suspects? Is *that* the true reason behind his warnings? I don't have the words for how I would explain it if not. The garden, the poison, the danger in the girl's touch, it all sounds like some kind of tale of terrors. I can't work out if he should *ever* know the truth if he doesn't suspect already. What good would it do? And more: What harm?

Clara meant something to Olea, that much is clear. Did they have the same something between them as Olea and I? This is a thought that makes me sick, a roiling squirmy jealousy. And how would I tell Leo that his wife was...*with* another woman? One she could not even touch. How would this have hurt him, when it's so clear he was committed to Clara despite his own confused feelings? He loved her—maybe not in the way a husband loves a wife, but in the way that matters.

I think of Aurelio's face in the library the last time we spoke before he died. The anger, the barely disguised disgust. I'm not sure if Leo understands how he feels even now. What if I tell him outright, and that's the way he looks at me, with that same disgust? Is it better than the not knowing? I curl inwards, pulling my knees to my chest, feeling the scab stretch on the back of my leg and the skin of my arm stinging like a healing burn.

I sit on the chair by Olea's bedside, too frightened to leave but too frozen to do much more than watch as she writhes in this torture of her own making. There are many more questions and I turn them over and over in my mind. Olea was born this way, so what caused her affinity for the garden? Is it simply because they have grown together that they are now tied so closely? Perhaps without the plants and the isolation she would have weakened and succumbed to the toxins in her blood as a youngster. Perhaps, then, Petaccia's insistence on her lonely existence is half the reason she is even alive now.

I wonder if she will die. She looks very much like she might. Her skin is paler, if possible, except for her cheeks, which blaze pinkish red. Her eyes are sunken, her breathing laboured. *Olea wants to die,* I think. *That's why she was asking about grief. Why she talked about ending it all.* Maybe that was always her intent in coming here with me. I allow myself a few tears, but still I remain and watch. What would happen if she were to die? Would Petaccia's research halt?

How would I feel?

Night comes and I finally move from my vigil by Olea's bedside to open the shutters in both the bedroom and the study. I gaze down across the garden, breathing the cooler air. Then I notice the difference. Where before the garden was wild but artfully cultivated, now it appears in the shadows like a jungle untamed. The weeds have grown leggy, taking over everything in their path; the black flowers I have often admired are wilting, their blooms drooping, petals scattered like wedding favours.

This, more than anything else, is what decides it for me.

"Olea," I say.

She peels her eyes open blearily, coughing. It is a wet, rattling sound.

"Can you walk?"

She murmurs something unintelligible but does her best to prop herself up on her elbows. Pain lances across her face. I feel a twinge of guilt but I double down, helping her sit upright and then beginning to dress her. I breathe through my mouth, avoiding the bitter garden scent the best I can; still, being this close to her makes me dizzy.

"Leave me alone," Olea mumbles. She tries to fight me off but there's no malice in it, and it is only moments before she relents and allows me to dress her like a child. "Let me die. Please, Thora."

"No," I say firmly. "I'm taking you back to the garden."

It costs us the better part of the night. The sun is beginning its pearly ascent by the time we reach the garden gate. Olea is near crawling, though I do my best to carry her weight where I can. She hasn't stopped crying since we left my rooms, though whether she is mourning for the future neither of us will have or because she knows I will not let her suffering end, I'm not sure.

She doesn't speak at all, the walk too tiring and taking all her energy. It takes all of mine too. Every second I'm this close to Olea I can feel my body's resistance weakening. Already I am hungry, so hungry I could eat three meals in one and still need more. And the sickness, oh, that intense, ravenous sickness. I want to tear with my teeth, bread or cheese or great bloody steaks—anything that might fill me up.

I won't let it stop us. The alternative is Olea's death—and, no matter what she has done, I simply can't let her die. I can't allow *my* inaction to be the reason for her death. She has lied to me from the moment we met, about her health and the garden and *Clara*, and still... Still I feel the thunder of my heart when she is near and I want nothing more than to wrap her in blankets, put her into the safety of her bed, kiss her and soothe her and *save her*.

And, whispers part of me. *Perhaps she does not deserve death.* The mercy of it, the finality. She is as much involved in all this as Petaccia is, as I now am. This experiment has become a monstrous thing, if it wasn't one from the start. We all have to play our role.

We reach Olea's tower as the sun crests the treetops. The garden is a mess. It has been barely a week and so much of Olea's hard work has been undone. The philodendron are ragged and weak; the coyotillo next to them are bulging with black fruits. I fight the urge to grab handfuls as we pass and smash them into my mouth, knowing what will happen if I do but longing for the taste anyway.

"In here?" I ask urgently, pushing at the door of the tower. I have never paid attention before, but it is old and wooden, though it doesn't creak as I push it open. Together we stumble across the threshold, past a stairwell that goes down into the basement and into a room that is filled with *things*. Books and pamphlets, figurines of ballerinas and mythical beasts made from pottery and plaster, and tapestries of scenes from the ballads—I instantly recognise Pollenides and Marta, the wounded couple in golden armour dragging each other off their battlefield at Clyde, the great dragon slain and bloody swords at their feet.

Olea is barely conscious. There is a work desk on the far side of this room, and a chaise by the window. I half carry her to it, letting her body fall unceremoniously, then I light a candle and slam the shutters tight, drawing the room in pure darkness. Olea lets out a sigh that might be relief, or perhaps simply more pain, her head lolling.

I carry the candle around the room, dancing between shadows, studying the collection of trinkets and tapestries. This is a life's work. The art is accomplished but a little messy—self-taught, no doubt. The tapestries range in size, but I notice one thing immediately: the smaller ones are all of plants. I spot *Atropa belladonna*, nightshade, with its black berries and purplish tubular flowers, and the clusters of starry flowers of the death camas—I don't recall their true name. There is a piece about the size of my torso featuring the stinging tree, *Dendrocnide moroides*, its large leaves and reddish berries drawn in the muted shades of moonlight. All the plants she has captured, every one, are caught in these same muted shades, silvers and greys, seen through the eyes of a woman who has barely seen them by light.

The larger tapestries are all from poems, ballads, old plays by the ancients. These stories Olea has cast in grand swathes of colour, reds and golds, orange and chartreuse, every scene highlighted in the unrelenting brightness of a midday sun. The effect is gaudy, near offensive, the whole tower room a rainbow cacophony thanks to its walls.

It hits me, all at once. The reality of Olea's existence.

I turn and stare at her, watching the steadying rise and fall of her chest, the sweat drying on her brow. This is a cage. A *prison*. She truly is just another one of Petaccia's little pets, waiting for her antidotes, for her chance at a free life. This is what it felt like when I was in Aurelio's home, the walls adorned with high-class art, statues, and scent diffusers. Gold-leaf everything. A library, an army of cooks and maids and valets. More human comforts than I had ever known. And yet...

Olea opens her eyes, sees me in her tower room, and her expression is one of open love. She throws her arm towards me, half beckoning, half begging. She pats the chaise, then her knee.

"Stay," she whispers. "Will you stay with me?"

I freeze. I fought my whole life to escape my cage, and now Olea wants me to share hers.

"I can't," I say. "I'm not—"

"You're already here," she says sleepily. "The garden welcomes you back. It needs you. You can help me, while I recover..."

I can't fight the shaking fear that grows in me like a seed, shoots of panic unfurling. *Stay*, whispers one part of my mind. *You liked it here, when this place was yours too. This cage is not a cage like Aurelio's. It is books and learning and knowledge—and Olea.* But if I stay, I can't continue my research. I'd be choosing the garden over Petaccia's life's work—a chance for it to become *my* life's work—and Olea's potential cure. And how do I know I won't get so sick that the garden takes me to death's door and beyond? *But. Olea.*

A golden cage, perhaps, but it is *still* a cage.

"No," I say. The word comes out cold and unfeeling, and Olea blinks, suddenly alert. "I'll stay until supper but not beyond that."

"Please," she begs. "I can't bear it if you leave."

I hesitate. The old Thora would have done as she was asked. She would succumb to Olea's begging, glad for scraps of love. Stay, wrapped in the safety of this barbed paradise. It was how I ended up in Aurelio's home, as his wife. I think of the way Olea said *You're my only choice.* Maybe she loves me—I'm sure she does—but I will not be caged.

I am not that woman any more.

"No," I say firmly. "I'm sorry, but I won't."

Chapter Twenty-Nine

I wait to head to the dining hall until fifteen minutes before it closes. My plan is to load my pockets and my napkin with food again, to keep enough stocked up that I can avoid it, and Leo's company, until I'm ready to face him. It doesn't work out quite that way.

The scent of fried onions and juicy steak makes my mouth water fiercely; I fight with one of the servers to get seated so late and manage to eat my way through two steaks in less than five minutes. I wash it all down with near enough a whole bottle of syrupy red wine, relishing the prickling sensation as my limbs begin to relax. I should keep a clear head, I *should*, but…why? I'm not going back to the garden tonight, and the dark emptiness of my rooms, suddenly silent after Olea's departure, fills me with dread.

When I stumble back out into the night with my napkins loaded with more bread and cheese, I am lightheaded, woozy. The air is as syrupy as the wine and swirls around me. I am queasy, and I am exhausted, and I am still so goddamn *hungry*. I've been with Olea too much, in the garden for too many hours. I should never have taken my mask off, I should have taken her back sooner, I—

"Thora...?"

I slam to a stop as I collide with something—no, someone. Blearily I peer up and—

"Oh, for god's sake," I mutter under my breath. Then I try to at least pretend I'm pleased to see him. "Leo. Hi."

"Are you all right? What are you doing out here so late? I thought you were working, but—are you *drunk*?" Leo peers at me from behind his spectacles; they reflect the lamplight in streaks of yellow and the effect is disconcerting. I can't quite see his eyes, though I can tell from the shape of his mouth that he is frowning. I step back, clutching my bundle of food to my chest.

"I'm fine, thank you," I say, slurring slightly. Leo says nothing, shifting from one foot to the other, glancing this way and that. "Let's talk tomorrow," I add. "It's l—"

"No." Leo snatches for my elbow. I let out a surprised hiss and he yanks his hand back. "I'm sorry, sorry. I just— Can we talk? Please? You're avoiding me again."

I hesitate, but Leo takes another small step back into the shadow of the dining hall. A gesture of trust. Of apology. I feel myself melt. Outside the glare of the lamp I can see better, see the concern etched into Leo's forehead, the lines around his mouth.

I haven't seen him since Olea's admission, and now all I can think of is Clara, buried in the garden's loamy earth. Leo doesn't know. He doesn't know. He—

"I've hardly seen you," he says, interrupting my spiralling thoughts. "I know you said you were busy with Petaccia. But..."

"But...?"

He leans in, his voice low. "Does she have something on you? Is that why you keep sneaking off there?"

My heart skips, blood roaring in my ears. "Excuse me? Who?"

"Petaccia's ward," he says, urgent now. "Does she have some hold on you, something worth throwing it all away? Are you in some kind of trouble? Because whatever it is, I can help."

"Leo, I don't know what you're talking about," I lie. My voice comes out shaky and uneven.

"Come off it, Thora. I might be naive but I wasn't born yesterday. You say you're working late in the lab, but twice I've been by La Vita this last week and it's still and silent as a sepulchre. Have you been going back to the garden?"

"Were you *spying* on me?" I say incredulously. "Leo, Petaccia has me in the lab all different hours. I'm working on really important hypotheses. Groundbreaking ones. It's science that could change everything. What's it to you how I spend my time?"

"But have you been seeing Olea?" Leo presses.

"What does it matter if I have?" I snap. "I don't need you constantly looking out for me. I'm a grown woman and I can make my own choices. I'm *fine*." I hate lying to him. He deserves to know the truth about Olea and her sickness and the failed antidotes and Clara—but I can't risk Petaccia's research, or Olea's safety. And I can't tell him the truth about Clara without explaining everything else, and I won't do that. I *can't*. Not now. It's too risky.

Instead I summon all my anger, at Olea and Petaccia and the failed antidotes and the poisons, let it fill me right to the brim, and then I roll my shoulders back and direct it at him. "I don't understand. You didn't *want* your wife, and you don't *want* me, so why are you being so goddamn jealous?"

"I'm not jealous," Leo argues. "I have a dreadful, *dreadful* feeling and you won't listen to me. I've tried to ignore it to keep the peace, but I can't keep pretending everything is fine. Maybe I'm wrong, maybe it's nothing to do with Olea and that damned garden, but look at you. You're exhausted. You've lost weight. You're never in class…I know you're besotted with her, and that you think you're the first person ever to feel this way, but you aren't. You came to St. Ellie to learn, not to become Petaccia's lackey and Olea's little garden pet. This is why I didn't want you going near that place. Olea's doing to you exactly what she did to Clara. She's corrupting you."

"Corrupting me?" I say, genuine disgust seeping into my tone. "Is that what you think my private feelings are? *Corruption?*"

Leo glances over my shoulder, furtive and afraid.

"Is that what you think happened to Clara? Don't be dim, Leo. You and I both know the way we feel isn't a choice. And whatever Clara felt, you said it yourself: she had one foot out the door long before she met Olea. Olea did not corrupt your wife; Clara was just as guilty." It's the closest I can come to telling him the truth. *Please*, I urge silently. *Please understand.*

"You're wrong," Leo insists. "Clara wasn't like that before she met Olea. She got in Clara's head, made her think differently."

"About what?" I demand angrily. "About sex?"

"Please, keep your voice down," Leo hisses. He makes to grab my arm again, to pull me farther out of the light, but I dodge his grasp.

"How do you know what Clara thought?" I go on. I hide behind my righteous anger although I'm making myself sick. This isn't how this conversation should go. Whatever Leo's thoughts about himself and his own feelings, he deserves gentleness to unpick them. He's only trying to help me—but he can't. I won't let him. So I push on. "Did you tell her how you felt? Did you give her the opportunity to understand?"

"No, but—"

I need him to walk away—far, far away from Olea and the garden and all this poison. But he won't. Not unless I make him. The thought is swift and brutal, and I know what I have to say. *Forgive me*, I think. "You know what? You're so damn insistent that I need to watch out for Olea, that she will hurt me, but what about *you*? Did you ever stop to consider if you're the one hurting people?"

Leo looks as if I've smacked him. His expression is a knife directly through my flesh, but I can't stop now. So what if he hates me? At least he will never have to know the truth. At least he'll be safe from the garden's clutches.

"You couldn't give Clara what she wanted and you still can't admit to yourself why. You kept her trapped and Olea offered her an escape. Can you really blame her for taking it? You're a coward, Leo. A controlling, frightened little boy. You drove your wife away and now you're driving me away too."

Leo is silent. It is a silence so loud it muffles the hot pump of blood in my veins, the screaming in my ears, the despair in my very soul. The worst part is, he doesn't argue.

"What the fuck did you think you were doing?" Petaccia demands. We are in the top laboratory in La Vita the next day, and I'm sick and tired and sweating profusely in the sunlit room. "Have you any idea the damage you could have caused? Oh, I knew you might be trouble, Thora, but I didn't think you'd do anything so *stupid*."

"With all due respect, ma'am, Olea is slowly wasting away. If I hadn't intervened she'd have found another way out—"

"Not just her," Petaccia seethes. "The fucking *garden*. Those plants are a lifetime of care and cultivation. How could you think you'd just throw that away—for what?"

"For your adopted daughter."

"I. Am. No. Mother." Petaccia's face is the blotchy red of a wilting rose. "How many times must I say it? Would you call me such if I'd never told you about Niccolò? Would you do it if I was a man?"

"Does it matter whether you're her mother? It's semantics," I spit. "Olea is in your care. She's out there right now rotting from the limbs up. Her body is shutting down, and then where will you be?"

Petaccia stills, her dark eyes flashing. "That is her choice," she says coldly. "Don't you think I warned her about all of this?"

"It wasn't just leaving the garden that caused it," I argue. "Her skin has been going bad since I first met her. Her hands—"

"You foolish girl," Petaccia snarls. She flies the short distance between us and soon she is towering over me. I do my best not to flinch, not to back away, but there is a feral rage in the doctor's face that is barely concealed. "You have such a hero complex you haven't stopped to think that maybe you're the cause in the first place."

"I...what?" Freezing water down my back. I shiver.

"Didn't she tell you the reason she isn't allowed visitors?"

"She lets them in too soon," I say, puffing out my chest. There are no lies between us, not any more. "And they die. It's a tragedy but that's not exactly my fault."

"No." Petaccia laughs. "Not just that. Those deaths were a tragedy, and they left their mark on Olea, I'm sure. But it wasn't the intruders I was worried about."

"You...you mean—letting people in is what's causing her

to…?" I can't say it. A warning rumble of sickness twists up my throat and I swallow fiercely.

"To wilt? Yes. I've always suspected it might happen," Petaccia says, "but so far the bouts of sickness have been few and far between, definitely not as pronounced as these days with you. I suppose nobody else ever spent so much time with her." She shrugs. "I started to suspect you might have something to do with what was happening. A symbiosis of sorts. It's a long way from a provable hypothesis, of course, but you're not a dimwit, Thora, surely you can understand. The garden has a strange hold over her. It doesn't want her to leave. You're a threat to that—and therefore a threat to it."

I falter. I came here to demand answers from the doctor about Olea's future, about the antidotes. I wanted to know if what Olea said about her friends beyond the gate and their deaths was true. I feel as if I'm drowning and can't find the surface. Nobody speaks plainly in this damnable place and I'm so tired of it.

"I won't visit her any more, then," I swear.

It isn't planned. In fact, as the words leave my lips I regret them, a screaming panic filling their void. Yet, I also know that I'm speaking the truth.

"I won't go there again if it hurts her. I don't care about the research if it's putting her life at risk. I didn't sign up for any of this, Doctor. I can't stand by and watch as innocent lives are lost in this pursuit."

"No…?" Petaccia's expression has gone coy. "You wouldn't risk one life to save millions?"

"It isn't working!" I shout. "For god's sake, can't you see that? What good is any of this doing? We've nothing but failure to show—"

"Ah." Petaccia raises a finger and waggles it, cutting me off. "Now, this is where, for once, failure isn't failure."

"What do you mean?" I drop my hands to my sides, tiredness snaking through me. Just that small outburst has exhausted me, and I long, absurdly, for the peace of the garden.

"Olea's illness isn't so black and white, I don't think. I've been watching her—and you. Yes, I know. I'm a vengeful old crone who deserves everything she gets." She rolls her eyes. "But I have a theory."

I shake my head, refusal making my whole body rigid. *She's mad*, I think. And the fresh truth of the thought shocks me. *This is utter insanity.* Petaccia cares more about the possibility of this achievement than she does Olea—or me, or herself, or anyone. Even if she succeeds, when the truth of her discovery comes to light—when the academy hear of her methods, her behaviour, her *callousness*—will this pain and sacrifice be worth it? Before I would have said yes in less than a second, but today it is Olea's face I see, contorted in agony, her body twisting in my bed, and I'm no longer so sure.

"I don't care about theories," I say sharply. "I won't continue to hurt her—"

"I think there is a different conversation we should be having here." Petaccia rolls her shoulders, rising to her full height. It's only now I realise how much bigger than me she is, how strong. I've no doubt she could crush me if she chose to. "My theory is that Olea's relationship with you has the potential to unlock another core level of understanding in how toxins in the body function as part of our system. It's clear, thanks to you, that removing Olea from the garden is *not* the way forward. And it was beginning to show that your presence in the garden had its own impact. The important thing is I need to develop greater understanding of why Olea's sickness has progressed in this way when otherwise she is more hopeful, dedicated, and happier than she has ever been since you arrived."

"You talk about her as if she's not even human," I seethe. "You can't make me be involved in any of this. If my presence is a danger to Olea, then I refuse to go into the garden again. Isn't that my right? It doesn't matter if you make me leave the university."

"No," Petaccia says simply. "That's not acceptable."

"How many times do I have to say I won't be involved in this?" I growl.

Petaccia is as quick as she is strong; her hands dart out and she grabs a hold of my shoulders before I can react, pushing me backwards until she has me pinned against the wall.

At first I'm shocked, unable to react. And when I do try to move, she shoves me again, hard.

"Thora," Petaccia says, warning in every syllable. "Don't test me. I think I've been more than patient with you. I thought I made it clear that we are partners and partners are supposed to trust each other. I made no fuss about you visiting Olea in the garden behind my back, and didn't even have a problem with you trying your own antidotes—but taking her from the garden? And now your refusal to assist me in fixing the mess you've made? That, my dear, is one step too far."

I spit in her face.

Petaccia continues, entirely unperturbed. It's unsettling how little she cares what I think. "Olea will need somebody in the garden with her. Especially if she is as weak as you say she is. And I need you to monitor her health. My suspicion is that your presence has a wilting effect—but the girl is too precious to the garden. I doubt the sickness will progress past a certain point. It's a punishment more than a concrete threat."

"And why, exactly, would I do anything you say now?" I say angrily.

"Oh, I have a few reasons."

The calculation in Petaccia's voice is new. Different than the annoyance or her anger. This is pure coldness and it stops my own anger in its tracks, leaving me filled with icy fear.

"Did you think I wouldn't have some sort of insurance policy, Thora? Do you think I would invite merely anybody into my lab, to share my work? I might care about empowering female scientists, but not at the expense of my magnum opus. And I might have known your father, but that was thirty years ago."

"I…" I didn't think. I did not think. *Thora, you stupid, stupid girl.* "Why me?" I whisper, meek now.

"I know about the library," Petaccia says. And those five words change everything. I know, instantly, that she is not talking about the book I stole from the library here at St. Elianto. My skin crawls with the memory I have fought so hard to box away. Like my grief, I have tied it with a ribbon and forbidden myself from ever peeking inside again. Oh, but my dreams, they keep the score. "I know, you're probably wondering why I would bring a *murderer* into my research, but I think it makes for a very interesting conversation, don't you?"

"I am not a murderer," I say, but my voice wobbles.

"I think perhaps that's a normal response, though I see the flicker in your eyes, my dear. I wasn't born yesterday. I know a coverup when I see one, and I am very, very familiar with guilt. I know the official story, that your dear new husband was killed during a planned purge of his private library due to *space*." She chuckles. "I'm also familiar with the family story."

I swallow hard. My mouth is dry as the dirt in the plant pots in that window bed, and my heart pounds with surprising tenacity. I'm half surprised it doesn't give out entirely.

"What happened to my husband was an accident," I say with as much courage as I can muster.

"Yes, yes. He was burning things he was embarrassed about, isn't that the official line?"

My cheeks burn, so hot I wonder if the fever is taking me again. This is all wrong. This is not how *any* of this was supposed to go. I regret coming here today, regret thinking that I could twist the doctor into telling me the truth and letting me go.

"But it wasn't *his* books Aurelio was burning. Was it."

This isn't a question, it doesn't deserve an answer, and yet the tremble in my lips and hands, the sweat at my hairline, beading on my lip—all these amount to guilt. *Fuck.*

"You're very quiet for an innocent woman, Mrs. LeVand," Petaccia says, putting emphasis on my name. Not *my* name, not any more. "It's very clever of you to swing it the way you did, pushing his family for a quick funeral to hide the man's supposed guilt, but I know..."

"You don't know anything," I say.

"No? Oh, I see the way you look at my ward. You think I don't notice you, sneaking out of her garden at the crack of dawn with your lips all bloody from her kisses?" Petaccia smirks. "You think I didn't expect as much, when I placed you in those rooms overlooking her paradise?"

Another fresh chill snakes down my spine. *I'm done*, I think. It doesn't matter what I want, not after this.

"I have some very interesting dirt on you. *Murderer.* Which is why," Petaccia continues, finally stepping back to her desk and retrieving her most recent book of notes, "you'll do exactly as I say. You will continue to visit Olea in the garden and keep detailed notes of her health. And you will report directly to me. Do you understand?"

All along, Petaccia has held the ace. I should have listened to Leo. And now I might as well be trapped in Olea's golden, poison cage with her.

Chapter Thirty

The library is burning.

In my dreams my breath is the hot smoke of a dragon's, golden fire and blue incense. The blaze started at my husband's desk—it was never meant to grow. But I never dream of the little flame, the moment that Aurelio's taper touched the dusty skin of my books inside their metal storage trunk. *Mine.* My collection, begged and stolen and hidden away for my pleasure alone. Not hidden well enough.

No, in my dreams it is always the blaze I see, so big and wild there is no hope for its end. My books are already gone. The feeling, watching their pages blacken and curl, is deep within me, an anger so big it fills every pore, every artery. The books are gone. But there is Aurelio, his face contorted in victory, even as the flames grow out of control.

"Do you see the sins you have facilitated?" he booms. He is so large he could swallow me whole. "Do you see what you have made me do?"

Oh, I see. I see my only possessions in this prison of his making turning to ash beneath his touch. I see his intrinsic hatred for everything I hold dear. I'm not hurting anybody, gaining small pleasures from my collection, content to walk in my husband's shadow against my very nature—but that is not enough for men like him.

He needs more. More money, more power. More of me than I can give. And I have tried so, so hard to be the dutiful obedient wife. I have worn his dresses and attended his galas. I have pretended to love him for capturing me and decorating the cage he has put me in.

It is never enough.

"Please," I beg, although it's no good. The books are already gone, ash and fire, the stench of scorched leather, my own musky sweat.

"This is not the worst I will do." Aurelio leaves the books burning in their trunk, his evening Scotch in a crystal glass next to it, and strides towards me. It is his second mistake, though he doesn't know it yet. The first, of course, was burning the books to begin with. "Look at you, cowering like a dog. You stink of it."

I shrink lower as he lifts his arm, raising it high above his head. My dream mind knows I must run, but it is stuck in the reality. I did not run. And I do not run now.

"Please," I beg again, this time quieter. "I won't do it again—"

"No," Aurelio growls. "You will not. I won't have it, Thora. No wife of mine will cuckold me, embarrass me. God, we took you in. Made a lady of you. And this is how you repay me for all I have done? It's a wonder I didn't find you in here rutting with the maid like a common whore."

"I wouldn't!" I protest. It was just reading. Just touching. Dreaming and imagining what it would be like to feel the touch of a woman. "I would never act on it."

"You already have." He brings his fist down, striking me directly across the mouth. It isn't the first time he has hit me, but it's the first time he's done it where it will leave a mark. Even in my dreams I feel the roil of anger, that rising tide of red. How dare he? After all I have given up for him?

Aurelio hasn't noticed, but with my head spinning and the stars in my eyes I see that the flames are growing. Already the blaze is becoming an inferno. If he doesn't extinguish it soon it will—

Too late. The curtains near the desk are the first thing to catch. And this is where the dreams divert. In real life I screamed, attempting to duck under Aurelio's arm to tamp down the fire; in real life he spun, too fast, stumbling into the scorching, heavy trunk atop the desk, sending his Scotch flying. The curtains went up like rags soaked in turpentine.

In the dreams it happens like this: I point at the curtains, already ablaze. Aurelio turns to me and his eyes are dark, black slits from side to side, his lips curving in a vicious smile. In my dreams I am the one who pushes Aurelio—I shove him with all my might. And as he sprawls his skull makes contact with the corner of the desk. The trunk careens against the curtains, pulling their excess deeper into the flames. The room is thick with smoke.

Aurelio is on the floor. Is he breathing? The heavy crystal glass lies not far from his head. It is only a thought, a split second of rage, but in my dreams it is not *only* a thought. I grab the glass and breathe—in and out, soot in my lungs, the taste of burning on my tongue. Then I slam it directly against his already-wounded temple.

Is that the dream? Or did it really happen? Either way, here is the story: I discovered my husband burning his collection of dirty books. Horror. He tripped. He banged his head. The fire grew. And I fled.

The end result is the same, in my life as in my dreams: the library is burning and my husband burns with it.

I wake with my hands slick with blood. I've scratched the scab on the back of my thigh in my dreams, the wound leaking all across my bedsheets, my hands, my nightgown. I give myself a few minutes to return to the land of the living—though it hardly feels like living. Is this what I wanted? Is this the future I always dreamt for myself?

Still, there's nothing left to do but throw myself back into the research. Wallowing won't do me any good. Sure, I could turn around and announce Petaccia's plans to the world, could tell everybody who will listen about Olea's dead "friends" and her poison touch, but who would they believe? Dr. Petaccia is a world-renowned scientist. As she's told me herself, her research in plant-based healing has saved thousands of lives in Isliano alone. And who am I? An undertaker's daughter with a dead husband and a marital family who couldn't wait to wash their hands of me.

No. The only way out now is through.

Eventually I drag myself from my bed. I am tired to my core, my eyes are sticky with shed and unshed tears, and I'm fucking starving. When did I last eat? I wobble at the thought of Leo, waiting for me in the dining hall. I wonder if he hates me for what I said to him. Or if he's somehow forgiven that and hates me for disappearing instead. *Again.* That's all I've done, over and over, the entire time I've known him. I've taken him for granted. It isn't what friends do, is it? Then I think I'm grateful that he won't see me like this. I know I look a mess. He would only worry about me, and that isn't fair either.

I boil water for tea, but I carry the hot water to the table before realising that I have no leaves left. There is nothing in this place to make it mine, not really. I have books, and notes, microscope slides I have stolen like lucky talismans from the lab. But even these things remind me of Olea. She has her tapestries and her trinkets, her whole life lived in that tower—it is all hers. Everything that is mine was either Aurelio's or hers.

I sink to the desk. The shutters are open to the darkness. I half expect to see Olea wandering through her plants, tending to them as she always does, but of course she is not there. I wonder if Petaccia will have checked on her. Who will care for her if not me? Has she *ever* had anybody care for her when she was sick?

I know it's half the tired sadness talking, but after everything I *still* want to be the one to care for her. I just don't want to feel as though my hand has been forced—and of course, that's exactly what has happened. Would things have been different if I had met Olea in another life? Or would she simply have been a different kind of danger to me?

I imagine what things might have been like if there was no garden, no poison. Just Olea appearing in the life I had before. What if we'd met when my father was alive? No amount of secrecy would have protected us from his lash. And if I'd met her at Aurelio's...? Oh, I would have burned the world just for a taste.

What if Leo's right and it's the toxins that make me want her? What then? But it doesn't matter how many times I ask myself this question; the answer is always the same: if the toxins make me want Olea, and make Olea want me back, then I would, and will, poison myself to death for her love.

The realisation does not, however, make any of this any easier.

"The only way out is through," I say, hoping that repeating the thought aloud will help.

It doesn't. I'm so hungry I can hardly think. It is too late for the dining hall. Could I beg food from one of the servers? I don't know if there will be anybody around in the kitchens to ask. I know what would fill me, maybe. A big, bloody steak. I can almost taste the juices. It comes to something, doesn't it, when even the offal I've used in my experiments seems like it might make a good midnight feast.

I absentmindedly lick my fingers, lost in my frenzied imaginings. The taste of blood brings me back to myself, iron-rich, like honey lubricating my tongue. The scent of it, too, is startling. I pause, bringing my palm beneath my nose so I can inhale it. There is something animal about it, something primal, both vital and somehow embarrassing. It isn't tacky like menstrual blood, doesn't have that same cloying smell. I close my eyes and I see the vermilion coating my skin.

And then the thought strikes.

It is so simple I can't believe I've never considered the possibility before. For all Petaccia's research, her theorising, her damnable hypotheses, I wonder if she's perhaps been too blinkered to notice what's right in front of her. The experimental antidotes with the highest success rates have been those using offal. Petaccia's theory about the success is to do with the body's ability to read and absorb these organs—and her theory of the failure is that rejection of an organ by the host body is equally common. It happens all the time in humans and animals alike, the body attacking even its own internal parts.

I stare down at my hand. How often does the human body reject its own blood? It's not unheard of, I'm sure—but truly, how common is it? The same goes for animals. A thrill of discovery trembles through me. Perhaps the carrier is not protein, not the meat itself. What of the haemoglobin found in blood? Low levels of haemoglobin, otherwise known as iron deficiency, cause—and I know this from my lectures in the halls of La Scienza—dizziness, shortness of breath, and muscle weakness or exhaustion. The exact same symptoms I've been suffering since I became a regular in Olea's garden, almost as if my body is trying to tell me what I'm lacking. This may be a coincidence, but it feels too fated not to try.

Haemoglobin. *Blood.* The perfect colloid.

I act without thinking. I change from my stained nightgown into a pair of dark trousers and a simple short-sleeved shirt, pushing my hair back off my forehead with a ribbon tied at my nape. I pull on my gloves and my mask, a hooded cloak over my outfit despite the heat. It is the middle of the night, but still the temperature soars, my clothing instantly sticking to me with the briskness of movement.

The last thing I grab is Olea's stinging tree leaf, now very badly wilted—near dried—from its empty vase. I remember what she said when she first introduced me to the tree in the garden, how the neurotoxin contained within its tiny hairs is so virulent it can be reactivated long after a sting by something as accidental as a little heat. I'm careful to pick the leaf from its vase with the tips of my gloves, wrapping it in a silk hair scarf and carrying it like a parcel instead of in my pocket. It will be perfect.

St. Elianto is always deserted at this time of night, though I have rarely crossed the square with such purpose after sunset. I am usually in the garden with Olea, or wallowing in despair in my rooms. Not tonight. And hopefully never again for either. I am going to help Olea, I'm going to hand Petaccia her damned cure, and then I am going to leave this fucking place—in that order.

I enter La Vita as silently as I can. I am not in the mood to deal with Petaccia after our last conversation. In fact, right now I'd be happy if I never had to speak to her again. I breathe another sigh of relief when I find the door to the Cave locked, the remaining salamanders left to their own devices for the time being.

The Tombs, too, is entirely silent. There are more empty cages than the last time I was here, and two more failed antidote vials on the shelf, both a thick green soup infused with what looks like some kind of algae. I scoff silently. For all her intelligence and perseverance, Petaccia's research is like a game.

I'm not one to boast, to crow loudly about any sort of achievement, but tonight could very well change that. I am filled with fresh zest, excited for the first time in days—*weeks*. I know that this discovery potentially has scope for the betterment of humanity, but it is Olea I think of first.

"I'm coming," I say aloud, and then laugh quietly to myself in the silence of the lab.

I work like a woman possessed, extracting what I need from the stinging tree with practised ease, cooling and distilling until I'm left with a neurotoxin so potent it would drive most people mad. Or to suicide, if Olea's tales of the tree are to be believed.

It pools at the bottom of the vial, the colour of saffron and texture of honey. Liquid gold. Weeks ago this might have surprised me, but now I only make notes as I swirl the liquid in the tube; the way it catches the lamplight reminds me of summer sunlight filtering through the high window over the golden cradle in our sepulchre—or, I realise, the bold yellow of the sun-kissed clouds in Olea's tapestries.

This is right. I know it the way I knew every other attempt I made wasn't quite there. But close, so close. All avenues have been leading me to this.

I have, however, got a problem. There are no more animals in Petaccia's cages aside from one anaemic-looking vole. The big brown hare I was hoping to use for blood is nowhere to be seen—I suspect the victim of one of Petaccia's failures. I curse inwardly. If I'd thought ahead I could have...I could have what? Caught a bird with my bare hands? The thought sickens me. The vole won't do: it barely looks like it will have enough blood to fill my vial.

I check Petaccia's icebox, filled to the gills with carefully labelled pig hearts and rat innards. The sight of it always makes me feel lightheaded, but tonight it makes me inexplicably hungry. I paw through her scientific stash, but there's nothing I can use. No blood.

I growl in frustration. The vole will have to do. I swipe off my cloak, wiping the sweat from my forehead with the back of my hand. It must be near dawn. I don't have the time to mess around if I want to finish this before Petaccia comes back. I peel off my gloves too; the vole is tiny and I'll need as much dexterity as I can get.

I carry the vial carefully over to the cages and prepare to extract what blood I can from the vole. I always start with a little prayer, one my father always favoured in his rites.

Hush now, dear one
Let the cradle carry you to the everlasting end
These golden hands
The sweetest of earth's honey
And the strongest bridle on Grief

It is only thanks to the hissing coming from the vial that I stop what I'm doing and finally pay attention to what is before my eyes.

My unwashed fingers, which have until now been beneath the gloves, are still stained with dried blood. I grip the vial of stinging toxin between my thumb and forefinger, both smeared red and pressed against the glass. The golden liquid thrashes wildly against the sides of the vial, near crawling towards the top like a storm, hissing and spitting all the while.

It takes everything in me not to throw the vial down and back away. Instead I grip it tighter, watching the stinging solution roil and bubble, clawing—if liquid can claw—at the sides. As if begging for my blood.

Immediately I abandon the idea of the vole. The stinging solution is—well, it's crazy, but the liquid knows better than I do. I prop the vial in the closest empty rack, washing my hands in the trough with rough soap and scrubbing them dry before seeking out Petaccia's sharpest knife.

I hesitate. If I do this, and it works, then there is no going back. In another life I would want more time, hours and minutes, days and weeks, to consider all the options before me: I have not, I realise faintly, any idea what this could do. If it works... If we release it... But it turns out I am selfish in this, and I have nothing to barter with except my potential success. I need the time to concoct it, and then to *use* it—to take Olea's future out of the doctor's hands.

There's nothing for it.

The cut hurts less than I expect it to, the bite of the metal in the pad of my thumb spreading a slow heat through my skin. I could, perhaps, have chosen a more elegant method, but time is ticking and every minute is one precious moment of discovery slipping away. I say another quick prayer and hold my thumb over the vial—

The blood drips.

The mixture writhes.

The scent that arises from the hissing colloid is not at all what I expected. It is not blood and nectar, but bread and honey. The sweetest fresh loaves with golden tops and rich, dark honey butter spread between warm slices. It rises to my nostrils, the aroma nearly dragging my head down it is so good and pure and whole.

I brace myself against the counter, careless now of the blood dripping from my thumb. My body sings at the proximity. It would not be an exaggeration to say I hear angels, or the soft timbre of my mother's voice calling me home. The fragrance envelops me and it takes all my strength not to pour the liquid straight into my mouth, drowning my tongue.

I force myself to step away. To inhale the clean, bland air of the Tombs. Every part of me strains for the antidote. *This is good,* it choruses. *Drink, drink, drink it all.* Instead I steady myself with another clean breath and another. There is a tray of unused pipettes in here somewhere, I know there is—*where* is *it?*

I grab one. There. I am as careful as my shaking hands allow. The antidote has stopped its unnatural writhing now, though the scent is still as strong. I wrap my thumb in a strip of gauze and shove it into my glove, then hold my breath as I draw a pipette dose of the solution out of the vial.

It is no longer that golden colour, not like sunlight or wheat or any of those. Now the colour is darker, rusty with my blood. There is a wholeness to it now, an indescribable quality, like the thickness of good cream, the bite of salt through butter. A completeness. It is red, it is orange, it shimmers strangely in the pipette as I lift it.

I know I should wait. Regardless of my hurry, this is—it is insanity. I am not qualified for this, nor do I want to be. All thoughts of bartering, of success, of *winning*, are gone, replaced with the knowledge that I should be afraid. I should wait. Yet I *can't* wait. Its siren lure is too much. I am so tired of fighting...

Before I have the chance to process my own actions, the pipette is on my lips, the solution in my mouth. The taste of warm bread and honey fills my tongue, slowly replaced by something deeper, something more primal—a bitter concoction of stale earth, tree sap, the bite of a green leaf. My tongue goes instantly numb.

I start to panic, but the numbness lasts less than five seconds. The taste dissipates soon after and I'm left with nothing but a sharp metallic edge. I swallow once. Twice. Nothing happens. The vial sits in its rack, the liquid a ruddy orange-brown. I might begin to wonder if I've imagined the entire episode, except for one thing: I feel amazing. No tiredness, no dizziness, no cloying sickness in the pit of my belly.

I wait five minutes. Ten. The night is growing thin and I'm eager to leave La Vita, but I make myself wait. Half an hour, a little more. I pull my hand from its glove and check the wound on my thumb— but it is gone. Not only is it gone; there is no evidence it was ever there. No scar, nothing but the smear of blood left behind. The same is true of the wound on my leg, now completely invisible.

I let out a caw of victory, startling the tiny, lethargic vole in his cage so badly he flees under his bundle of hay. I don't care.

"Olea, I'm coming."

Chapter Thirty-One

Olea is not in the garden, but it seems nobody has been through the unlocked gate since I last left, and I'm grateful for past Thora's carelessness. I let myself in silently, brushing through the overgrown tumble of weeds, the leathery green leaves of hassock breaking through in the red-brown earth where no marshy plant should live.

In my right hand I grip the vial, now sealed with a stopper of black wax. I daren't put it in my pocket; it is far too precious to trust its safety to a piece of cloth, to risk a rip, a hole, the smash of glass against stone. I feel frightened holding it, too, but the edge of my fear is dulled by the knowledge that this vial contains the future, and I have the power to create it again.

Olea's tower is entirely dark except for the faintest flicker of yellow candlelight around its uppermost window. I tread carefully, allowing my eyes to adjust to the lack of moonlight inside the walls. With every step I marvel at my body, how strong and effortless my movements feel. The air is so thick and hot it might as well be a wall, yet I am a hot knife through its butter, barely breaking a sweat.

The room at the top of the tower is tiny and cast in shadows, lit only by Olea's solitary candle on the window ledge. She sits on a narrow trundle bed with her back against the plain, dingy wall. Her hair is loose, hanging in straw-like coils. Her lips are dark as bruises, her eyes sunk into the sharpness of her cheekbones, a sheen of sweat on her forehead. She glances up when I enter and there is a brief flash of surprise, followed by the same old resigned melancholy. She has given up.

"Why are you here?"

"I came to help you."

"I don't want your help." She says the words with a sense of finality, as though she might have been repeating them in her mind ever since I left, but there is no force there.

"I'm sorry I left you," I say, stepping tentatively into the room. I grip the antidote in my fist so tightly I can feel the blood draining from my fingers. "I didn't know what to do...I suppose I was frightened."

"You didn't want to stay with me. I understand."

"I didn't want to be—"

"To be trapped?" Olea's eyes snap to mine, alert but somehow still dull, like the glass eyes of a doll. "You don't need to say it, Thora. I know how this story goes."

"It's not like that," I reply, though I know she's right. What did I say to Leo about Clara? "It's not that I don't want to stay with you. I couldn't be trapped *here*."

"*Here* is my home. I tried to leave it—for you. Look what happened."

"No, you didn't." This is Olea's fear talking. She is like a wounded animal lashing out, but instead of claws Olea only has lies. She'll make me feel guilty if I let her because it's better than admitting the truth: she is frightened the antidote won't work—and she's frightened it will. "*You* wanted to leave. I know you were afraid, but you still wanted it as much as I did. Don't blame me."

"I'm not trying to—"

"Olea, look." I raise the vial between my thumb and forefinger. In the candlelight it looks like treacle, tiny bubbles suspended within. She stares at the liquid, her expression unchanging, and then she glances away.

"So what? Just another experiment," she says. "Another failure. Always the fucking guinea pig."

"This *isn't* a failure," I insist. "I tried it myself. I feel great! Look at me. Really look."

I cross the room swiftly, crouching dangerously close so that my face is level with hers. She barely blinks. The illness that began its work in my bedroom may have slowed its attack, but her body is frail and her mind . . . She has the look of a convict, long resigned to a future inside four walls.

"Olea," I say sharply. "I know you're frightened, but please look at me."

"Why. Nothing works."

I'm no longer wearing my gloves, but the antidote has made me brave. I smell the bitter perfume of the garden, but it does not feel as if it is invading my lungs. I don't have any proof, but somehow I *know* that touching her won't hurt me. I grab her shoulder, and when she doesn't react I move my hand to her chin, lifting it so our eyes meet again.

"Olea," I say very calmly. "If you do not drink this mixture I will wash my hands of you. Do you understand me? I don't care if I'm being cruel; you're acting like a child. I don't care if you realise it or not, it's true. And I need you to do this for me."

"Why should I?" There it is, the spark of stubbornness I've always admired in her. Beneath the sadness, beneath her lonely, pitiable existence, there is a core of strength in this girl, like the roots of a tree delving deep into the heart of the world.

"Because if you don't I will tell everybody about your dead friends," I say, infusing each word with the rigidity of truth. "They will come for you, and your plants, and your catalogue. They will take everything you have ever made your own. And when I am done I will walk away from you, and this garden, and everything else."

Olea flinches, a deep hurt flashing behind her eyes. It is a minor movement, involuntary, but I feel it in the touch of her skin. I don't need to see how she reacts to know I've gone too far. Isn't this exactly how Petaccia has kept Olea meek and captive all these years? But how else am I supposed to get through to her?

She is about to argue, but even as she opens her mouth to tell me to go away, she can't resist the pressure of my hand against her chin; she leans into the feeling, the caress of my palm, the smoothness of my skin against hers, and she softens. I keep hold of her chin and I lean forward, guiding her face towards mine.

"Thora, don't," she breathes. "You'll—"

Our lips are so close I can breathe the warmth of her breath, taste the bitter sweetness of her on the tip of my tongue. A surge of desire rolls through me like thunder. Despite everything, I *need* her. I want her hands in my hair, in my mouth; I want my fingers inside her, to watch her squirm with pleasure. The antidote has made everything in me stronger—including this.

"Drink the goddamn antidote. It works."

Olea's breath hitches in her chest. I move my hand from her chin, down the soft slope of her throat, down until it rests flat right above her heart. I can feel the beat of it, wary like a bird. *You are mine*, I think. *And you will do this for me.*

"Get off me," she snaps. In one swift movement she shoves me backwards and I stumble upright. "Don't *touch* me. Are you insane? You think I want you now, after all you've done? You think I want the guilt of your touch, of your death? Fuck you, Thora."

"After all *I've* done?" I scoff bitterly. The anger that rises inside me is unexpected, but hot and bright. Strong. Everything is so *strong.* "You are a liar! Since the moment I met you, all you've done is tell a story—and I'm sick of hearing it. You've twisted me round your finger since the beginning.

"Everything I have done is because of you. When I came here all I wanted was freedom, my own life and my own future—and then I found you. You lured me in, you—"

"You can't blame me for that either," Olea snarls. "You were so eager to come into my garden you'd have eaten out of the palm of my hand when we first met if I'd let you. Don't you recall the way you begged, night after night?"

"Because of *you*," I hiss. "You're poison, Olea. Addictive, yes, but deadly. You take and you take from people, and the worst thing is, I don't even think you know you're doing it. What about your friends beyond the gate? How many of them knew what they were signing up for when they tried to befriend you?"

"I never meant to hurt any of them." Olea's voice is stone-cold, her eyes like liquid darkness.

"What about Clara?" I push. "You never meant to hurt her either? Even though she hurt you? Even though her death was an obvious punishment for what she stole from you?"

"She took everything from me!" Olea roars. "What should I

have done? I have nothing. Nobody to help me, to look out for me. How else am I supposed to protect myself?"

"Protect yourself," I spit. "And now you're going to just die? Tell me, Olea: What is your life worth? Is it worth Clara's? Is it worth mine? What about Leo, who's still mourning his goddamn wife because of you? How many more people have to sacrifice themselves to your cause before you realise that none of this is just going to go away? It doesn't matter how badly you want that."

Olea goes very, very still. "Do you think I wanted any of this?" she whispers. "I told you I was a monster and you said I wasn't. Do you feel differently now, Thora?" Her voice grows, steel edging her words. "Or are you too busy working with the woman who has kept me in this goddamn cage *my entire life* to see you're just as bad as we are?"

"You didn't tell me about her," I argue. "How was I supposed to know? I *asked* you if you needed my help—"

"What, I was just supposed to trust you?"

"You dragged me in!" I cry. "I never said you had to trust me, but you chose to be my friend. You chose to come to the wall, night after night. And now I'm trapped in this nightmare because of you, and all you do is lie. And, yes, Olea, lying by omission is still lying. You lied about Petaccia, you lied about Clara—and you're a—a killer—"

Olea's laughter is unhinged, throaty and so deep it sounds born out of hell itself. It echoes. She climbs to her feet, limbs gangly and gait uneven as she staggers towards me.

"I'm a killer," she repeats. "*I'm* a killer. Are you joking right now? That's your vindication for your behaviour? You left me. After all your talk of trust. I did trust you, the garden trusted you and welcomed you inside, and you fucking abandoned me, just like everybody else."

"Fine," I seethe. "You don't deserve it anyway. I was going to use this as a bargaining chip for your freedom, but since you don't trust me I guess I'll just focus on getting myself out, shall I?"

I don't know if I mean it. In the moment, perhaps I do. I turn away from Olea easily, anger burning away the regret, and I storm down the stairs. I don't stop until I'm standing panting outside in the waning light of the moon. I grip the vial, holding it up to the moonlight. Is anything worth this pain? It feels as if my heart is cracking inside my chest. If Olea won't drink the antidote, then I'll just give it to Petaccia as is. She'll have to let me leave the university. Then...where would I go? Anywhere would be better than here. Even if it means being alone. Part of me wants to smash the bottle.

Dawn is just beginning to purple the edges of the sky. Dark clouds gather and the air stinks of impending rain. I suck it down, filling my belly with it, the electricity of it zinging through me like the tartness of lime juice. *Fuck Olea*, I think. I crumple to my knees, great racking sobs crushing my lungs.

And then I hear her. She is slow, shuffling her way down the stairs and through the tower door like an old crone, her nightgown bunching as she carries it around her knees.

"Wait," she rasps. She stumbles as her damaged feet make contact with the earth. A zap of lightning forks through the trees. "I'm sorry."

For a moment I can't stop the sobs. They smash through me like gunfire, each breath a bullet.

"Me too," I say eventually. "I didn't mean to say any of it. I just want...I thought this was the life I had dreamt of and it's not. I need to get out of here, Olea. I want to be free. With you, if that's possible."

The truth is, no matter the lies that have spooled between us like thread, no matter the histories that have driven us to this dark place, I don't want to do any of this alone. Olea isn't much of an ally, but she's all I've got.

She kneels beside me. With a tentative hand she reaches for my knee, waiting to touch it.

"It won't hurt you?" she asks. I shake my head. "The... *That*." She gestures to the vial. "Does it really work?"

"I think it does."

"Can I see it?"

I hold the vial out to her. Gingerly she takes it, holding the glass up to the pale light of the coming dawn. How long has it been since Olea was able to enjoy the warmth of day without having to dress like the wrapped-up dead? I rock back on my heels. She pops the waxy seal and it tumbles into her lap.

I expect her to sniff it. To dip her little finger in and test the liquid on the tip of her tongue, as I have often seen her do out in the garden with nectars and fruits she isn't so familiar with. I half expect her to throw the vial away. I wonder if she can smell the bread-and-honey scent, if the flaring of her nostrils is intrigue or disgust. The liquid surges inside the glass, but Olea doesn't react.

"I trust you," she says.

Then she empties the entire contents into her mouth in one smooth gesture, swallowing it down in a single gulp.

"Olea—" I start, and then stop. That's more than ten times the dose I took. She lets the bottle drop with a heaviness. I watch her eyes, heavy-lidded and sleepy. She doesn't move at first, fists balled, curved lips parted as she inhales deep, and then deeper, drawing in the musky scent of the coming rain. "How do you feel?"

"I feel..." The words are slurred, drunken. She licks her lips and I think she must be tasting honey. "I feel *everything*." She grips hold of my outstretched hands, skin to skin, her palms pressed to mine and our fingers intertwined. "Did you feel it? It's like lightning in my veins. It's like..."

She surges forward and plants her lips on mine. The kiss is hungry and vibrant; I taste the nectar on her, running my tongue over hers. She presses her forehead tight against mine, nose to nose, breath mingling. Her skin is warm, warmer than I have known it outside of fever. She kisses me again.

I pull back, watching as the inky tendrils across her hands begin to dissipate. She marvels at the sight of her smooth, milky-white flesh returning. Pale, peachy nails, wrists speckled with a thousand tiny freckles. She beams at me with lips the colour of burning bush berries, pink and soft. Her eyes are warm brown chocolate cut with mint. She is as lush and fresh as a dewdrop.

Desire roars within me as she launches herself at me again, kissing my lips and then my jaw, my neck, the soft, exposed skin at my throat above my collar. She pushes me back into the dry earth, straddling me, a whoop of pure pleasure ricocheting through her, her hands on my chest.

"You did it!" she crows. "You actually fucking did it. Thora, you beautiful, beautiful—"

She stutters into silence. Her gaze has caught on the white circle of the sun. In its welcome light she is ethereal, her skin glowing in contrast to her dark curls—glossy and thick and near black as damp soil. I reach for her breast eagerly, but the expression on her face gives me pause.

"Olea?"

She grips my shirtfront with both hands, her whole body going rigid as some kind of seizure takes her. I scramble upright, nudging her off my legs. She lands in the dirt still shaking, trembling so hard that her teeth rattle in her skull.

"*Olea!*" I shout.

But my voice falls on deaf ears. The seizure continues, brutal and angry and hard, racking her body until she can do nothing but lie on the ground. I rush to help her, trying to hold her still or cushion her head against the earth. The new colour leaches from her skin as fast as it came, leaving her grey and cold.

"Olea?" I whisper. Thunder rolls in the distance. I feel the first fat drops of rain on my head and in seconds the sky is open and the rain is pouring, gushing, drowning us both in rivulets so thick and deep it might wash away everything. The vial, the mixture. But not what has happened. It is too late for rain to fix that.

The antidote has failed.

Olea is dead.

Chapter Thirty-Two

Rain lashes down hard. The garden becomes a quagmire amidst the deluge. I cradle Olea's body in my arms for what feels like forever but is in actuality perhaps only half an hour. The sun continues its ascent, and Olea's skin begins to grow hot beneath its touch. It does not redden or come up in welts, but I feel the heat radiating off her, like holding my hand too close to the flame of a candle—and it isn't long before the rain begins to sizzle when it lands.

At first I attempt to shield her with my body. I hunch my shoulders and curl around her like a browning leaf, but the sun is fierce—brighter and hotter than it should be through the rain. Its rays feel like knives against my skin, each prick drawing out what little energy I have left. I do not cry. I have nothing more to give.

Dr. Petaccia appears at my side like a wraith. I don't hear her arrive. The rain is like a roaring static inside my ears. Blink, water, blink, Olea, blink, water, blink—Petaccia. She wears dark robes over her usual outfit, black leather gloves, a mask over her nose and mouth, and a hood pulled up over her hair. I stare at her blearily, confusion and sadness and anger all blurring into one freezing emotion.

"She collapsed," I babble. "A seizure, I think—"

"Move," she says dispassionately.

When I don't immediately drop Olea's head from my lap, the doctor gives my shin a hard, fast kick. I yelp in pain. The agony is wrong, disproportionate to the violence; my whole body aches with it, tendrils of fire licking outwards from the bruising flesh until every part of me hurts. I scramble away before Petaccia kicks me again, fixating on the way Olea's lifeless hand drops to the dirt.

Petaccia lifts Olea's body as if her bones are hollow. Her dirty nightgown trails in the muck, arms limp and head lolling back. The doctor strides with purpose, not hurry, to the tower. Every step carries Olea farther away from the antidote, from me and our freedom, back to her prison.

I crawl after them, barely able to lift my arms. My strength has gone, sapped into the earth. Sickness swirls inside me and I retch filmy white bile into the dirt. My skin is fire, my innards a sluggish icy slurry. The pain in my head is a pounding so heavy, so loud, it pushes my eyelids shut. I will die from this grief.

I drag myself to the door of the tower and through into its warmth, and then follow the damp trail down, down the spiral stairs, step by step on my backside until I reach the basement. This windowless room is clearly a pantry of sorts, small sacks of potatoes and carrots and flour hanging from hooks on the walls, a slice of buttered bread half-eaten on a plate on the side. Petaccia has repurposed a thin low dining table, swept aside metal candlesticks in a clatter, and placed Olea on its surface, black dirt marring the white cloth beneath.

I sag against the wall and watch as Petaccia lights a handful of pillar candles scattered around the room, moving to them with grace and ease, as if she knows well where they will be. She works methodically. First she checks for a pulse in Olea's neck and wrists, shining a candle flame at her pupils and testing the reflexes in her knees. She bends away from Olea's body, keeping a careful distance between them as much as she can, touching only when necessary.

Olea's skin is alabaster, her hair raven. There is no colour in her lips. The inkiness on her hands and feet is gone, but the skin left behind is white as salt. She is almost perfect, except for the stillness of her chest. A storm howls inside me, a horror worse than any I've imagined in my life.

"Can you save her?" I croak.

Petaccia seemingly notices my arrival for the first time. She purses her lips and then shakes her head. "No," she says simply. "She's gone."

"But..." *You have to save her*, I think, though I know it's pointless. I saw her take her last breath. "You're a doctor. Can't you do something? Shock her, or—"

"She's dead, Thora."

Silence stretches between us, elastic. Words burble up my throat and turn ashy on my tongue. What else is there to say? I am a curse. I should never have given her the antidote—that damned concoction, brewed out of sheer desperation. I have been impatient, and my impetuousness has cost Olea everything.

Petaccia doesn't ask what happened, far more concerned with the facts than my story, and I don't volunteer the information, guilt clamping my lips closed tight. If I thought my future was dark before, then this is the blight that will end it all. I might as well join Olea in death, for there is nothing left for me now. I curl inwards, holding my stomach, fearing I might be sick again. The doctor continues her thorough examination of her ward's body, taking her temperature, studying her nails, teeth, and tongue, taking her time. I watch it all, trying—desperately—to keep from falling apart.

"Don't you care?" I say softly. My face is wet, and I realise I'm crying again. Petaccia, on the other hand, is a pillar dressed in black. She hasn't cursed or cried; she has barely acknowledged the horror of the scene outside. She turns slowly, her expression unreadable. "How can you be so heartless?" I go on, growing brave. "You *raised* her. Don't you feel anything at all? She wasn't just one of your lab rats—"

"Keep the Silence now," Petaccia cuts me off icily. "I will be back. I should think you know what to do."

She doesn't give me time to argue, as if she can't stand being around me a single moment longer. She storms from the room in a swirl of black cloth, the candles guttering in her wake. The rain continues to lash down outside; I can hear it although there are no windows to see the onslaught.

Olea lies on the dining table, still as stone. I can't bring myself to go to her, to feel the coldness of her skin. I sink down to the floor, knees to my chest, great sobs heaving through me until my head pounds afresh. This is all wrong. If I'd felt trapped before...

Eventually the sobs subside. I wipe my nose on the back of my sleeve, gulping, pushing the tears aside. Crying will do me no good now. Petaccia is right. Grief is my business. I gather myself, slowly, slowly, pulling my body upright. Every part of me aches, but Olea needs me now more than ever.

There is no incense in this place, so instead I burn the dried plants I find hanging from the low ceiling. They are fragrant and musky, their scent filling the room, banishing the dampness of the rain. I don't try to figure out what they are, common name or

Latin. I don't care. It doesn't matter. All that matters is the plumes of grey smoke that waft upward, cleansing this space, cleansing Olea's body.

I remove her nightgown with a pair of scissors and fill a small pail with soapy water. It doesn't take long to clean her up, mud slipping from her skin like she is greased. I find a bottle of perfumed oil in the room upstairs, a comb for her hair, a fresh dress just like all her others. It is not the first time I have wondered why she wears nothing but white nightgowns, but only now does it occur to me that she may have had no choice. This place is—was—Olea's home, but how much of it did she control? The food in the cellar is sparse, nothing fresh, only grains and vegetables that last for weeks at a time, and there is little to suggest it has ever been any different.

Hollowly I gather my treasures, carrying them down into the bowels of the tower where Olea waits, her body draped in a spare white cloth. I dab the perfumed oil at her temples, her neck, the crooks of her elbows and knees, and at the base of her feet. I dress her, panting, fighting against the loose heaviness of her limbs. When I am done I comb more of the oil through her thick black curls and braid them loosely. The floral scent—a cloying, jammy rose—gets in my nose, my throat, right down into the pit of me. Twice I rush upstairs and out, back into the pouring rain, to vomit my foamy guts up amongst the greenery. But the sun is hot, burning, *scorching*, even through the thick black clouds. Perhaps it is not the sun but the daylight itself, and I groan in agony.

The tower is safer. Cool and dark. But—there is Olea.

I push through the growing pain in my belly and sickness that comes in waves, folding Olea's hands across her stomach, pulling the white sheet up to rest beneath them. This is no golden cradle, no holy sepulchre cleansed by fire and ash, but it shall have to do. I pull a crooked old milking stool up to the side of the table, holding one hand just above Olea's head as I murmur the last rites my father burned into me as a child.

As above so below:
For the wicked and the pure
In this life and in death too
The same end must all endure.

I hold my hands in prayer, pressed to my forehead as though my thoughts might seep through my fingers and out into the grey-tinted air. The stench of burnt herbs is on my tongue. I close my eyes, darkness swimming with spots of greenish light, sickness roiling in me.

It is too hot in here. Sweat beads on my forehead, my neck. The storm rolls outside, thunder crashing. Everything down here echoes, but there is no life beyond me. No laughter from Olea, not a lecture on my pronunciation or a lesson in taxonomy; she is gone and waves of grief crash in me.

I would cut my hair to the scalp, hold my Silence for thirteen *months* if it could bring her back. I think back to our conversation about mourning, about the rites, and Olea's dislike of the traditions of death. Now I understand. Mourning has always brought me comfort. The loss of my mother, my father—neither unexpected in my life. I grew from babyhood knowing that one day I would hold their Silence, would shear my hair and throw it to the flames in their honour. And Aurelio...His death, my Silence, was as much relief as it was genuine grief. It was the end of something bad.

Olea's death is neither expected nor welcome. And it is my fault.

My hands tremble as a feverish cold takes me. My head pounds now with the force of a battering ram, my pulsing brain smashing inside my skull. I feel my forehead and it is ablaze, my tongue dry and swollen, lips cracking. Every tendon, every sinew, is shrieking in pain. And worst of all is the hollowness deep inside me, a gnawing, yearning pit of hunger that doubles me at the waist in untold agony.

Distantly I realise I've grabbed Olea's hand and I squeeze its coldness tight. It is not just grief—this pain, this disease, it has come from the antidote. Olea's dose was ten times mine, but she was ten times stronger, her life in the garden one long test. The inside of my skin feels as though it has been stuffed with a hundred thousand tiny hairs, each one barbed at the tip with poison; every movement, every breath, every *blink*, rubs my skin against itself and I roar in pain, breaking my Silence.

"I'm sorry," I sob.

I am a curse. This is punishment for my sins. For Aurelio, and the books—for the antidote, my selfish legacy, and Olea. I roll from the stool onto the floor, clutching my stomach, bile filling my mouth and nose. Blood drips from my lips and I don't know where it has come from. For one brief second I wish for Petaccia, for her to bear witness to my death. I hope she finds the vial. I hope she uncovers where I went wrong.

No, I think as another rush of pain drives me to darkness, ears ringing, thunder booming. I hope for neither. Death comes for us all, and that is the way it should be. I knew, I *knew* Petaccia's research was unnatural and yet I persisted, grateful to be noticed, glad for a future that was not marriage and death in the childbed. Selfish—everything I have done was purely for myself.

Would I change it, if I could? Would I take back the books, the slow twisting of the key in my locked-up mind, or these sleepless nights in the poison garden? Olea's lips on mine, her hand at my throat and the other at my heart? Perhaps it is the pain, the delirium, but in this moment I think—for knowledge, for freedom—I would not.

I fight it for as long as I can, until finally the blackness claims me.

Chapter Thirty-Three

I stumble through the maze of darkness, right up to the doors of the house of Death, but she refuses to draw me into the arms of Heaven.

The agony is endless. It isn't long before I am begging aloud for Hell to take me instead. Anything is better than this. *Please*, I beg silently. *Please, please, make it end. If there is a god, may he shepherd me away from this torture and grease the palms of those above—or below.* But if there is a god, he does not hear me, since Hell clearly doesn't want me either.

The pain is simultaneously hot and freezing cold, each movement I make fracturing my bones and mending them again so that they can break anew. My tongue is dry as dust, my teeth aching, too big for my mouth, blood seeping down my chin from my tattered gums.

In the throes of this pain, I dream of nightmarish landscapes, twisted roots blackened by fire atop writhing craters filled with maggots or the crush of soil overhead, crawling in my mouth and nose, spitting flies. In the next in-between place I find table after table heaped with food, roast chickens and succulent joints of lamb studded with rosemary. Thick wheels of yellow cheese and jugs of wine the colour of blood. I surge towards the feast, knowing there is a place set for me at the table although I am unable to see it.

At the head of the table there is a chair made of carved ivory, polished like a fresh duck egg. The seat of the chair is adorned with ropy red and black velvet, tassels creeping against its legs. Olea sits atop the throne, her head pushed back in ecstasy as she finishes chewing and licks the pink meat juices from her delicate fingers.

My heart thunders at the sight of her, but it is the feast that guides my feet. My body sways, a corpse-like stagger. I reach for the table. My nails are black and ripped down the middle and I claw at the meat, dragging a drumstick to my mouth.

I bite down, savouring the soft flesh between the sharpness of my teeth, the meat melting on my tongue. The taste of blood rushes down my throat, vibrant, still beating, beating like my heart should. The chicken in my hand goes limp, feathers drifting down my dress. I hardly notice that where before was a platter of cooked meat, now lies the body of a rabbit, another of a whole pig, barely cold.

Olea. Her face is bloodied, ruby droplets on her bare chest, rivulets running down past her navel and her hands slick with the dark display. She opens her eyes and they are the black of night, lips parted, teeth bared. She tears at something small and white and blood spurts down her chin.

The chair of ivory is a chair of bones, the velvet tassels the remnants of flesh. Olea leans forward in her throne and beckons me. *Come*, she whispers, and a familiar, aching wetness surges between my legs. *Come*.

I awaken, breathless, to the aroma of roses. Buttery early sunlight falls in beams around the edges of an ill-fitting shutter. I blink and slowly the room swims into relief.

It is not sunlight, but the flickering flames of candlelight; I am not in a bed, but somebody has laid my body across some kind of burlap sacking, which bunches between me and the hard flagstone floor.

It hits me then. I am alive.

I grope down my body, feeling the hardness of muscle and bones at my hips and the soft plumpness of my breasts. The dress I'm wearing is white and silken and I luxuriate in the feel of it across my skin, the fabric so light and sweet it is like spider silk. Every synapse fires within me. The candlelight is golden and glorious, my dress the most exquisite thing I have ever touched, my skin as soft and cold as fresh water. I pause.

My tongue snakes between my teeth, which are sharper than I recall. I cannot feel my heartbeat.

"Perfect."

The word comes out a purr, the voice without a face. Long seconds pass before I recall its owner. My hands drop to my sides, frozen. I would take the pain over this.

"What do you feel?"

Dr. Petaccia's face swims into view, only her eyes visible over the band of fabric she wears to cover her mouth, and my vision distorted by the angle of my neck. I try to turn my face away and she clucks disappointedly.

"Ah now," she scolds. "Must you really continue to be so mulish? Anybody would think you'd be a little more grateful."

I struggle to prop myself up on my elbows. My limbs are so

fluid they feel almost like water. No, more like running a moist-ened hand over glass. I judder, knocking my chin against my shoulder and biting down on my tongue.

The taste is…not quite right. It is blood and yet it is not. Some-how it is thicker, slower, honeyed. I try to hide my panic behind the action of sitting upright, but it doesn't work.

"Holy fuck."

I can't believe my eyes. I am sure I must be dreaming, another nightmare in the in-between taking over, for right ahead, upright on the table, legs dangling over its side as she peers down at me, is Olea.

"Well, quite," says the doctor, and I know I'm not hallucinat-ing. She steps away from both of us and lowers her mask to expose the rest of her face, clearly satisfied. Her grin is wolfish.

"*How?*" I exclaim.

Olea doesn't speak right away. It's clear she's just as confused as I am. She reaches up to her face, examining her nose, her lips, her cheeks, through the gentle touch of her fingertips. Her skin is barely a whisper darker than her nightgown, smooth and unblem-ished. Her lips are a healthy peach. When she opens her mouth, her voice is throaty with disuse.

"The cure," she breathes.

"Well done," Petaccia says to me by way of agreeing. "I *knew* all we needed was a little freshness. Fresh eyes, fresh passion." Her gaze travels between the two of us and her wolfish smile deepens.

"It worked?" Olea asks.

I touch the satin material of my nightgown again, rubbing it between my fingers as if I could start a fire and blaze this whole place to the ground. A wave of rage crests in me. *Did* it work? And what is the cost?

"I told you to trust me, my dear. Didn't I say—"

"Where are my clothes?" I demand. I attempt to climb to my feet but the effect is ruined by my slippery limbs. I sink back against the sacking, winded.

"I've taken them away to be examined, and likely burned. They were quite badly damaged—bodily fluids, you know—during your transformation."

"Transformation?" My anger dissipates in a cloud of smoke. "What do you mean 'transformation'?"

"Well, you're hardly the same as you were, are you?" Petaccia chides. "Look at yourself."

She points to the floor beside me, and there is a hand mirror, as if she's been waiting for the opportunity to draw my attention to it. I know I should ignore her goading, force my limbs to obey and stalk out of here, but I can't help the curiosity that holds me frozen as I reach for the looking glass.

I hold the mirror to my face, letting the horror—and the wonder—unfurl in my expression.

The first thing I notice is my hair. It is thicker and longer than it has been in months, now falling to my shoulders in gentle burnished waves. Where Olea's skin is alabaster, mine is like sun-warmed sand. Gone is the greyish tint it has developed over the last weeks, the dark circles under my eyes, that perpetual look of having not eaten enough. I am not plump, but the jut of my cheekbones now looks as if it has always been that way, as if I have been carved from gilded stone.

"The antidote…" I say. "It restored…" Restored, rejuvenated, *reanimated*. The thought is a stab right in my gut. I look at Olea, and the meeting of our gazes is electric, a flash of lightning under my skin. She understands. We are perfect, re-created in the Lord's perfect image—and that does not come for free.

"Yes." Petaccia claps her hands together in delight. "It remade you both. I'll admit I wasn't sure it had worked. Especially you, Olea." She shakes her head and clicks her tongue, this time in pleasure. "I'm glad I was wrong. I was starting to think that all my plans were for nothing. And when you took her from the garden..." She shakes her head at me. "It turns out loneliness is quite the growth inhibitor. Who knew? Well, I did. I began to suspect as much after the last debacle. I'm glad all that worked out too. And human blood! My god, I can't believe I didn't think of it. The *Dendrocnide moroides* was a nice touch—I have a theory about the powdering process, but I won't bore you with that now—"

"You," Olea growls. "You did this. You orchestrated *all of it*." She jumps off the table, making to march towards Petaccia with her fists raised, but her knees give way and she crumples to the flagstones at my feet. I scramble to help her, pulling her towards me, instantly aware of the coolness of her skin, the fire she creates in my touch.

Petaccia says nothing except, "Careful."

"What do you mean?" I ask, turning back to Olea. Her eyes are dark with anger.

"She planted you," she says. "In those rooms—right where she knew you would see me. For years she told me I shouldn't leave the garden, shouldn't have friends. For fucking *years* she isolated me in this place. And then one day *you* turn up, and you know about grief and dying and you want so badly to learn. I didn't suspect it then, but I'm right, aren't I?" She glares at the doctor. "You put her right there, for me. Like some kind of *prize* to be won."

"Is it true?" I demand fiercely, though I know she chose my rooms. It feels so...calculated. And, of course, I feel foolish for imagining the doctor would have taken me on if my father had merely *asked*.

"Eh." Petaccia shrugs. "That's hardly the worst of my crimes."

"How could you?" Olea shrieks.

"Calm down."

"Make me." Olea bites down on her inner cheek and spits a bloody glob at the doctor. Petaccia only steps to the side, as if she expected exactly this. As if this is not the first time Olea has spat or shouted at her, and as if she simply doesn't care.

"Oh, Olea, stop being childish. Isn't it time you admitted that this is bigger than you? Bigger than all of us in this room? This is about the future of humanity."

"I never asked to be a part of this."

"No, that is true enough, but you've been a part of it since birth and I'm afraid that was a sacrifice I was absolutely willing to make. I'd do it again if it got us here. Wouldn't you? Look at you both! Back from the dead in full glory. I know you feel a bit unsteady now, but in half an hour you'll be right as rain. I'd bet my doctorate on it." She laughs, as though this is the funniest thing she's ever said.

"What do you mean?" I ask, taking in Olea's stricken expression. What colour was left in her cheeks has leached away and the effect is eerie, like looking at a ghost. "A sacrifice you were willing to make—are you talking about *Olea*?"

"Florencia?" Olea prompts. "Tell me it isn't true."

"Well, I couldn't exactly try the microdosing many other ways, could I?" Petaccia sighs. It is a petulant sound, small, although it sends the story of Olea's life down like a house of cards. "I've always suspected it was part of the equation, though I'll admit I wasn't sure exactly how it would all fit together. I suppose I was wrong, in that way. But I did manage to prove that consistent dosing of the toxins can cause a certain level of synchronicity—"

"*You* did this?" I don't try to keep the horror from my voice. "You made her this way?"

Petaccia shrugs again. "It started during my pregnancy. The garden called to me then. So perhaps it wasn't all my fault—"

"Olea is yours?" I fight to my feet, leaving Olea slumped on the flagstones. I'm not sure what I intend to do, but the rage is blinding and I can hardly stop myself as I stride—or attempt to stride—across the room. "What happened to 'I am no mother'?"

Petaccia doesn't even back away. She holds her ground, and it is only then I realise she's not unarmed. In one hand she carries a knife with a blade so pointed it makes me feel sick. None of us know how this works, how the antidote has changed us, how precarious our fresh grasp on life might be. Flashes of my nightmares stutter and all I see is blood. I falter.

"Semantics, Thora. As you said yourself. She was the garden's before she was mine," Petaccia says matter-of-factly. "I have never considered myself a mother. I dreamt of this place constantly, and when I wasn't by the wall it felt a little like going mad. I made a mistake the first time, let Niccolò get in my head, let him lord his experience over me. 'Your father wouldn't have wanted this,' blah blah. As if he really knew what my father would have wanted. My father was the one who *gave* me the bloody idea. Of course, by the time I brought the child in, it was too late, and Niccolò never let me have enough time. By the second pregnancy I knew that early exposure was absolutely vital to maintain a certain level of health. Niccolò tried to sabotage me every step of the way, spineless little man that he was, nothing was ever good enough, but I learned from the first time, and frankly he looked better under his little burial mound in the trees." She smirks. Olea's face has grown still. "When I tell you I have never been so sick in my *life* as those months." Petaccia lets out a cheerful chuckle, as if the murder of her child's father, and the lifelong, systematic abuse of her daughter, is a fucking joke. "But I was determined. I couldn't do it to myself, you understand—too impractical—but a child? It turns out if you introduce them early enough, frequently enough, they can adapt to anything. Of course, I never meant for any of it to manifest outwardly. I was aiming for immunity, not conformity, but I suppose the end result is the same. In any case: a little poison each day keeps the outside world at bay."

Olea is entirely speechless. Is it disbelief? Dissociation? Or is that more resignation I see in her face? Tears well in her eyes but she refuses to let them fall, her throat bobbing with each painful swallow. Petaccia's singsongy voice shows no sign of remorse. In fact, there is nothing about her behaviour that even hints at apology. *She's fucking insane.*

"Let me get this straight," I say with as much fight as I can muster. "You microdosed through your whole pregnancy, then dumped your daughter in the garden and prayed she'd become a monster?"

Olea flinches at the word, but Petaccia does not.

"No." The doctor examines the blade of her knife with the same quizzical stare I've seen levelled at her seedlings. "I prayed she would solve the puzzle. And now look, here we are, albeit in a roundabout sort of way—"

"No fucking thanks to you."

"Entirely fucking thanks to me, actually." Petaccia glares, flashing the knife. Still, I can't bring myself to feel guilty for my language. "If it hadn't been for me, none of this would have been possible. And now, here we are, staring down the barrel of the greatest scientific discovery the world has ever known. Do you understand the door you two have just unlocked? I've checked both your vitals and you're doing excellent. A bit of muscle weakness, but I'm sure that will pass. I have a few questions about what the next few days will look like—I think we should treat this as a kind of clinical trial, given that we're already here—"

"The only door we've unlocked is the one I'm about to walk right through," I snap. "I can't speak for Olea, but I will not be sticking around to help you with any kind of trial. I never agreed to this."

Petaccia laughs. The sound is throaty, so like Olea's laughter when I first met her in the garden that I freeze in place. Olea has hardly moved, barely blinked; she stares at the wall ahead as though she's trying to imagine she is anywhere but here. I don't blame her, but it would be nice to have some support.

"You think you're just going to walk out of here? After everything I've done for you? I don't think so."

"You said yourself, we're perfectly well now. Why should we stay? I can't think of anything worse than being stuck in this place while you play doctor."

"I said you were doing excellently," Petaccia concedes, "but we still have the question of how your bodies will adjust to the added toxins. At the very least I need you here until we understand how the antidote interacts with the latent toxicity in—"

"We're still poison, aren't we." Olea glances away from the wall, finally meeting my gaze again. I hadn't considered this until Olea said it, but the possibility sinks in with surprising speed. Petaccia may have removed her mask, but she is still dressed with good coverage.

"Both of us?"

"I haven't had the time to properly assess—"

"Both of us?" I say again, louder.

"Early signs point to yes." Petaccia waves the knife in the direction of the door, where two hares hang unnoticed from the knob, their bodies limp; green-black tendrils extend from their mouths, marking their fur akin to tabby stripes, and their eyes are the cloudy grey of skies before a storm.

This is the final straw. I sink to my knees again, relieved when they bark in familiar, living pain. All I did to protect myself from the garden this time and none of it matters. I'm as toxic as Olea is. I don't cry, but sickness swirls and I dry heave a couple of times.

"Yes, well." Petaccia sheathes the knife, clearly no longer worried I'll attack her. "Enough with all that. There's no evidence yet it won't pass with time, so I suggest you both try to ride it out. I'll leave you to it, but do make sure you make a note of any symptoms over the next couple of days, positive or negative. I'll be back to check on you shortly."

I watch her go, considering—briefly—how easy it might be to launch myself at her right now. If I'm poison, then I can get rid of her, no problem. It would be immensely satisfying to see her collapse, her skin greying and that horrid inkiness spreading from my touch. She hasn't developed any tolerance for this new version of us, after all. But the rational part of my brain holds me in place. Without Petaccia we would be technically "free," but then what? The antidote was supposed to cure Olea of her deathly touch, not make me the same.

What if our toxicity doesn't pass?

Chapter Thirty-Four

I'm leaving."

Olea is still on the floor where Petaccia abandoned her. I know I should go to her. I *want* to go to her, but I refuse to let her convince me to stay here. It doesn't matter what Petaccia believes; I have to see the effects of the antidote for myself.

Olea doesn't react. She barely even looks at me. I reach the doorway before adding, "Are you coming?"

"Why." She punctuates the question with such force an answer seems near pointless. Then she adds, softer, "We can't go anywhere."

"I think it's long past the time we trust that woman without any sort of proof," I say snidely. "Don't you think? She's been lying to you your whole life and you still eat up everything she says. Why don't you grow a backbone?"

"You say that as if it's easy." Olea sighs. She looks frail—not in her body exactly, not like before, but she still holds herself as though she is exhausted. "Florencia's my—"

"You *don't* have to call her your mother," I cut her off. I try to soften my tone but I'm antsy now. I need to get out of this cellar.

"No matter what she says. This is a woman who's kept you on reins, poisoned you daily for her own scientific beliefs."

"She raised me," Olea says quietly. "Every thought I have, every belief, every doubt, is one she's planted there in my mind. It doesn't matter what she is to me—she's right about that. There were times I *wished* she was my mother, though." She lets out a bitter half laugh. "Can you believe that? I dreamt that she would come to me one day and say, 'Well done, Olea, you've done your duty. We've found the cure. The experiment is over. Let's take you home and you can meet your siblings and all of these friends who are waiting for you.' And we would ride off together to a little house on the edge of a big old city, and I'd never have to see or touch another plant ever again."

"Olea—"

"Let me talk." She blows out a puff of air. "How can I simply turn that kind of feeling off? She's the only constant in my whole life. Everything she told me, I believed. Every meal I ate, every scrap of clothing on my back, everything comes from her."

"She abused you," I say firmly. "You don't have to be grateful to her for this."

"I'm not grateful," Olea snaps. "But I can't just turn it off. I have to have some faith."

"She's not somebody either of us should *ever* be putting our faith in." I run my hands through my hair, feel its silky length with a resentful kind of thrill. "To think, she talked about supporting women in science. That's how she drew me in. I'd have taken anything she gave me, swallowed any pill as long as she told me to, so I understand a little. I was happy just to break free and be out here on my own. But no, she sold me a dream of partnership. And I fell for it. All I'm saying is, now isn't the time to wish we'd done things differently."

Olea stares at her hands in her lap, examining their new pallor. She doesn't speak. I stand in the centre of the room flexing the muscles in my hands, arms, calves, feeling the push and pull. Petaccia is right about this at least: I already feel stronger.

"Are you coming?" I say again. "*Olea*. No? Fine. I'll go alone."

I stalk up the stairs, taking them two at a time. I'm not sure I could have managed that before, but the thought is fleeting. I don't know what I'm planning to do; I don't know anything other than I can't stay here and I want to prove Petaccia wrong. I make it to the next floor, halfway across the room, before Olea catches up to me.

"Thora, wait." I turn, trying to hide my relief. I don't know what I'm doing, true, but I'd rather not have to do any of it alone. "You can't go out there."

The relief sours in my stomach. "Olea—"

"The sun," she blurts. "If we're still...If we're like I was before. I..."

"The antidote was supposed to *cure*," I remind her.

"Florencia said—"

"Fuck Florencia!" I shout. The word feels so good to say, ripping off all restraints. "For god's sake. Do you still believe *every* little thing she tells you?"

"You saw the hares," Olea says, as fierce as I am. "Stop treating me like I'm stupid. I'm not stupid, Thora. Just because I've been sheltered here doesn't mean I know nothing. Or have you forgotten that I'm the one who taught you half of what you know?"

"That was different."

"Oh, it's always different when it's what you think. I'm telling you to be cautious. At least grab one of the parasols."

I don't have the patience for this. I can't describe what's come over me, but it's like a fog has lifted. Everything stands in sharp relief, magnified by a thousand—even my frustration. I march to the window, ignoring Olea's protests. She backs away, grabbing a shawl from the chaise and covering her head and shoulders. I claw at the shutters. Maybe Olea is right and this is stupid; I remember the heat of the sun when she was out there, dying. But I don't care. I need to know, I *need*—

I fling them open.

Golden sunlight streams into the room, illuminating Olea's tapestries, her books and trinkets, the faded fleur-de-lis pattern on her chaise. She blinks, stunned, shielding her face with her hand.

"You see?" I demand. "Lies, all of it."

"No, but sometimes it's worse than others," Olea murmurs. "Some days it's stronger. You still need to be careful."

"She's a *liar*, Olea. She's indoctrinated you. Stop taking her word for it."

"Or maybe the toxicity is just waning, like she said. There are so many answers we don't have. How can you just assume she's lying about everything? She's the one who pushed for this; she's the one who said we could make it happen. We *died*."

"I only have her word that it happened to me too."

"You're being obstinate for no reason!" Olea exclaims.

"I'm not. I'm trying to establish that everything we've been told, everything we've believed, could easily be an untruth. I know you're frightened to go against her, but I'm trying to show you that we have to, Olea. The only people we can trust right now are ourselves. We're the ones who have to live with this. And I genuinely don't think us arguing about this is going to help. So, I will ask one final time: Are you coming with me?"

"No. Because you shouldn't go. If we're in this together, then why are you so quick to leave?"

"Why are you so quick to want to stay?" I return coldly. I shake my head, forging towards the door. Olea rushes after me, reaching for my arm and trying to pull me back. I shake her off, thundering out into the garden, where the sun is hot and bright but so, so much better than the darkness of the cellar. Olea chases me, reaching out again. "Don't fucking touch me," I swear. "This is your fault."

"My fault?" Olea gapes. "You're the one who brewed the damn 'cure' and made me take it."

"Oh, that's rich. I never would have made it if I wasn't trying to save you."

"I never asked you to save me!" Olea's throat cords and the laugh that comes out is verging on hysteria. "I asked you to *let me die!*" *This is good*, I think wildly. *Let's get it all out in the open.*

"Are you kidding me? You said you'd *kill yourself* if you had to keep living this way, knowing full well I was trying to save you. How do you think that made me feel? Have you got any idea how manipulative that is?"

"That was never meant to be a threat. I was trying to be honest. I couldn't take it any more, all the lonely hours and days. But then the universe intervened and now you're here with me. So why can't we stay?"

I fold my arms across my chest. "So you got what you wanted, then. You got *me* where you wanted. You never wanted to leave, did you? Or is it simply Petaccia's thoughts speaking over your own again?"

"How can you be so cruel?" Olea blinks back tears. "You know it's not that simple. I never wanted you to sacrifice anything; I just wanted you with me. I *wanted* you in every way I could have you. I thought you wanted the same thing. You certainly kissed me like you did."

"I'm not being cruel; I'm making a statement of fact. You wanted somebody to come and be with you in the garden, since you can't leave, and now that I'm stuck here I'm sure you'll be perfectly happy to go about your life as you always have. I can't understand why you're so content to just go on as normal!"

"Why can't we?" Olea begs. "Is it really such an awful life? There's nobody to bother us. You don't have to worry about money, or finding some replacement husband with your silly friend—"

"You think that's what I was doing?" I bark. "I told you Leo is my *friend*." *Was my friend*, I remind myself.

"You sure *seem* friendly with him," Olea says. "The way you went on and on about how much he mistrusted me, and how much losing his wife ruined his goddamn life. People don't have friends like that. You must have been looking for some kind of security, a backup plan, even if you didn't know it. That's your problem, Thora—you've always one foot out the door."

"A backup plan," I repeat coldly.

"Well, it's hard to imagine you wanting to fuck him."

Heat rises in my cheeks, but it's a mixture of anger and something else, something like lust. "What, like I want to fuck you?"

Olea is inches from my face. I can smell her, the mixture of sweat and rose oil, and the bitter scent that is so intrinsically *her*. She's right, though. It's all I want. It's all I've wanted since the moment we met. And, god, it's probably half the reason we're in this godforsaken mess.

"You can pretend you're over the feelings between us," Olea says. "Deny it all you want. It's not my job to convince you to love me. I'm just saying that this life doesn't have to be as awful as you imagine it. You have the whole garden. People have lived many lives in spaces much smaller than this. We have food, we have books. Florencia will get us whatever we want as long as we help her out with the research. And you can do your own research too! Whatever you want to do, whatever you want to learn."

"You've lived like this your whole life, but I haven't. Excuse me for having trouble coming to terms with the fact that I'll never be able to leave without posing a risk to other people. I won't be able to travel, to see new things. How will I be able to continue my research, or do any of the things I wanted?"

"Were you planning to do all those things anyway? When you arrived here you told me that learning, the university, was your dream. You're still here. That hasn't changed. Why can't you be content with this life, just for a little while? We can find a way around this, I promise. We just have to give it time. That's why I'm asking you not to go marching off like you're going to war—you don't even know what you're planning."

"I swore I would never allow myself to be put in a cage again," I argue, frustration making my voice ropy. It hurts that she's right but that she doesn't understand why I can't just roll over and accept this. "First it was my father and his sepulchre, and then my goddamn husband. This place, learning, was *my* dream, but it was never just about learning either. It was about the freedom—"

"You can still be free." Olea tentatively places her hand under my chin. She holds it, her grip surprisingly firm, so I can look nowhere except her soulful eyes. "In here...we can be ourselves. You felt that before, when you kissed me."

"This isn't just about our pleasure any more."

"Why not?" Olea demands. "Are you telling me things are truly better out there? A world with husbands and duty and social graces? The same world you've been running from?"

"You don't understand," I growl. "You've never been out there."

"I know enough to know that what we have would *never* be allowed out there. Clara said—"

I rip my chin from Olea's grasp and turn back to the gate. Olea is right. My father couldn't stand the idea that I didn't want to marry, and Aurelio was disgusted by me. Leo can't even stand himself. But are acceptance and love, if they only exist in a cage, good enough?

"This isn't about our pleasure," I say again, firmer. If I say it enough times, maybe it will sink in—and maybe it will assuage the flicker of acknowledgement inside me. "Don't you dare bring Clara into this. If it wasn't for you she'd probably still be alive, and I wouldn't be here."

"I'm just trying to say that the garden isn't your enemy..."

Olea trails off as I stop. My heart sinks.

"What?"

"It doesn't matter anyway," I say. "I'm not going to leave."

"Really?" Olea's hopefulness is an icy spear through my heart. I turn on her, a snarl on my lips.

"I can't go even if I want to. The gate is locked. She's padlocked it from the outside."

Chapter Thirty-Five

I sit at the gate until nightfall. I'm not sure what I'm expecting to happen, but the thought that if something *does* happen I'll be here to see it comforts me. Olea disappears back into her tower— it is still hers, isn't it? Nothing in this place is truly mine. For the first time since I arrived here I find myself wishing for my clothes, the ones I brought from Aurelio's house; they are the last shred of proof that I ever had that other life, that I ever existed outside this place.

Who will remember me? Only Leo might care that I'm gone, and honestly I wouldn't blame him if he didn't. I've treated him so badly I wouldn't be surprised if he took my absence merely as a sign that I was done with him. This thought saddens me most of all. The legacy I hoped to build for myself is gone, and the garden is all that remains.

Not that it is all bad. I realise pretty quickly that this new life comes with several perks. I rarely get hungry, but when I do, even basic bread tastes like the best thing I have ever eaten. I pick the fruit off Olea's trees with abandon, gorging myself on its sweet, pulpy flesh, spitting seeds and scratching pits into the earth. I

wake each day to the sun on my face, not a single ache from sleeping amongst the flowers, and know I could easily walk the length
of the garden ten times over without tiring—not that I do. But I
could.

I return to the tower only once over the next few days, in a
fit of frustration at some godforsaken time in the early morning,
when I thrash about the sitting room looking for a pair of scissors, candles, and a box of matches. Olea must hear me from the
upstairs room, but she doesn't come to see what I'm doing, and I
don't ask her for help. I can't bear it.

I carry my haul back out to the gate and sit in the crumbly
mud in the patch between weeds, still wild and rambling in Olea's
absence. I light the candle and hold my newly grown hair over its
flame, shearing great swathes into the fire, where they sizzle and
pop as normal hairs do.

"For Olea," I say. "For me. For my life and hers. For whatever
this is. I hold my Silence in grief." I repeat several of my father's
prayers and sit for the rest of the night in Silence, watching the
candle burn down. There is no breeze and the flame goes steady
all the rest of the night and through most of the following day. It
doesn't bring me peace as it once would have, but there is some
comfort in the old motions and I'm determined to try to lay the
past to rest. At some point I fall asleep. My dreams are peaceful,
and when I wake my hair is exactly as long as it was before, transformed while I slept.

"Well, fuck me," I say, enjoying the harshness of the word on
my tongue. There is some new freedom in this, too.

Olea isn't surprised when I tell her about my hair. When I
finally return from my garden vigil with my stubby candle, blunt
scissors, and the box of matches, Olea is lounging on the chaise

in the sitting room with a book in one hand. The other circles her abdomen lazily, tracing symbols of infinity across the soft white of her nightgown as she reads.

"So we're stuck in time as well as in location." Olea shrugs carelessly. "More fool me, I guess."

"Do you understand what this means?" I ask. After our argument I don't want to treat her as if she's stupid. She's right: She's not stupid; we just have different priorities.

"That you'll stop sitting by the gate like a little lost dog?" She wrinkles her nose endearingly, this time playing dumb. She's forgiven me already, I realise. "Or...that you're sorry you said such horrid things before?"

"Neither." I roll my eyes playfully. "Well, no. I *am* sorry. And I will stop sitting by the gate, waiting to feel strong enough to smash the lock. But, no, it means that our bodies are in some kind of stasis. So the antidote *does* work. It restores us to our 'natural' state, which is a kind of healing itself. It's just that the antidote, once in our bodies, thinks that our natural state is *its* natural state, which is, well, a mixture of poison plant and blood."

"I don't follow." Olea drops her book to the floor carelessly. Her eyes are fixed on me, but she continues the lazy circling of her finger, round her belly button, up her sternum, across the tops of her breasts. She's teasing me, I realise. She knows exactly what I'm trying to say but she wants to drag it out. I watch her fingers.

"The antidote needs the plant component to create the longevity and healing aspect," I say, only half paying attention. It's all fallen into place in my mind already. Now I am strong, I feel better than I have in years. I'm not lying about the padlock either: I'm almost certain, if I built up the strength, I could snap it with my bare hands eventually. "Plants are notoriously robust and can survive in some of the harshest environments, and they're also self-healing. When you combine that with the toxicity, which forms a natural safety barrier between the plant and the rest of the world, you get a colloid with one main goal: protection."

"So the antidote is protecting us," Olea says, her voice husky. "Making our bodies...stronger. Faster. Healthier."

"Making them *perfect*."

Olea's body really is perfect. Her nipples are soft peaks beneath the thin silk nightgown, her skin soft as perfumed oil. Her hair falls in coils over her shoulders, over the collarbones I once saw from my desk, and from the darkness of the gate. The sight of them then, and the sight of them now, awakens something inside me. Something primal. I clench my thighs hard.

"What I said before...about Leonardo..." Olea says.

"Shut up."

"I'm sorry—"

"Enough," I growl. I stride to her side, thrusting one hand against the back of the chaise so I can lean over her. My hair falls in a curtain around our faces and Olea looks up at me, that same lazy expression on her face even as the apology hangs between us. I banish it with a kiss, hungry and deep.

Her lips are soft and wet, parting immediately to draw me in. My tongue finds hers and the graze of her newly sharpened teeth on my lips is enough to make me ache so hard the agony is delicious. I kiss her until there is no breath left in my body, forcing myself to hold my hands on either side of her head and not move them lower.

"*Fuck*," Olea breathes. Her eyes are hazy with pleasure, her cheeks flushed a soft pink. "Do you— Is it..." She stops. Licks her lips. She's trembling. "Do you feel as if every part of you is singing?"

No. It is screaming—but not in fear. In pleasure. It is heat, it is light; it is static in every inch of my skin, almost too much for me to bear.

"Yes."

"I *am* sorry," Olea confesses. "For all of it."

"Olea," I grind out. She tenses. "If you don't stop apologising and kiss me again, I shall go entirely mad. Okay?"

She melts back into the chaise, one fist bunching in my night-gown, pulling me down so that my right knee lands between her legs. I push the nightgown up hungrily and Olea writhes as my knee touches the soft skin of her thighs. It is exactly as supple as I dreamt it would be. She grips my arm, guiding my body with ease until my leg presses against her softest part. It feels as natural as breathing.

There is no panic, no dutiful pretence like with Aurelio. In all my days and nights with my stolen books, my fingers curling tight inside myself, I never could have imagined this. The heat that grows between us, the frantic scrape of nails across my back as I grind my leg between Olea's, feeling her wetness and the feral joy it unleashes deep within me. Olea grasps my breast, her other hand desperately clawing my nightdress up and over my head. I rip Olea's gown like it is made from paper, the ragged tear of the material a symphony to my ears as I bite down on her neck. Her skin is slick with salt, bittersweet and tender against my tongue. She writhes in pleasure, wrapping her legs around my waist.

It is a frenzy. Fingers searching, tongues circling. I kiss my way down Olea's neck, her chest, first one nipple and then the other. I taste the cool, creamy garden scent of her skin, feel the tickle of the coarse hair beneath her navel. I stare into Olea's eyes as I dip lower, lower, and then dive between Olea's legs and suckle at the tender skin there as if she is made of honey. And, oh, she tastes as sweet. The sound of her moans drives my own hand between my legs as she begs. *Harder*, she urges, though she doesn't say it aloud. She doesn't have to; our minds and our bodies might as well be one. *More.*

More, more, *more.*

Olea shifts, scrambling upright and pushing me back. She forces me down with her hands on my shoulders, and in seconds she is hurling herself at me again, barely giving me time to think. She shoves me flat onto my back and climbs onto my face, at once grinding down and leaning back so that her fingers can make their mark on me in return.

Her fingers search hungrily, rubbing against the folds of my skin, grazing my most sensitive flesh as I lick and suck in return. The sight of her, head thrown back, mouth open in ecstasy...It is heaven. It is *ruin*—for I know I will never settle for anything other again.

"Shall we tell Florencia?" Olea says softly. It is late afternoon, though I think neither of us has any idea how much time has passed, too caught up in the map of each other's bodies. We have stopped more than once, lazily, enjoying the delay, in order to fill carafes with ruby wine, devouring grapes and plates of cheese Olea has brought up from the cellar, before returning to our frantic explorations. We lie now, in another blissful lull, naked in the garden beneath the canopy of poison trees.

"About what?" I ask, playing dumb.

Olea turns her head to me and the sunlight catches on her nose, her full lips still raw from my kisses. What might, in another life, have been awkward between us is nothing of the kind. "I mean. She asked us to keep records about how we've been feeling since we took the cure, and—I don't know about you, but I haven't exactly been truthful in mine. It feels too…private."

"I've not kept any records at all. Why should I?"

Olea rests her head on my chest and her hair is warm and heavy. It smells like flowers and cream. Her breath tickles my bare breasts and I feel another impossible surge of desire. I could do this all day, every day, forever and ever and still not tire of the taste of her, the scent, the feel of her soft skin against mine. For the first time in days it seems as though a future in the garden— even if just a temporary one—is not truly awful.

"I don't think we should tell her," I add. "This kind of strength…I don't think it would do her any good to know about it. And the other things, the feelings…I doubt this is what she's interested in."

"Me either," Olea agrees quietly. "I don't think we should tell her. Not yet, anyway. Not until we know more about how it might play out. It's like…It's like seeing everything in sunlight. The world is ablaze with it. I've never seen, never *felt* like this."

Relief rocks me. The old Thora would have wanted to turn over our discoveries immediately, desperate to please. The fact that the antidote has the power not only to heal but also to strengthen, to build stamina, to heighten every sensation, is *groundbreaking*. This is not just a cure for all. It has the potential to completely revolutionise humanity. No more disease, no more wounds, but no more hunger or true thirst either. And we still don't know the effects on aging or emotional conditions, or the true bounds of our new strength. I'm surprised, but truly happy, that Olea understands the need for caution.

"Not just that," I say. "We deserve this peace, don't we? Why shouldn't we keep it to ourselves for a little while. After all you've been through at her hands, the pain you've suffered in this place, why can't she wait?"

"You're right." Olea is quiet. "She lied to me."

"Right. And once we set this ball rolling, there will be no going back. Petaccia has no idea what she's unleashed. And besides..." I shrug, jostling Olea's head gently, trying to banish her grief. She has hardly spoken of Petaccia's revelation about Olea's origins, but I know she's hurting. "Maybe I want you to myself. Just for a little while."

Olea's breath slows as she whistles a cool breeze over the top of my breasts. I wriggle, clenching my thighs tight. Tentatively she pinches my right nipple between her thumb and forefinger, first gently and then harder until my own breathing quickens in response. Olea lifts her head and meets my gaze as her other hand trails the length of my body, sending electric zaps of energy right to my core. Her fingertips are freezing, sending shivers in waves as she finds the damp patch of hair between my legs, tugging playfully, then slips one icy finger between my lips. I gasp in delight.

"You can keep me to yourself anytime," she murmurs, and lowers her sharp teeth to my waiting breast.

Chapter Thirty-Six

In the days and nights that follow, I am aware only of the world in terms of *needs*. Hunger, thirst, lust, exhaustion: each need begins small, a kernel, but unattended it becomes a flame. We sleep where we fall, often with our limbs entwined, fingers and mouths sticky. When we are not sleeping, eating, or otherwise engaged, Olea and I raid her library, reading and performing the tales aloud. I have never heard Olea laugh as she does during these in-between hours, when we dress in fresh nightgowns and wrap our hair in towels to act as queens and servants.

We sketch and paint with Olea's battered charcoal and water-colour set, often setting up where the trees grow thickest. One evening we go as far as taking a bottle of wine and a blanket to the fountain, where we set up camp for several hours in the moonlight. I draw Olea amongst the blooms, a riot of lilies and foxglove captured in strokes of blushing pinks and purples. She lies back, resting her elbows on the ground and her hands across her bare breasts, her legs parted at the knees so I can capture the petals within.

When we return the following day the streaks of paint from our lovemaking still spatter the bright stones in a pastel haze. We are both so aroused at the sight of the evidence we left behind that we spend another hour lying amongst the wreckage, grass in our hair and thorns pressing against our bare legs. The scratches heal within minutes, but the pain they elicit is sharp and fresh and—*delicious*.

Petaccia returns to the garden only thrice during this time. More lies, for she claimed she would check in regularly, but I'm glad she doesn't. Mostly I'm too enraptured by Olea to care. Petaccia appears once while we are cooking, a figure dressed in a black hooded robe and ever-present black gloves. She speaks little, keeping a careful distance that neither Olea nor I care to disturb. We hand over our notes—almost entirely fabricated as they are—and then ignore her until she leaves.

The second time she comes, Petaccia brings food and wine, great sacks of pasta and rice, small potatoes and jars of brined olives and cheese. I watch her pull the little cart through the winding paths of the garden, its wheels oiled so it is near-enough silent. I glance at Olea, and her shrug is confirmation enough: This is normal. This is how she has survived all these years.

"She comes a different way, and at a different hour, each time," Olea says softly when she notices my expression, no doubt dark as thunder. "As a child I thought there might be other gates, but truly if there are I've never found them."

"So you could never escape if you wanted to." Sickness roils in me, warring with the heat of anger. The deeper I swim in this dream, the closer comes the sulphurous stink of hell.

"I didn't want to." Olea shrugs again and the gesture is so practised, so defeated, that I wonder if she believes her own lies. If that's the only way she can process the magnitude of ills Petaccia has burdened her with all these years.

When Petaccia arrives with the food on the small handcart, I'm ready and waiting outside. Olea hovers in the doorway, a ghost in the daylight. Petaccia waves and grins—as though this is the most normal thing in the world.

"Supplies," she says briskly. "Olea, unload the cart."

Olea moves jerkily to do as she's told, but I step in her way.

"You do it," I say.

"Excuse me?"

"You unload the cart." The old Thora would have cowered in shame at my brashness, but anger might as well steam from my pores for the good it would do trying to keep it in. "Olea's not your slave."

Petaccia straightens her shoulders and stares me right in the eye. "Do you think you're in a good position for bargaining?" she asks.

"You have more to lose than we do. If you want notes from us, confirmation of theories or contradictions, then a bit of work on your end wouldn't go amiss. We're sick of you treating us like chattel. And don't get me started on the way you've treated Olea— for saying she's your own goddamn flesh and blood." The words pour out of me. I can't believe I ever thought I could trust her.

Petaccia's dark eyes glitter with a mixture of what might be amusement and malice; it's always so hard to tell. She shifts so she can see Olea clearly over my shoulder.

"Is this how you feel?" she asks coldly.

Olea is silent. I turn, urging her with my eyes to agree with me, to back me on this the way I know she desperately wants to. She doesn't deserve to be in this mental prison as well as a physical one. But Olea stares down at her hands, fingers clenched—fingers that were, an hour ago, curled so hard inside me I wept from the beauty of it.

"Exactly what I thought," Petaccia says. "You see, Thora, Olea is not so quick to turn her back on the one who has nurtured her—"

"You call this *nurture*?" I gesture wildly at the sacks and jars of food.

"Olea has had access to everything she could possibly need. I really don't see your problem. Any other woman would be grateful for such an opportunity. I taught her to read and write myself; she has access to novels and plays and scientific treatises, books on art and music, and the instruments and utensils to practise. If she ever wanted for anything, all she had to do was ask." Petaccia pauses for a second, reaching up to adjust her protective clothing, and then points at me. "Isn't this the same thing you *wished* for?" she demands.

I balk. "It's not the same and you know it—"

"Is it not?" Petaccia bares her stained teeth in a smile that's half grimace. "I wasn't lying when I said I saw something of myself in you, Thora. A young widow, trapped in society's customs and graces, without the financial or physical wherewithal to get out. A woman forced to marry for the sake of seeming respectability. A woman judged and criticised for asking questions, for wanting to *know* about this world we live in. Olea has never been exposed to any of that. I wanted to give you the same opportunity—"

"There's no reasoning with her," Olea says quietly. It's the first thing she's said the entire time Petaccia has been here, and it has the same weary detachment as always. "Come on. Help me unload the food. It'll be quicker that way."

"No," I say, very calmly. "The doctor unloads the food."

"Thora, please—"

"Olea." I fix her with a gaze that I hope says it all. *If we don't stand up to her, if you don't stand up to her, then we are nothing more than guinea pigs in this place. We might as well leave.*

Olea doesn't move. She doesn't speak. Indecision thins her lips. She knows I'm right: the lock on the gate was deterrent enough to keep me from fleeing right after our awakening, but it is Olea that keeps us here now, her evergreen fear of life outside the garden masquerading as concern about the long-term clinical effects of our cure. Without Olea I would not still be here, and she knows it. But I know she has a lot to process, and, well, it seems like we might have time yet.

"I..."

"Oh, for goodness' sake," Petaccia snaps irritably. "I don't have all day. And since the both of you seem determined to play out this little routine, go on—I'll bite. Move out of the way, Olea, and I'll unload the food, and then I want whatever *notes* you'll deign to give me. How's that?"

After Petaccia is gone, we do not talk about what occurred. In fact, aside from our single conversation about keeping the nature of our new gifts from her, we do not talk about the doctor at all. Not yet.

The third time she visits after the cure, Petaccia is a silent presence, leaving behind fresh supplies of food and wine while Olea and I nap in the depths of the garden. She doesn't attempt to keep up the pretence of taking our notes—no doubt after the last visit completely aware we've been lying. Perhaps she is watching us, determining for herself the effects of the antidote. This occurs to me early on, given how fast she arrived in the garden for Olea's death and Olea's suspicions about other gates, but I've yet to gather any actual proof. And what does it matter? We will have to face her eventually: there isn't anywhere for us to go if we want the answers ourselves. Try as I might to rationalise it, leaving the garden is not the right decision. Petaccia is correct: here, we have everything we need, food, water, shelter, sunlight, recreation...Out there—who's to say the impact our toxicity will have on the world?

Olea pretends not to care either way, happy to be caught up in our pleasure if it means not addressing the truths of Petaccia and her childhood. Part of me knows I should be embarrassed at the prospect of somebody watching us; only weeks ago I stole that book from the library to read in secret, a book that had ended my marriage (and, admittedly, my husband's life) and could easily have ended me if the likes of my father had discovered the truth about my feelings. When Aurelio discovered it, it very nearly did.

Here, in the garden, we don't talk about the world outside. Not any more. It is remarkable how quickly we fall into days and nights of discussing nothing more than hunger and sex. We settle into a rhythm of casual chaos, sleeping and fucking without care, and I wonder: Is *this* freedom? Is this what I have searched for my whole life?

It is nearly three weeks before things change. It starts slow, barely noticeable at first. It takes me longer to fall asleep, worries about Petaccia and the antidote creeping in, thoughts of what she's doing on the outside, and whether Leo is worried about me. They don't all come at once, not a steady stream but more of a drip. So insidious I don't truly realise the difference from those early days of abandon until it is too late.

I notice Olea is sleeping less too. Neither of us has had her monthly courses (and truly I suspect we might never have them again), but our moods rise and fall with the same rhythm. Olea becomes irritable, prone to hours in the afternoons where she wanders out of sight and does not reappear until dinner. And the hunger—we both begin to eat more. It is fun at first, cooking together in the cramped cellar. We concoct strange dishes from potatoes and onions and dried pasta, mushrooms and rare fruits we pick from the garden's hidden hollows that Olea knows well. We cook vats of the stuff and then pick at it for days between sex and books and games. The weeks pass and the food lasts hours instead of days, though neither of us gains any weight. We fuck like rabbits, abandoning the books in favour of the garden more nights than not.

"It's not enough," I growl one night. We lie panting at the base of the stairs to the top tower room, since we couldn't even make it to the bed. Olea is stripped of her nightgown to the waist, her breasts covered in bruises that are already yellowing and faded. I regret the teeth marks in an abstract sort of way, and in the same breath long to create them again, to draw blood and taste its metallic tang on my tongue.

"It will settle," Olea soothes. She pulls the straps of her nightgown up, hiding her flesh away. A flash of annoyance takes me, a stabbing kind of jealousy, but I push it down. "These urges are... They're normal, because of the plants and the toxins. You'll see. I've had them in some form or other my whole life."

"Worse than this?" I ask. I narrow my gaze. "Are you saying you've *always* wanted to carry me halfway up a staircase and fuck me until I scream?"

"Well, no, but—"

"Because I can't imagine anything worse than this."

"You can't imagine anything worse than three orgasms in a row?" Olea raises an eyebrow.

"No, I'm sorry, I just mean—"

"I know what you mean." Olea swats my arm playfully. She grows sombre then, thoughtful. "It *will* pass," she says again. "It has to. I always thought the urges I had were my body adjusting to new plants, new toxins, different exposure to seasons and lights, pollen and dust."

"Do you think it's normal *now*, though?" I press. I hold out a hand and help Olea to her feet. We climb the rest of the way to the tower room and collapse together amidst the mass of blankets and cushions we've piled around the trundle bed, which is too small for both of us unless we're lying virtually atop each other. My stomach rumbles, although we ate not long ago.

"What, exactly, about any of this is normal, or has ever been normal?" Olea bites her lip. "I may not know much about the outside, but I know that."

"All right, I know it's not normal. But you know more than I do. And if we don't talk about it—"

"I don't like talking about it," Olea mutters childishly. "I just want to go on as we are. Why can't we just keep pretending?"

"I'm trying, Olie," I say softly. "This is all so new to me. It wasn't like this at first. The world's slowed down but we've sped up. Don't you get frustrated?"

"Of course I do."

We're speaking around the subject, neither of us wanting to acknowledge what we've both realised: something is changing. I can't be sure if it's because of anything we're doing, or if it would have started to happen anyway. Maybe the doctor was right: We should have been keeping notes, records, for how else will we understand the changes? Already those early days after our awakening feel like nothing more than a dream. It is as if we are growing, too much and too fast, and the tower and its gardens are getting too small to contain us.

"I can't stop thinking about things." I run my hand over my

face, and it's damp with sweat. We didn't sweat much at first either. My hands tremble with the exertion of our lovemaking—and this, too, is new.

"Thinking isn't going to change anything." Olea shrugs.

"I know it won't. But I can't shake the unfinished business. How long are we going to keep doing this for? I'm not convinced Petaccia has a plan for any of this. How long before you get bored of fucking me?"

"Unfinished business," Olea repeats. She raises herself on her elbows and looks at me. "Like Leonardo, you mean."

"Like *everything* I left out there." I throw my hands up in exasperation. "Why are you so scared of leaving? I know how badly you want to."

"Why are you so scared to stay?"

"I'm not scared. I'm tired of feeling trapped."

Olea goes quiet. Frustration gurgles inside me and my hands are clammy. I should have fought more about her mentioning Leo, but now isn't the time. Whatever she thinks my relationship is with him, it doesn't make my point less valid. Olea has never thought about the bigger picture.

"This isn't just a holiday," she murmurs.

"That's what I'm trying to say. It isn't a holiday, but we've been treating it like one. Is this what life looks like now? The same thing forever? How long do we do this for, until we die? How long before we get bored, before all of this feels too small?"

"It's barely been a month." Olea levels her gaze. "And you're already chomping at the bit."

"Aren't you?" I snap. "You were ready enough to come with me before. Why are you *so* insistent that we stay now?"

"You're adjusting," Olea tries to soothe. "You know why we

can't leave, Thora. I know this is all new to you; the toxicity of our touch is...it's terrifying. I know that. But it will get easier to understand, and at least we have each other. We're still finding the rhythm. It's bound to be like this at first, a little excess. Why not? You said yourself, we deserve it."

Frustration claws at my throat. "It isn't just a little excess. I need *more*."

"More what?" Olea demands. "More food? More sex? We can try different things—"

"More of everything!" I exclaim. Anger is a torrent, storm water destroying all in its path. I wriggle out of the blankets and get to my feet. I want to stomp my feet; I want to smash things. "It isn't enough. None of this is *enough*." There's a fire burning in my belly and I don't know how to explain it. It's growing, every second bigger and hotter, consuming everything in its path. I don't believe that Olea can't see it; it must be burning up my very soul.

"It will settle," Olea says. Her voice is like cool water, but even that is not enough to douse the flame. "You can't see it yet, but the anger is normal. It's normal to feel trapped. It will pass, though. It *will*."

The night is thick and black as smoke. Autumn is finally coming, bringing the unrelenting storms from the mountains along with the ice-pine bite on the wind. I carry two bottles of wine down to the fountain, staggering a little between the trees.

These are my sixth, maybe seventh bottles of the night. It's taking more and more of the stuff to make me lightheaded, never mind drunk. What I want is to obliterate it all, drink it into the blackness of oblivion. I want to see stars and wake up with a pounding head and the rank stench of alcohol in my pores. There's something so human about it, so *alive*.

It doesn't work like that any more.

I chug the first of the two remaining bottles before I've even slumped down by the fountain. Olea is going to be livid when she finds the booze gone, as we're not sure when the doctor will next be back, but that's not my problem until it happens. If she's so determined to live in the moment, then fucking let her.

The wine is rich, deep and spiced with nutmeg and cloves and hints of black pepper. I hardly taste it. It is like the early days of my exposure to the garden: everything tastes ashy, dry, and powdery.

The second bottle has a deep cork wedged in it. I spend long minutes picking at it, trying to shove it down with a stick, and in the end I give up. I smash the top of the bottle against the rim of the fountain, sending shards of green glass flying. They scatter across the ground beneath the paint stains we left only days ago—it seems like a lifetime already.

My thoughts turn quickly maudlin. Neither Olea nor I have really discussed the subject of the distant future. Olea won't talk about it, no matter how hard I try. Petaccia alluded to it when she took our notes, wanting clarification on the slow beat of our hearts—one of the few things we didn't lie about. A slow heartbeat after what can only be described as medically induced death... What does that mean for the rest of our lives? It's the thought that's been eating me up inside, every minute like a grain of sand in an hourglass of indefinite size. How long can this go on?

"Are we living?" I ask the garden softly. "Or is this death?"

Of course, the garden doesn't answer. I drink the wine from the smashed bottle, savouring this one a little more than the last. I'm careless, though, the swing of my arm loose and strong, and as

I bring the bottle to my lips I slice the tender flesh. It splits like the skin of an apricot, blood dribbling onto my chin.

I let out a startled laugh. The pain is a slash of brightness across an otherwise black night. I lick the blood, the wound already knitting, sucking the taste of it mingled with wine. The pain is too good, over too soon.

I snatch up one of the glass slices from the ground, holding it up to the sky. The moon is hidden and offers no light. I wish Olea was here; I'm craving the taste of her. But she isn't, and I'm simultaneously glad. My stomach aches, not with the hunger I'm familiar with, a sensation that will grow until fed and then retreat. This is a different, vicious sort of hunger. Untameable.

More wine. My lip is healed. I lower the shard of glass to my arm, hovering with indecision for just a moment. Enough time to convince myself that I need it. Need—it's a funny word, isn't it? What is the difference between want and need but strength? Where do they blur?

I need the cut. The pain. That bright slash of feeling. It is the most I've felt in days. I drive the glass into my arm, drunk with the carelessness of it. Thick blood wells at the wound, and the trigger of sensation—it is *everything*. I moan, writhing as I watch the wound heal, a pleasant tickling the only evidence as the skin stretches back towards itself. And then I lower the glass again.

I drink the rest of the wine, slicing and stabbing wildly: my arms, my inner thighs, the soft skin at the back of my knees, my belly and my breasts. Each new cut tightens something in me, something that has been unravelling.

I only stop when I become aware of the mess, slowly and distantly. My nightgown is scarlet, sopping, and the stains around the fountain are no longer of paint and lust but this reckless science.

I lick the blood that dries sticky on my hand and fall back against the fountain, spent.

Sometime later I come to consciousness, swimming upwards from dreams of sluggish red rivers cutting through soil, vines coiling, leaves scorched with sun. I am so hungry that it hurts, but this is not the pain of mere hours ago. It isn't hot and bright; there is no pleasure in it. It is dull, an ache so deep it might have doubled me over—if I were still myself.

I peer through the shadows of the foxglove, the long grasses hiding the edge of the trees and the side of the tower. Olea might never find me here if she didn't come looking. But of course she will. There is no space. I want—no, *need*—to run, to burn the hunger from my bones, but every way I turn there is eventually another wall. Could I climb them? The iron spikes atop it won't do me any lasting harm.

I flex my muscles. They feel…weaker. A lot weaker. I could probably still do it, though, scale them and swing myself over to the other side. Or I could find a way to smash the lock—though, again, I'm doubtful that it would be as easy today as it might have been two weeks ago. It's not as if I've not considered it before. Why didn't I?

It's the same question Olea and I keep passing back and forth, always dancing just on the edge. *Then what?* I come back to the thought now, circling it like a vulture. Whatever poison now flows in me is here to stay. Olea says to give it time, she is hopeful the toxins will fade outwardly and soon we will be able to join, and rejoin, the rest of the world. The cure has to fix the poison in our touch, doesn't it? That's what it was for.

The more time passes, the less I am sure. Olea might not be

able to feel the poison, for her it's a normal state of being, but I can. I know what to look for, that surge of reckless energy, that base urge driving me on. I *know* without knowing that if I were to touch Petaccia on her next visit to these walls she would fall down dead. And Leo, my only friend—

Olea's last mention of him bothers me. *Unfinished business.* When I'd said those words I was thinking of my life outside these walls, of learning and libraries and academic acclaim, all the things I left without realising I'd not likely go back. They are so close—sometimes I hear the scholars, the slap of their hard-soled shoes as they race across the square, and I can see the window of my old rooms from the gate—and yet so far they might as well be on another continent. My world has shrunk. And yet the first thing Olea thought I meant was Leo.

She's jealous, that's all. I have a friend outside these walls and she no longer does. Is it only jealousy, though? Is it insecurity too? She has me, a captive audience, she is my sun and my moon these days, and still she wants more. Does she realise the way this hurts? No, I don't think she does.

More. I said that too, didn't I? More. More. Nothing will ever be enough. If this is living, then what kind of life is it?

Suddenly my cheeks are wet with tears. I blink them back angrily, hot salt stinging. It is too late for crying.

A rustling in the grass shocks me to silence. I am so used to the peace of being surrounded by poison that it takes me a moment to understand what it is I'm hearing, but the second it clicks, my brain stops being my own.

Rabbit, it hisses. *Run.* I move without thinking; sticking close to the ground, I slink into the long grass. It parts for me, stalks twisting away from my body gently so I make no sound at all.

Bare feet in the earth. I follow the sound of the rustling, creeping closer and closer until I spot it.

It is a hare, like one of the ones Petaccia brought to us. It isn't dead yet, having by some miracle avoided most of the garden's tricks, though its movements are curiously sluggish. My stomach clenches, famine driving me onwards. The hare doesn't see me. It doesn't sense my approach.

I can smell it. Dirty fur, soil, and the scent of living, breathing flesh. Its heartbeat quickens. My mouth fills with water. And then I lunge, capturing its frail body with ease. It is hot in my hands, its fur soft. I picture myself sinking my teeth into its neck, the pulse of blood, the—

"Thora, are you out here?" calls a distant voice.

I stare down at the hare. It is still moving. It doesn't wriggle, but I can feel the trembling of its tiny heart in my hands. A swoop of hope overtakes me. It isn't dead. The bird that flew into the garden died almost instantly, but this hare still clings to life. I lick my lips, still tasting the imaginary blood.

I'm still watching hungrily as its movements grow still. It happens so slowly I don't realise straight away, but the slowing of its heart, the *throb throb*, the pause between each beat and the next is longer and longer until there are no more. Horror overtakes me. Bile rising in my throat. I didn't mean to—

Too late.

I am struck dumb, like a fish thrashing in a tightening net. Who—*what*—am I? I lay the hare down gently, crouching in the dirt, tears falling.

"Thora?"

Olea appears beyond the fountain. I smell her before I see her. Rage fills me, and then terror.

"Go away," I snarl.

"What's going on?" Olea climbs through the crumbling, empty fountain, her hand trailing the statue as she passes its centre.

"I said fuck off."

She pauses, her eyes growing wide. She's seen the hare, and the state of my gown. I try to cover myself with my hands but there's too much blood.

"What...Thora?" she asks. "Are you all right?"

"Do I look all right?"

"What happened? What did you do? Is that—"

"Fuck. Off." I infuse my words with as much venom as I can muster, and the sound is a low vibrato.

"We can talk about...whatever this is." Olea waves her hands, continuing to edge forward. She climbs over the rim of the fountain and past the broken glass and the bottles, and then into the long grass. The garden doesn't bend away from her as it did from me, long stalks swaying to touch her legs, a gentle caress.

"No, we can't. This is all kinds of wrong. It's unnatural. I've been trying to persevere, I have, but there's something so, so deadly wrong with us and you're too busy playing pretend and using me to satisfy your needs to see it."

Olea stops, her hands dropping to her sides. It is too dark for me to read her expression, but I can tell from her body that I'm pushing my luck. I don't care. I don't want her here.

"You're one to talk about using people to satisfy needs," she says coldly.

"Excuse me?"

"You heard me, Thora. You're storming around as if you're the only one this affects, yet you're just as guilty in all of this as I am. It takes two for a consensual tango."

I laugh, a caustic, bitter sound. "Oh, really? I'm guilty?"

"You brewed the goddamn antidote. We've been over this. And you're *just* as guilty, using me and your precious Leo however you see fit so you feel better about your reckless choices."

"Why do you keep bringing him into this? Leo is—was—my friend," I growl. "Not that you'd know anything about *that*. He's a good man, and his wife, thanks to you, is gone. And I don't think he understands why! He was right to be suspicious of you. You're manipulative, do you know that? Why do you only mention him when I'm unhappy? I'm sorry I thought it was appropriate to be a shoulder he could cry on, when he was there for me in return. Leo isn't *like* you. He doesn't think of me that way."

Olea's laugh is just as dark as mine. "Oh, come on, Thora, isn't it time you stopped lying to yourself? You were using him, stringing him along while playing house with me. You're so caught up with ideas of *propriety* and what's the done thing. You pretend you flout the rules of society, yet here you are because you were too afraid to sack them off entirely. Your dead father has the same hold over you that my...that Florencia has over me. Only you're too blind to see it. You talk about me being scared to leave even though it's what I truly want—isn't that what you've done your whole life? When I met you, you were still wearing your wedding band—why? Was it because it meant something to you beyond your marriage? Or was it because you were afraid to exist in the world without it?

"Admit it. You were half in bed with Leonardo before you ever fell into mine. If he'd asked you to marry him, and let you stay at the university, you would have done it—for *propriety*. Wouldn't you? Whether or not he wanted other things from you."

"That's not true!" I exclaim, ignoring the roaring in my ears that says she's right. Olea thinks she knows everything, but she doesn't.

"Believe what you want, Thora. At least I acknowledge that what we have is only possible because of our stupid choices, and I don't want to be so quick to just throw that away."

"What are you saying?"

"I'm saying that you're obsessed with the idea of freedom but you've never stopped to consider that the sort of freedom you talk about is a privilege. It shouldn't be, no woman should have to choose between safety and love, between safety and *anything*, but we *do*. You're so focused on the details that you haven't stopped to consider that this, what we have now, is what others like us can only dream of."

"You think women dream of this?" I lift my bloody nightgown and point at the dead hare. I don't like the way she says *women like us*. Are we so different? "This is killing us, Olea. I don't know if you can sense it like I can, but we're falling apart. My strength is failing, and I'm so, so hungry. It's not sustainable. It's not worth it. What kind of life are we selling to Petaccia? What if she takes the cure elsewhere? Do you think anybody would *want* to be poison like this?"

Olea takes one step forward, so I can finally see her face. Her eyes are hollow and they glitter dangerously. And then she says something I have never considered. It freezes me cold. "Poison," she says, deadly serious, "is the only thing that has ever kept me safe. I thought you of all people would understand that."

Chapter Thirty-Seven

In the days that follow I resume my vigil by the gate. This time I try the padlock, but either I'm wrong and I'm not as strong as I thought I was, or I'm tired, because the metal doesn't even bend. Olea barely acknowledges me as I come to and go from the tower. She doesn't go so far as to leave the room when I enter—the tower really isn't big enough for that kind of petulance—but she might as well since she refuses to speak. It is simply easier for me to spend my days and nights sitting amongst the weeds, deadheading the purple-veined yellow flowers of Olea's henbane and thinking.

I think a lot. Where the first days after the cure left me able to consider carefully the conundrum before me, even if I *was* too busy to do so, now my brain is slack and uninterested. The same thoughts circle round and round. I start to spend even more time by the gate. I could cut the padlock, maybe. Climb the walls. I do neither.

I feel like a rabbit caught in a trap. No amount of wiggling will set me free. It is a feral, animalistic kind of fear that sets in. Every sound, every distant caw of a bird, every imagined rustle amongst the grasses, sets my teeth on edge.

I creep into the cellar when Olea is in the upper tower and stuff my face with slices of dried meats, thick chunks of cheese, and as much bread as I can muster. Olives, pasta, porridge, and water. I eat like the starved, hunched over, barely tasting. Usually by the time I've snuck back outside my stomach is rumbling again. I think of the hare often, regretting that I didn't have the sense to take it home with us for dinner. It is too late now. I doubt the antidote would let us die of poisoning from bad meat, but the process, the vomiting and cramps, doesn't seem like fun.

Of course, the truth is Olea is right to hate me. The longer I sit and think my circular thoughts, the stronger I feel about this. It's fair of me to be concerned about what is happening to us, but Olea isn't solely to blame—and I've no doubt she is struggling more than I am. Yes, she has me now, but she has also discovered her entire life is a lie. The story she told me, of the deaths of her parents and her adoption by Petaccia...it seems especially cruel knowing the doctor would choose such a tale over the truth.

It is as I'm turning this over for the millionth time that the noise startles me. This is no phantom whisper on the breeze. It is the beat of footsteps, the slap of hard shoes. I spring into action, hurrying to the wall and out of sight of the gate.

I'm not sure why I hide. Perhaps it is an instinct, the antidote protecting me still, even though this could be a way out of the garden. The shoes do not belong to Petaccia, who rarely makes a sound even though her stride is long and purposeful. Still, the same voice echoes: *Where would you go?*

I press my back to the wall and listen. My heartbeat is the slow thud I've grown used to, but my skin prickles with sweat as fear floods through me.

"Thora? Thooooora?"

It might as well be a ghost for the feeling of dread that fills me up. I hold a hand over my mouth to silence my breathing, ears straining. Is it my mother? I grasp through the fog of confusion. My father? Perhaps the antidote never worked and this is Death.

When the voice calls again, it sounds closer. I stumble from my hiding spot and out into the open, running for the gate.

"Leo," I gasp. "Oh, it's you."

It *is* him. Cream slacks, white shirt rolled at the sleeves. He's missing his usual scholar's robe but has a dark jacket pulled up at the neck against the cooling night air. He looks thin. There are so many things I want to say to him. Apologies and excuses and desperate pleas for him to leave all burble one after another until the noise in my head is so loud my ears might burst.

In the end what comes out is, "Are you all right?"

"Am…am *I* all right? Thora, I've been looking everywhere for you."

"Oh." I don't know what to say. "I've been right here."

Leo's eyes don't stray from my face, but I know he's taken in the state of me: stained nightgown, dirt and grass and probably food too. Is there blood? I've not changed in several days. What's the point? My hair is thick and curling and I know I look better with it like this. I try to give him a winning smile—though I suspect I just look unhinged.

"Thora." It's all he says.

The reality of it sinks in like a stone in a pond. I wrap my arms over my chest and hold my elbows, hiding my breasts. I'm not cold, but the air has taken on a chill. I'm aware that this looks strange, it *is* strange, but the fog in my brain makes me slow.

"You shouldn't be here."

"What are you doing in there?" Leo asks. "And where are your clothes? Come here, I'd like to take you back to your rooms if you'll let me. You need to rest. You look..." He trails off.

"I look what?"

"You look unwell."

I can't avoid the laugh that breaks from my chest. Oh, if only he knew.

"Will you unlock the gate?" Leo presses. "I assume you have the key. I can call a doctor."

"Oh, a doctor," I singsong. "No, don't do that. We've had enough with doctors, thank you."

"We? Is Olea in there with you? Can I speak to her? I knew something wasn't right with that woman—didn't I tell you? I warned you."

"No," I say thoughtfully. "Olea doesn't want to talk to anybody right now. I fucked that." Another laugh breaks through my defences at Leo's expression, leaves me breathless. If only he knew that too. I fucked her. Then he'd run back to his little room on the other side of campus with his tail between his legs, too scared to admit he'd want this too, if Olea were a man. Maybe he'd set some sexy books on fire, just like Aurelio.

"Thora," Leo tries again. "Please let me in. I'm not sure what's going on, but we can talk about it if you want—or not. I've been looking for you. You've not been to any of your classes for weeks. I thought you were hiding from me."

"I'm hiding from everybody," I say solemnly. "Do you have any food?"

"Do I... have any food?"

"Yes, do you have any food?" I approach the gate. "I'm ravenous."

Leo takes a half step back. What has gotten into him? I'm only asking for something to eat. Something—

"Thora, there's something really, really wrong here. Why won't you let me in? Is it the plants?"

"The plants love me. Not as much as they love *her*, of course."

"Olea?"

"Olie, Olie," I say. God, the closer I am to the gate, the stronger I can smell him. He is aftershave and fresh, clean sweat. His floppy hair is like a hat. I'd like to take his glasses off and step on them. I wonder what he'd smell like if I grabbed hold of him, his neck, his hair—

"Right, I'm not leaving you, but I have to go and find somebody who can let me in. You obviously can't stay in there. I'll be back with Dr. Petaccia or Almerto, anybody who can help. Okay?"

He makes to leave and a wail escapes me. I didn't even intend the sound, like a dying pig, and the shock of it turns me to laughter once more.

"Clara's over there," I say. "You should come in and see her."

"...What?" Leo stops, frozen in place. I've never seen a look like this on his face. It is hurt and confusion and anger and betrayal; it is disbelief. Worse: it is the belief beneath it.

"Over there," I repeat, waving at the boggart's posy. "At least I think she is. Don't see why Olea would bury the ring there and not the lady." I snort. "She's all sorts of tricky. Did you know you were married to a thief? Olea kissed her, you know. She *kissed* her. Oh, but I don't think Clara kissed her back. Of course, she didn't have to. Damage, it was all damage. How does that make you feel? It makes me feel a certain kind of way."

"I don't understand what you're saying." Leo's voice has gone cold. I hadn't noticed the warm concern until it was gone, but it feels better this way. I don't deserve his kindness. Olea is right: maybe I *was* just using him. He might have married me, too, since he's so afraid of himself. He'll be better off without me. "It's clear you're not well. Look at you."

"Look at me," I repeat. I curtsy, lifting my nightgown higher than I'm sure is appropriate. I'm not a society lady, thank god. I never really was one. And anyway, Leo won't look at what's between my legs. "I'm fine. Better than fine. Stronger than fine. Well, less stronger than finer and less finer than I was."

The scent of him is driving me mad. I can't think. My stomach clenches so tightly I think I might have to curl into a ball, and yet I don't think that would make Leo very happy.

"Come here," I soothe. "Look at me. I'm fine."

"No. I'm going to get help. Stay right there, please don't move. I'll be back as soon as I can."

"Don't!" I cry. "Please, Leo, I'm sorry." I reach through the bars. They are cold, the rust digging into my flesh. I feel the prickle of pain and for just a moment I am myself. I lean hard against the bars of the gate, pressing my face up close. Leo is hesitant, but he hasn't fled yet. I beckon him with my arm. "Please," I whisper, dropping my voice low enough that I know he won't hear me unless he steps in. "Don't tell."

"I've got to do something. I'm…Thora, I'm dreadfully worried about you. Have you been drinking? You can tell me if you have. Or if you've taken something else, a pill or smoked some of the leaves. I wasn't born yesterday. I'd understand."

"Open the gate," I whisper. "Can you do it? I can't. Not tonight. I'm not strong enough. Nobody can know, though."

"You're not making any sense—"

"Can you do it?" I demand, a little louder. The fear is back and I know he can see it in my face. "Can you let me out? I don't want to be here. I can't…"

He lifts a hand to examine the lock on the gate. I know he's exasperated—I can *smell* it on him. It is like impending rain, a blustery kind of scent. I like it. I want to taste it. He rattles the padlock, which is attached to a thick link chain.

"I don't remember anything like this being here before," he says, then shakes his head. "I told you, I need to get he-elp."

The wobble in his voice surprises Leonardo more than it does me. He swallows hard and glances down at his fingers. They aren't touching mine, aren't even touching where my hands have been, but we are close: perhaps only centimetres apart. I can smell the dinner wine on his breath. I let out a huff. Petaccia doesn't wear a mask around us, but I suppose she's been microdosing herself a little, just a little, for years and years. But she does wear gloves. Leo isn't so lucky.

"Are you sure you don't have any food?" I ask sweetly. "I'm just so incredibly fucking hungry."

"Tho-ora," he says. His voice changes. "What did you do?"

His panic cuts through the fog, but it is only a second, a brief second where I understand: he is wilting. Like the hare. Only he doesn't know it yet. And then the scent of him slams into me like a brick; the weak flutter of his heart is the smoky fry of bacon, the rushing pallor of his skin is rich, salty whipped cheese on crusty bread. My mouth waters. I snatch my arm farther through the gate, grasping for his jacket to pull him closer.

It happens in less than a second. My fingertips graze the back of his hand and something in me is unleashed, something I didn't even know was there. It is a monster. I fling my arm wildly through the gate, scratching and clawing, grasping for more of him. Leonardo is in the dirt by the wall, panting and crying and trying to scramble away, but I've caught his trousers and I won't let go. A dark scream tears through me.

"Thora!" The shout barely breaks my concentration. "Thora, let him go!"

It is Olea. I know it's her. I don't want her here. She's right behind me, coming up fast. Her hands grasp my shoulders and try to pull. I send one elbow back and it connects sharply with her jaw, but she doesn't stop.

"Thora, you're killing him."

"Olie, I'm *hungry*," I grind out. "He smells—he smells so good."

"Fuck," Olea grunts. She wraps her hands around me, her body slamming against mine as she hooks her arms around my waist and pulls. Hard.

"Let me go!" I yell. I try to punch again but it's hard with one arm still through the gate. Leo lies on the ground. He's still crying. He's not dead yet. I can smell the fear in him, and, oh, it's like sweet pistachio cream. Nutty and delicious. I bet his blood would taste as good. I lick my lips. "Just a taste," I beg. "Please, just one."

"*Thora.*" Olea lifts one arm up and chops her hand down at the crook of my elbow. The pain ricochets through me and I cry out. She uses the opportunity to finally yank my arm back through, releasing Leo's trouser leg. He stays on the ground, stunned and in pain, his heart slamming about inside his pathetic little chest. "Thora, you're not yourself. Look at me. LOOK."

Olea grips my face with her hand, digging her nails into my flesh. I writhe but am forced to look at her. And when I do I see the pale oval of her face, bright like the moon, her eyes the colour of a chocolate torte with rich mint filling. They shine with fear and unshed tears. Her lip is bloody from my punch, already healing, and the honeyed scent of her sings to me. It soothes me.

"*Breathe*," she hisses.

I draw in a breath. Deep. Painful. My ribs are on fire. My belly is the pit of a fire, coal and ash and crumpled paper. Slowly the inferno dulls. I breathe again. Again.

"That's it."

"Leo," I sob.

Olea, still holding my face, looks to the gate. Leonardo is collecting himself slowly. His expression is that of a man who has just found out his sentence is death: he is greying, dark hollows already in his formerly olive cheeks, his eyes like dinner plates. His brush with my hand has not, thank god, killed him. Yet.

"Can you move?" Olea demands. Leo nods. "Good," she says. Then she thrusts me behind her, baring her sharp teeth as she rushes at him. "Then you should run."

Leonardo doesn't run. He stares at the two of us, the familiar touch of our bodies, the shine of our teeth. Matching moonlit gowns in the black garden. Poison in our veins—on his skin.

"What are you?" he breathes.

"Better you don't find out."

"But—"

"Leonardo," I growl, infusing my voice with every bit of malice I can. I don't want this to happen, I don't want our friendship to end like this, but—I nearly killed him. I'd kill him again in less than a heartbeat without these walls to hold me. "We don't want you here. If you come to these walls again, one of us will kill you. Do you understand me?"

"Thora—"

Olea hisses, and the sound is guttural. Primal. Leonardo shrinks back, clutching his injured hand to his chest. I can already see the black marks stretching across his skin, and distantly, the sane part of me hopes they don't get any bigger.

"Do you understand me?" I grind out. I show him my teeth again. "I'm going to give you ten seconds. Olea is right. If you value your life, you should run."

Olea slams her body against the gate. There's no hunger in it, not like when I did the same, but Leonardo doesn't know that.

"RUN!"

Chapter Thirty-Eight

After Leonardo is gone Olea leads me back to the tower like a wayward child, holding my hand. Half, I suspect, to guide me and half so I don't bolt. I don't tell her not to worry—after all, if you'd asked me an hour ago whether I wished any harm towards Leo, it would have been an emphatic *no*. I stumble and sway as she leads me into the sitting room and deposits me on the chaise. I know I'm not myself, but I can't think what else I might be.

"Do you want to talk about what happened out there?" Olea says once I'm settled. She's antsy, has barely stopped moving since we got back. Her fingers dance like butterfly wings trapped under a glass dome. She lights a couple of candles, but otherwise the room, with its bright tapestries, is left wrapped in gloom. I'm glad. I don't think I could face Olea's sunshine hopes.

It's too warm in here. I miss the cool breeze of the garden. I want to go back out there and run my hands through the loamy soil where Olea has watered the nettles. I want to bury my hands and my face in the earth.

"No," I say.

"Are you sure?" Olea comes to kneel at my feet. She takes my hand in hers and massages my palm.

"What's the point?" The touch of Olea's skin is both soothing and, as always, deeply erotic. I wriggle, withdrawing my hand. Olea's fingers gravitate towards my knee instead and I feel my heart trip. "You said yourself: It's my fault. I brewed the antidote. I'm the one who got us in this deep."

"You were trying to save me," Olea corrects me, her voice soft. She lifts one hand to my chin, the skin there no longer bruised but still surprisingly tender. I turn away.

"You don't have to console me."

"No?" She grips my chin harder and turns my face back towards her. I try to fight but she's surprisingly strong. Her eyes glitter; her lips—are they darker than they were a few days ago?

"No," I grunt. "I told you, I don't want to talk about it."

"Ah, we only talk when you want to." I can't tell if Olea is seriously angry or if she's trying to tease. Then I realise: it doesn't matter. When I hoped the cure would tell me if she was really for me, really mine, I missed the vital point. Regardless of the reason, Olea and I are joined in this. She is mine—even if only for right now.

"Fine," I say huskily. "Perhaps we shouldn't talk at all."

Olea keeps her grip on my chin tight as her other hand surges under my nightgown. She rips it up, her eyes glittering with anger and frustration and tenderness all in one. Her fingers are strong, bordering on cruel.

There is no shred of our gentleness in her touch. No hesitation. We have explored each other's bodies now in a hundred different ways. She moves her hand from my chin down to my neck. The pressure is pain and pleasure at once. I moan, encouraging. She squeezes harder. Her other hand pinches, scoring my skin in bright hot lines with her sharp nails.

And then come the teeth. *The teeth.*

We fuck until dawn, barely pausing for breath. Unlike our early lovemaking, this is not punctuated with wine and cheese, with laughter and acting. This is purely animal. Teeth and claws, grunting and moaning, using whatever we can find to draw blood, to punish, to maim. The healing of the wounds is as much a part of the ritual as the sex—and when we are spent, the tower walls, and Olea's tapestries, are flecked with dark blood.

The taste of iron still in our mouths, we lie together on the chaise, bodies braided together like twine. I want to cry, but I don't. The hunger within me consumes it all.

The sunlight hurts our heads. Olea's eyes are puffy. We block the edges of the shutters with the rags of our destroyed nightgowns and set up camp back in the cellar, blankets and cushions amidst the sacks of food. Our garden days, fucking in broad daylight, revelling in the beauty of the garden, seem years behind us.

"The antidote is fading," I say. "You can feel it too, right?"

Olea doesn't speak, but I know she's been thinking it. It's hung between us, this toxic miasma, for days. Our world has shrunk again, this time to the size of a pinhead.

"It could just be temporary..." she hedges.

I prop myself on my elbow. "Come on, Olie. There's naivety and then just plain stupidity, and I *know* you're not stupid."

Olea refuses to open her eyes. She lies on her back, a vision in her white gown, black hair braided and freshly combed. If not for the slow, slow rise and fall of her chest she could be a corpse ready for the cradle.

"We heal fine, though," she says.

"Sure. We do now. But... that could change without warning. You saw me out there with Leo. I was absolutely beside myself."

"You want to talk about it now?"

And, surprisingly, I do. Fresh from the ache of her inside me I am no longer so afraid to voice the horrors.

"I'm a monster," I say.

"You told me I wasn't." Olea opens her eyes and rolls onto her side. "You emphatically told me so."

"I *wanted* to kill him."

Olea kisses my bare shoulder, working her way down my arm with gentle precision and then kissing my palm and each of my fingers.

"No," she says. "You didn't. That wasn't you."

"How do you know? It certainly felt like me."

"I know," she assures me. "Because I know you."

"I killed that hare."

"Also not intentional."

"Isn't there a point, though," I say sharply, pulling my hand back and struggling upright, "where intentionality doesn't matter? Do you think the monster was always a monster? That he set out to hurt people? I doubt it. It doesn't matter that I didn't want it to happen. It doesn't matter that there were other factors. All that matters in the end is that it did happen. It may not be my fault, as you say, but it sure is my fucking responsibility. Maybe it's best that the antidote fails; maybe *this* is what we both deserve."

Olea is silent at that. I regret it almost instantly—but I'm right, aren't I?

That night, Petaccia returns to the garden. Olea and I are waiting for her. This time we haven't bothered to tidy our mess, blood and tattered rags of clothing scattered through the sitting room. The candles burn low, the shutters closed against the draughty night.

The doctor doesn't bother with pleasantries. And it's clear she's not here to bring supplies. She marches in with the air of somebody who has much more important places to be, barely glancing at us as she starts to unload a leather valise onto a side table. The candles gutter, casting long shadows.

"I want blood samples. Body measurements. Olea, you go first, strip and stand over there so Thora can measure you." She barks instructions as the two of us sit, unmoving.

When she throws a tape measure at me, I let it bounce off my shoulder and roll to the floor.

"For god's sake. What's the matter with you two?" Finally, for the first time, she looks at us. "Is this about your little visitor?"

"You know about that?"

Petaccia rolls her eyes. Of course she knows. She knows everything, though I still don't know how. I grip Olea's hand tightly in mine, one last squeeze, before standing abruptly. I'm weak, the muscles in my arms and legs complaining from their earlier exercise, and I sway a little.

"Why didn't you come to make sure we were all right?" I demand. "If you knew there was somebody snooping around?"

"Oh, he's hardly just a somebody." Petaccia shrugs. "I know he's your friend. Besides, you girls—and the garden—can look after yourselves."

Anger whips through me. "Not that you care."

"I've been busy in the lab," Petaccia says airily. "You're not the only ones who need my attention."

"You haven't." Olea is horrified. "You've made more of the antidote?"

"You've *used* it?"

"Not on myself I haven't." Petaccia closes her valise with a snap. "But every experiment needs a control group. I've made variants with animal blood—matching type to type."

"You can't!" Olea shrieks. "You haven't got the faintest idea what this could do. Look at us. We're…" She lifts her hands helplessly.

"I think the compound must be breaking down," I provide mechanically.

Petaccia glances between the two of us, taking us in with a clinical eye, and then all she says is "Mm-hmm."

"What?" I demand. If only I had more strength. I'd love to rip her apart. Briefly, for one mad second, I wonder if Petaccia has timed her visits like this on purpose, visiting early on, when we were confused and high with discovery, and now. The thought is too terrifying to probe deeply.

"What are your symptoms?" Petaccia says instead of answering. "Dizziness? Fatigue? Any shortness of breath, photosensitivity? Hunger and thirst all normal? Any cravings for steak, venison, or otherwise raw meat?"

Olea and I both stare, slack-jawed. Petaccia, with her hands on her hips, her skin covered nearly head to toe in thick black cloth, is the bringer of death. She knew, I realise. She knew all along this would happen. And I don't know why I'm surprised. I'm just like Olea, it turns out: ready to believe whatever lie the good doctor tells me.

"How could you keep something like this from us?" I attempt to throw myself at her, arms—clawed nails—outstretched, but Petaccia is light on her feet, sidestepping my movement easily so I stumble against the side table, knocking the valise. I grip it for support. "Don't we deserve to know what's happening? What else do you know that we don't?"

"Are we dying?" Olea asks quietly.

"I didn't keep anything from either of you that you wouldn't have discovered yourselves," Petaccia says calmly. "A good scientist should never be in the habit of sharing her suspicions with the subjects of any experiment of this type. It could colour the results."

"Is that all we are to you?" I slam my fist against the wall. Days ago, I'm sure, that would have left a mark—in the wall, and in me. Now the only evidence is an ache deep in my bones.

"Anyway, it's quite clear there's no need to keep the information from you. Even if you are both horribly hard work where gathering results goes. As far as your current symptoms: I suspected that given the unstable nature of the antidote you concocted"—she looks at me—"there's little support for a consistent outcome. The dose between the two of you was variable, which only extended the support for my hypotheses since you both had very similar reactions. Death, and undeath, shall we say. The healing of exterior wounds is, of course, a bonus—"

"What are you trying to say?" I spit. "Speak in the plain fucking common tongue, won't you?"

Petaccia looks a little put out but shrugs it off. "Well, to put it simply, the antidote doesn't come without risk. It seems to me, given that red blood cells take around four to six weeks to be fully replaced by the body, there may be some extra instability around that time as the body replenishes. Consuming another dose, made to the same strength using—well, to put it bluntly—*human* blood, would likely avert the more serious of the potential issues. Though of course of that part I cannot be certain."

"You suspected this. The whole time. And you've been keeping us in here, knowing that this might kill us both? Why are you doing this?"

"Please, Thora dear, stop with the righteous act. I warned you. Science is not always clean and easy. We've had to rob graves, use slaves, cut cadavers without permission to get where we are. How do you think your father learned the art of autopsy? Yes, I know we're not supposed to talk of all that, but it's integral to the craft. How do you think medicine has progressed as it has? This is depth of discovery we're talking about. How can you be offended when science, experiments like these, are the reason smallpox no longer kills thousands of people a year?"

"That's different!" I exclaim.

"How?" Petaccia raises an eyebrow, as though she's genuinely baffled. "What we're doing will change the world. When my own father died I would have done anything to bring him back—wouldn't you want the same? I know you idolised yours. And think of the accolades! Oh, I know you think that's silly now, but not long ago I know you'd have scratched my eyes out for the chance at this kind of fame. Why *should* death be the end?"

"My father never hurt anybody in pursuit of knowledge," I spit. "And I've no dealings with slaves or robbed graves. Nor have you, I presume. That stuff all happened years ago, and you shouldn't justify your behaviour by the immorality of the past. You can't just start experimenting on people without their permission. It's—"

"It's wrong?" Petaccia lets out a coarse laugh. Olea says nothing, but I can see the fury burning in her face. I know if given the choice she would never want to see this vile woman—her mother—again. Though, of course, *choice* is a tricky word. "You forget: I did not force you to do anything you didn't want to. You made the antidote. You both consumed it. All I'm trying to do now is make your concoction safe for others, to give the world a chance at something new. Don't you think that if I don't do it somebody else will? And I can assure you they will be a damn sight less accommodating of your...shall we say *lifestyle*."

Olea's face is frozen marble, but her cheeks are bright with colour. The mortification shuts her down, but it only drives me on.

"But it isn't safe! You said yourself. It's unstable, it's—"

"It is at the moment, yes. But, you see, once I have an idea of exactly how the breakdown plays out, I should be able to tinker with the mixture to stabilise it. And next time we'll simply add a second dose of the cure and see how long that lasts."

"Next time?" Olea asks.

"Yes," she says simply. "Whichever of you handles the red blood cell count better will need another dose."

Chapter Thirty-Nine

W hat are we going to do?"

It is night once more, darkness closing in around the walls of the garden, and Olea and I have made the trek to sit amongst the grasses and stinging nettles of our fountain. The air has grown cold, though we don't feel it as normal people do.

Neither of us slept after Petaccia's visit last night, and we spent the day today doing anything but talking. I'm still sore from our vigorous lovemaking, which I know isn't a good sign, but I'd rather have the pain than the lack of pleasure. We can't go more than a few hours without food or wine or sex: almost as if our bodies are trying to plug the gaps where hunger, where satisfaction, lie.

"I know it seems like an obvious question," I go on. "But what the fuck do we do?"

"If you want me to say that we can't just ignore it and go on as we are, then…" Olea shrugs, popping a cherry in her mouth. She holds the punnet between the two of us reverently, like a cradle; it is some of the last fresh non-garden food we have until the doctor brings more. "Well, then you're right," she says. She tries to smirk but the gesture is tired and sad.

"We need the antidote." I take a cherry and place it on my tongue. The skin is tough, the innards tart and watery. I chew around the pit and then swallow that whole too. I hate eating; it only makes me hungrier. "I have the exact ingredients we used last time."

"With the exception of the human blood."

"Yes," I say.

"Well. We don't *know* that it won't work with your blood again," Olea suggests hopefully. "There's nothing to say we're not human."

I point at the blood, my blood, which still stains the fountain. We've had one small round of rain showers since I did that, but it wasn't enough to remove the evidence. Just seeing it makes me want to do it again, rip my teeth into that hare too, taste the pulse of its blood—

"Thora." Olea smacks my leg hard enough to make it sting.

"Thanks," I murmur gruffly. "Why is it you don't struggle like I do? Sometimes all I can think about is…it's darkness. I don't like it." *But, oh, I do.*

Olea rests her chin in her hand, a ghost in white. "I don't know," she says genuinely. "It's not like I was a sex-crazed maniac before I met you." Even now, after the intimate places we have taken our bodies, she curls slightly inwards at the mention of sex. It's not embarrassment, I don't think, so much as the need to protect herself. She doesn't want to admit how much she needs it—like me.

"Oh, I don't know," I joke. "You did a pretty good job of seducing me."

"Says you with your filthy pornography collection." This would be a low blow from anybody but her. I know she doesn't mean it harshly and I let out my first genuine guffaw in days.

"I believe the scholars call it erotic fiction," I correct. She gives a gentle huff of laughter of her own. "Did you..." I trail off, but it seems silly to avoid the subject now. "Did you and Clara ever...?"

Olea starts to bristle, but I see the same realisation in her face as she softens. "No. She was—magnetic, though. I wanted to. Before her I never thought—that is..." She rubs her nose awkwardly. "Sorry."

"I won't be angry," I say, realising as I say it that it's true. "No more secrets."

"She was the first time I'd ever felt *seen*," Olea goes on carefully. "She was lonely, like me. She didn't talk about it much, but I could tell. She never had anywhere else to rush off to, not like the other scholars who used to walk past—back when your building was used for accommodations.

"Florencia stopped that, of course. But Clara found me anyway. She told me once that she used to come and sit for hours on the grass outside the wall before she met me. Only...she didn't ever get too close. She always used to smoke this little...these tiny little cigari—cigare..."

"Cigarillos?"

"Yes. She sat and smoked and read and smoked some more. And one day she was still there when I came to do my rounds."

"And you spoke to her, just like you did with me."

"I did." Olea inclines her head thoughtfully. "It was different, though, Thora. I'm not just saying that—it was. At first she was kind and patient, but it didn't take long for that to slip. After a while she was brash and sharp and, well, sort of mean. She told horrible tales about the ladies who lived near her, made snide comments about their husbands and children too; she told me stories about her hometown and how much she hated it here. At first I thought she was funny and charming, and I was so tired of being *alone*."

"It didn't last?"

"It wasn't long before I started to see through the facade, no. By the time I realised she never truly cared for me, I'd already decided I loved her, though, and it felt too late. I thought maybe if I let her into the garden, if I could touch her, it would be different, like when we first met. Maybe we'd get some of that magic back. So I invited her in."

"And instead she robbed you."

Olea nods. "Let's call it a mistake. I'm ... I still feel awful about it, though. She didn't deserve—what I did. I never meant for it to be punishment. I was just trying to protect myself—and the garden. I was sure, even then, that Florencia's cure would come."

"You did love her, though," I say gently.

"Maybe I did. It was puppy love. It's not like it is with you— and I'm not talking about now, all the ... the blood and the sex."

"I know. It's like the antidote has reduced us to our basest needs. It isn't who we were before."

"The garden had already stripped away many of my defences." Olea glances behind me, to where she can no doubt see the stinging tree in the distance. "What does it mean for the cure, though, if it's breaking down again in our blood?"

Always the cure. Everything leads back to the damned antidote.

"I don't know," I say honestly. "We can try a batch with our blood, but it congeals so fast I can't see how it'll be any good as a mixture. We'd have to water it down a degree to even get it to mix."

"We need human blood," Olea says, repeating Petaccia's phrase. "You said we could leave the garden if we wanted to. Get through the gate. I've always been too afraid... Please promise me you won't go without me."

"It doesn't matter about leaving the garden," I say. Olea eats another cherry and offers me the punnet, but I shake my head. I'm queasy and dizzy, my stomach all in knots. "I'm not sure where we'd find it anyway. Petaccia keeps only animal specimens in the lab."

"Promise me you won't go without me anyway," she urges. "Please?"

"Olea—"

"No." She is firm in this. "Please promise me."

"Fine," I say, shrugging. "I'm not so sure I can manage the gate any more anyway."

"No. I suppose not. It's like recovering after a long sickness, isn't it? Only we're not getting any better."

That's exactly what it's like. I had the flu once as a small child and I recall those aching days afterwards, hot and cold and feverish, starving and thirsty though it hurt to eat and drink. And the delirium... My father never treated me the same after that. It makes me wonder what I said during those hours. What I did.

"We can't let her do this," Olea says. I only half hear her, stuck in my thoughts. "My whole life she was the only constant I knew, aside from the plants. And I still don't understand how she could just... leave me to die. For all our talk of monsters—"

"That's it!" I cut her off, then grasp her hands in apology, startling her. "Sorry, sorry. But."

"But?"

"Petaccia," I breathe. "She'll have to come back to the garden with supplies soon. We can make sure we're awake, that she can't sneak past us. We'll find a way to get her blood."

Olea grips my hands right back, so tight it hurts, smearing cherry juice over my thumbs.

"You can do it, can't you?" I ask. "Even though she's..."

"Yes. And then we make the cure for both of us."

For the first time in days our minds are occupied—not with food and sex but with plotting. We work out how much food we have left, make a calendar based on the last drop, or the best we can remember it, and attempt to cover all our bases.

If Petaccia comes between dawn and dusk she will likely bring the food into the cellar, though we can't assume that to be the case. If she comes overnight, the likelihood of us being awake will be much higher, but she's more likely to abandon the supplies by the gate as she's done for Olea before rather than demanding we help given the new revelations about her hidden knowledge. She'd be a fool to assume we won't be working against her.

We plan to use strips of sacking and some of Olea's craft tools—knitting needles and crochet hooks amongst them—to create tiny alarms for the perimeter, hoping the jangle might alert us as we take it in turns to keep watch.

It isn't much of a plan, but given our limited resources it's the best we can do. Neither of us is particularly confident we'll be able to take Petaccia in a fight if it comes to it, and though Olea suggests she might be able to concoct some type of sedative from the garden easily enough, we're not convinced we'd be able to get her to consume such a thing.

Still, it's better to have something of a bad plan than no plan at all. We quickly lose ourselves in security, taking turns keeping watch near the gate. Our couplings are urgent, quiet, and brief.

Neither of us suggests taking a break from them and for this I'm grateful—without Olea, the smell of her tangled in my hair, on my hands, I'd go mad.

We wait. The days stretch, and with them the last of the fresh supplies. We run out of milk and meat first, then fresh vegetables and fruit. Then we start to run low on staples: potatoes, pasta, wheat, and oats. The hunger is another form of madness, gnawing, desperate. We return to fucking louder and more often between explosive, repetitive arguments, burning through our frustration every way we can, almost hoping Petaccia disturbs us in such a state. Then it becomes harder to do even that. We are exhausted, unable to sleep, eat, or drink anything but water from the well.

It takes another week—five, now, since our initial exposure to the antidote—for me to realise: Petaccia isn't coming back.

Chapter Forty

I study Olea as she sleeps. We've given up the shift watches for the last couple of days, mostly out of necessity. Neither of us can face being out in the sun for more than a minute or two, coming up in great red welts that take much too long to heal, and we won't have the strength to do anything if Petaccia does turn up. Instead we sleep together through the daylight hours, burrowed in our blanket den in the cellar, the constant reminder of our steady starvation all around us.

I've considered more than once how I might be able to leave the garden. I don't like to think of breaking my promise to Olea, but the more days pass since our last delivery of food, the more likely it is that I will have to. Olea does little except sleep now, and that she doesn't do well, tossing and turning, crying out until her sobs echo in the tower.

There is no doubt that while my mind might be the weaker of the two of us, more prone to giving in to its animal urges, Olea's body has endured much more punishment. The plants may have protected her since she was a child, but they have little control over what we have done to ourselves, and it hurts me to admit that

Olea will almost certainly succumb to whatever the end may look like first.

And in truth, I'm not sure what scares me the most. The idea that she will waste away quickly, her body scooped hollow from the inside with this dreadful hunger, that she will starve before I can do anything to help her; or that the agony will linger, her mind unravelling alongside her body as I'm forced to watch.

"Maybe Florencia miscalculated because of how much we've been eating," Olea had suggested tiredly at dawn as we snuggled down to try to sleep, still desperately clinging to her hope. "I know she's been watching us, but maybe she got it wrong. We've not really had a schedule. I used to eat—oh, not much at all. Peck like a bird. Do you think she might just be delayed? Perhaps she's had to travel..."

I didn't answer then, but my would-be response has been playing on my mind ever since. Petaccia may have been watching us, especially at first—and she may have fully intended to see which of us would come to death's door first—but the longer it goes, the more likely it seems to me that she isn't coming back at all. When she implied she would wait to see which of us lived, this time she wasn't lying.

It has been more than five weeks; if the doctor cared as much as she said she did about blood cell counts and the life of the antidote inside the body, she would be here, right now, observing us.

Instead she hides in the shadows, not even brave enough to enter the garden to provide us with food. Not even to gloat. No, it seems to me that the doctor hasn't told us the entire truth, yet again. What's to say she hasn't already brewed another batch of the antidote to administer to test subjects elsewhere? The stinging tree might be rare, but it isn't the only one of its kind, and a doctor with her network and experience would have little trouble tracking down another.

And, of course, who's to say the stinging tree is a necessary part of the colloid? It frustrates me so very badly to have only half the information, even though the damn thing's very existence is almost entirely my fucking fault.

Olea tosses in her sleep, rolling from her back to her side and then onto her front, arms splayed as if she is trying to fly—up and away from this place. She is so frail. I haven't noticed before, but the bluish shadows under her eyes are bruises, and the skin is pulled gaunt across her face so it is all skull, juts, and hollows. I can see her ribs, and the collarbones I once saw in the garden—a view that had seemed so untamed it bordered on the obscene—are now deeper, more pronounced than ever. She is skin and bone.

All at once, I bend over breathless, my stomach clenching as sobs force their way up inside my chest like bubbles of air.

"Olie," I say softly. I stroke her face, forcing back my tears. "Olie, darling. Can you eat?"

She rolls onto her side again, opening her eyes. They are dull with sleep. When she sees me she doesn't react. I hold a glass of water to her lips and she takes a hesitant sip.

"Tastes like nothing," she murmurs.

"Can you eat?" I say again.

"There's nothing left."

"There must be. Any more of the crackers? No, we finished those yesterday. Oh, how about the oat dust in water?"

"Leave it, Thora," Olea says tiredly. "Let me sleep. Maybe Florencia will come tomorrow. I'm so tired. Won't you just leave me?"

"No," I say. I'm frantic now, but Olea hardly seems to care. She's closed her eyes again and pulled the pillow up over her ears. I search around desperately, look for something—anything. "Olie, I'm going to go and find us something to eat. Okay? I'll figure the gate out. It'll be fine. I'll come back with steaks and sausages…Olie?"

"Thora," she warns. She opens one eye like a cat and stares at me in my panic. She doesn't move, only watches. "You know food isn't the real issue."

"It's not helping!" But I know she's right. I feel it in the twist of my gut. It's the same thing I've known for days and days and refused to acknowledge. Food *isn't* helping. Because it isn't food we need. It isn't even just the toxins, for chewing the stinging tree leaves does nothing except tingle our tongues. We've tried it. It's the blood. *Human blood.*

"Petaccia's gone," Olea says. "She has, hasn't she?"

"I think so. So we've got to go too. We could leave and try to follow her—she won't disappear without a trace. If we find her we can still get her blood, still make more of the antidote."

"She'll come back," Olea assures me without force. "She has to. All her research is here."

"How do we know? You said yourself she travels a lot. I bet she's got other gardens exactly like this one."

"She doesn't."

"How do you know?"

Olea rubs her face, that single movement exhausting her so she lies with her hand over her face. "I suppose I don't. But how do we know leaving isn't going to make things worse? Your Leonardo might have told people tales and if we appear it'll only be—"

"Worse?" I bark. "How could things possibly get any worse? Olea, we can keep having this argument a thousand different ways, but the answer is always going to be the same. Aren't you sick of it? How long before we go mad?"

"I don't know!" Olea wails. "Please, Thora. Just let me sleep."

I'm silent for a moment before the rest of it bubbles out of me. I try to keep it in but the fear, it's too big. "Olie, if I get us some blood from somewhere...Will you take it?"

This, finally, wakes her up completely. She thrusts herself upright and stares at me in horror. "Where from?" she demands.

"I...I don't know. One of the scholars, maybe."

"Right. And what are you going to do, just walk up to one—in the middle of the night, might I add—and ask them if you can borrow some blood?"

"I...well. I hadn't thought—"

"No," Olea snaps. "You hadn't thought about it. Thora, I asked you not to go out there without me. What if it happens again, like with Leonardo? What if you lose control and really hurt somebody?"

"I won't! I can't let this happen without fighting it."

"I will not let you do something you'll regret either. There is another solution, we just haven't thought of it yet. Let me sleep and maybe I'll come up with it."

"Olea—"

"No," she cuts me off. "No more. It isn't even a discussion. We can make tea from the nettles and eat the fruits off the trees. This is not the end."

She lies down without another word, rolling away so she doesn't have to look at me. I fix my gaze on her back for the longest time, long enough that she eventually falls back to sleep. But I can't stop thinking about it. The blood. We need it.

We're running out of time. If I don't do something, Olea will die.

Chapter Forty-One

While Olea is sleeping, I sneak into the garden. I figure I have perhaps an hour or two before she's built up the energy to come looking for me, and by then I'll be safely back in the tower—hopefully with a broken padlock to show for it. I'm not sure what I'll do after that; I haven't got that far in my imaginings: step one is *possibility*.

I gather the biggest knives we have in the kitchen, though they are all dull now. I have a pair of scissors too—not that I'm expecting much from them. With every silent footstep I curse myself for not breaking the padlock when I had the chance. It was sheer stupidity, negligence. I wanted so badly to believe Olea was right and Petaccia wouldn't abandon us for the sake of discovery. I should have trusted my gut.

I head straight down to the gate with my weapons of choice, not stopping to check on the plants as I know Olea would like me to. I'm not the gardener she is, and without her tender touch the plants have once again gone wild. A horrible thought tickles my brain: What happens to the garden if Olea dies?

When I've had the thought before, it was from a scientific

vantage. Now my concern is purely selfish. This place is our home—my home, now—and without the border of poisons to keep people away, would I lose even the sanctity of this space? Will I end up in chains worse than this gilded prison?

I push the notion away. It won't happen. I simply won't allow Olea to die. I've worked too hard for the scraps of this life regardless of whether it was what I wanted to begin with.

When I reach the gate I pause, stacking the knives and scissors against the wall so I can examine the padlock. I remember it being thick and heavy with a wide link chain. Perhaps if I can pry apart one of the links, that would do better than breaking the lock itself.

I stop. It takes a second for my exhausted brain to register that there is no lock. There is no evidence that there has ever been a lock, although I know it's true. The gate rests closed on its latch, not even Olea's original lock and key still present. A latch. A simple goddamn latch is all that stands between me and outside.

I suck in a deep breath. There is a fresh hint of rain on the breeze. I let it fill me, palms pressed against the rusted metal. In, and out.

It makes no sense, but my first thought is Leonardo. Is it possible he's been back and found a way to unlock the gate? This is followed by a rush of pain. I double over, gasping like a fish out of water. I nearly killed him and this man is so kind he has come back to help me anyway.

But no. It's much more likely that the doctor unlocked it herself. I swallow, wondering if in keeping our watch here amongst the weeds we somehow startled her—if she'd brought supplies but refused to leave them when she heard us. This is something I could not bear, if in our efforts to protect ourselves we have doomed ourselves instead.

Fuck, I think. *Fuck.*

Faced with the missing padlock I stare at the gate for what seems an eternity. What now? I'd only planned to destroy it and take the evidence to Olea. I hear her pleas, a steady buzz in my ears like the hum of a fat little carpenter bee. *Promise me you won't go without me.*

Can I bring myself to betray her trust if it has the potential to save her life?

I'm through the gate before I have the time to process what I've done. It has only been just over a month, but the world feels different since I last felt its unperfumed air on my face. Out here the air is brown and grey, not the lush green of the garden.

I stick to the wall, trailing along past my old rooms. They belong to a different time. A different Thora. The only thing I miss is my book, but I've hardly thought of it since those first days of our passionate lovemaking, when I referred to it mentally a half dozen times a day. As I pass the building and come out the other side I say a silent prayer—never truly able to abandon my old familiar grief. I hope the next owner of the book, if I'm not able to retrieve it, has as much love for it as me.

I go slow, treading delicately in bare feet. My movements are sluggish but steady enough. I keep my hands held firmly at my sides, regretting my lack of forethought. I should have brought a cloak, or gloves—though I'm not sure Olea has any—to protect anybody who might cross my path. Until I'm ready to...

The thought slows me further. I come to a stop at the edge of the campus square, hiding from the slanting moonlight that filters through the buildings, my back to the stone. What the hell am I doing? I'm out here dressed in nothing but a silk nightgown with no plan and no tools. Olea was right. It is a fool's errand.

My breath comes fast, lungs aching. *It doesn't matter,* whispers my starving brain. *Keep going. Something will come.*

I don't know if it's fear or madness that drives me on. Perhaps both. Perhaps neither—perhaps it is some higher power, the Death that would not take me.

Whatever drives me, I walk with purpose. Out of the campus and down, down into the village. A few months ago this might have taken me an hour or two, but despite my exhaustion and the hollow coldness in my bones, I make the journey in much less time. I'm sweating, and I become aware as I walk of the scent that follows me: it is the bitter, almost chemical aroma of Olea's *Aristolochia goldieana* foliage, whose flowers almost never bloom. It is seeping from my pores like sap. Like poison.

I keep to the trees where I can, and the hedgerows where I can't. It is perhaps two or three hours until dawn and the village is shut up tight. I pass houses on the outskirts, little more than shacks on half-acre farms, that grow into villas with tangled olive trees out front.

If I can find a house with an outback larder or, better yet, an icebox, then I can grab my fill without alerting anybody to my presence. Failing that, perhaps I could carry a lamb—or small sheep, given the season. That would tide us over, wouldn't it...?

But now that I am here I know it wouldn't. Olea is right about that too. Meat, vegetables, milk—they are just prolonging the inevitable. I could eat and eat and it wouldn't fill this longing inside me. Without the antidote we will wither, just as Leonardo did at my touch.

The trees grow sparser as I sneak into the main thoroughfare. There is an inn at the end, just past the bakery where I bought the poplinock pastries for us both. The memory brings a fresh pang.

Exhaustion ripples through me. My legs tremble with it now, each step jerky and unwilling. I'm going to get stranded here.

I need blood. I need it. How can I get it? The lights are dim in the inn windows. Everything must be locked up tight. I wonder if there are travellers who come this way, perhaps to visit St. Elianto for conferences. Could any of them be a suitable—

A suitable what?

I don't even know what I'm thinking. Who in their right mind would give me their blood just because I asked? It doesn't matter that I don't need much, just a small vial—maybe two. I'm not sure how long the antidote would stay good when mixed, and we'll likely need a fresh batch next time. If there is a next time. *Next time.* This thought alone is enough to send me into another spiral. I sneak to the side of the inn, trying to peer through the windows. They are shuttered on the inside.

I won't find anything here. Not without taking it. The sort of person who might willingly give me a vial of blood is probably also the sort of person I do not want to be around dressed only in a silk nightgown. I rub my hands over my arms, suddenly afraid. The feeling is so out of place, a type of fear I have not felt in the entire time I've spent in the garden with Olea, that it momentarily freezes me.

I could break in, I reason. Find one of the bedrooms, break in, and—and what? Not only am I physically weak, but is that something I could do even if I wanted to? I've hurt animals, but that was for science. I hurt Leonardo, but that was an accident. Do I have it in me to hurt a human on purpose?

The shutters in the bedroom at the back of the inn are not closed. I don't remember how I got here, sandwiched between two cypress trees, their lemony tendrils scratching at my skin. The scent is driving me—that same scent I smelled on Leonardo. It is the salty, smoky goodness of fresh bacon. I inhale deeply, my forehead pressed to the stone sill just below the window so they don't see me. There are other scents too: the honey-flour of fresh bread; the tart ripple of blackberry jam; the sweet kiss of Franco meringue... My nostrils flare and I drink it in.

Maybe I could do it without hurting them, these unknown travellers in this hillside village inn. If I sneak into the bedroom I could perhaps use the wilting power of my touch to stun them, or to bargain, playing on their fear. It is better than bartering with the sort of people who might expect other things in exchange; if I surprise them, then I might get the blood for the antidote before they're even aware of the danger I pose.

It isn't a plan so much as a desperate wish. The voice in my head goads me. *Yesss*, it hisses. *Go, go. Hungry. Go now while they sleep. Don't you smell their dreams?*

I clamber through the open window without a second thought. The scents from within threaten to devour me. My mouth waters, my stomach rumbling so loudly I'm surprised the inhabitants don't hear me. The room is pitch dark, no moonlight filtering through the trees. Beneath the human scents, as temptingly delicate as they are, I smell the grime of the road, dusty luggage and trap-wheel grease, spilled ale and overdone pie crusts.

It takes a moment for my eyes to adjust, my body so weak I have to blink blearily several times before the room comes into focus. The scents guide me, pulling me in. I let my hands loose from their spots at my sides, fingers twitching, the urge to scratch and tear barely held at bay as I rub my fingertips together in circles.

I'll just find the person who smells like meringue. They smell sugared and kindly. I cannot say why it is, but I know they will give me their blood if I ask. The saliva in my mouth is thick, my nostrils flaring, sucking the smell deep into my lungs. Yes, meringue will do it. Meringue will give me what I need. I bare my teeth, oh, sharp enough I think to do the job. If I can just—

The figure closest to me opens her eyes. I glance frantically about the room, taking in the scene. A bear of a man—honey-flour—and his wife—tart blackberry jam—lying side by side, both deep in their cups and snoring well. And at their feet in a trundle bed not much smaller than our bed back in the tower is the sweet, compliant Franco meringue.

A child.

Chapter Forty-Two

I flee.

Straight for the window, I dive back into the night in a scream of white, slashing my arm on the jagged corner of the open shutter and leaving behind a spray of scarlet blood. The child's terrified whimpers hunt me into the darkness. I fight the horrified sobs that build in my chest and threaten to engulf me, not stopping to breathe deeply or wipe my eyes until the terra-cotta-and-cream turrets of St. Elianto are once more in sight.

A child. A *child*.

I'm losing my mind.

I've been gone from the garden for less than a few hours and already I have proved Olea's fears to be true. If that girl had not woken when she did...I shudder to think of what I would have done. I have visions—of teeth pincering her tender flesh, the taste of her sweet blood on my tongue. Down my throat. In my belly.

The fire that burns there shames me, but beneath it lies the hot coal bed of *need*. I should have tried one of her parents, the black-berry mother—

I'm glad I didn't hurt the girl, but I can't pretend I don't regret the rest. The walk to the village and back has left me frailer than ever. My mind is abuzz, a cacophony of pleas. *Feed me. Feed me. Feed me.*

"Shut up," I growl, thrusting my palm at my forehead. It is smeared with blood from the healing injury on my arm. Healing, not healed. I inspect the wound cautiously, pulling at the skin. It is red and puffy, the tear leaving a scar. This can't be good.

What will I say to Olea? "Sorry, darling, I broke your trust to go on an adventure and am returning home with—nothing." Not blood, not the antidote, not even a fucking leg of lamb. I chuckle darkly, careless now that I'm back in familiar territory. The square spreads before me like a moonlit piazza. I remember standing in this same spot only months ago, life and possibility spreading before me.

I come to a stop as a new scent overwhelms me. My nostrils flare. My heart beats fast, faster than it has since the transformation. I'd almost forgotten what it feels like to be so, so—*alive.*

My head jerks in the direction of the deliciousness. It comes in wafts, faint at first but then stronger. Notes of oak-smoked whisky, barrels of the stuff, overriding the subtler scents of salt and honey and chilli-flaked whipped feta. I inhale deeply. This isn't the same as what happened with Leo, not even the same as the travel-worn family in the inn. This is strong. It's fresh. It's...

I see him. It's a man, I think, a dark pool of scholar's robes on the other side of the square. A puddle. He's on the floor, unmoving and *injured*. It's the blood I can smell, leaking from the gash on his head. Beside his crumpled body lies a bicycle, handlebars bent and twisted around his leg.

I'm moving before I know it, bare feet gliding across the cobbles. I don't bother to hide in the shadows of the building or trees; I cut straight through the square, nightgown flapping against my legs. The air is full of the taste of him. He's not just injured, I realise. He's drunk as well.

I halt just beside him. My toes grip at the stones underfoot as I try to steady myself, the headiness enveloping me. It isn't like Leo. It isn't like the child and her parents. It is a *sign*.

I did not want to cause the others pain. Leo was an accident, pure instinct. The child...This proves I can control myself—doesn't it?

This man is already bleeding. If I can find a vial or pot of some sort I can take what I need without hurting him. He's drunk too, maybe even unconscious. It won't hurt him—and it could save Olea's life.

Desperately I search about for something to put the blood in. My blood thrums, heartbeat urging me on. Faster, faster. There is no time. Olea—every second I waste is one that might end her.

I navigate the man's body, keeping my distance in case he wakes. In the basket of his bicycle he has books and a sandwich pail—empty—plus a pot of ink with a stopper that's somehow survived his crash. That will do in a pinch, but it isn't clean. I reach for it jerkily and then stop myself. No, it's too risky. I don't know enough about the antidote and I won't get a second chance.

Then I spot the jar. It's rolled out of the basket, or perhaps out of his hand, and come to rest beneath the nearest tree, nestled amongst its grass-laden roots. Small, about the size of the L of my index finger and thumb, the jar is perfectly straight. Somehow this, too, survived the crash. *A sign, a sign.*

I rush to it, frantically grappling to pick it out of the dirt. I smell it; a mixture of booze and spiced cloves assaults my nostrils. It's amarthal—a sour whisky and apple cider blend that is notoriously potent. That's as clean as I'm going to get.

I don't have time to waste. I don't have *time*.

The closer I get to the man, the stronger the smell of his blood becomes. There is an iron taste to it under it all, but still whisky barrels and chilli feta. Garlic—I can taste that too. I'll just lean in and press the jar to the wound, careful not to touch his skin, careful—

The scent of him pounds at my skull. It envelops me. It is a crashing wave, swallowing me down into the ocean bed. I struggle, mouth closed, lips clamped tight. I try not to breathe. This is Olea's. It's for her.

But I can't. And, oh, I don't want to do this. The fight is too much. But—he won't feel it, I promise myself. It's for Olea. It's worth it. I'll just move his head, just once, that's all I need.

I grab his chin with one hand and twist his neck so it is arched towards the moon. The man groans. *Olea*, I think. For *Olea*. The smell of him only makes me hungrier, ravenous, the pain so large I can't stop. It isn't just for Olea. My body screams with the need.

I've dropped the jar. His skin touches mine and the singing is in my blood. I can feel the thrum of his blood in his veins, pulse-pulsing just below the skin. Thin skin. Salted like whipped feta.

Without thinking I push his head farther, popping his neck so I have better access. Pulse. Pulse. I graze his flesh with my teeth. Sink them in. Oh, the taste of him is glorious. *This is it*, whispers the voice. *You need blood, fresh blood, and LOOK. Your body can cure itself. It is a marvel. A wonder. You are a GOD. You might not even need the stinging tree. This is a cure all its own.*

It is glorious. Like the golden heat of sunlight warming my bones. Like a tummy full of fresh bread and butter after a vicious illness. Like the end of pain, a soft white light, it fills me up.

I drink deep and sate my hunger well.

It doesn't hurt. That's the first thing I notice. Unlike the original cure, this melding of my body and his blood is entirely painless. The taste of him fills me up and I am *strong*.

I stumble back from the man, finally coming to my senses. I'm drenched in his blood; it is on my hands, in my hair, and drips down the front of my nightgown. More of the ruby liquid spills from his neck—two jagged wounds carved into his flesh that ooze and gape. My teeth. These aren't like the practised bite marks I inflict on Olea during our love; these are crude and uneven, tears that glisten with red and the pink flesh inside.

Mechanically I reach for the jar. The edges of the wounds are green-black, tiny dark veins reaching out to the paler skin. They look like—vines.

It is only when I've filled the jar halfway with blood, when I've wiped my hands on the cleanest part of my nightgown, when I've checked the man's pulse and found it lacking—only then that I realise what I have done.

I sit back on my haunches, horror and panic filling every part of me. My nose is clogged with the salted scent of him, my tongue thick with his precious lifeblood. I run it along my teeth as I grip my knees, flexing my fingers and feeling their same loose-limbed smoothness, rocking back and forth and sensing the core of my body grow taut and strong once more. I'm going to be sick.

It didn't hurt him. That is the thing I want you to know. It didn't hurt him—just as it didn't hurt me. There's no way it could have. And now that I have the blood, I can save Olea. I will, with-out a doubt, willingly trade her trust in me for her life.

I should say a prayer, shouldn't I? For this life I have taken? Or for the life the pavement may have taken if not for me. I should grieve for this man, since it is one thing I can do for him.

But I don't. It is too risky out here in the open. I can sense the stirrings of the scholars in their beds, the beginnings of dawn creeping. Olea will be awake soon—and if she isn't, then she needs this cure more than ever.

I grip the jar of blood like a talisman, and then I bolt, flying like a bat in the night.

Chapter Forty-Three

I creep back into the garden through its silent, rusted gate just as dawn is pinking the sky. The moon is a ghostly figure; only she looks upon me and knows what I have done.

Olea is still sleeping in the tower's cellar, her body wrapped in thick blankets to ward off the night's chill. I no longer feel any of the cold, hot blood pumping in my veins, glory on my breath. I check that she is breathing—she is, though she's sicker than I realised. The rise and fall of her chest is painfully rapid and her skin is glossy with a fine sheen of sweat.

I change out of my ruined nightgown to avoid contaminating everything in case any of the blood is mine, and then waste no time scavenging dried cuttings of the stinging tree from Olea's catalogue, pulverising the leaves and their fine, poisoning hairs to dust, just as I did before. Or as close as I can recall.

It isn't accurate. Without the lab and the equipment it can't be. Panic makes my movements jerky, my pulse pounding in my throat. I don't have time to second-guess. I have one shot, and it has to be *now*. I let my hands guide me, relying on the muscles as I pound and grind and measure.

Then: the bubbling and sizzling as I add the dead man's blood, still fresh but already congealing. I shake it well until the fizzy mixture begins to dance. My stomach lurches, heart racing. It's ready.

I test it first, one mouthful. Swallow. It is sweet and pure and good and light. It doesn't hurt. It doesn't seem much different than the blood. Joy overflows, brightness in every inch of me. I've done it. I can save her.

"Olie," I sing excitedly. "Oleeea. Wake up, my darling. Here I am with your medicine."

Olea doesn't respond. I drop to my knees, scooting along the flagstones. I check her breathing. Still fast, but slower than before. Her arms are like marble, stiff to the touch as I try to lift them.

"Olea," I urge, this time less gently. "Wake UP."

I jostle her, her body resistant as a statue. Panic overwhelms me. I push it down, shove it so hard I can't breathe, until I am nothing but a machine. This can't be it. I can't have run out of time. I did everything right!

"Olea," I growl her name like a curse. "Come *on*."

I grasp the antidote with one hand and her chin with the other, prising open her lips with sheer force. Her teeth are as white as salt. They begin to chatter as I hold her tight, forcing the rim of the jar to her lower lip. I pour all of the rest of the antidote into her mouth. Her chin jerks and I hold it steady.

"Come on, darling, drink it for me. Drink it, drink it, *drink it*!"

Finally—the bob of her throat. She swallows it down in one. There is a brief second before she begins to cough, spluttering and retching. She rolls out of my lap and onto her side, her breath hitching.

"Breathe," I say. "Come, now. You can rest easy."

It is another moment before she is herself. She wrests herself onto her elbows and stares at me with eyes as black as a moonless night.

"What did you do?"

"I saved you," I say. It's hard to contain my excitement. Already I can see the faint pink returning to her cheeks. She throws off the blankets angrily and her skin is smooth and cool-looking. I want to touch it.

"How?" The suspicion in her gaze cuts me to my core.

"There's a hospital," I lie. Thank god for the antidote, which greases my brain as if I were, actually, a machine.

Olea is silent. I can see her thoughts coiling and uncoiling, but she is precious minutes behind me with the antidote. I'm sure the fog in her mind will clear, but for now it's my job to sell this reality. I watch her as she kneels back on her legs.

"How?" she asks again, this time gentler.

"I bartered for it." I leave this open, waiting for her to fill the silence with her own assumptions.

"Oh, Thora," she says softly.

"Don't you feel better, though?" I prompt. "You looked so unwell. I thought...well, it doesn't matter what I thought. I'm glad you took it."

"You didn't give me any choice."

I rub my jaw, annoyance brewing in me. I said I would risk losing Olea's trust to save her, and I don't regret it, but I didn't expect her to be so...sad.

"You would have..." I can't even bring myself to say it. The thought of a future without her alive...It is more painful than I would have ever thought possible. We have been forged anew in this same fire, and I can't let her go.

"How did you even get out?" Olea asks.

"I broke the lock. With tools from the kitchen." This is not such a bald-faced lie, but Olea reacts to this one with far more suspicion. I don't know *why* I lie; I suppose I don't like the idea of Olea knowing how easy it was for me to betray her.

I reach for her, laying my hand atop hers. Olea stares at my hands for a moment. A horrified thought strikes: What if she can see the lingering remnants of the dead man's blood? Is it dried around my fingernails? I washed my hands, but... And then I notice her gaze is not on my hand but on my nightgown. Not entirely dissimilar to the one I wore earlier, but not identical either. She was so out of it, though, surely she can't remember such a detail...?

So I do the only thing I know how, throwing myself into her arms and smothering her face with kisses. She resists at first, shocked and amused, but in seconds we are tumbling into the blankets and cushions, mouths together, fingers searching.

"I love you," I say breathlessly. "And I'm glad you're okay."

I wake to the sound of Olea making her nettle tea. The sun is just beginning to disappear, a sunset-gilded cloud of rain moving in from the east. The chaise is stiff beneath my body, a book buried somewhere in the bolster, which we no doubt lost during our second round of lovemaking.

I crack my eyes against the golden-hour sun, but it doesn't burn like it did only a day ago. For a second, just one blissful second, all feels right and good.

Olea hands me my mug, both of us uncaring of the heat that scalds our palms. She sits at my feet, sips from her tea, and then she says simply, "I want to know why you lied."

"I didn't lie."

"You're lying to me right now, Thora. I thought we were past this. I thought we had an understanding. No more secrets. You said yourself: How many times are we going to have the same conversations?" The antidote has cleared Olea's mind, just as I thought it would. I'm briefly angry, but it is a fleeting emotion with no real bite.

"I did what I had to do," I say simply. "You didn't need all the details. You were recovering—"

"Oh, cut the bullshit," Olea chides. "You promised you wouldn't leave the garden without me, and you did. You told me you got the blood from a hospital. And, what, I'm just supposed to believe you?"

"I saved your life," I repeat the mantra again.

"You didn't give me a choice." Olea's stare is cold. Whatever frustration we burned through during sex is back and roaring like an open flame. I was naive to think I might be able to recover from this. That *we* might be able to. "Once again, nobody ever asks me what I want. Did you ever stop to think that I didn't want this? You poured that fucking stuff down my throat. Just like you forced me the first time."

"I didn't force you!" I exclaim. "I *never* forced you."

"No, the first time you just manipulated me into thinking it was my only choice or you would leave. Last night you forced me, and I didn't appreciate it. I'm so fucking sick of everybody acting for me."

"Would you have rather me let you die?"

Silence. It spreads between us like poison. Not the good, trusting poison of the garden, but the kind of poison little children are taught to fear. Olea doesn't say anything, only stares at me, at my nightgown, at my hands. Guilt, it's written all over me. And the worst part is, I'm sure Olea can sense the same thing I've been thinking nonstop since last night: I would do it again. I almost *want* to do it again. I want the taste of blood on my tongue, salty and hot and good.

"Thora, I'm not saying you're not trying to do the right thing. I'm not even saying I'm not grateful, because now I'm here... Well, it's hard to wish I wasn't. But I want you to know that you do not, ever, have the right to make that decision for me again. Do you understand?"

"So next time it happens I *am* supposed to let you die?"

"There won't be a next time."

"Of course there bloody will." I gulp a mouthful of the nettle tea and relish the warmth in my throat. "Next month, like clockwork. You heard the doctor."

Olea is already shaking her head before I've finished speaking. "No," she says. "She'll be back. Maybe not right away, but she'll want to check on us, to see which of us..." She swallows. "Look, all I'm saying is you've bought us more time. Next time we will have Florencia's help and everything will be fine."

"When are you going to learn she doesn't care about us?"

Olea sets her tea aside. "It isn't that I don't know that. I'm not stupid. But if we just abandon this... You understand, don't you, what will happen? I simply can't bear the thought of her doing this to somebody else."

It is now, in this moment, that I realise something. It's a thought that has been growing for some time, but last night has sealed it: if we continue to do nothing, we are just as responsible as the doctor for what happens next. We have no guarantee that she will come back to us. Petaccia has our formula for the antidote, and she knows it doesn't kill immediately. Olea is right about this: I'm sure she'll find no shortage of subjects willing to do just about anything for the chance at a cure for all.

And with that realisation comes another swift on its heels. Olea will *never* do what is necessary. In our arguments she is always the lock and I am the key. She is shackled by her past, trapped in this garden in a way that I am not and will never be. I am not my father's child any longer, a girl so wrapped in the intricate rituals of death that she does not see the way it stunts her; I am not my husband's wife, trapped by his short temper and shorter leash with no way out besides books. I am a woman who has tasted her dreams—and her nightmares.

I want so very badly to kiss Olea, to distract her as I did last night, to feel the pleasure of our crushed bodies. I want to taste her, to hold her, gentle and slow and holy. Instead, I place my tea on the side table and climb to my feet. I throw a few things into a bag: cloak, gloves, several empty vials, a bundle of rags.

"I knew you wouldn't stay," Olea says sadly.

"You know I can't."

She looks at me imploringly, her lips slightly parted in the seductive way she knows I like best. I force myself to look away, anywhere but at the painful, endless beauty in her face. I can't stay—because if I stay, even for a moment more, then I will never, ever leave.

"Where are you going?"

I am a monster, forged by grief and transformed by science. This is my duty. More than grieving, more than hiding and learning and knowledge. I was made for this.

"I'm going to find your mother," I swear solemnly. "You can stay here if you want. Guard the garden, and the catalogue, and the recipe. I will find her. I'll make her help us. And then..."

And then?

Olea's lip trembles but she is the calmest I have seen her in weeks, perhaps ever. She knows this is right the same as I do; it's written in the curve of her shoulders, the resilient grip of her hands around her mug. We both know what must be done.

It must.

"And then I will stop her from spreading this, this…" *This cure. This gift. This unholy offering.*

The touch of Olea's hand against my elbow is cold as marble. I finally look at her face, etched in the blue of sunset.

"This endless agony," she says.

Acknowledgments

Writing any book (and having people read it) is a privilege that I feel very lucky to have experienced—more than once! So I would like to start here by saying thank you to my readers. To those of you who read and reviewed and supported *Wild and Wicked Things*, and to those of you here now. I'm so very grateful to each of you who have taken the chance on this bloody, unapologetically sapphic book. You are the reason we writers get to exist and I'll never tire of saying thank you.

Writing this book in particular was difficult for me. I got COVID shortly after committing to write my second book with Orbit, and I was diagnosed with long COVID not long afterwards. This book is not the book I originally planned to write thanks to the severe brain fog I experienced in those first months of drafting, but it is a book I love deeply. I fell head over heels for Thora and Olea in all their darkness, and writing their story felt like an obsession.

That being said, I've not been very good at hitting my dead-lines, so an extra *huge* thank you to my agent, Diana Beaumont (and the team at DHH), for being my untiring champion while

I recovered and for all your support while I drafted, redrafted, scrapped, and drafted again.

Huge thanks also to the entire team at Orbit Books in both the US and the UK. To my US editor, Alyea Canada, for your endless patience with my deadline shenanigans, and my UK editor, Emily Byron, for all your hard work and kindness. I'd like to shout out my production editor, Rachel Goldstein; my US publicist, Ellen Wright; and my UK publicist, Nazia Khatun, for showing me some of the coolest cakes and snacks in London. Thanks also to the design team who have now been responsible for two of the most beautiful book covers known to man: Lisa Marie Pompilio and Lauren Panepinto.

The industry at large is full of people I love. Thank you to all the bloggers and reviewers who have made my career such a joy so far, and to the teams at Goldsboro and Waterstones for choosing to back my books. And also Nivia Evans: thank you for taking a chance on *Wild and Wicked Things*, and for writing the tweet that inspired this novel.

Endless thanks and cups of tea and whatever sweet treats y'all love best to my fellow booksellers. I could not do what I do without the support of booksellers around the world, and you guys are the best cheerleaders anybody could ask for. A special shout-out goes to my Waterstones friends, Jo and Michelle, who have supported me unwaveringly throughout my career. And to Callie, thank you for always being one of the loudest advocates for my books, and for your continued encouragement.

As always I'd like to thank my non-bookseller friends for not taking it personally when I cancel on our life plans to do something boring and stay-insidey, like write a book. Tom, Sarah, Alex, you guys are my world and I'm endlessly grateful for you.

My family deserve even more endless thanks. I love all of you so freaking much, and yes, I know you know I'm on deadline again so I'm going to be busy. I know. Sorry. Mum, Dad, Steve, Alisha, thank you, thank you, and I love you.

The list of animal friends I have to thank grows every time I write a book, but I'd like to acknowledge the fact that I literally could not write anything without my furry pals. They keep me sane, or help me foster the right kind of insanity, every single day. For everything from welcome (and unwelcome) distractions to necessary cuddles, I'd like to thank the dogs (Bella and Mex), the BIG dogs (Circe, Quintus, Tarquin), the cats—and BIG cats—Jet, Atlas, and Morph. And for the angels we've lost since I wrote my last book: Zeus, Xena, Juno, Fizz, Shadow, and Athena. I've spoken a lot on social media about the impact these losses have had on me, but who knew a book so mired in grief would make me think about them lots...! All I know is every second of the grief is worth the time spent loving them.

Lastly (and definitely not least-ly), I'd like to thank my fiancée, Clair. You have supported me through countless ups and downs over the last couple of years, and I'm forever grateful for your unwavering support of my writing. Thank you for sitting on the floor and plotting with me until way past your bedtime—I literally could not have done it alone (and not just because Morph wouldn't let me). Thank you for helping me to be excited when I'm exhausted, for cleaning up after me when I'm in "let me just do this one thing" mode, for cooking when I'd rather not, and for juggling the animals when I really do just need to do "one more thing before I can help." There aren't words to say how much I appreciate you (or maybe I just can't find the right ones), but please know that this book exists largely thanks to you. Thank you, and I love you.